I0532807

The Geto Love Song

The Geto Love Song

WHEN LOVE HAS AN EVIL MELODY

Written by P.M. Don

Copyright © 2016 P.M. Don
All rights reserved.

ISBN: 0692470689
ISBN 13: 9780692470688
Library of Congress Control Number: 2015944377
mack williams, Sacramento, CA

When the windows towards a man's soul closes we often find it hard to communicate...even when most relate. Yet and still our silence is often times our loudest voice.

    Through my travels I've met folk who feels as if giving up is better... even when they're awfully close...almost to one of the world wonders has now become a trivia question. Like how is it that we've come so far just to die so easy? Success is a choice and so is failure. No...we will push, pull and strive. Because we can't stop and we won't stop! Who says? We say. Well who are we? Will-Ticket Publishing Inc.....

Better than the beds of roses your beauty inspires us still. May god forever hold you close.

In Loving Memory….

Pauline Moore	Herman Abraham
Mack H. Williams Sr.	Clark Robins
Barbra Thomas	Anthony Abraham
Betty Lou Peterson	Sammy J. Davis Jr.
Jimmy C. McCoy	Lavina M. McCoy
Cathren Williams	Adam L. Jackson
Samuel James Peterson	Voltaire T. Phillips

Virginia Greenly

CHAPTER 1

Marva

For Marva a day this beautiful would only go un-noticed or even cared for. The sky azure, a clear sapphire at its finest. The air was crisp, not one visible cloud in sight. Birds were heard singing all of their wonderful symphonies as they tweet their melodies of mating. Spring time had now sprung; flowers were in full blossom, and giving off their perfumed scents of exotic fragrances. Any other time this would have been the perfect day for an outdoor cook out. She'd invite a few friends to sit on the patio while she stared through the smoke at her true love Javier. As the thoughts ran through her mind she couldn't help but snap back to her present state.

"Javier why did you do me this way," she thought as she laid on a cot that was provided to her at the woman's shelter for battered women. The W.E.A.V.E program it was called. Women escaping a violent environment as the acronym would have it. Never did she ever think her relationship would end this way. She never thought for a minute that she would ever see the inside of a shelter, whether it be for the homeless or the battered. Yet, as luck would have it she had drawn the daily double. With her Prada tote bag filled with clothes and other provisions that Javier thought she would need when he was kicking her ass out helped her remember just how homeless she was. And to think that he waited until she was off running errands to pack her belongings kind of pissed her off a little. Oh, and all she would have to do to remind herself that she was battered was to look in the mirror to see the puffy cheeks and the swollen eyes which started off a purplish hue, now took on a dark black tint, there's a joke in that. Like what do you tell somebody with two black eyes? Nothing, because somebody done already told them twice. In her case she found very hard to see through the ones that God gave her because they were nearly closed. Not to mention if she rolled over fast enough the cracked ribs would be an instant reminder that she was indeed battered, so yes, for her the daily double it was.

"Javier why'd you have to treat me so bad," she cried still refusing to accept her reality.

As Marva laid on her cot she thought of all the sacrifices that she made for Javier, her being charcoal black and him of the Spanish decent being one of them. Marva shook her head in memory of the continuous ridicule that had gone along with being in an interracial relationship. The curious stares that felt like daggers after a while, those coming from the brothers and the senoritas alike was another was pretty compromising. Feeling as if love needs no explanations so the two pushed on joined hand in hand. Even though everyone had their own opinions to how these two should get along or how these two would part but no one had more concerns than those of her best friend "Mia." Who warned her not to give too much, too soon just in case Javier cured his curiosity for the black stallion and wished to return to the sorrel that he was used to.

It wasn't until she saw her suitcases and tote bag parked outside of the house that she shared with him and then later the vision of the toddler did she realize that his curiosity was then cured. It was only sensible to believe that her place was now being taken by Javier's baby's mother.

"But he didn't have to beat me and drag me across the house and stomp on me like that," Marva thought. The only thing that she could think of was how afraid she was to let her home girl "Tamia" see her in such a condition. She figured it best to wait awhile before she resurfaces and start life all over again but this time, on her own.

"Yeah, I'll be back. This time I'll be stronger, faster and much, much smarter." Although it hurt, she still found reason to smile. Just on confidence alone, she was able to smile through it all. Confidence being one of the intangibles that she possessed but her tangibles, oh my goodness. It was said that God paid way more attention on her then he could have ever spent on Eve. Her dark chocolate complexion, which also took on the tropics for its smoothness was so damn tempting. Her eyes were green with gold specks, and her teeth were so white and so even, that her smile by itself would land her on any runway in Paris. At five foot ten inches, her smooth legs ran on forever, starting from her size nine, well pedicure delicate feet that she would hide in pumps, stiletto heels, boots or the comfort of the cross trainers. Those she would lace up to head out every morning to put in her five-mile trot in, and even those were a good look on her.

Feet that kissed her ankles, then gone up to her bowled legs and thighs that often times hid themselves beneath the skirts that drove most men bananas trying to solve the riddle. Like what could possibly be the use of even wearing a skirt to begin with? Seeing that her micro minis were often times found shorter than the other micro minis on the market. Yet, somehow Marva brought the word classy to such a sexiness, which had actually become the riddle. So, how does this particular woman wear clothes that were made specifically for a hooker, become inviting enough to call her "ma'am" or "Ms." and lord help everybody, but even "Mrs..." Oh yeah, her tangibles were real, five foot ten, one hundred and fifty pounds of everything that a man loves so much about a woman, well-toned and cared for. So much, that any man would've loved to ask Javier what exactly was it that cured him. Because, certainly very few of the brothers wanted any of those remedies and fuck that kind of medicine. Just to mention that you were calling it quits to making Marva one of the happiest women of all time was unheard of, it was more than ludicrous it was a sacrilege, and one punishable by death.

With all of this beauty one would look towards her for the absence of brains. Well, Marva for her scruples helped Javier launch a successful business in the field of landscaping. As crowded as the grass cutting, bush trimming business was, what had set Javier's business apart from others was Marva's business wit and good looks. Which brought bids from Parks and Recreations, and twelve other churches with large lawns and all of this just to make her man happy? Really she was doing all of this for her, because it took a while for her to stomach the fact that she could have a man who could plant the shit out of a flower or mow the hell out of some damn lawns. It was something about him that she liked and everyone concerned had known this because, she sure terminated her lease in order move in with him, oh Javier.

Maybe it was his ponytail or his accent or even the fact that he could cuss her ass out in another language, which to her this was always a treat, just not this time. Oh, how she liked the way he ran his hands up and down her body avoiding no parts of her anatomy, just not this last time though.

Marva rose slowly into a sitting position trying to collect and arrange her thoughts. Especially the big one, the one that would show her how to elude the police who promised to resurface once she felt a little better, and Marva was given no reason to believe that speaking to the police was anything but an event waiting to happen.

"If that's the case, I'll see y'all motha fuckas next month sometime," she thought but knew better. Because, if the Sacramento Police Department wanted to lock them a motha fucka up then they'll see you bright and early... in the morning. They'll have coffee, doughnuts and a motha fuckin' note book. Nah, this wasn't what she wanted to go through at all.

"I got to get out of here; this place is crawling with pessimism." Marva said to herself while making the very slow process to her feet. She unzipped her tote and rummaged through it until she found her cell, contemplated for a moment then placed the call to her best friend "Tamia."

TAMIA

For Tamia, life wasn't all the peaches and cream either. In fact, it was a norm for two o'clock a.m. to find her in front of her desktop researching anatomies and cures for one health problem or the other. Tumors one day, spleens the next, tissues and hemorrhages on Tuesday, organs by Friday and brain samples bright and early Saturday she'll rest come Sunday then she'll start the ball all over again come Monday. Motivated, well of course, plus she possessed this mental attitude that nobody ever said that anything worth having was going to be easy to obtain so, her grind was real heavy.

Her days were spent calculated and concentrated because she also knew that it would be hard work that would place her in the top three of her class, which to her was non-negotiable. Speaking sarcastically the idea was a brilliant one considering that the top two, one of them was her Asian class mate Chu Chin, who was a shoo-in with both of his parents being in the medical field, and then there was the whiz kid, Brian Bernstein, who have yet to fail at anything scholastic. Brian brought his psyche all the way across the globe to compete. All the way from Poland he would say, by way of Moscow, Budapest and Frankfurt because his background brought military to the table.

All of this was challenging for Tamia who grew up in Oak Park, tenements and dilapidated buildings up and down the street no matter which direction one shall look. Pestilence, both physical and mental ran rampant where she came from. Drugs and violence had seized the place a long, long time ago and vowed to never let go anytime soon. Pessimism that started from childhood had grew right along with the collectives, so much that soon a vast majority of these tenants would leave this community to go to either Thompson's or Morgan and Jones, both are very popular funeral parlors. If not the morgue, they'd eventually end up lost in the penal system, which is a system that to this day boasts of over crowdedness.

So, for a back ground Tamia Peterson got off to a rough start. She attended high school at Luther Burbank which was a layout that took on its own personality. From a distance or to any outsider you'd think this school was a prison for the youth. Bars made of the finest steel was placed everywhere to one had to wonder if this variation of methods, and the use of penal system tactics was placed to keep crime out or to immure these kids to keep their crimes in. This way the officials would bring statistics that crime is easily controlled in the city from eight in the morning to three in the evening. Luther Burbank as a high school was indeed equivalent to any youth authority; here riots would break out on the school grounds just like in prison. Only in prison the convict warred with a shiv, these youngsters though, another story .40 calibers, 357 desert eagles .44 magnums and hell, toss in a few M12s and M11s and what you'd have is a complete visual of the campus where Tamia made her plans to become a doctor and nothing else. Never did she try out for the cheer leading team. Never! Even though her looks and build was sure to draw the attention needed to distract an entire stadium. If one was to match her beauty with her athleticism, then she was sure to be on the top of the pyramid yelling.

"Give me a B and give me a U" nah, for Tamia there was nothing else. Biology class, science and mathematics were her strong suits and for recreations and hobby she made the track team only to lead the girls to the state finals and that was because there were girls at their rival schools doing a whole bunch of trash talking.

Well, by the age of thirteen anybody could say that Tamia knew that she was going to attend the University of California Davis where she would do her under studies as well as achieve all of her degrees toward being an MD, and nothing else. When Tamia looked at her young life in hindsight there was one resentment that crossed her mind time after time, a memory that pushes her morning until night, which also brought her taciturn personality under speculation. Just one regret, she could playback the one day when she wasn't able to save her mother who suffered from chronic asthma from dying of suffocation. A time when her mother found it very hard to breathe, even harder to explain to a nine-year-old Tamia that she was in a desperate need of the bronchodilator that was in her purse.

In a state of shock, the young Tamia watched as her mother collapsed, then eventually shook and she died. Enduring a loss so great she learned, that any child could take personally the devastation and hold fault all the way into adulthood, a stage in life where alcoholism or drug addictions comes to plague an individual's life. Tamia released the idea of blaming herself because what child actually knew CPR or could even understand the pantomime that her mother offered? Even though any fool could of saw that something terrible was going on with her mother, enough to dial 911 and ask somebody over there to help her. Ultimately her mother passed away from being a chronic asthmatic.

Since Tamia came from an awfully small family, there were very few people to turn to. Her aunt Mimi was on drugs so bad that all of her kids were already in the system. She had an older brother who went off to prison when she was only a year old for killing an ice cream truck driver. Tamia growing up had never seen the sense in that, I mean who kills a Popsicle dealer? Then there was "Nana," who came to the house right away, just in time to meet the coroners as they were wrapping up and preparing for transport. In the same state of despair was how Tamia watched as strangers traversed in and out of the residence that only she and her mother shared, which was the same house that she was brought to call home as an infant. It was "Nana's" strength that was passed down to Tamia; before the coroners had her mother in the bag they asked her "Nana" if she would like to view her daughter's body. It was the words that left "Nana's" lips that brought a sense of calm to Tamia. The coroner was kind and soft spoken, when he said,

"Ma'am, would you like to see, ahh, the body before we transport her down to the mortuary?"

"You said that my daughter was dead, right?"

"Yes ma'am, I'm sorry to say."

"Then no, I don't think me seeing her would change anything, y'all go on and carry her body to the mortuary while me and this child here pray to God that my daughter's soul makes its way home safe and sound."

"Yes ma'am," and for that Tamia watched her grandmother with pride as well as astonishment, genuflected and begun to pray as her grandmother instructed. Once they were finished aiding their loved one safely into heaven by way of prayer, Tamia's grandmother sat Tamia down and said.

"This is a horrible thing for any child to see and I hate mostly that it was you who had to see it. But baby, I need you to believe that God knows what he's doing, always has and always will. So you just find a way to avoid putting the blame on either yourself or on God. Though it may be hard at times, but you still got to believe in these words that I'm saying right now, so go on in there and pack you up some clothes and all of your favorites, with the understanding that you would never come back here again. You could take your time if you like, now go on and mind me for what I say now, hear." Tamia nodded her head in response and went about the chore of packing with the swiftness of one who was ready to go.

As Tamia reflected on her life she started to smile. She thought of the roller coaster ride that life presented her a ticket to ride and even though the roads were bumpy to begin with, her "Nana" instilled in her some very fine qualities, and because of this she found stability. Although her financial situation wasn't as stable as she would like it to be but she was a long way from being financially embarrassed. It's been awhile since she lived in Oak Park, though she made frequent visits to her friends and associates who weren't fortunate enough to escape the tentacles of such a place. Because of that alone she would make the trips from the North Natomas area to Oak Park if not but to remind herself of where she had started from. Not that she needed reminding just that it was always good to know where home was.

Her smile grew even more once she thought of her fiancé William. Oh how he made her so happy, just the thought of him helped her wrap her arms around her midsection to hug herself. William was so kind, so loving and understanding. Yes, she was very, very, very happy with life. Just a few years ago he'd became the only true family that Tamia now had ever since her "Nana" passed away. He had become her baby, her "tooga wooga" as she was so quick to tell her friends in regards to him.

Through thick and thin he's been there, when "Nana" passed she leaned heavily on William for supports, that of all natures, moral, mental, emotional and in some cases even spiritual support. No matter the reasons, he was there and she loved him so much in return for that. So, as far as family history and excellent back grounds to aid her with reaching for the moons and the highest heights were concerned wasn't so big the facts were that her circles were small but she had "Nana" and that was it. Yet, that was all she needed. "Nana" wasn't a doctor or even a nurse, she wasn't rich or even sort of middle class. In fact, she was the furthest thing from prestigious or influential. She'd never held a job more than a house cleaner, a baby sitter or a maid and all of which was when she would work for prestigious people, raising their lily white babies while cleaning up a house that she grew too poor to even dream of. No! "Nana" didn't have trinkets or glitter, but what she did have were all priceless, her sense of determination, priceless, her desires to meet life on life's terms, again priceless. Her desires, integrity and inner beauty were all priceless. It was love that she gave to all people without measure, and all of these things are what she passed down to Tamia at a very young age. So one could easily understand how Tamia as an adult could exude these qualities so effortlessly.

So when her phone rung so close to midnight her concerns grew immediately to a panic while wondering who could possibly be calling so late, and on a week night. As far as she knew, William would be at work, he worked the grave yard shift at the post office sorting mail, so what could have gone awry there.

"Hello,"

"Mia, oh Mia!" Marva cried into the phone finding relief to have reached out to her friend.

"Marva girl are you all right?" Tamia's concern grew wilder as she listened to her best friends' sob. So close was these two that they were sisters to everyone else who didn't know any better. The sobs only grew louder and even more complicated to decipher what exactly was the cause for this trepidation.

"Oh, Mia!"

"Girl, now calm down and tell me what's wrong, where are you?" Asked Tamia

"I'm in a shh, shh, shelter,"

"You're in a shelter!" Tamia shouted into the phone "uh, uh what the hell you doing in a shelter? Which one I'm on my way?" Not at all believing her ears, Tamia searched the background for clues.

"He beat me so bad Mia, I'm embarrassed for you to see me like this"

"He did what! Oh hell no, where are you, at least tell me that, oh no he didn't!" Tamia took off running throughout the house grabbing pieces of clothing along the way dressing on the move. Then out the door she went and straight to her car with Marva still on the line. Noticing that not only did she leave the front door wide open but she also ran out of the house without the keys to the car. Repeating everything that Marva relayed to her adding that to memory to ensure her friend that she would be on the way and in route, just as soon as she found her keys and locked the house up. Figuring that she would call William along the way and leave a message, just in case he caught a break and decided to call home and become instantly worried unable to get through to her. It wasn't that William was the type to keep tabs on her no, this was just how they got down, all the way up and all the way down. They would always put each other first, an affair that wasn't in the least a one sided one. Do me like I do you was how they viewed their relationship. They had a bond that was communicated through example, and this simple practice was envied all over Sacramento.

These two had become a paradigm, a superlative, and nonpareil. I'm talking about the archetypal of how a love affair should be, a groove that should never be disturbed. Yet, as equal was the way Tamia felt about family and Marva was just as close to family as anyone could get. The things that they shared in common are what created a bond that was so strong. They both were raised by their grandparents, both of them had deceased mothers, they both attended Thomas Jefferson Elementary, and both had gone on to Kit Carson middle school. They even entered the draft together and gone to war at Luther Burbank High School. Both were often times envied and 'hated on' for their Gods given physical attributes, Marva more than her. That's only because Marva done two things that Tamia would never do.

One being, that Marva wore the kind of clothes that if "Nana" ever saw Tamia in, would have expired her on the spot. So Tamia never wore 'ho' clothes or sashayed around town seeking attention. She'd never pick an interracial relationship as an excuse to escape where she came from, not at all prejudice or racist to say the least. Tamia just felt that if she was to entertain a relationship of such, it wouldn't be to escape yesterday, no, it'll be to enrich tomorrow. Not that she held anything over Marva's head relenting that Marva's relationships were hers and hers alone, but getting beat up behind it was different all together. So to her friend she was going to help.

CHAPTER 2

RASAAN

RASAAN WATCHED AS NAHJEE MANEUVERED his navy blue 745Li BMW through traffic on highway 99 coming from Stockton, California without once touching the brake pedal. This had Rasaan a little nervous I mean with the traffic being as thick as it was This being pretty much the best time of the day to realize that an automobile of this quality came equipped with a lot of safety features, namely a braking system. Never one to question his comrades driving abilities but he did know that accidents were called 'accidents' for a reason. Rasaan as it just so happens wasn't into chances or anything else unintentional for that matter. So he calmly double checked the latch of his seat belt which has proven to be the life saver of many of accidental or unintentional occurrences. The kind of occurrences that just so bizarrely and peculiarly happened. Satisfied with his discoveries, he had but to perform just one other task and that was to bring calm to the four fifteen inch sub-whoopers and the other twelve mid-range, door mounts and six by nine speakers before he said.

"Playboy, how about slowing this bitch down a bit." Rasaan said to Nahjee, who appeared to have been deep in thought. He was basically driving on instincts. Rasaan noticed as he locked his stare on him before he said "Dog, I know that you weren't just day dreaming was you?"

"Nah, nah, I mean yeah, but I'm back now, my bad," and just as Rasaan suggested Nahjee brought the machine to a humbler pace.

Rasaan knew better than to ask Nahjee about his business, feeling that if there was something that Nahjee needed him to know then he was sure that he would inform him sooner or later. Rasaan just turned the beat up and let Roger and Zapps' "Computer Love" put the whupping on the other travelers as the two drove by with the trunk acting as a holding compartment for Godzilla, who was ferociously growing tired of being cooped up and tried to beat its way out of that motha fucka to the crispy snares, high hats and rattles that resonated throughout the interior. To prove that Nahjee was indeed back from his star-ship ride, he reached into the ash tray to activate the lighter in order to put the bright orange utensil to the tip of the dark brown hand rolled Swisher leaf that was used always by these two to wrap around the dark and very sticky high quality Kush. Replacing the lighter and cracking the sun roof he put the blunt into rotation. He inhaled deeply then exhaled. The extreme coughing fit reminded him that the THC level once again had proved to be too much for two lungs to compensate. Nahjee still managed to get most of the smoke through the roof before passing the blunt to Rasaan who accepted gladly, until he too joined Nahjee in a losing battle of keeping the powerful smoke contained by lungs alone before passing it back.

Nahjee and Rasaan were thick as thieves. Where there was one there was the other or the other was close by. Those were the certainties that these two were known for. What was uncertain was just how these two acquired so much leisure time to do which and whatever their hearts desired. While everyone else worked these two were at play and while everyone slept these two were at play again, and this is what confused everybody. For starters both pushed their dream cars. Nahjee the 745Li, Rasaan the S550, and both put shoes on their whips, Nahjee 22-inch Diablo rims and Pirelli tires. Rasaan sported 22 inch Asanti rims with Yokohama tires. They both had monster beat installed, both had a walk in closet with hangers that were blessed with some of the finest of fabrics. These two also had an additional closet made strictly for their shoe game. One that had to stay on point or all hell broke loose, and both no matter where they went in life, they always had a jeweler in their pockets along with their many other connections.

If they were in Modesto California, a jeweler, Oakland California, a jeweler, Los Angeles or even Seattle Washington, a jeweler, Cleveland Ohio, you bet ya, a jeweler. So, needless to say that they both sported the high quality rings, chains and watches. This type of thing bothered everyone including the Sacramento's Police. Once Rasaan was pulled over across the street from 'Oak Park Market' for a reason unknown to either Rasaan or Nahjee and was asked via loud speaker to put their hands on the dashboard and on the steering wheel respectively. They remained there still and in the same position for nearly thirty minutes waiting on a backup unit to come. Once back up arrived still they remained in the same position, this time waiting on the K9 unit to show up. This left Nahjee to decide that if nearly an hour was long enough for his feet to go to sleep and his back to grow stiff. Then it had to be long enough to at least know why they were being detained and pulled over in the first place. He decided to recline in his seat appearing to be way more comfortable than Rasaan who grew tired of being bent over the steering wheel so long that he forgot that they were even pulled over by the police. He also reclined his seat after locking all of the doors and cracking the window just wide enough to slip his license and registration along with the proof of insurance through. Once the officers became observant to their detainee's fractious behaviors they became unsettled and announced for the two to resume their positions on the instructions that were given an hour and a half ago had found their commands to be easily dismissed by the two as being merely unimportant so they continued to resist.

These two acts of defiance were of no comparison to the all-out display that the SPD were exhibiting without once informing their malcontent captives of their reasons to why exactly, should the two compromise their comforts. There was no gun in the car, neither one sold drugs, so there wouldn't be drugs in the car and they never made it to weed spot so they knew that there wasn't any weed in the car, so, these captives weren't frustrated at all.

Although Nahjee's guess was as good as Rasaan's to why the cops were irritated with their commands going ignored I mean with all of the complaints that they have. Watched when the cops decided that they needed to approach the car with extreme caution. They made wave like maneuvers until the car was surrounded by gun waving and highly pissed off police officers yelling at the top of their lungs something about if anybody moved that they were going to get their heads blown off.

To pour salt into an open wound the dogs were released, which didn't make sense to anybody especially not the two occupants that everyone was interested in, who was sheltered safely in the confines of a locked car with the windows rolled up with absolutely no desire to exit such a dwelling place what so ever.

"What do you think they want?" Asked Nahjee,

"I don't have the slightest idea, I mean I have a pretty good guess coming on if that would help any," both were looking through the windshield at the four officers who had them covered.

"Nah, I don't think it'll help any but your phones ringing," said Nahjee, then smiled at his potna "you want to take a guess who that is?"

"No, I could see her." Rasaan replied as he saw Tahj waving her phone in his direction.

"I was wondering if you saw her," Nahjee continued to smile.

"I do, what's so fucking funny, I mean you think we should at least ask them what they want?"

"Ok, so far we got a bunch of guns drawn on us... Whoa, and now you got a dog running and jumping on your shit. The fuck! Tell me, what you think would happen if you opened the door to ask them anything."

Nahjee was always finding reasons to smile and was doing pretty good with the visions of his man getting shot a bunch of times for being nosey. Just the thought of Rasaan reaching for anything less lone a door handle under these conditions drew some pretty funny pictures if you asked him. But relief came when the two saw that from the twelve officers, one of them had to have been the Sergeant, because he proved to be not only in strict control but also the most educated in affairs like this. Through all the chaos, the panics and disorder it was this officer that asked the lot loud enough for all to hear.

"Does anyone even know who the occupants are?" Comedy was the look that was passed around like a hot potato. Seeing the confusion, the deputy in charge immediately brought order to a scene where there was no crime what so ever, which meant that the dogs were called off. Yet, they were still being covered by officers as the deputy with the most brains converged on the car and said,

"Don't mean to inconvenience the two of you but is there a licensed driver between the both of you?" Rasaan slid the deputy his license through the crack of the window.

"Ok, good, good, now my next question is the money one. Does this car belong to anyone of you? Now I could understand if it doesn't, with this being such a fine vehicle..." Rasaan slid the rest of his credentials to the deputy, including his registration and proof of insurance. He watched as the officer took all of which back to his car with him and after a spell returned all of Rasaan's paper works.

"On behalf of all the officers here Mr. Sherman I'd like to apologize. You are free to go, and sorry for the delay sir." With nothing further to say, the Sergeant waved over all the other officers around him and began to bark obscenities in their direction while Rasaan started up the car and drove away placing a call to Tahj, the love of his life.

To say anything about these two, one could easily draw them up as drug dealers. One could easily draw them up as flesh peddlers, which means that one could easily only speculate towards their occupations as well as their spendthrift and clandestine ways. Even if one was to implore instead of speculate, would have only gotten them blank stares or shrugged shoulders for it says it right there on Rasaan's license plate "no comt." which stood for 'no comment.' For these two didn't trust anyone but each other.

Although they had other friends and other associates who they barely talked baseball, basketball or relationships with, who were just as curious as all the rest. Still through all the curiosity and all the tedious speculations and vacuous conclusion, what was ever so plane to see was that these two were hustlers. These two didn't sell drugs, but they knew somebody that did. These two didn't like the gun either but if the time came for them to need one, both Heckler and Koch would show up. If the time presented itself for these two to incorporate women into their schemes, then only the most beautiful would do without compromise.

So, were these two flesh peddlers, with just another fancy name? Well, never has anyone of the two ever put a price on a woman, because no one can. It's a wonder how women compromise so often, because these two knew that a woman was and always will be... forever priceless.

The understanding being something that alludes and never fully grasped by all of mankind had always came down to these two major factors and keys to life. Not all the time did where you come from genuinely gets you where you need to go. Who you know is what gets you there faster and being loyal and trustworthy is what kept you there even longer. Knowing this helped these two set out and meet some people from Spokane to Spain, from the Golden Shores of the Pacific to the frozen doors of the Atlantic. These two left knocking on doors, and the doors that went unanswered, were kicked in, rude announcements and all.

The other thing that these two learned along the way was that God had over done it when he created man. Wisdom was so high on his list during this creation of 'Adam' that he created man with two brains. One on his shoulders and one between his hips, somehow the production of 'Adam' should have been recalled due to faulty parts. Because inside of the human anatomy there isn't enough blood flow to occupy both brains at the same time, and being spaced so far apart makes it even more complicated for the flow of oxygen to keep both brains creative and fully functioning. It was one trick man has yet to master and because of this a lot of deals that were made, where the stakes were high? Either Rasaan or Nahjee would make the comfortable reservations of four star hotels, transportation and the company of a well-kept beauty. Who would indeed accept the money for a favor that wasn't sexual at all. Majority of the times sex was used only if that's what the hired help wished to do in order to get the prize posses-sion of 'information' and 'leverage'.

Sex would never be recommended by either Rasaan or Nahjee leaving this strictly up to the hired beauty. To them it was the combination of who they knew; jewelers, executives in large firms, attorneys, people in small places, dark places, high places and faraway places, which forced many of women to be enlightened by the mere notion of a pure 'come up' and it'll be their own doing to provide pleasures along the way.

What they've learned and sometimes the hard way was that regardless of the situation to always remain silent. People would probe, speculate, beseech, and reach for even the farfetched and use even that to destroy. These two knew that they would have to live under those conditions if for nothing else but to survive. Worse would be to live amongst business associates, who'll fail to trust you because you have loose lips. A lot of successful people have skeletons in their closets that they'll wish to take to their graves. So to be labeled as a blabber mouth in a world of secrets would discourage any potential client, prospect, or merchant which would ultimately stunt the growth of any venture. So much that any business could become dehydrated and money spots dried up until it was all over, on the count of those kinds of lips.

They knew to never make promises that you either can't or wouldn't be able to keep. Never say you could deliver unless you were sure that you could deliver. In life shit happens and everybody knows this. No one accepts the whole rose garden but they do however expect the roses. By knowing this these two knew that if the April showers never came to be wise enough to supply the water. These two had become reliable to their many acquaintances who've called upon their services regardless of any-thing prompt, discreet and honorable would be the main ingredients to any handshake deals, back room deals, and porter potty or where ever the deal was made. They'd offer what you could expect and in return you deliver what they'd expect, cold hard cash. That's it and see ya' next time, if there was next time. Nobody hurt, nobody harmed and business is good. Never had a deal gone awry because everything was always sat down mutual. I got the goods; you got the money, now let's make the switch, and a deal is a deal. This being the prime reason why they were donated so many things like Jewelry, cars, clothes, foods and expensive liquors. To see what these two have become accustom to, many would give a right arm. These two had an insurmountable desire and an advantage over other hustlers because a lot of these brothers lacked balls, but not these two.

As it is clichéd, everybody wants heaven but nobody wants to die. A cliché that was arguably not invented for these two. A phone call is normally made in secret, in strict confidence. A friend of a friend is in deep trouble; someone could of home invaded them and took this friend for everything. Some prized pieces over a month ago and they would love to have them back. The pieces have surfaced maybe a fence was sought and a buy has been arranged, these are the piece's yadda -yaaa, they're worth fifty grand to us could you cover? Great I'll send you a car. Sounds simple right? But what if the friend of a friend, the one that was home invaded was spitting mad and vowed revenge and really could care less about these possessions not as much as they would care to squeeze the culprits head into a vise and watch their eye balls pop right out of their sockets. Would these two care or even give a fuck then? No! So, a car would show up with the keys in the glove box with carry out instructions nobody the wiser. A kid napping could take place or heaven help us, just a simple recovery.

Sometimes these prized possessions would be paintings or jewelry or just regular ole respect. Whatever it may mean to one, it meant dough to the other. Suffice to say that to these two, it was always, only business. You stole or took from a friend or even a friend of a friend, their jewels or whatever, these two would come and get them. The merchandise, whether diamonds, pearls, rubies, watches or wooden teeth. To make sure that it was all returned when they got there, and to alleviate the arguments they would bring a set of pliers to act as a remedy for that. You'll put the jewels in a safe but these two would put your jewels in a squeeze and really wouldn't care if they had indeed busted your balls...literally.

Sometimes a ransom note would be passed to a friend saying this amount of dollars, a tip would be made in confidence and you could have their friends' son if that's what you picked. To balance everything these two were known to make a few phone calls and have your whole family as captives. Your grandmother, mother, step brother, kids and the damned gold fish. You could either release the merchandise or ultimately, you would lose it all in the one way that would hurt "you" the most.

In a world outside of the ghetto some of the strangest things takes place but none more surprising than how it's so easy for some of these prissy fucks to find sleep at night knowing the sordid acts that the rich inflicts on the rest of the world and this was crazy, crazy, crazy.

Rasaan always took the calls, and he always spoke for the both of them and the two has always delivered. Not even a trip to Stockton would change their morals or their integrity. Stockton California a place reputed for two things; their ports and their ever inclining murder rates. Their ports would bring the guns and the drugs and the thugs would murder because of this, and for a town so small one could easily get lost in it.

The call came nearly a week ago; someone has been hurt and a deal had gone oh so terribly wrong. A brief case was taken and someone was shot on the count of this bad deal. The brief case has plates; five of them were all see through facsimiles of US currency worth thirty grand a piece to their friends. It took a week of taco and burrito trucks, fast foods and junk foods before Nahjee said morosely,

"I had enough of this bullshit," and got out of the car and walked across the street pulling his shirt over his high powered 9mm Browning. Rasaan saw as Nahjee gone to the sleazy motel they were casing on Eldorado Street, right between Charter way and 8th street. Catching up to him he said,

"What you thinking just a crash and grab?"

"Exactly, fuck this shit, we trying to be all nice and shit while this bitch in here putting blocks on our knots. I'm thinking, why don't we just go in and Rambo that fucker and run like hell? So, how you like my plan so far?" Nahjee finished while retrieving his soda purchase from the vending machine while giving Rasaan enough time to make up his mind.

"So far it stinks; I mean how much time you think we'd have to smash the door, lay him down and check the case? What if the plates aren't even in the case? As you say, there's always a chance for the "what if," remember?"

"Ok, I'm listening but I'm going to tell you ahead of time, I'm going to veto anything that doesn't give it to us right now." After a lot of improvising the two had finally gone in and captured what they came to get from a cranked out doper. One that nearly had a heart attack when the cleaning lady met morphed into two extended fire arms, one of them yelling lay down or else, the other yelling for some plates. So frightened was this frail looking fella with the menacing tattoos that he trembled so much under the watchful eyes of Nahjee that Nahjee was soon expecting the doper to give up the ghost.

"Don't kill me man! Look, all the plates are there! I knew someone would come sooner or later so there you go, you could take them, so you don't have to kill me, right?"

"Punk why did you shoot him," said Nahjee loving the control that he held over the druggie while Rasaan scanned the plates.

"I haven't shot anything but some dope brother, look at me, do I look like a hard case? Shit, I liked to shit my pants when you two came in, no sir I haven't shot anybody and you guys don't look like the ones interested in these plates but if you want them go right on ahead."

"How you know, bitch" Nahjee poured the rest on him now.

"Because I would have been able to recognize two brothers out of all of those white people readying themselves to die over this damned case. I'll tell you that if you let me live I would give you a strong word of advice; the person that was shot was the rightful owner of this case, everyone else was only trying to get the plates for free, you see they came to strong arm them…"

"How you know mother fucker?" Nahjee was in full rhythm now,

"Because the one that was shot was my little brother and I would have known if he made a deal with one of you."

"Quit lying before I shoot you in your face."

"If that's what you want to do but I lie to you not, you go on and take the plates but ever since I came near them it's been one problem after the next. Now I need to bury my brother, so whether you are careful or not is up to you and if you need to kill me seeing that you already have the case then maybe you didn't just come for the case..."

"Hello," Rasaan finally broke through to Nahjee while waving the brief case, "It's time to go now, I mean not that I'm trying to you know, fuck over you guys little friendly thingy, but you know the police and everything, maybe we could all consider that. I mean, what you guys think?"

So now that the two were on their way back to Sacramento Nahjee continued to go in and out of spells, so much that now Rasaan needed to know what the fuck has gotten into his potna.

"Ok, at first I wasn't going to say anything, but now I wanna know what the hell got you dropping ashes everywhere? You've been spacing out ever since we got on the freeway, something you think that I should know about?"

"You know what I'm thinking?"

MECCA

THE RENDEZVOUS WAS ONE OF the most happening spots in all of Sacramento. The disc jockeys played only the latest and most popular music and the patrons came from all walks of life to celebrate, unwind or to rinse away life's woes. Whatever the case may be, the Rendezvous was indeed the place to be and everybody who claimed to be somebody had known this. Way before their self-proclaimed or street legend ever formed or took shape, the Rendezvous was right there, but for Mecca this was her home away from home. When one asked about her occupation, sure one could easily see that her vibrant personality would place her in the "hands on people business," but no one would have picked for the life of them that she was a bar tender. Every time someone asked she'd say proudly,

"I'm a bar tender,"

"Nah, hell no, dancer maybe, but bartender never," they would always say.

"Oh, I'm a dancer too," she'd tell them and lord knew that she had never lied because one of her other talents was that this babe here, knew how to get the party started.

"So, you mean to tell me that you are a bar tender, you say?" And to the unbeliever she would produce a card that would grant them free admission for a one time visit to "The Rendezvous."

Over the years over five thousand of these cards had been passed around by her alone. Which at first the idea would drive management the fuck nuts, now has not only become a welcoming idea but a heavily recommended one.

"So, you say with this card that I'd be able to get in free? Well what if I brought a date does this card work for her too?"

"Surely does."

"Nahhh,"

"Uh huh, come and have a drink with me," she'd say. So, the club stayed jammed packed with people celebrating, and jubilation was always present due to the occasional cameos coming from recording artist. Who would tour through this particular club even if it wasn't on their schedule because it was known to come through and pay homage's to one of the most cracking spots in all of Sacramento.

Anyways, on this day Mecca sat in on a conversation between two of the regular patrons. They'd always show up a tad early in order to drink in peace, and would make themselves scarce once the club became too crowded for their liking. This wasn't a problem for either Mecca or her home girl Lerin nor the other bar tenders or management who knew that some customers would love their drinks in peace. No matter what, the club was going to open at the same time every day, Sunday to Sunday at twelve o'clock noon Pacific Standard Time. By five o'clock in the evening Mecca, Lerin and Jerry the other bartender would have then poured hundreds of drinks.

What nobody knew was that these hours were the business hours, and Mecca knew business when she heard business and when she saw it. Believing that just because these old geezers pulled up in those old vans or trucks never constituted that these men were on the sidelines waiting for the casket to call them. No sir, a lot of these old timers had old money and some really, really old money. Whose biggest assignments weren't making money but remembering where they hid all of it.

So, while these two gentlemen were discussing portfolios and money markets, while these two talked escrows and the 401k, Mecca was tuned in closely. It wasn't that she was a stranger to such talk, and it wasn't that she was listening just to be listening either. No. Mecca always liked and admired brothers rather old or young who talked with a sense of purpose, with the education needed to challenge this ever evolving world. Those that could use their minds to be successful, because Mecca well knew and was a firm believer that in this life only the brain way would prevail.

Sure an individual could indeed become successful through hard drudgery work, that was always good too, but Mecca liked the brothers that worked for their money plus knew how to make their money work for them. So with that said, note that she never listened just to be listening, she was listening with admiration and a deep, deep respect. As a bar tender Mecca has heard every story one could imagine, for a bar tender must wear many hats, being a broker, a confidante, a philosopher and a psychiatrist was to name a few, and Mecca wore each one with the authenticity of the natural owners of such occupations. And this being another reason that "The Rendezvous" was the place to be, for even the employees as well.

Tahj

"Come on, two, three, four, five, six, seven, eight, again, two, three, four, five, six, seven, eight, spin, yes, leap, yes, drop, ok, now back up. You're slow Unique, you're slow, come on, again, we're gonna do it until we get it right people." Tahj only had two loves in her life and she held them both close to heart. One of the things was this girl loved to dance. It didn't matter the kind of dance, Jazz dance, the Salsa, Waltz and lord could this girl Tango. Yet, it was her urban dance and Tribal steps that she was famous for. She drove religious men on first class tickets to sinning. It never mattered, she needed to dance, she needed to teach people how to dance and show them how to bring her vision to life.

Many people sought out her expertise. Musicians came from far and wide, both colleges and high schools came calling for her rhythm. The only demand that she would put on any pupil or group was that they would work as hard as she did. The energy that she would put into teaching she only asked that you'd put the same energy and enthusiasm into learning.

Now that this hot group had come all the way from Georgia to be cured of their monotonous stage routines, Tahj figured that she may as well push them to be all that they could be, even if it took all night.

Famous for the yard stick that she used as a pointer, she would tap the floor in perfect rhythm to the synchronized movements, which would help aid the dancers as well as help aid the dancers who were out of sync. In this case it was the lead singer Unique, who brought her laziness all the way to Sacramento from Georgia. This was a problem that Tahj was sure to get rid of before the group left California. Maybe in Georgia the peaches grew nice and sweet but in California, the competition being what it is, lazy is the first thing to get you sent packing.

To let Unique tell it Tahj had singled her out only to make life miserable for her. What Unique didn't know was that her record company had already forwarded the footage of their prior tours and Tahj fought hard to stay woke through the viewings of such footages. If it weren't for the angelic voices that these girls possessed, then finding slumber would have been a synch. One other thing the girls didn't know was that Tahj was gonna push them until she pushed their stardom right into perfection, because dance is the one thing that she could do, and could teach.

The other thing that Tahj found a rhythm for, which was in perfect unison, was her love for Rasaan. Nothing has ever come between the two, though a lot of people have tried, these two always stuck together come what may come.

The facts were all well known that she loved everything about him. The fact that he never pushed and always rolled with whatever, and never had he made any demands what-so-ever. Even though Tahj was sure that if he decided to start she would arrive every beck and call. Because she had the comfort of knowing, not believing, but knowing that Rasaan would arrive in the very same fashion if not quicker.

Although they lived apart their hearts were always joined together. When men live away from their spouses there's always the idea of unfaithfulness and infidel or unctuous behaviors. Not that Tahj never entertained this for a thought. I mean what woman wouldn't? We won't even bring up the fact that he pushes a ninety-thousand-dollar car or the fact that he could make a down payment on a Lear jet with just his watch collection. Toss in the ice blue ear rings that went flawless two carats apiece, the same ones that dripped like water from his ears, then we could start talking warheads.

Never mind the fact that Rasaan was what the French called "debonaire," get rid of the idea that he was always draped in purple labels. We could even toss all of his material things in the river and still Rasaan was a boss. No secret, Tahj well knew that it wasn't what was on a man but what was in a man that made him chief. Tahj wasn't the only one to know this. As far as she was concerned every woman in California knew this, because Rasaan wasn't what one would call local, uh uh, Rasaan was what one would call national and bi-coastal. So, trying to convince Tahj that there was absolutely no competition aiming at her man was a waste of time. She'd believe it more if you were sending her a snowman for the fourth of July, then to try and convince her to take it easy on thinking that nobody wanted Rasaan but her.

Sure they lived apart and sure at times Tahj became uneasy on the count of this, but when she expressed these concerns he just gave her the keys and the security codes and told her to come through whenever she liked and do you think that she didn't. Midnight, five in the morning, nine in the evening, when he was at home, and when he wasn't. She would stop by and do 'his' laundry and 'her' snooping, until she got tired of that bullshit. Five in the morning, she would let herself in only to find Rasaan asleep, solely, in his king sized bed with nothing but his boxers and a necklace on, rolling over always glad to see her. Rasaan was the type of man that could send a woman's intuition into "Helter Skelter" because he is everything that he says he is. No matter how heated the passion he was the truth. All the way in and all the way out.

WILLIAM

William did however catch a break, though not from work uh uh, no. Work was only the throw off and the decoy in case his main bitch got wind of his game bitch. He always used work as the alibi; I mean it was true he'd always have love for Tamia, but for him she had grown too touchy feely and too suffocating which was the furthest thing from William's liking. The only thing that she thinks about was work, work, work, fuck, fuck, fuck and school, school, school. Oh she was fine as hell but so was this nice piece lying next to him right now. The difference between the two; Tamia was stiff and ever so regular and traditional but Aretha, the fine piece lying next to him now, "shit" was the best way to explain her spontaneous, inadvertent, sudden and spur of the moment activities. Definitely it's what drove William crazy the most, because William was into that instant gratification stuff.

Oh he was hip to the hard work being all that paid off only nobody said how long that shit would take for the pay off. Shit, nothing ever came easy for him, hell no. He'd dropped out of high school to help raise his little brother and to keep his doped up stepfather from molesting his little sister while his dope fiend momma just stood by and craved more crack. This left him to steal, beg and barrow just to feed his self and his siblings. The money that was meant for food and other supplies was spent on drink and drugs at his house.

William wanted to go to school, wanted to make the football team and lord only knew what would have become of him then, but as it stood now he worked at the post office, just a quarter past minimum wages. He had to hustle on the side to get the ends to at least speak to each other, didn't really have to be the closest of friends, just to "meet" was enough for him. So because of this, on his fake work days Aretha could easily count on him to surface and begin to service the many dope fiends that straggled up and down her street in search of a "jet plane," which was cooked cocaine rocks, to take them as far away from their realities as they could possibly go.

William could only wish that he could share the same enthusiasm for life as Tamia. He wished he shared the same beliefs in God as Tamia. Many people say that they made the perfect couple, but what they never knew was that William was dying inside; life was taking too long to make him happy. Everything about him was fraud. If you asked him that punk ass Chevrolet that was parked around the corner was fake, the smile that he wore was fake too, even the stories that he told Tamia was fake. The fact that he says that he liked going to work was as fraudulent as the stories he had told Tamia. All of this didn't do nothing but remind him of how far he was left behind; feeling as if life had taken off without him.

So, now that he finished sexing Aretha all the way to sleep, he figured that he could bring his phone to life and after checking his messages did he wish that he never done it.

"Who the fuck does this, who she thinks she is," he thought to his self. "Baby I'm going to pick up Marva from some shelter. I believe that she'll stay with us for a minute until she could get her stuff together ok, see you when you come in." Not baby is it alright for Marva, not sweetie I don't want to make the decision without you, considering you pay most of our living expenses with that shitty check that you get. None of that was said at all. She just made the decisions for the both of them and left him to live with it like it or not.

So justice is served. She behaves like 'that', so I behave like 'this' and with that William raised the quilt high enough to reveal the buttocks of Aretha. He slapped them hard enough to awaken her and just as she was taught, when daddy slaps those cheeks that meant the legs must open wide. No matter when or where and this night would be no different. Her eyes were still sleepily closed, but her legs found their way open and inviting enough to allow William entry. Before long she was fully awake and in full groove with the man that she called daddy. No matter who was present, even if her real daddy was in the room it was real, she knew better, and this is what William liked in a woman. One that run off halfcocked was never then and never would be, the kind of woman he'd call wife. These were his thoughts as he gyrated in and out of Aretha, in slow, but powerful strokes until they both lay spent.

"Mah, you are not going to believe this shit," William said to Aretha.

"What, what is it daddy?" Was her reply,

"Listen to this shit?" William replayed his voice mail sending it to loud speaker so the two could hear, and then said, "What you think of that?"

"Well, at least she called you baby before she made the decision for you guys. You got to give her credit for that."

"Tell me, if that was you that left the message what would say?" William smiled as though he already knew the answer.

"Well, first I would have said daddy, gave you your respect and all."

"Is that right?"

"You know I would, don't even play me like that."

"Ok, ok, what else?"

"I mean if that's my girl and all, she would understand it if I told her that I would have to wait to communicate this situation with you first. I wouldn't run off full steam ahead like that and then ask you to deal with it. No I wouldn't do that." Satisfied with her answer William said,

"That's my baby."

"I know. The way I see it I'm the Queen Bee, and she's the other bitch. Soon you're gonna get tired of playing around and you're gonna come home, I ain't even worried about that."

"Is that right?"

"Yelp, and you know it too, don't start playing up in here."

"Ok I hear you, dig it though, we're not gonna worry about what she over there doing like you say. What I need to know is what are we doing? That's the question. What are we doing?"

"What you mean by that? What you mean what is we doing?"

"Just like I said what, you trying to buy time or something answer the question?"

"Daddy you call all the shots around here. I'm doing what you doing and you know all of this already. So why do you continue to test me I haven't a clue."

"So, what if I went and got all of my clothes and shit right now?"

"I'll be sleep when you get back but you know how to wake me up. I'll be willing no matter when, you know I would. So?"

"So, what you mean so?" William snapped out of his reverie, a chimera that let her words go unheard. As soon as William asked the question, one that he'd swear he knew the answer to already, he left mentally in an effort to try to imagine how life would be without Tamia in the picture, even though she proved to be ever so stiff and straight as an arrow, she did possess the determination to be successful at her endeavors. Though the thought of her reaching for a Doctor's Certificate was a bit much, still she possessed a drive to be something. Then he thought of the negatives. She was stiff, too formal and traditional for him, in a world of spice she was bland, and never did she ever like to do anything exciting. To her exciting were the spots on an unhealthy liver or how to fix a cleft or a club foot, "Yippy, hooray," how exciting.

Never mind exciting, she rarely had time to do anything. The sex was rushed, too obvious for him. He knew what she was gonna do, how she was gonna do it and when she was gonna do it. Somehow she loved to manage the money, including his, as if he only had one inspiration and that was to pay bills which was something that a man knew better to do anyhow. If you were to ask her, a man never thought of copping' those new Jordan's that just came out, those Retro Sevens or the new LeBron's. To her men had better never be caught entertaining such a crazy idea as to pay over seventeen dollars for some sneakers. It would be just plain out right foolishness to pay one hundred and seventy-five dollars for some damned shoes no matter how fly they could look with your outfit. William learned all of this when he made it in rocking the new Griffey's that came out. Liked to gotten his head busted on account of that one. Tamia didn't seem to care about the over time that he put in just to cop those joints off East Bay at the low, low, discount, buy now and save twenty-five percent and no shipping and handling. She still went bonkers, took her all of three days to speak to him. She didn't want to sleep next to him, allowed his laundry to pile up as if the dingy socks weren't beginning to get to her as well. Just to send the message across she'd behave like a spoiled brat. This to William was too much to forget so easily. She possesses all of these strict grown up qualities then behave so childishly over some tennis shoes that he bought with money that he decided to stay later than usual at work in order to purchase.

Then it became the war of the roses at the home front. So if William was to look at the negatives one would of thought that he should have been long gone by now. Ah, but the pluses, the positives. Let's see, hmm well she could balance a damn check book in two point two seconds, and that homemade gravy that she runs crazy over those chops were always bringing him home before dark sets in good. She knows how to keep a house in order and William always liked that about her. Though she proved to be too frugal for his liking, there's times that calls for that. So in that regard she is special because Lord knew that if it was up to William, everything in the house would be up to date. There'd be eighty-two inches' worth of television, surround sound, the works. The warriors on "call of duty" would look like little midgets flying across the TV tossing hand grenades and firing life sized weapons at the evil villains. It would be pay per view fight nights every Friday and "guys night in" every Sunday.

Let him have his way shoot it'll be his and her Retro's all over the place. It'll take a whole moving truck to carry the boxes out of there if they decided to move just in shoes alone, I mean with all the hard work that he's been doing. Nah in life no one needed those kind of irresponsibility's. So to her credit she does keep a nice leash on not going above and beyond, and the sex when she really got into it, it was always explosive, trembles and wobbly legs at the end of those sessions, my goodness. Just the thought of this makes him hate that he was entertaining the thought of walking out on her. To do that he knew would definitely break her heart. He would be leaving her for Aretha who too is all the pennies in a dime, but she lives, eat, sleeps, breathe, drink and think Oak Park. Fine is one thing, fine with a sense of direction is a whole "other" outfit all together. Aretha doesn't even care that she receives county aid. She figures she could push this coke or this crank for the rest of her life or she would use fine as a weapon to land her a nigga that she feels would take her to the top without dropping her ass off.

The sex with Aretha was continuous and all day not to mention good. Her head game was incredible, but try to take her out on the town if you want to. She'd see a woman that she knew and it would get loud and obnoxious, depending on the woman. If it was a woman that she knew to be an enemy, then all hell could break loose right there on the spot. Which went past obnoxious, it took William most of two days to realize that he was never taking Aretha out in public ever again. Once her and her ex-man's sister tore up the whole China Buffet and wouldn't stop until the cops showed up with riot gear to usher everyone out, one table at a motha fuckin' time. So to leave Tamia, solely for Aretha alone was not going to happen, no. It had to be an upgrade in it somewhere. Aretha alone wouldn't equate the loss of Tamia not even close. Tamia's negatives were way better than Aretha's' positives and this he'd known.

"You know what I mean by so. What were you doing? Where did you just take off to dang, so are you or what?"

"Am I going to get my things right now? Nah not right now, but I'm seriously thinking about it. I mean for real. She's doing too much 'in the way' stuff right now and I could honestly see it getting worse before it gets any better. But I need you to understand something; it would be hard for me to crib with you until I've lined up all the ducks. I can't, I mean I can, but it wouldn't be smart for me to just go off halfcocked and I want to make the best decision available. I mean I like what you and I have going right here. We are getting this paper and we doing the buildup thing. Let's continue the build and let this other situation play itself out, feel that?"

"I hear you. I'm just tired of you leaving me that's all daddy and I want to be with you all the time."

"I know you do sweetie. I believe I want that too mommy, but something is telling me to be a bit more patient. I mean when I come in don't you want me to come all the way in?"

"Yeah boo I do, but when though? That bitch is taking up all your time only to stress you, and then you come running to me all banged up needing me to patch you back up and stuff."

"I know baby. Let's see what happens in the next few weeks ok, Sweetie?"

"Ok, daddy you know I got you."

CHAPTER 4

Marcel

THERE WERE TWO THINGS THAT Marcel knew about; paper and how to get paper. That's why the whole hood called him "Cash" even though he could have simply drawn other handles like "Danger" or "get ta playing" or "one punch" or "havoc" even. Cash seemed to be most sensible because a lot of times he would be found counting some of it. For Marcel money was always easy come and easy go, therefore the "true value" of it was no more than the "face value" of it. If it was a twenty-dollar note, great that's how much Remy Martin cost for a pint. If it was a c-note, perfect that just so happen to be how much those camel color Roc boots were that he saw on K. Street the other day. Lord helps him if he hit a righteous score then its shopping spree for real. Then guess what happened once he went broke? He would pull his banger out and anybody could get it. Over a hundred times it was recorded that when he came down hands went up and he always said,

"My nigga, you better send it all, "get ta playing" and make me find it myself if you want to." Because everybody believed that he was screwed up enough to make good on his words of wreaking havoc. No one ever "got ta playing," shit nah, they would just fork it over, all of it too. Marcel was known in the hood for his "cash," his "banger," his "licks," and for his "hands." Barely into adulthood, had Marcel already been up and down the coast, across the Midwest and down South.

By age twelve Marcel was sent to Juvenile Hall. By the age of thirteen the Sacramento Police Department was so tired of hearing his name ringing and had grown so tired of arresting him that they sent an old white haired man that everyone called "Pops" to visit him with a proposition saying that Marcel would be released immediately on one condition, that he'd be released to the custody of the Police Athletic League. Marcel was young, but he was far from dumb. He signed those papers without reading them, he was in the presence of his lawyer and though his mother was on the phone still she played an influential part in talking Marcel into signing the papers and coming on home to behave. What Marcel thought was a break, found out soon enough that he had only been "duped" "hoodwinked" and "lead astray" or what his grandfather would say "son you just got hustled that's all."

Yeah, Marcel had been hustled alright, had Marcel known what the athletic league was he probably would have just sat this one out for the entire eight months that he had coming for a burglary in the first degree. There was something in the name he thought, 'Police Athletic' sounded appealing, sort of like he was signing up for some kind of basketball or better yet a football team. One that he always saw kids going to the Salvation Army about. Lord knew that Marcel knew how to catch, run and tackle; just thinking about it he couldn't wait to get his hands on one of those little bastards because at thirteen Marcel was already maturing. He was the tallest student in all of middle school whenever he decided to go.

Already five foot eleven, scaring the shit out if six feet, a long and lanky fella he was. Understandable was the reasons why the police wanted him on their athletics because Marcel knew damned well that he wasn't there to provide them with information. If that was the case, then they'd look good taking his ass right back to Kiefer Blvd. Like on the double, he was sure that they had a cell in juvenile hall for him waiting.

When "Pops" showed up to his crib for the first time, which was the right time to wake the roosters, only to bring Marcel to a gym that was equipped with a heavy bag, a speed bag, a very real boxing ring and other knock out apparatuses. Marcel put his two's together and figured it all out for himself, he stood in the middle of the floor flabbergasted. It wasn't even six o'clock a.m. and there he stood looking at posters of Leon Spinks,

Sugar Ray both Lenard and Robinson, Ali in his prime, George Foreman, Ken Norton, Rocky Marciano and for some strange reason Rocky Balboa the television legend. Everything in the gym was sponsored by the great company "Ever Last." At five in the morning who the fuck really cares was Marcel's thought until "Pops" put something else on his mind, a two piece sweat suit top and bottom that he tossed to Marcel then pointed in the directions of the locker room then said,

"Hurry kid we haven't gotten all day," not quite understanding why the big rush to get dressed into some clothing that weren't his own. No, Marcel had a behavior problem, but he was nobody's charity case. Sure he decided to go along with the rest of the routine I mean since the two were already huddled up at dark thirty in the morning. But wearing someone else's sweaty garments shoot, good luck and this is what he told "Pops."

"Suit yourself kid," was all the old man had said before pointing towards the door to which they had come then said,

"You're ready I'd reckon?"

"Sure, not quite sure for what though, but I'm sure that I'm ready to do whatever I need to do," was Marcel's reply.

"Great attitude kid, I like a man with a great attitude and you son, have a great attitude. Now follow me and if you follow me you're gonna go far." What Marcel didn't know was that the old man had said this to everybody, it was his own personal inside joke and one that Marcel didn't think was very funny after a while. He soon found out what "Pops" meant by follow him; he discovered that the motha fucka meant that shit literally. Once they were outside of the gym "Pops" hopped inside of an old share cropping truck and set the pace for Marcel to follow him. First Marcel ran alongside the truck, and then way behind the truck realizing then that when "Pops" told him that if he'd follow him that he would go far, the old fart actually meant that shit literally as well. The old guy took Marcel to the streets before they came alive.

The Police Athletic League was located on 5th Avenue between 35th and 38th Street. Pops took Marcel clad in Levi's jeans, a plaid button up and some Hush Puppies down Broadway all the way to 65th Expressway, right on 65th going south to 14th Avenue. Stopping and waiting before continuing on for a spell before God gave the old dude a conscience which made them break for water. Then the old guy sobered up in time to lead him west to Franklin Blvd. Making a right there, leading him north to 2nd Avenue where God showed up again to give Marcel another break, and a drink of water. Plenty of pissed off by now and couldn't give a flying fuck when "Pops" kept saying,

"You're looking good kid, you're looking good, you're special I tell ya." Marcel soon realized that the old fucker always said this motivational shit right before break time was over, then he would take off again.

Now that Pops had led him back to the gym, Marcel found that he was more interested in the time so he searched and found a clock and found that it was ten minutes to ten o'clock. So irritated was he that he barely recognized that the gym was now occupied by other athletes and trainers. So aggravated was he that he barely heard Pops say,

"Follow me," this time Marcel was more hesitant and reluctant to fall for the same trick twice, just shook his head and fell in step with the old man with the very deceptive and broad sense of humor.

"Come I want to show you something," and by something Pops lead Marcel into a kitchen that was hid in the far corner of the gym, crazy and silly was the idea of having a kitchen built inside of a gym he thought. The aroma had reminded Marcel that he was operating on an empty stomach. Which begun to make this idea a very beautiful one after all. He followed Pops to a stop at a counter where they both took a stool. Marcel was now soaking wet in sweat understood fully the need for the sweat suit, for his jeans, shirt and shoes were now ruined and felt clammy to his skin. He still stuck to his guns as if he didn't have a care in the world, sat and listened as Pops spoke to him.

"Kid I need to ask you a very honest question and in return I'm gonna need you to give me a very honest answer. Do you hear me?"

"Yeah, what's up?" Marcel didn't see the need for a heart to heart, but he went along with it anyways.

"When we were on the road just now how many times did you feel like quitting?" Marcel who was expecting something else began to laugh then remembered that he was dealing with a fox and not any ole fox either but a slippery one. So he sobered up right away and gave thought to the question and with honesty he said,

"Well when we went down Broadway to 42nd I sort of wanted to quit, I was sure to quit once we made it to Green fair, luckily you gave me a break or I was gonna head back at 65th. I was too pissed off to quit once we got to 14th. I didn't want to quit then, my ass wanted to fight and I rolled that feeling all the way back here. Why'd you ask?"

"Well, why didn't you quit?" It was Pops expression and questionable look that made it easy to ask but easier was moving a ton of bricks than to answer, and no matter how long Marcel contemplated, this question was too complex for such a young mind. So he just looked Pops in his eyes and said,

"I don't know,"

"Yes...you... do, you just don't want to say it, but I'll say it for you. Kid you are so into proving "your" self-worth to someone else that elusive and vacant is the need to prove "your worth" to "yourself." When you look out there in that gym you would see twenty people out there just like you. Twenty kids who feel the need to be, but when I told you that you were special I wasn't lying to you because out of all twenty of those kids, let me see ahh, well, all twenty of them hopped in the back of that truck way before we made it to 65th and I brought them back here and I showed them the same thing that I'm gonna show you, you know what that is?" Marcel was still trying to pull the sting from the words that came tumbling from the old man's mouth that he couldn't do much but shake his head in the negative. Though young he may have been but he was wise enough, even young, to know the truth once he heard it and whoever coined the cliché which stated that the truth hurts were a genius. And whoever coined it was far more popular than the jerk that coined that one saying "the truth that shall set you free" because whoever made that shit up was an idiot. Marcel remembered telling the truth twice; the first time they gave him two months and the second time he got three.

"Ah, but you do know what I'm going to show you. You just don't want to say it," Pops finished appearing to know "Marcel" better than Marcel.

"How do you know that I know? Since you're so smart ole timer tell me that, huh"

"Well not because I'm so smart but because you're so smart that's how I know. You just don't want to be. It's either because you'd hate to be or because you don't want to be. I am smart enough to know that much. Now, I'm going to need you to work with me on this one. I told you that I wanted to show you something and I brought you to a kitchen and I did this because of why? Come on kid work with me now?"

"So we could eat."

"Close, so I could show you how to eat. I don't mean which utensils to use. I need to show you which foods to use and because of this I'm gonna cook for you every day. First thing in the morning and in the evening only it's what you eat away from here that could ruin everything that we'll work so hard for or it could help. Do you follow me?"

From that day on Marcel showed up to the gym as a regular. First with the help of Pops then once it became routine Marcel would meet Pops at the gym at the same time, every day, even on Sunday. Because of this, as an amateur, Marcel had an impeccable record sixty-two wins and no losses. The old man had created him to be a monster in a world of sheep. Chiseled was his body, lightning fast were his hands that packed TNT in both of them. He had a mercurial style that was fickle enough to create match up dilemmas for any trainer. Never mind the opponent.

Marcel had found a true love in Pops and a true love for the sport of boxing. Many scouts came from abroad to get a firsthand experience of the Sacramento's Boxing Club that the Police Athletic League had manufactured. Which was a club that was burning a trail through Northern as well as Southern California alike? In four different weight classes there were undefeated records in Sacramento waiting on their professional debuts. Then fate spoke, and God had sent one of his angels to claim the life of one of the best trainers in boxing history. Pops at the age of seventy-nine was called to service where he would join some of the great warriors in the sky.

Marcel was so distraught, so out of sync without the guidance of his best friend. Due mostly in part to some diabolical events, this young man failed to hear the message after death entirely. He failed to carry on and dedicate the rest of his days to one of the greatest things that ever happened to him. That one day in November, just two days after the announcements that he was going to join the United States of Americas' Boxing Club in the great state of Main for the Olympic try outs. Marcel had borrowed a truck from a friend just after celebrating way too much. So much that Marcel struck a fire hydrant and high tailed it the hell away from the scene where he had sent water flying over fifteen feet high. "Oops, sorry," oh, no, no, no buster, an officer was in hot pursuit and pulled over the very drunk and highly intoxicated Marcel who blew a breathalyzer field test that registered somewhere around Mars so to say, which so happen to be passed the California's legal limits.

Fate played its cold and heartless tricks once more by adding into the boxing rule books policies that prohibited performance enhancing drugs or any other drugs for that matter and it just so happened that the Committee for the Board of Boxing needed a urinalysis sample. One which Marcel provided after knowing that he had over done it at a party where there was marijuana and cocaine a plenty.

So after discovering what he already knew, that he failed his urinalyses deposit. The committee gave him no choice and publically removed him from the tour and blasted him all over the News, the Newspapers and all of the radio stations. The barber shops and anywhere else people met up all had their own opinions. No one could believe that anyone could be so stupid as to blow away the chances at becoming an Olympic champion to go along with the status of his golden gloves.

"How could he do such a thing like this to us, he disgraced himself and all of us," they were saying. What they didn't know was that Marcel was waiting on the chance to walk away from the sport. Not quite sure of what he would do in its place, but he knew that he didn't want to fight anymore. Pops called all the shots from the corners and Marcel would answer the bell to execute the mission with the beautifying precision of a sculptor.

Pops replacement had never quite gotten through to Marcel. He never stood a chance really and often times found tossing the towel to Marcel in disappointment a better option before calling it a day even after less than an hours' worth of training. He believed the kid had lost his steam, his snap and his enthusiasm.

Eight years' worth of hard work and high expectations just washed away. Yet, if you let Marcel tell it the entire fault lies in the bosoms of our father who art in heaven. To prove it the church on 42nd Street and Broadway haven't seen him in months, but if they were to go looking for him all one had to do was wait for him at the liquor store right off of Fruit Ridge and Stockton Blvd. I mean the store clerks saw him every day, several times a day. With the way life has turned out for him, with all of its twist and turns of events had all led Marcel to miss the perfect opportunity to be called "Champ."

Without boxing or training Marcel's days were spent wreaking havoc on a society that once felt betrayed by his foolishness but now felt afraid because of his foolishness and blatant disregard for human life, including his own. With this new life style which in fact was actually the "old" one that he reverted back to after taking the scenic route. You know with boxing in the way and all. This is when Marcel proved to the world that negativity begets other negativities and that negative people well, there's a reason why you'd never find them in the plus section much. In this life one must seek and find all of their people of the same ilk. There is only one thing that a thug, goon or whichever one of those street niggas respects, and that's "street shit" and for Marcel this saying was as good as platinum. Because what had grown old was "hustling" as he called scaring the b'jesus out of people for their money with an old crusty .44 Magnum, the high powered hand gun that Clint Eastwood favored in The Good, The Bad and The Ugly. A hustle that paid often and always once a target found his or herself on the business end of such an antagonistic and gladiatorial looking weapon.

It was because the victims gave it up so quickly that the sport of armed robbery had become monotonous and simple. Life had come with no further excitements at least not until he came across another hoodlum who was on his shit twice as hard as Marcel. Although looking at him would be a deception all its own, he had introduced himself to Marcel as being "Sean" which was the name that his parents gave him, but the hood called him "Scope" because he wore really thick, old school pop bottle glasses which made his actual eye balls shrink three times their regular size. When one was to look through his glasses, everything was magnified and brought up close and personal, always the butt of the jokes when he was younger was Sean, but as he grew older the jokes quickly stopped. Same glasses, but what was entirely and ever so different was the man. Sean became just as dangerous as Marcel, which to the community of Oak Park was not a good thing at all. He was one of the best drive by shooters ever created, he became a "Jacker" and a good one, before he turned twenty. When he was still a teenager, no one would have guessed for no one would have believed it anyway that he would even live to see twenty-one. Sean wasn't as tall as Marcel and wasn't as skilled a fighter as Marcel, but the influence that he held over the streets of Sacramento was like a thunder cloud, one waiting to bring a storm as wicked and as violent as a hurricane and Marcel knew this.

So instead of bumping heads with each other, the drinks would be on Marcel. The two could discuss future business plans that could get them both a few ducats which wasn't a bad idea, as Marcel now reflected because hustling had now regained the zest that was lacking while hustling on his own.

By the time the first drink was poured a reason to celebrate had materialized. The Rendezvous, proved to be the perfect atmosphere for such the occasion. The music was loud and so were the patrons. The dance floor was packed and the party goers spent most of the night with one tracked minds. That was to party like there wasn't a tomorrow coming.

The ambience was always flavorful. The rendezvous opened the doors for members of each echelon of classes, middle class, lower class, and upper class. Creating a motley environment that proved to be effective and the antidote against melancholy or a place to hold colloquies or to impress upon a future business partner, as Marcel was doing with Sean. Because at "The Rendezvous", drinks could easily flow for free even though one would have to rank in the class of wealthy in order to buy the bar because at this club there are bottles that could easily run fifteen hundred dollars a pop or ten thousand for a case. Yet often was the times that wealth would find its way through the door and force the bartenders to work awfully hard for their wages. While discussing an upcoming "event" or "lick" or "hustle" Marcel couldn't help but to notice the constant burn that sent his senses into a very uncomfortable and out of alignment frenzy. Constantly he found himself breaking the flow of conversations in order to locate the source of such discomforts.

"You're all right cat daddy," Sean said to Marcel recognizing his agitations. He was shaking his head trying to figure it all out while paying close attention to his inner voice.

"Dog, if I didn't know any better I would say that I'm caught off guard. I feel like an enemy has found me," Marcel reluctantly shared with Sean.

"Like somebody watching you and shit?"

"Yeah, you too,"

"Nah, but somebody is watching us though. Only he's with me, no offense but until I knew for sure that you were talking square business and all." Shrugging his shoulders, Sean concluded by saying "life is what it is."

"I could dig it. I guess this means I could relax then? Now that you said what you said then, right?" Marcel continued his study of Sean, still looking for signs, not receiving any caution signals or any other warnings of hazards, he managed to relax.

"That's exactly what that means my nigga. I like what you are talking about. I just hope you could find respect to be mutual I could respect your mind just know that I got a mind of my own and we would get along just fine."

"My man, so tell me, who do we have for the referee? Do you trust him enough to be here or what?" Marcel asked no longer scanning the room for a potential enemy heard when Sean told him without breaking eye contact that the one, not group but one single man, who played the part of chaperone to ensure that Marcel and Sean both kept their punches above the belt, was indeed trustworthy enough to be assigned the most precious of all items to Sean, which was his life.

"I could dig it even more. Now that you drew it up so well, at first I thought offensive was the only way to take it, but I could only imagine a person of your reputation, must remain on both of his nickels and assurance is the farthest thought away when meeting on enemy grounds. But I need you to know that I wouldn't ask you to meet me here, if you couldn't meet me here. Now, how about clearing the curiosities and invite your folks to sit with us. Let a friend of yours, be a friend of mine, let your brother be my brother, your "Mah Duke" be mine. What I offer up is integral, where as I embody your system and you inherit mines, this way we'd be strong, remove the equivocations that I speak with eloquence only to con you, no, far from the case. So, I say if you accept my brotherhood as innocent and not as a way to emasculate your system, but to ameliorate it." Marcel finished by holding Sean's gaze, for Marcel knew that he spoke from his heart and not his greed, he spoke with sincerity and honesty that was not to be mistaken for deceitfulness, and to assure Marcel that a bond had been reached and that the message has been conveyed through the correct channels and in a very cogent fashion. Sean stood to beckon for his home boy who was more than a brother to him to come and join him and their new friend in Marcel.

Marcel followed Sean's gesture only to discover that he had struck out completely. The heat that he was feeling from the brother who occupied the perfect booth, one that provided the best view in the event that something, as Sean had said was to "pop off" was pure heat, but deceptive as hell. What Marcel found to be Sean's body guard was the furthest description from his mind and to his credit the only reason that he couldn't spot the gentleman that brought on such an eerie feeling was due in part because the brother that headed in their direction had found it very easy to conceal himself considering that he was officially two full inches past being a dwarf. Marcel stood as the little man joined them and extended his hand to the brother who introduced himself as Fabian, who took on the appropriate moniker as "Stomp." At least a million thoughts crossed Marcel's mind as the three took to their seats. He beckoned for a waitress to come and take the empties and replenish them. He reminded her to keep them coming. "Now just how dangerous could this little man be," thought Marcel who sat and listened while Sean brought Fabian up to date.

"Did I leave out anything?" Asked Sean to Marcel who reached for his glass as the waitress brought their refills. Raising his glass waiting for Fabian to take hold of his, then the three raised their glasses in a toast.

"To health and wealth," said Marcel.

"To health and wealth," the two repeated. Marcel found trouble with the way that he viewed Fabian, who he discovered was the oldest of the three which wasn't the only thing that Marcel found out. Fabian, whom barely weighed more than a sack of potatoes, had the heart of a lion. He spoke with conviction and he listened with the same mannerism. The trouble didn't come due to the fact that Fabian was concise, with a taciturn personality. The trouble came when Marcel pre-judged Fabian believing him to be acting body guard because somehow he snuck a pistol inside of the club, which by the way wasn't all that hard to do. The trouble showed also in the way that he looked into your eyes as he spoke. It was such a burning sensation which was trouble by itself. That made it easy for Marcel to feel such a stare penetrate even from across the room as such a deadly warning. At first when the troubles were how to place a finger on such a vibe that was once allusive but now accessible, pretty much an aura or over tone that spoke way before he ever did. It was the same climate and characteristics, the exact same mystery, atmosphere, that of a killer. A killer that had murdered before and on maybe more than one occasion may indeed have brought on another trouble.

CHAPTER 5

TAMIA

"GIRL I'M GONNA NEED YOU to slow down and tell me what the heck is going on with you. I can't understand a thing that you are saying through all of this crying that you're doing." Tamia began to get flustered and almost impatient with her friend. She found it very challenging to listen, decipher and ignore the black, blue, purplish and yellow bruises that formed a now horrific view of Marva's face, arms and neck. Yet, had she been able to check for other bruises and frankly could care less. The sight of Marva's face was enough to send Tamia's anger towards capacity, and a very dangerous level that was.

"He, he, he doe, doe, don't want me no, no, no, no more," Marva stammered.

"So he beat you like this? Ooh heck no, what did the police say?" Marva shook her head and waved off the notion of involving the police department and if Tamia didn't know much of anything else she had for a true concept that regardless to the direction in which their lives were headed what was clear was the fact that they were "hood" first.

"Well, shoot, what you need to do is have somebody go over there and beat the dog... mess out of him." Marva noticed that Tamia had to catch herself from letting the ghetto seep out of her. She found a comfortable seating position so it wouldn't hurt so much when Tamia switched gears or turned so sharply and said,

"I'm gonna be alright, but somehow you're letting the way you feel go straight to your feet. Girl could you at least slow down for the speed bumps?" Tamia saw as Marva braced herself to protect her mid-section. She slowed the car down in order to crawl over the speed bumps then pulled the car over to a stop. Illuminating the car with the interior lights until it was bright enough to see Marva clearly.

"Ok, raise your shirt and let me see." Sensing Marva's reluctance Tamia said, "I'm not playing girl raise it up right now," more demanding this time. Through reluctance and all Marva raised her blouse giving Tamia the perfect view that she needed to poke and probe and search for signs of immediate danger. Tamia noticed that every time she poked Marva below her breast bone Marva would react as if Tamia hit her with a hot poker.

"Now how come you didn't go to the hospital again?"

"I'm gonna be alright, I'm sure of it."

"Yeah, yeah, yeah, just look a lot worse than it really is, perhaps a crack or a fracture. I didn't feel a lot of danger or else I would have made a U-turn and took you straight to the Medical Center. I don't know what you did to deserve all of this, but whatever it was he sure laid it on you good." And as an afterthought she said, "So why did he do you like this? You know you're my girl and all and I'm too inquisitive to let this go." Tamia put the car into gear and drove away from the curb.

"Girl this motha fucka sends me all over Sacramento. He sent me to the cleaners, to the mall, to the store, and then the Post Office. While I'm doing all of this, that son of a bitch gathered up all my shit and threw bags together. He got his baby mama all situated in the house that I helped put together, got their little wet back rug rat running around the house jumping all over my shit. I liked to pick that little funny built motha fucka up by his head and tossed his ass over the couch is what I should have done."

"Wow. So you mean you guys were fighting in front of his baby mama, and the baby?" Marva smiled at the thought of that, leaving Tamia to say,

"What the heck do you see that's so damn funny?"

"Girl, I must have had an out of body thing going on, because I floated right over to that chubby bitch and before I knew it I had her hair in a fist and was whooping the shit out of her, you should have seen it."

"Ohhhhh, so that's why he did this to you? You were scratching up his little diva."

"I made that Spanish speaking bitch speak five minutes of good English." Tamia smiled at the thought and said,

"His special Prima-Donna and you are the very Cinderella who stayed out past the stroke of twelve? So now you're turned back into your old self?" Tamia chuckled at her own sense of humor then smiled at her friend and pinched her on the cheek and said "Don't worry girl, ole "Mia" got you, just like always when you run off and get yourself all messed up and into cat fights, like how you be doing or when you..."

"Alright, alright I get it, geez; just beat me across the head with that. I get it. Yes, you are my best friend and savior but do you think I need reminding every five minutes? What about that time when..." Marva froze mid-sentence as she reflected through time? Tamia waited until she waited long enough before she looked over to Marva, smiled then said,

"I'm listening; go ahead you were at what about that time."

"You know when you.... Umm"

"When I umm what? Go ahead take your time, I'll wait."

"Shit."

"Hun, I could barely hear you."

"Forget you."

"When I what? I ran off with a married man. When I do that?"

"Forget that girl, you know good and well that he wasn't married."

"When I broke my lease to do what? Move in with Rico? I didn't break my lease; my lease was up already."

"You get on my nerves," Marva said now hating the game Tamia was playing, but Tamia was already in full swing and loving the game.

"When did I run out of Macy's? I didn't run out of Macy's those people just left the tag and the beeper on the jacket and I lost my receipt. I don't know where those pants came from, somebody set me up." Laughter filled the car for the first time since Tamia arrived at the shelter to collect Marva and her luggage.

The time Tamia pulled the car into the drive way she knew that it was best to let Marva know ahead of time that she had yet to inform William of the fact that she was extending such a hospitality at least not in full detail anyways. She was banking on the fact that he was aware of the relationship between the two old school friends.

"However the case girl you know I got your back."

"What? You think he gone flip? I mean I can't stand to see that on the count of me. I could appreciate the offer but I'm thinking that the shelter wouldn't have been so bad after all." Marva thought about the contrite feelings that she would have if William came off grumpily and not only black balled her but became physical with Tamia.

"Girl I could never live with myself knowing that I left you in a shelter knowing that I got a place for you to stay. What you need to do is come in this house and let me nurse you back to health because right now you look sickly and thirsty and busted and…"

"All right already. I get it for crying out loud; I look like shit, well doc what do you recommend for such a sickly person?"

"Not yet, and don't jinx me either but as a med student I'm gonna go as far as to recommend that you soak in a hot bath with the bubbles in it and a dash of Epson salt. Then I'm gonna recommend that you apply plenty of ice to your ribs and your face and the other swollen areas that you aren't telling me about. After that you need to take the soup for the broken heart. A nice liquid Band-Aid if I don't say so myself. After all that, I'm gonna recommend that you forget about Hector or Jesus, Paco, Pedro whatever his name is and find out who you really are. That's what I recommend."

"Javier, girl you know that his name is Javier. Well whatever you say you're the doctor I mean the medical student, sorry."

"No you're not. You said that on purpose because I forgot Mr. Hernandez first name like I really cared to know all of that. The only thing that I knew is that he was "your" man and that he always smelled like tomatoes."

"I use to hate that. Man, grass everywhere got on my damned nerves."

"You're gonna miss that pretty soon watch."

"I hope not. That would really mean that I'm out of my mind."

"I've saw you do stranger things." Tamia said exiting the car and make way for the trunk. Marva was now out of the car knowing full well that she would feel way better to just leave that one alone and even though she knew better she just couldn't find it in her to let it slide at all. She closed the door making sure it was locked before making her way to the rear of the car and said,

"Oh yeah, like what?"

"Nah, uh uh boo don't even get me started on that. Here, you could carry this little bitty teeny bag can't you?" Said Tamia as if she were speaking to a child,

"Nah, I need to know. What kind of stranger things that you've seen me do? Don't just through that out there like I was gone give "strange" a free ride. Uh uh," she said while accepting the bag that Tamia held out to her before closing the trunk.

"Girl please, here this is the key open the door and please hurry,"

"Nah I wanna know what kind of strange things you think I do?"

"Marva, girl I swear to God I will name off about ten of your foul ups, follies, bloops and blunders if you just hurry up and open the door." Tamia not as visible any more due to the task of trying to carry all of Marva's bags at once. She looked ridiculous trying to find a hole in the luggage to speak through while thinking of the good sense that Marva had lacked on occasions. She barely escaped a folly herself trying to make it through the door and across the threshold before dropping the heavy load and joyfully reaching for her back as if in pain she said,

"I'm getting too old for this stuff," side stepping Marva who stood with her arms folded sternly across her chest desperately seeking to know what it was exactly that made her strange. For Tamia it wasn't but four seconds that may have passed before she wished that she had never said anything about her friend's bazaar, non-sensible, preposterous, grotesquely and extremely farcical personality, because she already knew Marva would stay up late badgering the hell out of her until she was informed of the way Tamia or anybody else shall view her other than queen of the universe.

"Excuse me," said Tamia as she noticed that her agile attempt at side stepping Marva failed to succeed. Marva was disallowing her passage from the hall way through to the living room where the nice puffy and ever so comfortable sofa was located. Marva didn't budge an inch but looked Tamia up and down with full confidence that strange was the farthest thing that she would ever be.

"Humph, that's what I thought, the great Tamia has failed to produce evidence just blah, blah, blah, blah." Marva turned to head towards the living room granting Tamia all the time she needed to recover.

"Girl pa-lease you want some evidence, what about when you tied yourself up to the fence? My bad a barbwire fence trying to snoop on Hector. Who was it that had to cut you down? Huh? Luckily you were able to get your wrist free enough to call me or you would have still been up there."

"That ain't even funny; I knew I couldn't trust him and his baby mamma at the same time."

"Yes, it was funny. What about the time when you cried bloody murder when the guys kicked you off the football team? You cried because they didn't want you to be the hiker anymore. You thought you were slick. The only reason why you wanted to be the hiker was so D'Marco could continue to touch you on your 'cooch', girl pa-lease."

"You remember that?"

"Yeah, you thought he was gay because he'd rather have the men hike him the ball instead of you. That's what gave you away right there. I was so embarrassed for you because you were so dumb that you didn't understand that you needed to block for him too. You were in it for the jollies while poor D'Marco he was getting his neck rung on the count of you. Shoot he had to make a life or death decision. I'm sure he liked fondling you only I think he favored his neck just a little bit more. You called him all kinds of faggots that day, gosh."

"Well, I see that we got our own definitions of strange because you know D'Marco was fine girl don't even deny that."

"But not fine enough where I wouldn't wear undies just to give him easy access to the honey. Un uh Yogi was gonna need to be more than fine or a quarter back to get this jar of honey."

"No he would have to be a mailman and sort of cute." Marva cracked at the fact that Tamia fell in love with William, who barely knew how to get anything professionally.

"I know you didn't." Tamia snapped "Mrs. Green acres honey I love you but give me Park Avenue, married on a tractor, straw hats and grass residue, always smelling like green onions and horse radish, honey I'm home, Ricky Ricardo, I love Lucy, look I planted you a rose garden, help me get a green card and I'll promise you a tamale and a taco Mariachi band playing in the back ground...."

"Tamia, alright hell, get a hold of yourself," Marva interrupted.

"I'm just saying don't be talking shit about my man. I will pick him twelve times in a row over Hector "Macho" Camacho. Look at you? Up here looking like Rocky, what you need to do is take your 'I don't get it' ass up those stairs and run you some bubbles while I get some Epson salt and hook up some soup and fix you a place on that couch because un-like somebody I know I got some sleep that I need to get. Yes, ma'am. While you're in here tossing and turning don't even bother waking me. There's some extra strength Tylenol in the bathroom just toss a few of those back and holler at me in the morning."

"And what about your husband when he shows."

"I left him a message maybe we'll get into an argument, but he'll see things like me I'm sure of it."

"If you say so, I'm gonna be situating myself to get myself together soon enough. I see this as a setback in order to bounce back. I'll have to find a job right away which is my first start then I'm gonna get my head and hold that up really high and be the boss bitch that I know I am."

"There you go toots. How about we let your first start be to go up those stairs and run that water like we both know you need, and next we'll wolf down that there soup like we know that you need and you know, pack that ice and do all the things that you "need" right now." Marva headed up the staircase and moments later the sound of water running was heard throughout the house. This was the last thing that Tamia could remember second to the sound of the microwave announcing the completion of a cook cycle with its sharp beeping indicating to the operator that the contents were now complete. This particular content just so happens to be a bowl of Campbell's chicken noodles.

By the time Tamia came to, normally she would roll over to greet William. Only not this time, normally she would roll out of bed and head to the shower only not this time. Because this time what she wanted to know in her own panicked way was just where exactly was her man, her lover and soul mate. Never had he ever let the sun beat him home and his cell going straight to voice mail ain't helped out a whole lot either. Still she knew, worried or not the day must go on so she edged out of bed and to the shower she went. When she was finished bathing her happiness and comforts were restored at the sight of William stretched out on their bed looking whupped, and in desperate need of sleep. So she allowed him at least that although she had a million questions that she would love to ask him. Most of them were in regards to his tardiness and inconsideration. Still in all she loved him and not too much was gonna change that so she walked over and placed a peck to the tip of his nose and left.

As for William he was tired, awfully tired. The grave yard shifts had always brought him home in this condition. Regardless where he done it at; on the grind or at the post office, same thing, late was late and tired was tired. Even though he knew what to expect with Marva the intruder in the house, he wasn't ready to deal with it. He figured he'd go directly to the room, collapse on their bed and search for sleep right away. Sure he felt when Tamia placed the kiss on him, of course he did, it was like a kiss from a Cobra. Although he remained still, he felt the urge to pull back and wipe the venom from the tip of his nose but he knew that it was always best when in the company of a viper to remember to remain real still. So he stuck to the doctor's orders and waited until Tamia slithered out of the house and out to the car before disrobing enough to find comfort between the sheets allowing sleep to get the best of him.

By the time William came to it was nearly six o'clock and the tint of the night was beginning to cast its curtain over the city. The room was quiet and so was the house except for the sporadic footfalls he'd hear tipping around downstairs. He laid in the very same bed that he shared with Tamia and couldn't help but to wonder for how much longer. William knew that the worst thing that he could do was to up and leave especially on a whim without preparing for such an enormous step. He didn't have a clue towards his next step. He's been saving his night shift money just in case something crossed his mind. He even entertained being a bachelor with a fly ass bachelors' quarters. He even thought about moving in with Aretha for whatever that was worth. He knew that he would be well sexed and well paid because the hustle took place on her street; something about laying his head where he "shits" at sort of rubbed him the wrong way. He even entertained the thought of shutting the fuck up and stacking some more paper until he had enough to buy him a cool spot and let his punk ass postal job create a stability face after all he was going on his third year there. "Yeah, that's what I'm gonna do," he said to himself. "I'm gonna stack up me some more of this paper and then cop me a condo and fly that the fuck out." With his mind almost completely made up William rolled out of bed and searched for his pants, then headed to the restroom to relieve his self. Knowing that Tamia would sense him to be awake and would begin her "con" campaign to get them to provide room and board for her friend slash sister who always seems to need one favor or another.

Finished in the restroom William prepared to meet Tamia on the other side of the door once it opened was surprised once he discovered a blank space that ran blank all the way down the staircase. Relieved plus irritated at hearing the two as they chattered about like old magpies. William figured that he would put on a shirt "considering that we got company and all" he thought before he took to the stairs. The women's voices grew louder and louder the closer he got. It wasn't until he came into vision of the two when the silence fell.

"Oh, honey you're up, are you hungry?" Tamia switched instantly into her obligations from friend and loving host to loving spouse.

"I'm starving," said William but in his thoughts he said, "Now let the artistry of the cons begin."

"Well good, I made your favorite smothered steak over rice; we're out of bread so I baked some honey biscuits."

"Girl you had me at smothered steak. You didn't hear my stomach when you said smothered steak, it rumbled in syllables."

"You're so silly. Go ahead and have a seat. I'll make you a plate the yams and greens came from a can and hopefully you don't like them as much as mine."

"You say some greens and yams out of a can, yuk, yuk, yuk."

"So you don't want any?" Tamia said teasingly.

"Girl don't play with me; I don't care if those Jones came in a box all I know is you doing a lot of talking. You see sweetheart around here we be about it," playfully William stood and put his hand on his hip in a joyous confrontation before retaking his seat and a hold of his eating utensils banging the table in a childish display singing we want steak, we want steak."

"Alright, alright steak it is and you bet not like the greens but you better love the steak." Tamia gone to the microwave and removed the plate a tad bit prematurely and served him. As she took her seat across from him she opened up with,

"So, you made it in a little later than usual I was worried."

"Oh, did you put some kind of curfew on me when I wasn't looking?" William replied between bites and sips from his beverage.

"Not like that baby, not like that at all, like I said I was worried a bit with me calling and all."

"I mean the hot ticket item is that I made it in right and look all in one piece."

"I was hoping you wouldn't be upset with me bringing Marva here. I mean I was banking on the fact that you know that she's my best friend second to you, sort of hoping that you wouldn't mind me extending our hospitality."

"Not a problem." William said with all the sincerity that he could find at the time before saying, "But these greens whew. Are you sure they come from a can?"

"Why you like them?"

"I'm scared to answer your honor."

"You better," was all Tamia said before she stood to accompany Marva in the living room.

CHAPTER 6

"WHAT? WHAT DO YOU MEAN how do I feel about dying? What the fuck kind of question is that?" Rasaan not believing his ears once Nahjee decided to spill the contents of his thoughts. Not all the way comprehending any of Nahjee's way of thinking, but he also knew that Nahjee had a way of seeing the unforeseeable and if Nahjee ever said anything to raise Rasaan's antennas, checking on his life span sure had a way of waving them fuckas sky high this time. I mean it's not that Rasaan ever thinks about dying.

"My nigga you know I don't bullshit you, not one time have I but I need you to think really hard though. Was there anything different about the arrangements when you took this job because I could think of one inconsistency right off the top of my head?"

"Dog, I'm thinking and I'm not finding anything. I mean I'm trying to but I can't find anything especially now that you spooking me like this. It all seemed so regular to me, maybe there is something but you talking this how would I like to die shit ain't did nothing but fucked me out of my memory. The only thang I could think about is what kind of shit you got me into."

"What kind of shit that I got you into?" Nahjee said unbelieving.

"You know what I mean. If you never ever said anything my mind would be crispy right now."

"My nigga if I never ever said anything your mind could be blown and I mean that shit like any minute now." Rasaan noticed Nahjee take the March Lane exit.

"Ok I'm confused. What is this all about?"

"Well seems to me like we owe somebody an apology."

"Ok, who?"

"I'm going to show you. This time I'm gonna need you to really pay attention."

Rasaan stayed with Nahjee all the way until Nahjee pulled into the same motel that he swore the police had just left from and could still be close by.

"Now I'm really confused. Dog what the hell are you doing? Are you insane? Tell me you're kidding. My nigga, tell me that you are playing right now."

"Well hardy har, har, come on and hurry up," the two showed up to the room door. One expecting and the other non- believing, still there they stood until Nahjee knocked politely on the door.

"Who is it?" Came the voice from inside of the room, scared to say house cleaning for fear of rejection. Nahjee had to think quick finding the words to say sent him into character right away.

"It's the Stockton Police Department." The two heard rambling around before the door was cracked enough for the hype to peek through. Nahjee and Rasaan pushed the door open while watching the surprised fiend back pedal into the room startled.

"Ohh no, oh, no, no, no, no, no,"

Looking around Nahjee could tell that the fiend had just finished getting high and here they were returning to fuck his high all the way up again."

"Shut up and sit down!" Said Rasaan,

"Ohhhhh, Ohhhhh no, oh no, no, no, no,"

It was gonna take way more than some mean and threatening words this time because the fiend was making a stand. One thing he knew for sure was he wasn't going to keep getting high only for these two sons of bitches to show up and fuck it up, shit no! And Nahjee put most of this together all but quick and decided to put some stuff on the fiend. He pulled out a bill and stepped to the fiend.

"Listen, I'll cop you whatever the fuck you want just calm the fuck down and be cool."

The fiend looked at the bill and toned it down a notch.

"Well that ain't enough because I need a sixteenth." the fiend took his shot at Nahjee.

"Alright, a sixteenth it is then."

"I meant an eight ball. That's what I meant, I meant the eight ball."

"Ok, no more after the eight ball alright."

"Ok, what do you want. I don't have anything else." The fiend said reaching for the wad of money that Nahjee extracted from his pocket.

"We want you to tell us why somebody just tried to kill us just a while ago. Who did you call?"

"I swear to God ah-mighty that I didn't call anyone. I told you that those things were bad luck. I told ya and don't say that I didn't because I did. Don't you dare say I didn't?" The fiend became animated.

"Well what we want you to tell us everything that happened when your brother got shot. How it happened from the beginning to the end." The fiend knew that they were ever so serious when Nahjee removed the jacket that was draped over the chair and tossed it to the fiend.

"Come with us we'll bring you back it's not safe for us to talk here."

"Ohhhhh noooo, Ohhhhh noooo…."

"Ohhhhh yes," Rasaan cut him off before the fiend convinced himself that he wasn't going without a fight. Which Rasaan was sure to offer considering the dangers that Nahjee was convincing enough to prove that they were involved in. "Don't worry if we were gonna hurt you that's how we would have walked in right off the bat. Now come on before we change our minds." The fiend must have registered that Lucifer lived in the eyes of Rasaan, put on his jacket and followed the two out of the door and to the car. Nahjee drove aimlessly until he parked in the lot of McKinley Park.

"Ok from the beginning." All of the passengers exited the car and they took a bench. The two listened as the fiend took them on a mental tour of the unfortunates, one that the fiend experienced in repetition, from the day that his brother took the call all the way to the gunshots that put him in the morgue. Rasaan was asked to pay attention but that request was an understatement. Rasaan was tuned all the way in until everything began to make sense and the thought of him dying became even more realistic. Had Nahjee not peeped the crookedness of the job that they had accepted they could have easily walked into some the same type of shit.

The maneuver was so obvious and so transparent that any child could have put those kind of two's together and got four. What made their friends adopt a diabolical way of doing business and stray away from the norm? Their anomalies were inexcusable. Rasaan became immediately angry. The thought of representing a group so conniving and unethical and mendacious really found a way to his heart in a bad way. Thinking about their position and their near future and both appeared to look bleak. He now understood oh so much that this last job wasn't from the regular friend or a friend of a friend as they would call their associates. This employer was a boss of malevolence and nothing else, the kind who may even lay in wait to off him and his potna.

"I got a question," Rasaan escaped his reverie then said "What is it about those plates that got people losing their motha fuckin' minds about? That's what I'd like to know." Both the fiend and Nahjee looked to Rasaan as if how stupid could he be to ask some crazy shit like that.

"Dog, it's about money!" Nahjee did all he could to work with his potna but was sure that Rasaan could have put all of this together on his own.

"Right, some fake money though that shit doesn't play everywhere, just the fools right. The FBI like it, the hood niggas that don't know any better likes it but why would anybody else like it?" Nahjee knew that Rasaan was referring to their friends also. This brought some good logic to the table and questions that even Nahjee would love the answers to.

"Well?" Nahjee looked to the fiend, who took his cue and said,

"Haven't you seen the plate," Nahjee hadn't but Rasaan had who said.

"Yeah they look like money but so what?" The fiend grabbed his head in his hands as if he couldn't believe these two doe doe's and said,

"Yeah, they do don't they, wow what do ya know, who would have believed it."

"Ok smart ass, is there anything so, so special that these guys are willing to kill over?" Nahjee tried his patience on the fiend, who gave him the same blank stare that he gave Rasaan.

"Yeah, they make money, Jesus'."

Money that nobody cares too much about,"

"I wouldn't say all that."

"Fake money is what I mean."

"Again, I'm gonna say that I wouldn't say all of that," Ok now this got their attention. Rasaan was the first to recover.

"So you're trying to tell us that those plates make real money?"

"At first I was until I discovered that no matter what I'd say neither of you are gonna listen anyhow." Rasaan wore his academics hat today.

"Then if those plates make real dough then why did you fork them over so easily then?"

"Because when my brother made those they weren't the only set that rolled off the press, I'll tell you that much. Have you ever seen a thousand-dollar bill? Know who's the president on a thousand-dollar bill? James Cleveland, that's who's on a thousand-dollar bill. Do you want one of those too?"

"No. What I want to know is on a scale of one to ten how would you project our survival rate if we took those plates back to Sacramento and trade them to the guy who says that they belong to him?" Nahjee just had to ask.

"Well on a scale of one to ten I'm gonna say a one. That's only because you didn't say on a scale of zero to ten, then I would have said zero. If you really, really think about it you would say "zero" too. You know why, I mean you just said it. The guy that told you that the plates belong to him is a liar. If not, then tell him to give you a Cleveland like I just offered to you. If he'd lie, he'd cheat, if he'd cheat he'd steal if he'd steal, then killing isn't that far off is it?" Silence grew over the three. A dope fiend he may have been but dumb, stupid or retarded, he was not. He had scored big with Nahjee and real big with Rasaan who started to pace the graveled lot, stopping in front of the fiend.

"So the plates are good. What's the trick behind it all?"

"The paper,"

"And if the paper is good?"

"Then hello car lot, hello floor seats at any arena and a mansion and the motherfucking FBI like you said if you don't do it right."

"And doing it right means?"

"It means don't let the FBI know you got them for one and two, don't let the FBI know you got them. Did I say don't let the FBI know that you got them? Because if I didn't, let me tell you to never and I mean never let the FBI know in any kind of way that you got them because if you do," the fiend began to shake his head vigorously then wagged his finger to the both of them "just don't slip up. I hate to think of the time that you two would get just for possessing them alone. With possessing being nine tenths of the law, even if you rolled over you could still get a hundred years."

"So, the papers the trick, you say." Nahjee asked half expecting the fiend to give up all of the details. He was rewarded when the fiend said,

"The paper and the ink, you see the trick is in the print, once you know what you are doing then the process is money in the bank, money in the bank I said!'

"You mean to tell me that this fake money could pass the professional eye of a banker? Somebody who deals with money all day every day," Rasaan was new to the counterfeit game but he wasn't brand spanking new because he does come from the streets, where one would fair way better being as grounded and well-rounded as one could possibly be. The more you knew the better off you were. And to the fake money game Rasaan saw it work and he had seen it fail. When he saw it work he just shook his head in an unbelieving manner. When he seen it fail he shook his head too and too in disbelief that somebody could be so stupid as to try some shit like that thinking that they could get away with it. Even the drug dealers now hold their earnings into the light in search of the smaller "ghost face" that had better look identical to the big face that sat in the center of a bill and if not then this could mean some serious repercussion for the shyster who attempted to "play stuff" on the dealers.

Somehow the street gamblers aren't so patient because the dice games held on the corners were always fast paced and could easily avoid detecting such a sham. But Rasaan was sure that if it were ever detected even then the repercussions could be similar, if not worse because a lot of the hood niggas Rasaan knew all wore a toaster in the holster and were always itching for the moment to bring it out, and gaming on them was as good a reason as any. The problem with this was that not all of the time could one catch a game in full swing where as one could make the swap at such a large volume as would be needed in order to yield a satisfactory profit. So, to believe that a banker, one whom deals strictly with money and money related issues could be fooled by some paper, "the right paper" and some damned ink was not going to happen, no matter how hard he tried, or how much Rasaan wanted to believe he just couldn't fathom the idea of any of what he was hearing to be plausible. A dogma that he would begin to base a future on, no buddy, the fiend raised his head to assume eye contact with Rasaan.

"Yes, even this money could and would pass through to anybody in the money business. You know why? Because those are legit plates the real deal, duplicates but the real deal. If those plates were the Mona Lisa, you or anyone else for that matter would pick those prints over the actual Mona Lisa. Even Leonardo Di Vinci himself would select those prints over his own creation. Those prints are a phenomenon and you ask, what are the qualities of them, why are they worth killing or dying over, I just explained it to you. No one wants those plates to surface, no one. The power that those plates could offer is unlimited. A bum could go from rags to riches in the span of a week. The powerful could wipe out all of its competitors in just one fell swoop. Hell, if a cop had the sense he would get his hands on those plates and retire on the spot and may God help us if a lawyer got his paws on such an item. It'll be a law practice and good drugs on every darned corner." Nahjee began to share into Rasaan's thoughts.

"So, even if you had other prints, why give us this kind of action to all of those luxuries that you talking about now?" Rasaan added in total agreement to both the question and the timing of the question. It was the same question that sat at the tip of his tongue so he sized up the fiend and waited for the answer though other issues were nagging at him. It was taking him awhile to put his finger on the cause or the realization that was troubling him, and then it struck him like a jack hammer. Rasaan had met many fiends during his life, crack addicts and crank heads were just alike. He met the "Black" addicts those that chose "horse", "Boy", "Dog Food" or "hop" or as they say in the Bay Area back then "Leven Five" not "Black" as in African American, but Black as in Tar. Rasaan could even recall when he sat down to eat with some of these addicts for he was never one to think that he was better or more blessed than anyone. He would simply ask a pan handling fiend exactly what was they asking for the money for.

His favorite ones were the ones who spoke the truth leaving the decision to be left strictly up to Rasaan to decide rather to up the change or not. Some would say that they needed milk and diapers and Rasaan would ask them what kind and what size only to see the fiend struggle for an answer. Some would even say that they needed a drink or a "jet plane" meaning a shot of dope or a cooked up cocaine rock. Not all the time, but some of the time does Rasaan become so sympathetic with a fiends request that he would up the going rate for one pass port. Anything after that the fiend was on his own or a fiend would address it's need for a meal, not all the way trusting of any fiend Rasaan would simply ask what the fiend would like to eat and he would go and cop meals for the two of them adding as much nutrition to the meal as possible and would sit and have the meal in the company of those whom life has run over. He'd do this solely to make sure that the fiend would indeed eat their portion but Rasaan saw none of what he was accustom to while looking at this fiend in front of him. No foul odor and no attempts at finagle except milking the sixteenth to an eight ball, he sported tattoos but past that nothing else matched. Oh, he was sure that this dude was a fiend because he saw the syringes and the cotton swabs and the rubber strap used to tie his self-off so with ease he'll be able to hit himself but that was all. He spoke with education. He wasn't sickly, he was well mannered that and groomed. The fiend now took a stunned deer caught in the headlights appearance to his self just shook his head and said,

"Well, if you remember right the two of you showed up waving guns and demanded that I give up the plates. Which I was sure that I was gonna have to do anyways seeing that I never said that I made a clean get away. I could only hope that who should ever come a knocking that they would be ever so kind enough not to send me off to meet my maker with the understanding to the secret that I just relayed to you of the extras. I mean, what kind of future would I have if the two of you decided to end my life? Those plates would just go on without me is what I'll say and then there's also the other thing. Lord help me but I got to tell you and don't take this the wrong way because business isn't all the time business as usual and the two of you should know that by now or you wouldn't be asking me all of these here questions. The truth is and you're gonna have to hate me now but I was knowing full well that you two would be too damned stubborn to listen when I told you those things were bad luck and that the two of you would go off and get yourselves killed and the plates would be in the hands of the murderers. The ones that killed you and not me was the plan once you two left. They would kill you and never mind me who by the way would have other prints whereas I could just go on living in a peace and harmony. Now I know this being cold blooded but so was the guns you guys used demanding the plates. Now that's what I thought at first, now that I see that the two of you is just too darned stupid that was a bad, bad idea like leading a baby to the slaughter house, a very innocent little bitty baby. So, now that the two of you are here let me tell you again that the plates could get you killed. Plus, I could tell you that they could get you in position to make life a whole lot better for the two of you. If and I emphasize "If" you guys do it right. If you do it wrong that's good for me because the bad guys would know the plates has now been confiscated. If you do it right, you would have to get rid of the bad guys who would push and push and push until they've got rid of you or you have got rid of them.

I don't know how you gonna do it, but I do know that you two really has no need for these kind of problems and that you two were either coaxed into this situation or you were pushed into this situation. However, you two have landed in a pile of shit, and the easy part is the worst thing that you could ever do and that's hand them over. For whatever reason that you could conjure up to do so just know I already got one of my kin over there on the ice and I can't see any reason why the two of you would fail to find a slab of that ole ice yourself in the same fashion perhaps and for the same reason.

See what you need is a plan, my brother really trusted those goons to do good, honorable and respectable business, but he sure did learn the hard way didn't he. You have never seen demons like these guys they'll shake your hand and stab you at the same time. Surely would piss down your back and convince you that it's raining outside, no sir what you need is a plan if you're doing any dealings with these guys you sure will, uh hun, or you would only get ice and your back wet." The fiend gave his speech to two very attentive listeners in Nahjee and Rasaan who both found good reason to believe every word that the fiend had spoken. Rasaan who grew tired of speculating just had to ask,

"So if you got all of this insight, what the hell are you doing in that run down motel? Don't seem like a place for a person of your wisdom."

"Ahh, but it does, I could tell that you're taking into consideration that I push the needle and you're confused because of the education that you detect...."

"And the London fog jacket is a giveaway and the Frederique Constant, didn't help out a lot either nor is the Salvatore Ferragamo's that you some-how got a blood stain on, you sure know how to mess up a nice pair of flats." The fiend stopped in his tracks as he listened to Rasaan's summations, took aback by the young man's taste of attire took a peek at his watch then said,

"So you recognized the old Frederique have you?"

"It's bothering me, so why do we find you in such a low class place where prostitutes and bums go to roost?"

"Well, my house is in French Camp, I live next to nothing but farmers and blue collar folks. Never, from the twenty years that I've lived there have I ever spotted a drug dealer, there may be one that lives there on the sly, but never have I spotted one that I knew for sure had the good stuff."

"So you come all the way down to skid row for the junk?"

"I do, but enough about me have you considered how you two gonna make it through yet?" The blank looks that the two shared with each other told the fiend what he needed to know.

"You don't have a clue do you?" No answer "I could help if you like."

"We're open for any suggestions," said Rasaan.

The two listened to the fiend even more attentively because these two were in firm belief that their very lives depended on it. They watched as the fiend paced and listened as he went in and out of dialogues. What the fiend didn't know was that these two to which he kept referring to as kids. Had the elements of a strong force behind them, one of them being the will to survive. These two have gone through so much together that they've found no sense in dying so easy. Gratefully, Nahjee had called a good one, his intuitions were on point so It was he who perhaps saved them from going in both feet in an ethical fashion to their death beds.

When dealing with the unethical one never knew what to expect for an outcome. So many deals had gone bad on the count of this. These two could have very well been set up by their friends. It was them that knew that these two were dependable and reliable to a fault, honorable to the end and would deliver, no doubt. Though the question of why not just pay them and get the goods was in question? But a question that has been eclipsed by the question of why they didn't just pay for them to begin with, No! They both knew it in the gut that this could be the very first deal to go all so bad that they accepted the suggestion of staying in Stockton California for the next two weeks. This way they could check the impatience of their so called friends who has never been impatient before and two weeks was the time needed for Christopher now that he finally introduced himself to print some more plates, plates that would have flaws and could be deemed useless to anyone of importance. So for two weeks Stockton California would be even more infamous for their taco and burrito trucks.

CHAPTER 7

THE DOORS TO SOLANO STATE Prison opened at eight thirty on the dot to allow visitors, and for Mecca this was a regular for her Saturdays. Even after a long night of working and partying she still managed to make it up to visit her younger brother Desmond who managed to throw away his life for just a few pleasures more. He was once a high school phenomenon and broke every Sacramento Unified School Districts passing record, every last one of them. Desmond Collins had the most passing yards in a game and the most passing yards in a single season. For the most touch downs in a single season and in a single game; guess who, Desmond Collins? Who tallied up the most total yards in a game, Desmond Collins? As an athlete he was phenomenal but academically? Well, nobody said that he was su-perman but as an athlete is where he was his regular ole shiny self. He was so quick that he ran the hundred meters at a nine, nine flat in high school. He played center field, and in between innings he'd run over to the track, participate in a four by four relay and win that, then back in time for the next inning to begin. Up to bat he'd knock a single, a double or maybe even a triple and depending on how he really felt he may even sit one down in the bleachers for you. If he decided that he just wanted to embarrass the opposing team. He was a place hitter by trade so to push one into the right field corner then take off like a bat out of hell, just to show up on two shoes for an infield homerun was in the archives as well. He had more stolen bases than anyone before him and yet has anyone come close to eclips-ing that. But in math, he, ahh, nah, not at all, he was groomed to be the athletic player of the year and nothing else. If you were to pay attention to the stats and look over his GPA which in the great state of California and "The Capitol" especially was never going to happen, not even as an afterthought. Blazing speed, dead on accuracy at forty yards out, touch passes and timing routes were impeccable; a thing of beauty, but it was something about science that proved to be evasive. In fact, it appeared that Desmond had hopped in line twice when the good Lord began to pass out physical attributes and athletic capabilities, but grew lazy when it was time to stand in such a lengthy line, when the good Lord passed out the brains and other intellectual functions.

However, Desmond was dyslexic and this was his excuse. You could show him things and he got it, tell him things and he got it, write it down, now you were only showing off. Colleges took a look in his direction, I mean you couldn't ignore his athleticism, but one peek at his bio and a small gander at his academic background and the colleges high-tailed it so quick that it was like they never came. All of this natural talent and the most that Desmond could mount were to be the starting quarter back at Solano State Prison.

The joke has it that he had enough "skills" to make it to Penn State only he had "sense" enough to make it to the State Pen. Not everyone knew this, and surely not the group of teenage girls who hoped like hell to attract the attention of an upcoming figure and a rising star, one that they'll be able to cop they ass a free ride through life from and nobody was a better score than Desmond. I mean if you were into newspaper articles and final scores that is.

One night Desmond and a group of his teammates found fun for the weekend, just before most of them signed their letter of intents. They attended the best party of the year, booze was down stairs, and sex was upstairs, free and willingly until it all got out of hand. Desmond could still remember the day like it all happened only moments ago. First the young lady was willing but when the different bodies began to hop up and down inside of her, somehow she sobbed up enough to scream bloody murder and the worst handle of all was "rapist." For months and months

Desmond was in the media, first in the positive, then in the not so positive, and then his name arrived in the awfully negative. It was as if some sort of cosmic force took a hold of such a young man to bless him, only to make a mockery of him so that all the world could see that God don't like ugly but he wasn't all that high spirited on the pretty either. It is the meek that shall inherit the earth they say. Strenuous testing was done for DNA that never once showed a trace of Desmond partaking into the act of the actual event or the crime of rape, but the girl stated specifically that it was he who disrobed her, that it was he who laid the ground rules saying that, "if you fuck all of them then you could have me," oh boy, once the judge and the jury heard all of this they all thought Lynch mob all the way after that. There wasn't anybody that powerful or prestigious in the world they say and if there were they better not walk into the superior court of the damn County of Sacramento, no sir. Try if you like and your kids would have great grandkids the time they decide that you have been rehabilitated enough to "finally" be released into a society that would have technologies that you'd be so far behind that you could move your eye lashes a certain way and that's enough to trigger NASA responses.

So to think that this dumb kid could remove a young lady from her innocence was gonna fly in this state and in this town without paying heavy for it would be some bull damned shit. That jury brought back twelve to none saying guilty. It took them all of half a day for jury deliberation and for the judge to cast his spell on Desmond to be worth thirty-eight years with eighty-five percent, a sentence that he would need to bring hence the California's very popular three strikes law. Desmond, who was not so good at math was caught counting on his fingers when the bailiff hiked him up and whisked him away as abruptly as possible and never to be seen again.

For all the jurors it was back to living a normal life and as for the young lady? Well, she went back to living too only she was now doing it really big at the Mustang Ranch where her hustle was made strictly for the paying kind. Those who didn't pay would have hell to pay she'd say. She always knew how to extort a man, this game came to her with ease because she knew that she would forever possess a man's weakness and to her this was as good as sitting on a gold mind. So if the money never made it out of a man's pocket then she was damned sure that the District Attorney had a wide purse with plenty of money in it. They would pay handsomely for a good testimony as she now knew. Let her tell it that little motha fucka should have cashed her out like she demanded and his little dick ass wouldn't be off to prison. She recalled the tears, the loud shriek, and the piercing high pitched scream that shook the whole party. That's what that nigga gets is what she'd tell anyone right before she'd pull away in her Nissan Altima a car that anybody collecting cans or other recyclables could purchase.

Wow what a life is what Desmond often found himself saying when sharing his story in support groups. Anything detestable that a person could be called, he's been called both privately and publically. For Mecca though, to her he was still her little brother and still worthy of her support and she knew that come hell or high water or both. She knew that she was going to do everything in her power to make sure that she held him down, even if it meant to leave work at two o'clock a.m. get to sleep by three then up by six to make the hour drive to visit to eleven, then get back just in time to grab a nap, only to start her shift come six o'clock in the evening. So down packed was her schedule that for the past three years it's been the same thing, so much that even Desmond's request for other visitors were the same.

"I love you sis' but look at me, I'm a grown man now mommy I need me a 'wifey pooh' now. Why don't you hook me up with one of your home girls or something" is what he would say ever so often if not too much. Only this time the request was a little different. Mecca had convinced one of her ole school home girls that used to have a thang for her brother to submit a visiting form which she so gladly obliged considering that she was down on her luck, just out of an abusive relationship and cribbing with their other mutual friend. I mean why not? This was just the break Mecca needed she was thinking when Desmond made it through the door. Spotting her he came to take his seat next to his sister, "always a pleasure to see you and always the misery to see you depart" one of those kind of moments.

"Guess what?" He opened up,

"Uh uh, I just went to sleep ten minutes ago my brain ain't doing nothing. It's just sitting there ain't spinning or anything,"

"Well, tell Marva that they approved her for a visit and that I'm dying to see her."

"Don't say that Des',"

"What, that I'm dying to see Marva, why?"

"No don't tell me that she got approved. Don't play with me like that I just felt my brain kick in yelling something about a vacation."

"Ahh tired of me already."

"Des', I was tired of your ass a long time ago."

"Well I got a break for you, all you had to do was say that you were getting tired girl I mean, you know."

"So, looking beat up and whooped wasn't communicating anything to you?"

"Well, ain't nobody told you to work so hard and so damned much, you should quit."

"Boy, please, that's the only bright spot in my life, I like going to work, plus it takes a lot of the stress off of me."

"That's because you are around all that damned alcohol, every time you need a fix you could just pull over and pop the top and get it in really quick then wolf down some peanuts and get back to cracking' I always knew that you'd make a good bartender you were a natural at mixing those damned drinks, lord."

"You're just saying that because I gave you that kiwi strawberry Mad Dog 20/20 and told you that it was a drink called 'Fancy Day' and you were dumb enough to go for it. Plus, you were already two cups in before I stunk it up completely with the gin and juice. All you knew was that you wanted some more and some more, didn't even care if it was lopsided or not, it was just gimmie, gimmie, gimmie was all you kept saying."

"Yeah, I remember, but that Crown and Belvedere, Hypnotic and Cran-Apple, now that was a fucking drink, man! The thought of that shit alone gets on my damned nerves."

"Then, there was the Remy, the 151 Bacardi light and Grey Goose and apple juice that you liked so much."

"That's because you didn't know the secret to that. Now that you are all grown up sis' I may as well tell you, the trick was them damned grape Jolly Ranchers, the 151 used to melt those thangs so quick and set the whole thing off. Watch, drop a few cubes in a glass of that fire water and pop it on your best customers and what's going to happen is they gonna want that shit again and again."

"Some Jolly Ranchers you say?"

"Some Jolly Ranchers, watch, spring it on them then back up and you'll see,"

"We'll make a name for it if they like it."

"I'm telling you they gonna want it, I know my shit girl.

If you mix it, I'm gonna drink it and if it doesn't go then dammit it just doesn't go and that's all there is to it. But I'm telling you now that this thing here goes so dummy, shoot call that thang the Retarded Bus."

"The Retarded Bus, that's slick but how about we call it Fed X?" Desmond laughed at such a silly joke because Fed X was his high school handle, they say started from his receiving group who would swear on their very lives that their quarterback was talented enough to ship it to them anywhere on a football field.

"But for real though, the Retarded Bus sounds better,"

"Ok then it's settled, only if they'll like it like you say,"

"Oh, they gonna like it and I put that on my word."

"Yeah, well I'm gonna slip it on them tonight, I'll put it on the house just in case."

"Then watch the feedback on that thang, they are gonna love you for it forever I swear."

"Ok, so umm, Marva, you were saying something about her being cleared for visits?"

"At first I was, and then your funky ass went all Niagara Falls on a nigga, fantasizing rainbows and Peacocks and banging some village leader name Rah Foo Abu. Shit I'm scared that you would leave and find that long village ponytails are irresistible and never come back, over there swinging from shit while I'm in this fucka stressed the fuck out wondering if my niece or nephew is one of those dirty bare foot black as hell motha fuckas with some light green eyes, smelling like oysters and old tamale pies."

"Boy you so damned silly,"

"No I ain't you know damned well that you are the only one that visit or even bother to write for that matter. I don't know what I would do without you." This was oh so true Mecca thought, she couldn't find anybody that would take money to come and see her brother, not their mother who seemed to have wrote her son off the very minute the judge said guilty. The impact of such a discovery ain't did shit but turn their poor mother into reclusiveness, a damned hermit.

Never bothering to know the whole story, all she knew was that the lady in that black robe said what she said and that was too much for her so she closed up feeling as if she had failed somehow her only son. Mecca thought for a minute on what could it possibly feel like to have for a reality, everything that you've ever known or ever loved and held dear to heart, had all but vanished and fallen away, from even a memory.

"Yeah, I know that Des', but, so what, ain't I all you need though?"

"Shit no! So when could Marva get up here."

"What! Ohhhhh-kay, I hear you, well let's see if she come up here every week then, see if she on your appeal attorney like I am for your black ass, that's five small a month remind you, see if…"

"Whoa, whoa, whoa, fuck, dammit, all right already could you cut me any deeper, since you put it all like that tell that bitch to stay the fuck away from me and any attempts to reach me would only force me to get a restraining order active immediately."

"I thought so."

"I mean, you just turned green right in front of me. I'm scared to say that you sounded a tad selfish without you ripping my arms off."

"I'm just letting you know how not to get us mixed up and you let down in the end."

"Hmmm, sis' I think I wanna take my chances."

"You think you gonna get some of that ole pussy huh, don't you boy." Mecca reached across the table to give a friendly tug to her brother's cheek before relenting a bit "I guess a visit every now and then you know once or twice, I was just tripping off of how hard it is to get people to come see about you in the first place, I really didn't mean to hit you off like that Des'" but Des' already knew the reason, even seen it when her wheels spun in the direction of how easy it was for friends and family to let him down so easily. He knew this because often was the times that the very same thoughts flowed in and out of his mind and by people Des' knew that Mecca was referring to their mother, aunts and uncles, never mind friends.

So by him knowing this already it was easy to detect it on his sister whom he's known all of his life. Desmond knew two things that he could count on. One, being his love for his sister, the other being her love for him. So, regardless of the disappointments these two have felt, he knew that she was right in her regards, she was really all he would ever need to get by, everything else was just wants and conveniences, and if he didn't know much else, he knew the big picture was his motha fuckin' freedom and his sister and those two went hand in hand. Not one greater than the other and Des' not being the smartest nigga in the universe or even in a small school for the mentally challenged, even dumb as a rock he was smart enough to know that it would never be a bitch alive who would hammer his attorney like his sister, plus post the monthly payments like his sister, so, no, his sister was irreplaceable, he knew it and she knew it. Although she never hinted on her fatigue of making the trips to see him just right after a long shift, he was able to see it in her eyes. Knew that she wished that there was a switch that she could hit to make everything go back to yesterday, activate a different reality then the one that has only become more and more depressing each step of their fight.

"Nah, I know what's going on with you and I need you to know that I understand, Mecca I really do. I know that it's a hard thing to do you know, come and go only to have to come back again to relive the same ugly dream. Trust me when I say that I could see it on you which is mainly the reason I requested another outlet, maybe help out a little bit. Mommy the dough was bait not to replace you, there's nobody in the world or maybe even in the next world who would be able to do that, you are the only family that I got and you are the only true friend that I got Mecca I love you for all you do but bigger than all of that is that I love you for being a beautiful person period. The truth is you do need a vacation, listen I've been dreaming about this place you know, every time I hear stories about this place I get excited and wish that I could see it you know, how about you go see it and tell me all about it."

"Oooh, you spooking me Des' what are you talking about,"

"There's two places that I vision the most in the world, and they are in the Virgin Islands, see there's St. Croix and then there's St. Thomas and I'm thinking that the beaches would serve you righteously. Get your little relax on for a few, plus the stories that I hear you would come back with recipes for eight or nine different drinks, you could then solidify yourself as the best bartender in the damned world."

"I... am... the best damned bartender in the world so get it right, are you serious. How the hell am I supposed to get to the Virgin Islands?"

"I hear you'd have to tip into Frisco and fly out to Miami, it could be another way, but that's the way that I hear about so much and it's the way I would take, the way I see it, when I rest you know." Mecca scanned her brother for the faintest sign of a prank with confidence, that if she didn't know anybody else in this damned world Desmond she knew, and it was because of that did she begin to get a little nervous and a bit fidgety. Because she also knew when her brother was dead serious too, and mm hmm, oh yeah, he had his dead serious look on.

"On an air plane?" she managed to utter,

"Yelp, on an air plane."

"I'm gonna go ahead and take it that you're saying all of this knowing well enough that I'm a bartender…right."

"Uh Huh, and the best one in the world …right, now is that on the record and official or just some shit that you made up, I mean I need to know what to tell the guys."

"Uhh uhh, Virgin Islands," Mecca was deeply rooted in her one opportunity to leave far behind any misery, whoa to stress, and anxiety be gone only to achieve this she needed Desmond to refocus,

"Well that last puzzle was a serious play, just like I knew it would be, what I'm gonna do is take this ball out of my boot, Mah it's a hundred, one hundred dollar bills. I need you to sort of run interference for me while I dig it out." A hundred, hundred dollar bills! My nigga no problem, Mecca thought before walking to the podium and commanding the attention of both of the correctional officers. She had it all worked out, she would fake a crush on the old geezer with all the confidence in the world, figuring that his job security was enough to land any woman he pleased.

Mecca would always stop to tell him that she was on her way to the vending machines. She'd often asked him if she could offer anything, perhaps a cold drink, smiling he would always decline. His partner a younger Mexican lady always viewed Mecca a bit differently, in one of those 'I wish that you would just die' visions. She would always decline way before Mecca made the offer in her direction, but together the two would follow Mecca to the vending machines with their eyes. This was always good enough for Desmond to make his move and dig out either money or information that he or another inmate needed to send out without the monitoring of a phone call or the surveillance of the ever rigorous mailing processes, saying that some things just aren't everybody else's business.

The time that Mecca returned with their refreshments Desmond had already loaded the cash into her coat pocket, now accepting the snacks, he said,

"Look Mah, that's a dime, use two to load me up, take one to our dude."

"Ok, ok, are you sure about this?"

"About the reservations,"

"No, about the other thing, that's a lot, the most so far."

"Which would still never be enough, you could get Marva to bring it, give her all the details and spare her nothing, I mean the last thing we need is her to step in and foul everything up, not right when it's starting to look like help."

"No, I'll just do it, if she screws up that would hurt us real big Des', I'm saying,"

"Na, I want you to enjoy yourself, if it doesn't look good I'll send her ass back to get some more schooling, we can't take those kinds of chances, not now, not ever. I mean my life depends on this, right?"

"All right, all right, I swear to God if she blows this I'll kill her myself."

"If you game her right, then I could reel her in from here."

"So, I'll score the 'bucket' wrap it up, lace her on how to behave then…"

"Go make reservations, tell your boss that you're about to collapse from being over worked, I mean it, get me some of those damned pictures, and just maybe we'd be able to go together soon enough," a smile spread across Mecca's lips before she said,

"Look at my bra bra, sending sis to the Virgin Islands and stuff."

"And you should take momma with you maybe that'll get her out of the house. If not, then go and treat yourself."

"Man, the Virgin Islands though, I have never thought this to happen to me."

"Girl, you know I got you."

"Yes, I do, but now let me get out of here before you change your mind."

"Mecca!"

"Desmond!"

"We need this, yeah?"

"I know; I love you Des' you hear me?"

"I do." The two stood and embraced before departing, both fighting back the tears that were stinging in their eyes.

CHAPTER 8

It was one thing to be burgled or even stole from, but to be all out robbed was in a class by itself. Even more so when one was being robbed in broad daylight. This is what the 'Rabbit' eared boys' grew a notorious reputation for doing, robbing people in broad daylight. The 'Rabbit' eared boys, a nick name that the whole Oak Park had for a stain on their brains. Every hustler was wide awake to this: the pimps, the whores, the coke dealers and the methamphetamines dealers where getting it the most. If you were caught selling marijuana in nickel bags, then you were prime time ready and lord help you if you had a bag of change, and be the undisputed quarter pitching champion of the world and here they come.

These boys always showed up as if they were led by cash sniffing blood hounds; one that always kept his nose to the ground in search of the dough. In this case this hound had a platinum nose because there wasn't a safe hustle spotted for blocks and blocks. Everyone wished it stop but this plague done nothing but grew stronger and stronger. The Police needed it to stop, because never had a 911 dispatcher been so busy with such a high volume of calls from people crying for help and for justice. As for the villains to these capers, the 'Rabbit' eared boys aka Cash, Scope, and Stomp they didn't give a fuck one way or the other, which was the reason their success rate was so high, because the victims of these encounters knew this as well, that either of them gave a fuck. If a child was implicated into the situation and a gun pointed in its direction. Then only these boys' demands being met is what ensured the child's safety and nothing else.

These criminals needed to die is what the community would say, someone needed to kill them, because nothing else would stop them. Everybody who hustled felt this fear because in reality these three dudes were aiming at them the most. What the hustlers didn't know was that these occurrences weren't as random as the people led others to think because never is it ever told correctly. William H. Bonney left bodies all over the place twenty of them if you let society tell it but if one was to actually check the history books one could easily find those numbers to be not so astronomical as the rumors has it and awfully exaggerated and neither are the drug bust of two kilograms of any narcotic worth one point whatever million dollars in street value as the arresting officers would leave a community to believe.

These same exaggerations and conspiracy theories also applied to the now fearful 'Rabbit' eared boys. Were their actions random? No, these occasions were planned and well strategized for everyone shall know that every dog has its day and in the back of each so called victims head oh how they all awaited theirs. Even though they were hustlers they were wrong, somewhere down their crooked lines of works, there was one kind of malicious mischief or the other and there was one person that knew about it all, no matter how dark the secrets there was illuminations just waiting right around the corner.

Not that the victims acknowledged any of this while under such a vicious assault no, no but Marcel always knew that he would come to visit. He even knew what to accomplish while paying such a visit. So, if they came down this only meant one thing, that you were on the list. You either ratted or rolled over leaving somebody to be the burden bearer and sufferer of a bitch niggas mischief and iniquities. Some either murdered to bring gains, whatever it was that landed them on the list Marcel had the answer for it, it was called revenge for the ones who would not be fortunate enough to reap it on their own due to lengthy stents in Pelican Bay State Prison, New Folsom, Or High Desert and then there were those in exile or they were dead.

Whatever the case, there was a way that these fallen soldiers would live on through Marcel, who had every connection there was to information.

His phone buzzed daily with collect calls from one prison or the other which only mills out reliable information, so much that there was work to do every day for these three who spent all day hopping out of cars or kicking down doors yelling, "Ok, show me the Rabbit ears." This meant the two front pockets pulled out to the whites. Never has an event made it pass the pistol whipping, nothing as heinous as rapes or foreign object activities as the rumors had it, just regular ole ropes and robbing and sometimes duct tape in case the ropes weren't available, but the police never cared. They hear foreign objects and that's enough to put an all-points bulletin out on three black males wearing dark colored hooded sweatshirts and dark colored clothing. Hell, with this description nobody knew how to help, because what the news just did was described half of Fourth Avenue and all of Thirty Third Street. To the three who operated from the hit list of things to do whenever the time was right, was held up a bit because the time was not right in fact it was wrong, wrong, it was all wrong because the heat from the police just got turned up a lot.

A devil may care way of living was their style. Yeah, being stupid and outright foolish was not. A break was needed and everybody knew it because of the constant raids and police harassments made this decision a no brainer. Over the weeks these three learned a lot out about each other. Of the three, Stomp was held the most active when it came to street politics, he wasn't liberal at all. He had gone to trial twice, homicide in the first degree then later homicide in the second degree, both times he walked away from it, scathed but unfazed. Scope knew how to drive, I mean, bank robbery and getaway car kind of driver. In reverse he was as exact and precise as if he was driving in the forward direction. Twice, the three were in high speed chases, once for no reason at all, Scope just didn't feel like pulling over, but both times it was convincing that they would live to rob another day.

Once Scope and Stomp found out that Marcel was the elite boxer that everyone spoke so highly about, concluded that they were fighting back the desires to shoot the shit out of him themselves, still found a joy of being in the company of such a local hero. Marcel also found out that Scope really and truly had a mind of his own, one that saw past the right now, a real two steps ahead of the game kind of thinker. Everything with him was calculations and on the clock; this is how much time on the clock we could use before the risk increase type of thinker. He was down to do anything, ready for whatever, rob a bank? Hell yeah. Rob a funeral parlor? Let's do it. To him everything was a challenge, a game that he would bet his life on. If he wins he'll get money but if he shall lose, it'll be his life. Crazy as these games may appear, let us let the record reflect that yet has he lost his life and oh how many attempts, one would think that he should have been erased a long time ago.

Started off as a car thief, you name it and he'll pull it off, never been to jail or any place else for incarceration, never been on parole or probation, in fact his record was squeaky clean. No one believes it, not even the police when they do get a chance to speak to him. The cops always hated this because never do he ever let an officer search anything of his, not his car, not his house and not him. Believing that if an officer felt endangered by the presence of him then he must have a reason to make an arrest. "Can I pat you down for my own safety? No sir, can I speak with you a moment? No sir, no one ever knew that this works, no one has to stop when an officer decides that they'll just like to talk. Now if you fit the description of a cat burglar as a cop would say just to get you to stop that you know that you fit the description and all. Well, that's another thing but know that you could always deny, deny, deny as Scope does. Because if he didn't, his first try out would have landed him level four points in Salinas Valley some damned where, which is also a maximum security prison that's stuck way the fuck out there in the middle of nowhere. Scope was sharp, well read and well educated and he came from a home of the well to do. His mother was a social worker for the county. His father spent a lot of time at the law library aiding the insufficient as they came through needing help with divorce or landlord problems, "it would always be something" his father would say. Growing up Scope had a silver spoon in his mouth, no brothers, and no sisters the only child that grew spoiled rotten. Other kids used to hate this, so they would make it as uncomfortable as they could, which only gave birth to an incubus or an anathema. One could easily argue that Scope had exactly no reason to be in the streets like he was but he had his own aspirations, he stole cars because he needed to learn how to drive. He needed to learn how to drive so the Police wouldn't catch him. He needed the Police not to catch him because he knew that his life would be filled with high risk activities. The rush from adrenaline was too intense in his life, for Scope was into the edges, bungee jumping and sky diving stunts always excite him no matter where he saw this, in books on television or real life.

So, to ride suicide on a motorcycle or in a car became as natural to him as breathing, eating, and sleeping. You can only wonder why it was so easy for him to turn left when he was raised to go right, one should wonder no more because Scope was an extremist to the fullest and nothing ever excited him in the Suburbs. Quiet by nine o'clock in the evening, no guns going off, no helicopters aiding ground patrolling cops, no crime unless they were the ones being victimized, no clubs, no nothing. Just work, eat and sleep. 'Fuck that' he thought, he wanted street credibility and fame. He wanted to be remembered forever like "Hard Rock" "SD" and "Chunk" or like "Steve O" "Demon" and "Carl Webb" these were the guys who've influenced him. "Steve O" robbed banks before, "Demon" orchestrated a whole Mafia Movement on Fourth Avenue, "Hard Rock" was killed on Fourth Avenue but alive, he was a hope to die hittah. Scope had a love for the streets so did Marcel and so did Stomp. No other place they would rather be and if you were in the streets with them then you were gonna respect them just like they did. If you had your own agendas, then you could expect to see them.

To them turf wars were for the birds. If anybody from Oak Park were to open up a strip to trap and get money in Oak Park then know, that this particular strip was designed for anybody from Oak Park to eat off of. If one wanted all the cheese like a dirty rat, then a rat trap was set and poison pellets were placed in the path to halt the flow of the rats greed, and if that didn't work then you're on the list. Better to rid the faulty then to be poisoned on an accident is how the game was explained and these three had no problem what so ever at enforcing this structure, this way of life. Rather you chose this life or this life chose you however, you were gonna respect these streets, that was it and that was all. There were codes and ethics to everything; in sports, in politics, or in courts it never mattered the field of one's choosing, there were rules. These three didn't make the rules, but they all knew the rules and no way in the world where they gonna abide while the faultiest slithered through, No! They didn't make the rules but they were born to enforce the rules.

The code in every hood that one needed to stick to was the "G Code" whatever field one may select just make sure that you kept it "G" and one hundred percent, nothing else was better. It was not only their field to these three no, it was their desire. To them it was an honor to die in the streets of Sacramento where they were soldiers at and where the many other soldiers died before them. Dudes like "YB" and "Poony" "Cadillac Tone" and "Killah" "Perk" and "Big Dirt" a lot of soldiers wrote the check and cashed all the way out so the hood could be a place that once had no voice, now screams louder than a motha fucka. What's in the hood is now depicted on televisions of all walks generating big, big money, hood music is selling everything from cars to cell phones. Hood dances are flying throughout the whole country to entertain folks from the other side of the tracks in order to sale, regardless of the products just know that it would need hood clearance first.

If you are into politics tell me where you run to when you need votes. The hood has its own powers and sometimes it silence is its loudest voice. Before the Polices brutality of Rodney King the hood used to scream Police brutality at the top of its lungs to no avail, no one paid attention to the hood then. Not even when it was showed to America on video did America listen but when the hood decided to cook Los Angeles to a crisp creating billions of dollars in property damage than they were like "Oh that's what y'all was talking about the police is tapping on you guys a little bit, well that's all you had to say the first time." These were the attributes that made it very difficult for these three to be impervious too. It was the hood in a whole that was the lure, the decorated cars, the sassy and jazzy women were the art forms. Everyone knows that where there's smoke then there's fire and in the hood it's no different and has its draw backs. There were bums, drugs, whores and the rats, people that relied heavily on government funds to provide information and affidavits to the law officials and those kind of rats. People who'd commit scurvy and other acts of scandal for a few dollars more and sometimes even just because.

Looking at the whole picture one could see the beauty even through the tenements, for its beauty is ever so potent and sure. Though looking at the same picture one could without a doubt see where this beauty could be marred and defaced, destroyed and easily ruined for the interior acids coupled with other toxics has always found its way to the heart of such a beauteous picture. It's always the artist who's the first to recognize these ruins of such a master piece and it is also the artist who must find a way to correct the damages that had been done. In this case there were three of them, all three held the same desire, all three stuck by the same code. Though equal in peril and street savvy these three held the streets of Sacramento as a banner to the reasons why they lived, and as ridiculous as this may seem balmy or asinine one may think, but all three knew that they were going to either die young, in this case awfully young or they were going to grow old and rich. For them there were no grey areas it was one way or the other and either of the three really cared which one it'll be.

For the resting spot and the best way to beat the heat not the regular heat either no, this was the gang task kind of heat. This was the under covers on feet, bikes and horse's kind of heat. The drug dealers hated when the heat was turned up so high, but knew better than to roll over and fink or their careers would be finished. For them to beat the heat the three headed out to North Sacramento in the Del Paso Heights district and to an underground hide out that Stomp had been renting just for occasions like this. There was always food supply and the perfect seclusion to allow the heat to die down. Scope needed the phone right away so he could get in contact with his game chick before dude that she would swear up and down that was only her trick daddy come through and eat up all her time with his petty poke.

"Hello," said the voice on the other end of the line.

"Hey, is Trick Willy with you right now?" Scope said in a joking manner.

"Don't be disrespecting my company like that, his name is William."

"I know, Trick Willy, right?"

"If you say so, what's going on, baby you all right."

"Yeah, yeah, yeah but you know my concerns right?"

"Yeah boo, you know that I got you. It's only a few dollars right now, but don't trip he's gonna come back through and I'm gonna sock it to him then, ok?"

"Is that right, a few dollars what's that about come on talk to me?"

"It's like three notes, that's all but like I say don't trip because I will get more I will sock it for you baby, you know that."

"Aretha?"

"What baby?"

"Don't let Trick Willy be the reason, you hear me?"

"I wouldn't even be fucking with this dude if it wasn't for the paper Sean and you know that, shoot let me have my way I'll be right there with you right now."

"What about that other nigga though, when he 'pose to come through" by the other nigga Aretha knew that Scope was referring to Marvin her other play thing who pays heavy to lick her like a lollipop as she calls it. Not only was Marvin ex-military but he lived in Nevada where it was awfully easy to cop weapons and ammunition and this was always good because this kept the "Rabbit Ear Boys" locked and loaded.

"Well, at first he said he was going to come through tonight, but he postponed until tomorrow. I'm telling you now because I don't want to hear your mouth."

"I could feel that but yeah I'm gonna sit up with my dudes and them, what I need you to do is keep what me and you doing first, feel that and don't forget to remember that it's a lot going on too that we can't afford any foul ups, you still feel?"

"Yeah, I got you boo, so when are you coming this way? You know that I need a fix Sean, the only times I see you is when I got some money for you and baby that ain't right."

"Three hundred dollars is some money and you still don't see me, so why are you talking like that?"

"Because I'm horny for my baby, you got me humping on these in the way ass niggas; I need a real nigga in my life you know this already."

"What's on your mind Mah, you know all you got to do is say it, I mean where you get all these bushes to beat around I don't know, sounds like some Trick Willy shit. He teaches you shit like that over there?"

"I don't know what's gotten into me, I just know that it hasn't been you and like I said I need a fix and only you could fix it so what's up?"

"Is that right? Hold on a minute," Aretha heard Scope exchange conversation with another person in the back ground before coming back on the line. He said,

"Look, dig it, when you get a nickel come through 'safe ways' all right?" Aretha now knew that Scope was in the north area at the safe house. Learning this gave her a sense of security knowing that she didn't have the police to worry about.

"What if I could get the other two hundred sent to me then?"

"Then I'll see you when you get here."

"Then I could have you all to myself?"

"You know that I got my niggas with me don't get 'ta playing."

"Because the last time I was hella sore, y'all didn't care for my little pussy at all."

"Well?"

"Well what?"

"You coming or not?"

"I'll suck they dick, but only you are getting the pussy, is that a deal, if not I'll wait until you come through here."

"You don't have to come through, just wire the chip to me, do that western union thang for me."

"Man, all right I'll bring it, first let me call Marvin to see if he would send it if not then I'ma call William to see, if that's not happening then I'm just going to wait until tonight."

"Yeah, yeah, yeah that's what I like, that's what I like. You know, only a real bitch is what works for me too. I make you get down not for what you would do I'm trying to see what you won't do, hear that?"

"Well I'm never gonna cash out the next nigga like I do you. That's for sure and I'm never gonna charge you like I sock it to those other niggas for the high prices even if they think they getting it for free. When they ain't looking I'm stashing on they ass, so, you don't have to worry about that. You made me I won't ever forget that. The game I got, I got from you, and you created me. When I was ever so lost I was found and all of this by you. I wouldn't care what I got to do you ask and I come running that's it and that's everything. So, you could look for everything that I won't do for you all you like and there will be nothing. What I won't do is disrespect you or your gangsta."

"Yeah, yeah, I hear you."

"Then what did I say Sean?"

"You said you love me more than ever only in a lot of words."

"Ok then tell me about it."

"I was paying attention."

"Well?"

"Well what?"

"I know you don't have another bitch over there with you Sean, I know you don't, you gonna fuck around and make me come over there and whip her ass."

"Girl, if you don't go on with that bullshit."

"Oh, I got your bullshit, who's all over there with you then, tell me that," again Scope disappeared from the conversation, then he was back on the line.

"Mah, I'm gonna need you to chill the fuck out for a minute."

"Fuck that I know that you ain't breathing all hard and shit while I'm on the phone, what bitch you got over there Sean don't play with me like that."

"Never mind that shit…"

"Never mind! Never mind! Ain't that about a bitch I bet you I will come over there and whoop that bitch ass right motha fuckin now."

"What bitch, wait a minute, hold on a minute" Aretha noticed that Scope covered the phone when he spoke to whoever the fuck it was that required his attention which sparked the flame of jealousy in Aretha. What she didn't know is that Scope was preoccupied reading rapid fire text messages and could not focus on the conversation with her and never made it any better when he came back on the line and said,

"Mah, look don't make the trip right now but go ahead and make the calls like you said and call me back when you're done don't make a move until you hit me back I think I got something else for you to do, Ok."

"Why, why I can't come spend some time with you like you said?"

"You could just not right now like I said do that thang you do then we good give me time to sort out this little situation that just came up."

"Put that on something that there ain't another bitch over there."

"I put that on us."

"What? What do you put on us Sean?"

"I know what you're doing already."

"What am I doing then?"

"You're trying to stay on the line with me so you could play the background. But I'ma tell you that there ain't no other bitch over here if there was I would tell you that and you know better so quit it."

"Ok, I believe you baby. You know how I get when I ain't fixed right, you already know especially having to wait on you like this, and you make me think stuff that's all."

"I'm hipped, so now what are you thinking?"

"I'm thinking that I'm gonna hang up and get this money right for you then call you back with the results."

"My baby," was all Scope said before he hung the phone up, unsure to what it was really that had his potna Cash pacing a shortcut through the alley way in the carpet. Whatever the text message was it was something real serious, because now even Stomp appeared to be fidgety and Scope had barely ever seen this for a practice with Stomp but never has he seen it in both not at the same time, he looked at Marcel and said.

"You guys win; I'm the only one that doesn't know what's going on, what the fuck is you pacing for?"

"Didn't you see the text nigga?" Marcel said as if saying that explained everything.

"Yeah, who the fuck is Lod, I don't know that nigga."

"Nigga ain't nobody named Lod, that means emergency, E-MER-GEN-CY" Marcel couldn't believe that Scope didn't know how to read a good text message. Not really, Scope didn't have to because he had a bitch to do all that technical bullshit decided that even as remedial as it looked Scope would be lost so Marcel continued with saying,

"Lod ain't a name, Life or Death see it, now the NH what that means is Need Help, then you see SOD that means stacks on deck then there the RS, and that means regular spot. And then there's the "SYWIGT" see that, you know what that means?"

"What, I love you..."

"See You When I Get There," Scope finished not understanding the rest when he saw the TNO as far as he knew those were the sender's initials, confused he said.

"TNO the fuck is that?"

"Trust No One, get it?"

"Shit, they could say that again," Scope said then added "My guess is that you gonna fill me in on the CGU then?"

"Uh huh, that means that it Could Get Ugly."

"Ok, stacks on deck, don't trust nobody and it could get ugly hell. I mean that's the storyline of my life don't know 'bout you niggas. So, where's this regular spot and how do you know all of this, you read shit like that before, you know this nigga?"

"Yes, and the spot is Club Rendezvous," the phone ringing startled the room and wasn't until Scope answered the phone did calm find its way back. Even Scope found relief once he identified the caller to be Aretha feeling that if it could get ugly then he was sure to need to sneak a banger in the club.

"Mommy listen, this is what I need you to do."

CHAPTER 9

FRIDAY NIGHT WOULD BE REASON enough for anyone to celebrate, but for Marva this wasn't just a reason to celebrate, shit Nah. This was a reason for a full blown festival a damned fiesta, talking about the whole motha fucking carnival. Her spirits were high, her moods were ripe for prime time stepping, ain't felt this good in ages thinking that finally her life begun to take shape again. Her contacts were more influential now, her purse a bit puffier now. She was on her shit something terrible now, and she knew it so it was about time that she let everybody else know it. So, when Tamia suggested a girl's night out only solidified the reasons to why she would hit the mall like a freight train where she strategically selected her outfit "Hmm, let's see Stella McCartney" she hummed "Yes, and all the way to the hand bag" because miss Queen over everything was back and to prove it $1,700 worth of leather and silks left the mall right along with her. Tonight was gonna be the night that she stepped out hot dammit, one Salvatore Ferragamo's step after the other.

The past month was made for healing and hustling and creating new ways to generate dough and, this is what she stayed true to. Oh never mind the cost of this night because if you let her tell it this night was all on them. In her basket, the one that she weaved, were cash traps made specifically to get that all mighty dollar and every trap must accommodate her worth and she was selling huge stocks at high prices.

"Three grand for two weeks' worth of work simply doing nothing but talking, holding hands and kissing," she soliloquized, then again

"Hell, piece of cake," for she knew that she would of took the chances for far less as down as she was on her luck, and this is when the idea struck home. "Hmm, maybe if I spread my wings a bit, instead of going to one prison she would get four of them into her scheme. Her and Mecca was locked in a split pot venture, which was cool because Marva understood well the attempt to help Desmond and his lawyer fees, great no sweat, as long as she got something out of the deal, but now the rest of her game was all her.

Solano State Prison sat right next to Vacaville Corrections and Medical facility, which is an older prison than Solano but just perfect for the only purpose that Marva would ever care about. She took out the newspaper articles of the lonely desperate incarcerated brothers, mm hmm, and that's exactly what she did, and just five weeks later she was in heavy correspondence with three other prisons that met her convenience. Her designs were immaculate, impeccable detail and harmony, a shopping spree, one that spoke in the French dialect, oh my God she was Wayne Gretzky at his finest. She would leave Solano which was indeed in walking distance to its older mate, walk in that motha fucka and do the very exact same thing, hug a little, talk a little and kiss a little, and then there was the business. In Vacaville, waiting would be Deontae who at the sight of Marva mumbled the words 'lord have mercy' and at the sight of this Marva knew that she had him. All he wanted to know was when would be the next time he'd be able to see her again. Marva's memory was vivid she recalled sitting Deontae down after treating him to a lunch supplied simply by the vending machines and said,

"Sweetie, as handsome as you are, and the way you take such good care of your body. Shoot, soon as you hugged me I got all moist and stuff and that's what I like in a man. Somebody that could make me feel that way with just a touch, you know. But, I got to be straight up with you it's a recession where I come from and I'll be lucky to make up this way for Christmas." As soon as Deontae heard the bad news his wheels begun to spin. Christmas didn't sound good to him at all uh uhh it was only March, 'Oh my God' he thought 'I can't let the baddest bitch in the whole visiting room slip through my fingers,' concluding his mental travels he looked Marva straight in the face and said.

"A recession, what is that, I mean in here there's never a recession, in fact this is where the dough is. I mean if you down I could help you get a bucket full of it."

"Oooh, I'm listening, I mean if it would keep me next to you I'm down for whatever, you need to know that."

"Cool, now you got to listen," and for that Deontae told Marva everything that she already knew, although she played virgin to the whole thing so she let him explain away and once he was finished Marva let him know what she would do and ever since then she's been three steps in front of Deontae. She would send him packages for commissary while he sent her cold hard cash which indeed was a lot of help, then there was the ad that she took out on a brother who was locked up in Folsom State Prison which so happen to be located a few minutes away from Mule Creek Correctional facility. Marva always liked going to Mule Creek where she would visit with Dennis. Marva really liked Dennis because he was about as dumb as a mule, it really took some working with him for he wasn't a quick sell at all, and this got Marva to like him right away. The fact that he was so dumb he was hard to get mad at but what Dennis had to a fault was he was very old fashion, so Marva had to exploit such a weakness she said,

"I see that you've been gone for such a long time that you've about forgotten how to take care of a woman, haven't you?"

"Take care of a woman, nah, nah, nah, now how could I forget some shit like that? Take care of a woman...pa-leeeese."

"Well, tell me how could you take care of me if I were your wife from in here then?" Marva saw the stars hit Dennis in his head for a minute, she waited for him to swallow the hook which took a few more pecks on his ear lobe before he drunk it. It took a second for him to get it but once he did, believing that he had a wife coming was motivation enough to send her the money in droves and been unbelievable ever since.

Then right down the street was Malcolm, now Malcolm knew what he wanted in a gal, somebody to bring him drugs and send him luxuries through the mail and it just so happen that for the right price Marva was photogenic as well. She had sexy garments flying every damned where about sticking to the money. Malcolm was so up front about the hustle that Marva forgot the lie that she made up, but she did learn that Folsom was a place starving for drugs because Malcolm would run out way before she would make the trip to refresh him 'his idea and not mine' she would say and she made sure to stay ready for him. Now that her financial net worth was now closing in on the ten-thousand-dollar mark with more on the way saying that her next load would net even twice as much. Oh yeah a drink was definitely in order, a few cheers, meet a few people and sit her charm down and get some of this "on the street" money she figured. Then, at least I could get a 'nut' and even then it would be in the name of the game and only for the dough.

It's been three months since Javier was out of her life yet she was already considering putting a down payment on that new Jaguar X type. In her phone she could scroll down her call log and find a long list of prospects and all of them was willing to treat her like a lady, chivalry far from dead when it came to her. Just on a whim she would scroll down her list to see how much money she could generate and seven calls later, she'll be on her way to express pay to collect a couple of grand and to make the peter sweeter and make it all more interesting just a few days later she would make the same calls and pull the shit off again. Oh yeah she was on her shit something awful all right. She had a surgeon who'd call her to the hospital so he could have her suck him off in the elevator and in return for this a tennis bracelet with ice running crazy through it and this is when we get to think Tiffanies for an introduction. Add the awfully healthy allowance, and ok, yes, on her shit she was. Marva reflected back on the day that she first met this particular mark; she was just cured of the black and blue bruises and she still put the 'woo-doffle' package on him and ever since then he sure displayed a funny way of feeling sorry for her.

Then there was the construction worker. Told her that he'll drink her bath water, loved her legs he'd say, and all the time Marva thought the gentlemen was only with the joshing but discovered him to be a man of his word. A word that showed him how to burp bubbles for a week and, even he bore gifts and guess what'? You better know it, a healthy allowance; boy was she wasting time cleaning grass stains from the carpet every Saturday. Only once did she fail to fight the impulse to ride down her old street where she could see her old house perhaps even see her old man. The impulse was too potent to resist, so, she waited for the right time that Javier would pull into his drive way, just in time to see her hit the horn and drive away vindicated while she left a bit of that exhaust fume leaking from a Chrysler 300C with the fully loaded package that she went out of her way to rent just for the occasion, conquering her task and loving every minute of it she drove away. To her, men was no more than a stepping stone that she would step high and hard on and over to find her way through life. Men owe, is all she would ever say in regards to the other half, and never would she ever let up was the promise that she said to herself, never. As long as they kept her chipped up then and only then, would she tolerate them? She was made to keep men broke and out of order, so a lady's night out was the perfect medicine, throw back a few of those drinks hit the dance floor and she was gonna wiggle with it. On occasions she would pause to see who landed in her web, this way she could add to her already overflowing call log. If it wasn't anything else left in the world that she could do she knew that she could always entertain herself with wrapping men around her finger because she knew that a big ass and a little class went far, wide and a long way. It just so happened that these very two attributes that could get her to travel to those distant places she had the best of, and she knew how to use them.

Tossing the bag inside of the rented VW Beetle, which then was the ultimate chick car, had a banana yellow paint that made it look boss with the black interior which by the way was just what she wanted to do and that was to stand out and look boss. Why not use the colors of a bumble bee knowing that tonight she was out to sting? Once inside the car she placed two calls, one to Tamia who didn't answer and was probably getting her hair, feet and nails done and couldn't answer it. The other call was to her new thang that proved to be the perfect hook up in order to keep her traps with bait on them.

For Tahj this was a night for her to celebrate as well. Once she heard that her man was on his way home her dancing feet took off without her permission. Upon hearing this they slid across the floor to help put her cell phone back on the charger, the happy music that only she could hear found its way to her shoulders raising them, then releasing them. Then her feet two stepped the rest of her in the direction of her closet where she knew the perfect set was hanging, for the perfect occasion. Tonight, she had to be a knock out; she knew what she had to do. Her man been gone nearly a month, she was gonna be eye candy for him and this she knew, the very, very, edible kind, she thought then smiled at her own humor as she sized up her outfit against her very powerful figure.

Accepting her selection of shoe to ride with her costume she immediately phoned into the beauty shop where she knew it was gone be hard for Ms. Lynn to squeeze her in for a pampering, but she was sure that she could make her understand if not by word then an extra $40 for a tip would suffice, a trick that she was sure would work. To her surprise it didn't take much coaxing for Ms. Lynn not only liked Tahj's company or even the fact that Ms. Lynn connected with Tahj's' occupation for in the day Ms. Lynn was a real glider herself. Ms. Lynn just so happened to have received a last minute cancellation and seeing how this was a rare occurrence Tahj rode her luck all the way out to the Jeep and headed off to her appointment. Tahj took the day in and found it one that she could appreciate. Her singing group had already landed safely in their home town over a week ago. She was happy to be rid of them but satisfied that they finally came around enough to represent her as well as themselves when they kicked off their 50 city tour dates. The check cleared just the other day, her man was just on his way home which high time she thought, and just as soon as she was beginning to grow restless he called to let her know that he would be arriving soon. Plus, one shot at a walk in at the world's busiest hair salon was all it took to beautify what was already beautiful, oh yeah she was having a good day.

Yes, today is a beautiful day, she said to herself while looking in the rearview to see what she would request to be done with her hair and eyebrows. The light turned green so she pushed off. Then the thought hit her, Rasaan sounded a bit pressed like there was something he wanted to say but somehow couldn't. He always left, yet when it was time to return he always sounded excited as if yearn has taken over him. This time he sounded flat, this time he sounded dreadful and this time his abnormalities created an instant concern. Normally Tahj knew that no matter what transpired that Rasaan always found a solution even when the situation proved to be sullen. Maybe she was reading too much into her phone call and maybe she was willing the wicked spirits just to have something to worry about, or maybe this last trip came with more than he was prepared to handle. She very seldom asked any questions when it came to Rasaan's disappearances, the lest that she knew the better off that she would be and this she was sure of, but this uneasy feeling she was getting was driving her nuts. Is Rasaan in danger, she thought as she pulled into the lot of the beauty shop. She also thought about calling Rasaan to confirm his safety but she knew that it was never him to talk so openly on his phone. Letting her thoughts seep from her mind, she hopped out of her Jeep and headed through the doors of the shop into the always pleasant and, always cheerful, Ms. Lynn.

Lerin got the call about the surprise party that was being thrown for Mecca so she was on the phone to Tahj immediately, who already said that she was gone fall through anyways, who called Tamia who thought the whole idea of the going away party was cool but felt a tinge of jealousy for Mecca who was on her way to the Virgin Islands. So, Mecca called Marva who was just looking for a reason to celebrate which was cool so Marva hurriedly called Tahj to make sure that they weren't wearing the same raiment's, because Marva already knew that Tahj had a notorious reputation for having every outfit in the mall, no matter what mall and was excited both ways. One that Tahj wasn't gonna rock anything 'Stella' even though she was certain that the new costume that she had just purchased wouldn't be in Tahj arsenal but wasn't into taking those kind of chances. This excited Marva even more and the second revelation was the fact that it's been four and a half years since Marva saw Tahj, but managed to call periodically due to a very, very monogamous and tamed domestic relationship with Javier, a relationship that kept her in the house or close by it anyway. Tahj, hearing this phoned Lerin who grimaced at the sound of the news that Tahj was delivering to her. Oh the fact that they were gonna hit the floor and showcase their group moves together, that was the good news and Lerin knew that Mecca knew all of the steps so they were gonna murder that. But the problem was that Lerin knew so many things, about clothes, about drinks, and about the streets as well. Who's winning? Who's losing? Who's on the move, and who's straight up and who's scandalous, she knew everything. If God ran a little late, he'd tap into Lerin and she'd update him on current events. Not that she was nosy, not at all, but she was the home girl and she was the home girl because she was street and she was street because she came from a long line of hustlers and thugs. All of her brothers were certified hittah's; the ones that didn't speak much but was prone to knock a nigga down really quick and with this kind of popularity Lerin knew how to capitalize on such an asset. She wanted to work at the club because she liked being sociable, she liked being sociable and cordial because she knew, that one could catch more flies with honey than one could with vinegar and by listening to Tahj relay their intents she was cool about everything on the list except having Marva for company. Lerin listened then expressed her discomforts to their home girl being a part of the celebration, and she listened when Tahj reminded her that it's been years since either of them had a chance to kick it with their home girl. Lerin even heard how Tahj emphasized the word home girl as if Lerin didn't know where she was headed with her cogent arguments and even heard Tahj when she said,

"Now you know you're my sister right?"

"Unh hun,"

"Lerin, I know when you're holding back."

"Is that right and what gave me away?"

"The feathers,"

"What, what you mean by that?" Lerin was slow.

"You sound like Sylvester, you know I Twat I saw a pooty cat, I did, I did saw a pooty cat, only this time you finally got the bird in your mouth."

"Uhh, the cat that ate the canary, I heard that," Lerin finally got it.

"So, fill me in."

"Trust me you do not want to know."

"Ohh, oooh, oooh," Tahj became immediately excited.

"What the hell going on over there."

"You bitch, I know you, every time you say that, something juicy is on the horizon and you be right all the time, once I hear it I wish you hadn't told me, but the shit be so juicy though."

"This ain't any different either,"

"Shit!" Tahj felt caught in the head lights.

"Yeah," was all Lerin was willing to say.

"You mean to…"

"Un hun,"

"Noooo,"

"Scan-docious"

"Marva,"

"Umm hmm,"

"Our Marva,"

"Uhh uhh girl, please don't say that."

"Alright, but our Marva?"

"You sound like you wouldn't believe me anyways if I told you."

"You're talking about square as four squares Marva?"

"Bitch, what four squares Marva?"

"Whoa, Oh my God,"

"Hmmm,"

"I sort of want to know now."

"Trust me."

"Why, is it best that I don't?"

"It was good bitch if I didn't but you know me a magnet for the bullshit."

"Oh my God so what should I do?"

"I don't care what you do, but as far as I'm concerned she's paying for every damned drink that she consumes and fuck her."

"Whoa, whoa, whoa, whoa, whoa, whoa,"

"Ok, if you say so."

"Whoa."

"I heard you the first time."

"Girl, I mean you may have said stuff in the past, but you've never said fuck us."

"Oh, well remind me how I said it this time so I could lock that shit in."

"Un unh, not like this,"

"Uh hun, just like that,"

"No, no, hell no, not like this ok."

"Like I say, I mean if you say so."

"Why do I got this burning sensation to know what's going on, but my stomach is bubbling at the fear of whatever you are gonna tell me is gonna make me sick on top of piss me off."

"You could say that again."

"Why do I got this burning..."

"Tahj, would you get a hold of yourself."

"I know, because if I was to repeat all of that I would have thrown up and I don't even know where you taking me with all of this madness. I know that you ain't tripping off her relationship with Rico Suave, I know that ain't where you going."

"Uh uh, girl I didn't care who she shacked up with, I loved it if she liked it I support my girls don't even play."

"Ok, so is it really, really bad, so bad that I should cancel out on the idea of a reunion?"

"It's bad enough for you to cancel out on a funeral."

"Dammit Lerin," the phone went quiet for a spell then Tahj said, "Tell me this, does it have anything to do with you?"

"Uh uh,"

"Does it have anything to do with me?" Tahj braced herself yet prepared herself to explode in the event that Lerin found something that was a threat to her happiness was completely satisfied when Lerin said,

"Nope,"

"Ok, if it doesn't have anything to do with me and nothing to do with you why should you care then?"

"Hmmm, all right then, maybe you're right. I mean I hear that though. It sounds as if it's your turn in the chair; I guess I see you later on tonight."

"Uhh Uh, that's not for me, I'm waiting on the conditioner to set so about you rushing me off the phone. I know you only do that when you are more than convinced and stand firm in your shit, I know you girl. I wish you'd stop being so simple for me and at least gimmie a challenge."

"Whatever."

"So, are you gonna hang out with us if she's there or what?"

"I'll step with you guys, I mean we gotta get the party started and since were celebrating our girls going away I wouldn't ruin that but you will find that I have a lot of work to do."

"Ohh, that's the way it is?"

"Mmm hmmm,"

"I think I want you to tell me now, forget that mommy. If you're this strong in your convictions, then I need you to run it by me before it's my turn to rinse."

"Ok, but don't say that I didn't warn you." Lerin tipped in and out of information, giving Tahj the full pictures of how and when, even why. Then she told her of ways that she could cross check in the case that for the first time Tahj failed to believe her stories. Tahj listened attentively without interruptions, the more she heard the more sickening that she was becoming which meant the more pissed off she was getting. She said,

"Look girl, let me go ahead and get my shit together, even though it's hard to believe that a girl could change so much and so fast but I do believe you, and I'ma ask that we send our girl Mecca off in good tidings without messing over her party. But do know, that I really wanna whip that bitches ass for being so scurvy, but I'm not gonna ruin nothing. You know Mec' it'll take her years to forgive somebody."

"Hell yeah,"

"But now I'll see you tonight."

"I know; I hear your husband is on his way back."

"I'm not gone even ask you how you know that, but yeah I'm happy as hell too."

"I know you aren't gonna keep letting that fine ass nigga out of your sights like that. I would have been put a stop to that, when he moves, bitch I move, God dammit just like that."

"Not after you done ran his ass threw the ringers like I did. Shoot I wrung that man all the way out. Been hiding behind parked cars and telephone poles long enough to trust his ass at the Play Boy Mansion."

"I heard the fuck out of that, alright then girl I see you tonight."

If anybody had a reason to get out the house and stay gone long it was Tamia. Every day, books, study and lectures. The finals were looming and her hard work was soon to pay off. She couldn't find an escape more suitable then to go out and hang with the girls, toss back a few and enjoy the night. One that started of troubling, her hair at first didn't want to behave properly, and then her wardrobe was a bit shabby and outdated but after a little mix and matching her day had begun to take shape. Now that she was cleared for takeoff with everything checked off, she done already called her baby, honey and sugar plum and let him know about Mecca's' leaving to the Virgin Islands and how the idea being a good one to celebrate her departure the night before she left just in case she decided not to come back. Tamia told him and ever so easily she thought, he agreed. This was the other reason why she needed a drink, because as of late so much has been out of sync, she found herself nervous a lot lately without reason. She couldn't help but to wonder if William really had to work so much overtime. Sure he's been having the funds to account for it, yet and still Tamia found concern in his need to always be away from her.

Even after Marva had moved out and into her own place with the help of Mecca who too had a tendency to come through in the clutch saying Girl God blessed a child to have their own and this made Tamia particularly proud of Marva for rebounding like she had while proven to be bigger than the broken pieces that was then, her life. She collected her pieces, glued them back together and kept on keeping on, not saying that Tamia approved of Marva's new way of going about things, but was understanding enough to remain silent and constantly in prayer. Believing that every person has a right to live their own life as one shall deem fit, besides she has her own problems now that William called in to work again, crazy as it all seems but if Tamia didn't know any better she would swear that she was allowing her man to slip away from her. "Dear God don't let me lose one of the best things that ever happened to me." Tamia said a quiet prayer before getting fully dressed. "Well, here we come y'all," she said then headed out of the door.

CHAPTER 10

ONCE THE OCCASION FILTERED THROUGH Oak Park that Mecca somehow lucked up to the Virgin Islands and that a surprise party was hopping off, the streets emptied and the place to be was at The Rendezvous. One thing for sure, anybody who was somebody knew not to be caught dead inquiring about the night before because they misread the street signals. Because on this night, every vibe, every signal, every pantomime and gesticulate all pointed towards "The Rendezvous." The maximum capacity of the club being 500, employees included was threatened shortly after the club opened the side doors which inserted the party goers.

By ten o'clock the disk jockey was putting on one of his better   performances in months because he strategically selected the whole nights play list. Every song was a 'Stepper' for he knew that tonight he was gonna keep the 'P' in party. This was the time Tahj showed up; dying to see Rasaan, but that was another story because tonight it was all about Mecca. Shortly after Tahj showed up Marva made her appearance. She was turning heads from men and women alike as she walked through. Drinks flowed throughout the club in abundance; limousines dropped off passengers only to await their returns. Cab drivers found a decent amount of the sprinkles too. The time Tamia showed up she walked straight to the bar and had Mecca fix her a drink.

"What you want girl," Mecca asked her, not believing her eyes, feeling as if something awfully fishy was going on because twice already she served friends she hadn't seen in years.

"I don't care girl, hit me off." Tamia needed to loosen up.

"Well, there's a new drink that took the club by storm, you want one of those?"

"Yeah, what is it?"

"It's called the "Retarded Bus," it's a nice drink trust me, it would ship you where you need to be."

"Well, that sounds like the one for me, well beam me up Scottie." Tamia reached for her purse to extract money from it.

"No, no girl this one is on me. Where the hell you been? All of a sudden now you wanna come see your sister. That's pretty messed up all that we been through, Mecca rambled off all of her complaints.

"Girl if you don't get me the drink. I had enough on my plate without your guilt tripping me, that's what I need right now is a Retarded Bus..."

"That bad hun,"

"Yeah," Then the area erupted as Lerin and Tahj came into view of Tamia and Mecca, happy to see each other they all embraced and jumped around in jubilation before taking their drinks in a small huddle.

"Guess who else is here?" Mecca yelled just loud enough to be heard over the loud music. "Marva's here, could you believe that?"

"Where?" Asked Tahj as they all scanned the club and found Marva already on the dance floor doing what she said she was gonna do, all the while spinning her web in her wake. Not even giving them a chance she wiggled and she dropped it like it was really hot, one powerful step after the next while the old clique just stood and watched her in amazement. The disc jockey came over the microphone announcing the reason why everybody came together on this night and once the realization hit Mecca the club took on a chant. Instead of 'it's a small world after all" the entire club chanted that "she's the best one after all" and Lerin wasted no time clearing the bar of empties and patrons alike. The disc jockey seen this and sent them a newly released stepper that sent Lerin to the top of the bar and how in the hell did Tahj leap so high in a set of heels to land on the counter top next to Lerin still boggles everybody's mind to this very day.

The rhythm found their feet, but the greatest wonder was Tamia. How did she remember the moves after being away for so long was also impressive, but the "Retarded Bus" had done more than shipped her there, it brought out her inner beast for she was step for step with Lerin and Tahj and Mecca was just waiting for a moment like this to present itself, she hit the counter top and fell in step right along with them? Marva had a lot of work to do, but this moment was too pure to pass up so she hit the countertop next to Mecca where one song led into the next one with the crowd cheering them on. So caught up with their performances that Tahj never saw when Rasaan and Nahjee made it through the door but Marcel, Scope and Stomp did, they beckoned for the two to join them at their booth. After a few pleasantries they all huddled and listened as Nahjee expressed his concerns and tumbled over their beliefs until a suitable solution prevailed, for Nahjee left out nothing. The fact that they were dealing with murderers made holding back a luxury no one could afford. He informed the three to the dangers of such an assignment and he also painted their rewards, and during all of this Aretha covered it all from the next booth over, not to protect Scope from the two, but from the other enemies that they had made along the way.

The music played loud and she could barely hear what was being said, but she was sure she heard the words diamonds and jewelers and that somebody was dead wrong and she couldn't help but to wonder who the two were "with their fine asses" she thought. Then saw as the two handsome men made their way to the bar in order to join the onlookers as Tahj, Mecca, Lerin, Marva and Tamia relived yesterday together and in perfect sequence. Which gave tonight's party goers a reason to cheer and enjoy themselves even that much more, for nothing excited men more than beautiful, vibrant and sexy dancers and nothing excited the women more than watching as other women commanded undivided attention by using their fruits to mesmerize. So, on this night both genders had received an over dosage of excitement, for these five beautiful women tore this club completely, the fuck up. No matter the number the DJ came with these five had a step for it even when he slowed it down with a slow jam, an old school number from Adina Howard who rocked her T-shirt and her panties. The men lost their minds and the women laughed at their weaknesses, concluding the show with as much impact as a car bomb. The club applauded the group and returned to their celebrations, everyone wishing Mecca a safe trip. Tahj found her way to her man and held him so long and so tight as if she thought that she would never see him again. Still she rejoiced internally as he held her just as tight and after a long kiss he said.

"I see you guys done went into cahoots to set men back another twenty years."

"No, no, no baby, just fifteen, why am I so glad to see you."

"What's the occasion, this club is jumping."

"Mecca's going on vacation."

"Is that right?"

"Yeah, look at you; you look like mama needs to feed you. I felt your ribs through your jacket."

"Oooh, would you please, I'm hungry right now another burp and I'ma starve to death."

"Oooh, right now, ok, let me go tell the girls I'm out."

"Nah, nah don't do that, enjoy yourself I would never hear the end of it if I steal you away right now.

"Are you sure?"

"More than sure,"

"Ok, if you say so, hear give me a kiss." The two pecked and Tahj joined her long lost friends and play sisters to celebrate the rest of the night. To Mecca's satisfaction management had called in the other bartenders to fill in for her and Lerin giving them the rest of the night off which was alright with her because this was one of the better nights Mecca had in a long time. Just as Mecca began to soak in the ambiance, there were other things taking place, something cosmic, something epic, something unseen but deeply felt. Lerin had the devils eye on Marva, who had the "googley" eyes for Nahjee, who seemed displaced even nervous, so much that Rasaan didn't know what the hell had gotten into him so he decided to buy him a drink, he said.

"Dog, are you alright, you look like you've been struck by lightning, what, you need a drink or something?"

"Naw, naw, I'm good with this one." Nahjee said pointing towards an empty glass. Rasaan felt took because he didn't even see Nahjee order a drink, he said,

"Who gave you that?"

"That bitch was just sitting there."

"You just drunk somebody's drink?" Rasaan couldn't believe it.

"Yeah, I think so." Nahjee was still out of reach with his mental facilities.

"What the fuck is wrong with you, you are struck by lightning, look at you trembling and shit, alright who is she, I ain't playing with you where is she?" Rasaan couldn't believe it, he scanned the room for the mystery lady who packed the magic.

"I said I'm cool Dog, I'm cool for real." Even though Nahjee said that he was cool twice, Rasaan still refused to believe it but decided to change the subject, shaking his head he said,

"So, tomorrow it is then."

"Yeah, tomorrow it is, are you worried about it?"

"Like a motha fucka."

"My nigga,"

"You too,"

"Hell yeah, because if it doesn't go right It could be blood everywhere I'm telling you. You know 'Cel and those niggas don't play that shit."

"Fuck it."

"For real,"

"Not our problem if they don't play right."

"For real, for real"

"So, if that's not what got you trembling then when you gone show me who she is?" Before Nahjee could respond a bartender brought Nahjee a drink and pointed in the direction of Tahj, Lerin, Mecca and Tamia, but it was Marva who raised her glass in solute. Nahjee looked at the drink then at the circle of women then pulled the bartender close enough so that he could place an order. The bartender heard him correctly when Nahjee said,

"Nineteen ninety-eight Dom Perignon, the Vintage Rose' please." This particular bottle was always kept in a metal briefcase. A case that stayed refrigerated for the conveniences and this was for a customer to enjoy right on the spot. Which was just one of the mini perks that the Club Rendezvous offered to some of their most privileged patrons. Seeing this Rasaan couldn't believe his eyes, he knew that Nahjee was impervious to a woman's fruits and all of her attributes, became more than interested so he paid close attention to the whole play, saw when the bartender stopped in front of his friend and said,

"For you sir, from the very beautiful lady down the bar," and he also saw as Nahjee grew hesitant to look in the direction to which the drink was sent. What took the cake was the 'Dom P' a bottle of Rose' in the '98 "I heard the fuck out of that" Rasaan said to himself, but Nahjee heard him. Who still hadn't touched his drink, in fact he knew for sure that it would grow mold before he would entertain it. Rasaan was confused by his friend's action said,

"Dom P... my nigga?"

"Well, hell what did you expect?"

"A screw driver, a martini or a long island, something like that, but Dom P and a Rose' to boot, I ain't gone even tell you about the sticker on that joint."

"You don't have to I know what I'm doing."

"$390 a bottle, a bottle to a chick that you don't even know, boy if you ain't got your cape just a flapping in the wind tonight, oh yeah you need a sound track."

"Uhn uh, $460 and, I ain't ever wore a cape and you know better."

"At first I would have said that then you started getting all fuzzy on me, I mean she is hell on wheels look at her she got it but $460 though?"

"Look at who,"

"The chick that sent you the drink, nigga what you mean look at who?"

"You don't know who that is my nigga?"

"Uh, uh,"

"Yes you do."

"I do?"

"Yelp."

"I don't think so I'm sure I'd know if I knew her, look at her in that cat suit looking like red beans and rice."

"Something to eat to you, I bet you better not let Tahj hear you talking that shit. Let me see, it was right before we took off when Tahj called and said umm, what did she say?"

"Shit I don't know, be good, don't do nothing she wouldn't do, hell she said hella shit."

"Well, to me she said Nahjee do you still got the condo that you got tired of in Green Haven?"

"Naw, that's her. So that's why she sent you a drink because you let her rent your place." Rasaan finally recognized her.

"I don't know why she sent the drink because I never met her a day in my life."

"Then how do you know that's her?"

"Because I saw her move her things into my place, you know I need to know what's going on."

"So, she doesn't even know that she's living in your place?"

"Nope,"

"Then we're back to square one, I mean I never saw you nervous or trembling on the count of any woman and especially one that owe you some money every month." Nahjee just stared at his friend as if he didn't have a clue to what it was he was talking about just said,

"We need to get out of here; we got a long one in the morning." Without tossing back his drink Nahjee stood and waited for Rasaan to communicate with Tahj before the two hit the exits followed by Marcel, Stomp, Scope and Aretha.

Marva couldn't believe for a minute that her small investment of a shot of Hennessy could yield so much, but she did see with her own eyes the frost that left the briefcase before the bottle was revealed which didn't do much of anything but heighten her education to fine wines because she didn't even know that Dom even made a Rose'. Although she did know that she could find it in a Moet was more than impressed by the expensive looking bottle. She allowed her excitements to grow once the bartender popped the top and filled the five stemmed glasses leaving the bottle before retreating to be of service to the many other impatiently waiting customers.

"Uh uh, ooh girl, I told you that he was the one," said Mecca to Marva.

"Girl you sure did, I like to thank God for even making this stuff it taste so good, what's that $100 or something for the bottle?" Marva's ignorance to such a high quality liquid was on display.

"Almost $500, it's the '98," said Mecca matter-of-factly.

"The '98? 500 damn dollars. Well let me go thank him a little more properly." The girl's laughter filled the air that followed Marva to the exit, not Lerin though, she had her own little secret for she had been a bartender long enough to know that it was customary for the sender of a drink to share in a drink and looking down the bar she could see the untouched shot glass that had once sat in front of Nahjee. Mecca noticed it too and nodded once Lerin pointed it out for they both knew that Nahjee only accepted drinks from the people that he knew and nothing else. Tahj didn't overlook the glass either but was just as confused because she knew Nahjee like a brother and in a lot of ways he was her brother and never has he ever appeared to weaken to the likes of a gold digger and to give in so easily was brand new.

She tossed around a scenario hoping that Nahjee wouldn't start paying house visits to Marva and especially after pointing out so vehemently that it would be best that they kept their business dealings, strictly business. Mecca was caught up in playing match maker; so much that she barely heard Lerin when she said,

"I don't know what you doing standing here looking all cheesy for you need to hit the door right along with them."

"Hmmm,"

"You heard me."

"For what, that's Marva's thang."

"Uh uh, not that bitch, Aretha, remember?"

"Aretha, who the fuck is that," Mecca's expressions took on its concerns.

"Ohhhhh-kay,"

"I mean for real, who the fuck is Aretha?"

"Desmond's Aretha,"

"What!" Lerin didn't bother to answer just pointed towards the exits, watching as Mecca weaved in and out of crowded traffics trying to make it to the exit. When she finally made it to the exits her and Marva stared into the parking lot together, Marva was watching as a Navy Blue BMW made its way out of the parking lot followed by a black Mercedes. Mecca saw the same thing, only she paid attention to the beige Altima that followed both vehicles. Back in the club Lerin, Tahj and Tamia began to take in the night.

"Wow." Tamia said, "What a night."

"I don't know what you wowing about you need to hit the exits too."

"I sure do girl it's getting late."

"That's not all it's getting," said Lerin, since the night was coming close to an end she may as well end it with a bang, some fireworks.

"Oh," said Tamia suspiciously.

"Aretha knows you too." Tahj heard this and decided it was time to grab her coat and go. Tamia looked Lerin in her eyes and read them before saying,

"Oh."

"You heard me." Lerin hated telling her friends these things, but she damned sure hated to watch them play the fool even more, felt the singe once Tamia said,

"Tell me you're lying, Lerin don't play with me like that." So Lerin let her silence do the conveying. Only then did she see the tears form in the wells of her friend's eyes. So she took Tamia in her arms in a sisterly gesture and said,

"And that's not it."

"Ok." Tahj had enough, she done all that she could to stop Lerin but nothing worked. She attempted to excuse herself,

"Well, let me get out of here, you two take it easy, and Mia I know what you are gonna do, but I'ma tell you it's not worth your time or your anger."

"What is it Tahj, Lerin. No. Tahj you ain't gotta leave we could all sit here and talk... can't we?"

"Hell naw! Girl I gotta go, Shoot, I almost pulled my mace out once I heard it the first time don't make me ruin such a beautiful night." Said Tahj in a very serious and non-playful manner,

"Lerin,"

"Hold up, let me get us a drink and we'll sit and talk."

"Tahj,"

"Shit, 'Mia shit, shit."

"Wow, that bad hun?" Tamia said then took a seat watching as Mecca and Marva came in to announce that they were leaving. Mecca took Lerin aside and the two exchanged hostile and very animated conversation before Mecca grabbed her coat and fell in step with Marva through the exit. Tahj sat quietly next to Tamia and got the attention of a bartender who was removing his apron and glad to be finished for the night.

"How may I help you ladies," said the bartender.

"Leroy, everybody's leaving so you don't have to be so formal," said Tahj.

"Girl what you want it is closing time and you know what that means."

"It's gone be a long one for us, how about giving us a few."

"This is what I get, shit, what you want and what you mean by long one, like you need me to stand around and wait on you to get shit faced kind of long one. Or were you talking about get you a drink and I could leave you here alone because you having a long one, you know, by yourselves?" He asked but was very glad to see Lerin come from the back with a bottle and three shot glasses and said,

"Go on Leroy, I got us and thanks for coming in tonight."

"No problem you guys drive safe," he said then vacated leaving the girls to sit and share drinks while watching as the club grew desolate."

"Well," said Tahj "there' no sense in beating around the bushes, Lae-Lae something you want to tell 'Mia?" Tamia faced Lerin and braced herself as Lerin ran in and out of dirty deeds inflicted onto her by her man and Aretha, though Tamia sort of knew something was going on she was not ready when Lerin told her that at night William finds himself changing hats to that of a drug dealer, just when Tamia began to get light headed and queasy Lerin told her that Marva goes into the prison with drugs in order to afford life. Although Tamia knew this already, but what she didn't do was how put the two together fast enough for Tahj who said,

"Do you see what she's getting at 'Mia?"

"You mean…"

"Yeah, that's exactly what she means." Tamia thought about it a moment then said,

"You mean William and Marva?" Oh she was really queasy now.

"At least five times a week, how do you think she gets her packages, and for free too?" Lerin was not into the punch pulling business she was a bartender which is why she said what she said and poured them all a drink.

"Oh my God,"

"That's the same thing I said," said Lerin.

"What am I gonna do?"

"Now, that's what Tahj said," Lerin said pointing in Tahj's direction.

"Lerin," Tahj snapped, "None of this is funny."

"Yes it is, put it together, now look. Tamia brought Marva into her home and to prove that that was such a horrible mistake she lost everything."

"And that's funny?" Asked Tamia with pain dripping in her voice,

"As Hell, I could see you holding the snake by her tail now, girl you so stupid you 'pose to hold a snake by its neck stupid." Lerin got a good hardy laugh of Tamia holding the snake by the tail only to see her get bit in the process. Lerin poured another drink for the three then replaced the bottle under the counter. Raised her glass and said,

"You must always hold the snake by the neck from now and on." Their glasses were raised until each one hit the counter empty.

"Well, I still have the same question," said Tamia.

"What you're gonna do is put on your jacket so I could lock this place up, and we could get out of here and if I was you I'd keep the mystery in it until you're ready to pounce, this way you could get ready for Nahjee. I know I'm not the only one that saw him hypnotized by your belly roll and I know I'm not the only one who saw you add the extras oh, and who else saw him reject the drink that Marva sent him?" The two, Tamia and Tahj both said that they had, in unison.

CHAPTER 11

Nahjee would lay awake all through the night; he tossed and turned through the wee-hours. Nothing that he used for a remedy seemed to prove effective and for the first time in all of his life had warm milk prove to be of no use. A force that had taken over him, a force that he hadn't developed an answer for, it was something enormous, epic and colossal. A force that penetrated his hardened exterior and proven to be an anomaly? Something intangible had consumed him. His thoughts were imbued, finding it very difficult to put his pieces in order. His life has always been lived as meticulous and methodical as possible, now; on this night he found his organized style to be cramped the fuck up. "Man," he thought "God sure has a sense of humor."

He located the very one, the one that makes his heart skip a beat, the one that stole his breath away, he reminisced. It was the way she moved, the way she slid across that counter top and gyrated to the heavy drums. It was the way pure and wholesome seeped from her pores; the way that she locked her eyes on him right before she dropped it really low for him which didn't go unnoticed either.

"She's probably happily married," he said to himself then rolled over as if sleep had suddenly found him but he knew better. He knew that in order to get her off his mind and I mean the only way was that he somehow died before the morning. Nahjee had shared the company of pretty women by the plenty, but none like her. Nahjee has had his mind altered before by a woman but not quite like this. Even met some awfully sexy dancers, but not at all like this. Never had he ever gulped down a drink that's been left unattended like he did and found himself thanking God that the one that he stole wasn't a loaded one meant for somebody the fuck else but he slipped that night, and as it stands here he was, numb. Staring into the darkness, wondering what exactly the future held for him knowing that his future could all end in the morning.

Nahjee couldn't help but to wonder if Rasaan was suffering from the same symptoms, but knowing Rasaan like he did he concluded that his friend would have been asleep by now. Instead of fighting his restless state he decided to crawl out of bed and head through the adjoining door and to the room where his weight set was located and began to work out, both, physically and mentally. Physically, Nahjee decided to go hard starting with two forty-five-pound plates applied to each end of the post to warm up with, doing sets of fifteens until he got his blood to flowing. Then he added another forty-five-pound plate to each side where sets of seven was now the lucky number.

After reaching his seventh set he down sized to two plates and here he'd reached his seventh set before downsizing again to one plate then brought to a satisfactory conclusion his bench press routine. Nahjee picked up his jump rope and decided to give some to his cardio for fifteen minutes, and then he was on his tower and brought pull ups at fifteen reps a set until he had reached his lucky number, seven. Through the window the dawn began to reveal itself, the roosters began to crow and all of this had gone unnoticed by Nahjee. Which brings us to mentally, my God, a maelstrom condition was putting it lightly, an oversized understatement, it was like a nerve damage free for all. All through the night he guessed and second guessed. He would realize and then the next moments question his realizations, never has he ever suffered so much uncertainty. Never has he wished so hard for a peace of mind for never has a woman dominated his mind set like that lady from last night and, even more sad was the fact that he didn't even know her name but knew that it was gonna be hard to trust his self around her and may want to give this lady plenty of space for safety and security reasons, man.

Rasaan spent most of his night wide awake as well, far from restless, hell no; the facts were that he knew that he needed all the rest that he could get only the romantic laws prevailed. His absence for such a lengthy amount of time never sat well with Tahj to begin with. I mean, she wouldn't crowd him no, but, she was damned if when he made it back that they didn't spend every minute, every second and Nanosecond all of which together and wide awake. Rasaan had known this more than anything which was why he went directly home after leaving the club to catch a few before Tahj came through. Happy that she took her time about it because the little knap that he did achieve gave him the energy he needed to at least be respondent towards what he thought would be Tahj's ultimate advances. Really what Rasaan needed was a vacation; he needed to be on the same plane as Mecca but in the window seat on his way to a few weeks of rest and relaxation.

His life was always lived on high speed no pauses at all just go-go, and go. So much that he was having mixed feelings about giving Tahj the heads up to his returning, but, knew that he missed her about as much as she missed him. When this deal was done he was sure to find him a nice quiet secluded spot where he could relax and get his mind right. Ever since the two made it back him and Nahjee, it's been one meeting after the next one in an attempt to discover who were all the players in this ruthless attempt to rid them of their lives and why, for these two has been nothing but straight up. Then there was the fact that Marcel came through with an outsider was of concern though it appeared as if they were trying to conceal her in the next booth over but occasionally she would be caught leaning into their conversation, a colloquy that she invited herself to time and time again. Her insolence lead Rasaan to assume that either Marcel has now all of a sudden deemed him and Nahjee to be untrustworthy or just maybe he, Rasaan was reading too much into this new way that Marcel decided to meet with them because if he knew Marcel, a friend is and forever would be a friend and the same shoe fit the other foot when it came down to his enemies hence the reason for concern. Something that he knew he would address the first thing in the morning.

Then, there were the plates, the flawed ones and the flawless ones and then there was Christopher a real deal hope to die printer gone badly. Who had game galore, but even he stood on pins and needles waiting on the afternoon to come and go for Rasaan knew that this dude could make all three of them some very, very wealthy people. Then there was Nahjee, Rasaan hoped like hell that his friend hasn't lost his zest to choose wisely. From what Tahj had told him about the very same woman that was now a tenant in his Green Haven condominium. He gathered that she was a messy and unethical woman which goes against everything that Nahjee stood for. Fine as hell on the outside, but from what Rasaan has gathered mommy was all so ugly on the inside. Basically no different than the rental whores that they'd call up to gain position or leverage over a potential tradesmen or merchant. Rasaan thought long and hard about it, Nahjee had never come between him and Tahj concluding that it was never any of his business each time. This being just one of Nahjee's finer qualities and one of the strong reasons why Rasaan digs him like he does, so, in return Rasaan will extend the same favor of minding his own business. But, if miss thang gets too far under his skin and wedding bells and chapels become the topic of their everyday conversation, then he knew that he was gonna step in and bust that shit up all but so fast though. Rasaan heard the water stream from the shower being cut, meaning that Tahj was sure to come to him with only one thing on her mind, to get everything in one night that she's been missing all month and one thing for sure, Rasaan wasn't going to argue with her but knew that she was gonna have to surely understand that the morning held his life or his death.

For Tamia, she didn't give a fuck if sleep found her ass or not, all she knew was that William wasn't home, nor was he at work, nor was he answering his phone. Tamia felt the pain so, so, deep that tears flowed so easily from the wells of her eyes. Tears rolled down her cheeks in abundance and all she could do was let them. She cried until Gladys Knight and Aretha Franklin turned into Teddy Pendergrass, and when TP turned into Mary J. she just about had enough of this bullshit and to prove it she took to the stairs and took those two at a time until she was now in the kitchen making her a meal out of a sandwich and a salad taking both to her desktop. "I came too far and a long, long way and I fail to see why I should let the way I feel be the reason I should stop running," she thought. If William really cared about her then he wouldn't hurt her so badly, he has proven his worth by not only going outside of their home to find love elsewhere, but he even found reason to disrespect the home that the two shared together, may have even dishonored the very bed to which they slept and shared their promises. Watching as her computer booted itself up and came to life, she immediately began to peck at the keyboard attempting to erase folder after folder to rid her machine of any trace of her and William together. She promised herself that she wouldn't cry, wasn't gonna shed not a tear again but to herself she lied.

As she removed photo after photo, song after song, plan after plan and goal after goal and through her teary eye sight, she made sure that she erased every trace of them completely, until there was nothing left of them. Her desktop had now become solely hers, and nothing after that. Finishing her light meal, she began to run through her assignments for the next day which would then be the first day of the rest of her life, alone and on her own. With her to-do list neatly organized and schedules set, Tamia took to the stairs this time heading north until she reached the hall closet where she searched through her belongings and found the two boxes that she sought, the ones that held her dreams. They were wedding bands that she saved up for was enough for. They weren't very fancy, just bands but to her it was plenty for never did she ask for much. One thing that Nana had always taught her, if nothing else she sure showed her how to keep a receipt and Tamia had always paid attention to her Nana. Again she searched through the closet and again fruitful with her findings "I'll stop by the mall in the morning to redeem my funds and to hell with these rings, I'll search for a place and I'm gonna be ok Nana I promise." Once she made it to her room she was cured of her tears yet the pain remained, nothing she could do about that it was what it was. She laid in her bed and traveled through the night that she just had, save for Lerin dropping the bomb on her like she did the night was otherwise a good one. Tamia smiled at the thought of Marva running to the exits to run down the handsome brother that she, Tamia had hypnotized with her sexual prowess's, although she was only teasing, she did indeed find the brother to be an attractive one, and by the likes of the bottle that he sent he was an attractive brother with extremely good taste and an extraordinary way of expressing his knack for the finer things. Again Tamia found reason to smile, it was the class that this brother projected only to be run down in a hot pursuit by the likes of no class at all, Marva.

"So what Mr. whatever your name is she got me already. If I was you I would run nigga run, and whatever you do, don't let her bite you you'll have to remember and never forget to hold her by the neck and nowhere else."

Mecca paced back and forth in her tiny apartment, sleepy? Hell the fuck no, concluding that sleep could kiss her ass. For one, her flight is due to take off soon, but what she wanted to do was see her brother in that prison before she left, so she could tell him all about the horrible night that she just had, but knowing him he would only look at her as if her air plane must be parked right outside of that motha fucka then remind her every five minutes of her broken promises which would be the extreme version considering it'll be the first time yet, and still he would try to get her to chill and fuck that she didn't want to chill, her ass wanted to fight and fuck chilling. How the fuck could Lerin do some shit like this of all things, wait until the party was over to point the bitch out allowing her to make a clean ass get away? Lerin knew how bad Mecca wanted to finally get the chance to get her hands on that bitch "Just gonna let her get away like that" Mecca yelled through her room, upset because the search must start all over again for this whore bitch. "I should call Lerin and cuss her ass the fuck out" she thought, but knew that to be a waste of time because she knew that Lerin would only hang up on her like she always does. She thought of the face on that whore bitch named Aretha and done everything that she could to place her somewhere, she wondered who could help her locate this bitch again. Mecca thought about what she would say to this person when she did finally get the chance to meet her. This person has destroyed her whole family, wrecked it so bad that the damages were irreparable. She thought about the bribe that she could offer to help her brother, but smiled once she pictured the bitch playing hard to reason with. Oh how she would love to ring that whore's neck until her eye balls popped all the way out and her life seeped through Mecca's fingers like a fine grade of sand.

Mecca put a halt to her pacing knowing that four o'clock in the morning wasn't gonna get anything accomplished so she checked then re-checked to make sure that she gathered everything. Satisfied that she had, she sat on her sofa and stared into her fish tank where a lot of things crossed her mind as she saw the gold fish chase each other. Although she blamed Lerin for letting the bitch get away deep inside she knew better. Lerin argued that she barely recognized the bitch on the way out and would have definitely hipped her sooner if she knew better but, Mecca was too pissed off to hear her friend for her words and blew everything out of proportion. She reminded herself of all the things that the two been through as friends and this made her feel even more like an ass hole because Lerin has always without faltering had her back, and that was one reason. The other reason was there would have been no better time to see the club go bonkers then to have the bartenders declare war on the bitch and Lerin would have been an overnight phenomenon once her report hit the gossip column. Mecca concluded that she owed her girl a deep, deep, deep apology. Mecca stared through the fish tank and couldn't help but imagine Desmond in the same light, that of a goldfish, cooped up and confined to such a minimal amount of space, whose boundaries were suffocating. Mecca stood to escape the idea of her brother in the same predicament as a goldfish, who would sooner die in such confines. Shaking the thought away from her mind she located a pen and a notebook and made a few notes then spent her remaining time writing a note to her brother this way he would know that she was on her way to paradise.

For Marva never has a night been so pleasurable, she was batting a thousand and she knew it. The oldie station played softly in her ears, still feeling the "dranky-drank" as she called it, loving every minute of the buzz that influenced her. Life was being awfully kind to her, she had gone from homeless to suburbia in the span of months, she had gone from flat broke to a stash spot that carried a real live growth potential, one that would soon land this ole girl on Wall Street if patience prevailed. This bizarre twist of fate was only heightened by the fact that even now as she reclined on her sofa with her legs spread eagled receiving an oral massage from William, who, in her opinion gave the best head this side of the Rocky damned mountains and would pay in spades to make her say that. Life felt so good, so right, so Queen and so rich. Although she knew that if Tamia ever found out that it would be hell to pay, but Marva rationalized, it was the way that he made her feel and how he paid to make her feel this way that made him undeniable and a forbidden fruit that she always loved to digest. This was a risk that Marva was willing to chance, his tongue brought her senses alive, she took both of her breasts in her hands to massage her nipples as her desires increased.

"Oh my goodness, if this nigga wasn't so damned weak minded, shit," she thought "I would pay his ass for having a mouth like this." But as it stood, the packages that he gave her were merely worth hundreds to him but what he didn't know was that those same packages were worth thousands to her, and a bunch of them. With this as a thought Marva reached for Williams head and began to gyrate ferociously feeling herself ready to explode to the thought of money and to the thought of her defying every common law and because of that she felt, well, bitchy. The laws of friendship where crossed on the very same table that her girlfriend for years fed her at. She could still remember that vibrating sensation as she released with her legs draped over Williams shoulders while she fed him her lunch after catching him counting what appeared to be "thug money" and oh how she liked thug money, but never as much as she liked the idea of disrespecting men. So much that she came again just thinking of the power that she possessed over this man. Her explosions were intensifying. In this oral way she would violate the laws that of respect for man in another way because Javier had just left moments before William arrived. Oh how when she masturbated herself while Javier pounded inside of her was pretty disrespectful to William. Plus, fuck Javier too because she was doing this all while she was entertaining the thoughts of that fly ass nigga from the club. Figured that she would let Javier come and fuck her while she played make believe that Javier was 'Mr. Dom P' with the handsome face and the BMW.

Marva smiled as she thought of how heavy she ran on the perfume, passing her fragrances on to Javier letting him leave smelling like he was in the intimate company of another woman, but knowing that stupid bitch over there she may miss such a clue but the lip stick on his boxers would be hard to explain, even to an idiot. She began to tremble at the thought of this, her orgasm erupted heavily. The thought of Mr. Man combined with the dough was sending her unbearable shivers. The thought of her degrading man was sending her high levels of exhilaration, a felicity insurmountable by anything other than sheer power. So powerful was her fruits that she squeezed William into not caring one way or the other but the fact that he was a paying customer even though he was paying for way more than he had bargained for. In this case he had even paid for the fruits that of even Javier. Sensing this, Marva's eruption was at its most high and when William attempted to insert his penis into a very, very slippery vagina he done so to no avail, Marva closed up like a sentry safe saying.

"Nuh unh, you know what I like," and true William did know what she liked. She liked head and money and not too much more after that, so he said,

"I got some licking for you anytime, but I wanna hit that though."

"Well, toss in a few more pieces and you got that honey."

"A few more pieces, don't worry about that you get that but dig, I'll make the pot even sweeter if you come through and wake me up right, wake me up to some head, wake me up to some good pussy, I know how you love fucking in Mia's bed, because I know how you like disrespecting your home girls house, so how about it. I hit this pussy tonight and you come through and wake me up in the morning and I'll have the pieces for you then." Marva thought for a moment, "Funny but this man sure knew how to speak the truth and with that for a thought her legs spread wide.

While William was across town socking it to Marva on the smooth, Scope, Marcel and Stomp was putting a combination platter together on Aretha, who like a professional worked her lips, hips and fingertips and all of those at the same time. Only once did she allow all three holes to be filled at one time her anal, her vagina and her mouth. Hell, everything that she said that she wouldn't do she was doing plenty of it. The only break that she got was to sip some more Hennessy just too wet her whistle, and then she was going back in. If you let Marcel tell it, Aretha was his favorite bitch in the world because she kept him stuttering each time she took him in her mouth. She was getting on his last nerve with the tiny mites of pain that accompanied gigantic amounts of pleasure when she nibbled then licked then pinched and sucked, better was to sell her recipe throughout the country. Stomp always liked her doggy style so he could smack that ass when he hit it, wouldn't mind distributing her recipe, because every time Aretha gave him anything orally he'd come in a matter of minutes. So he knew that if he was gonna do anything it was gonna have to happen from the back, he wouldn't even trust his self near her lips. Scope knew firsthand the problems that his home boys were having just that he had already become immune to such a skill set, just sat back and let Aretha service him until he was sure that everybody had enough. Satisfied, he arose and stepped away from them to go to his stack of funds and counted his trap for the third time.

"Now that's a boss bitch, and the best bitch in the world," he said to no one particular. She knew what made a nigga happy, sex, money and more money, which she would surely need to go and get him some more of. The time he finished counting and poured himself a shot of the fine liquor and sipped from it, he noticed that his small band of street family was now getting dressed, so he gone to Aretha and took her into the bedroom and laced her to the upcoming events. He told her that he was really depending on her to be brave; she thought about it a minute then smiled and said,

"Anything for you Scope but can I get some before I go, you know how I like it baby."

"Yeah, I do but not right now, I need you to go get some more of this shit here," Scope said pulling out a wad of cash, Aretha who've become immediately disappointed pouted and said,

"Then when? I have been waiting for me and you time for weeks now."

"Soon as we do this business I could see us on a vacation just me and you, you know." These were Scopes plans especially when the worst case scenario told him that everyone would split ten stacks. If that was the worst case scenario, then he was rooting against the traditional payoffs. He voted heavy on the transactions being some fuck shit because this way the payoff would be a little different, because this way they would bring the pound down and collect it all. Which was the way he liked it, fuck fundamentals, traditional and ethics right now, some good old fashioned fuck shit right now was his only wish.

CHAPTER 12

RASAAN HUNG UP THE PHONE after speaking to his friend, his very over excited friend he would later tell Nahjee. It was close to noon. Tahj, who wore a very concerned expression, decided that she would just go and leave Rasaan's business up to Rasaan. Though his concerned expression upon hanging up the phone gave her all the information that she needed to know; she figured that she would fair way better to know what the hell was going on. She was also a woman of sheer intimates and knew that the best way to discuss matters with Rasaan was over a meal, so she took to the kitchen and prepared a very big one seeing that her man had a lot of explaining to do. Rasaan made another call this time he phoned Nahjee, who already had a jump on the day, answered his cell through a lot of commotion which told Rasaan that Nahjee was already in the company of Marcel, Scope and Stomp going over the details in its entirety. Details that were held out the night before in the presence of a nosey intruder, was now being brought up.

"Cat Daddy, I see you decided to come around, what's going on with you?" Nahjee sounded a bit cheerful and to Rasaan this was always a good thing said,

"So, what you doing laying the floor plans or something,"

"Yelp, already on the third one," by the third one Rasaan knew that it was Nahjee's job for the day to lace Cel, Scope and Stomp with as much information as possible about their so-called friends in case the bottom fell out of this "Plate" deal. The bottom falling out was something that everyone felt in their bones was sure to happen. Information was Nahjee's strong suit because Nahjee was one for detail which was a quality that saved their lives on many occasions and a quality that Rasaan would never argue with.

"Wow, already on the third one? Shit, when did you get started?"

"Not too long ago, what's up did you line us up or what?"

"Just got off the phone with them, seems like they've grown impatient with us. What you think about that?"

"We knew that they would, so I don't think shit about that playa all I'm concentrating on is us. If it's open season then its go, and you'd be surprised to the knack that these niggas got for shit like this, really I'm just on for the ride I could have just stayed home and just told them about it, maybe I could have got me a nap or something."

"A nap,"

"Hell yeah, I ain't been to sleep since the day before yesterday."

"Not last night?"

"Hell to the naw, I tossed and turned all night." Rasaan had an idea that Nahjee would possibly lose a lot of sleep the way the night ended for him.

"I think I know what kept you up all night, I figured that you would have shaken it loose by now, I mean come on champion now that you talking this "up all night" shit I can't help but to say it. I mean, you're my nigga and all so I reserve the space to say that I think you could be making a big mistake."

"Is that right?"

"Hell yeah,"

"Why you say that?"

"Don't get me wrong, you know my first impulse was to kick back and mind my own business until Tahj came in and told me about the night that she was having after we left."

"What happened, is, she alright, where's she at now?"

"No, I mean she's cool, but not really." Nahjee became really interested in the conversation now because Tahj held her very own place in his heart so he was honed in and holding on to every word as Rasaan continued with,

"The truth is she's worried to death about you and in a way so am I."

"Is that right, I don't get it why is that?" Nahjee was smiling at the revelation that Tahj and now Rasaan were both arriving at the wrong conclusion.

"Well, for one we think that you could be making an awfully big mistake with Ms. Lady from last night she's like wrong, wrong I mean dead wrong like wrong then motha fucka."

"Whoa, that sounds serious bro, why you saying all of this, how you know?" Again Nahjee was smiling through the phone loving the ride that he was taking his dude on had to straighten up before he gave himself away, but the sense of hate filled his body once he heard Rasaan say,

"Tahj came in last night with her head hung low talking some shit about how ole girl came across a sad case of the fuck shits, and I mean she fucks shit literally. All of them that was on that countertop at the club last night were all girls, you know, grew up together. They all made these pacts and shit, never would they ever cross each other over a man and shit you know that kind of shit, and never, you should have saw how she put emphasis on "never" would they fuck each other man and shit, you got that?"

"I hear you so why was Tahj all upset then, you ain't been humping around while I wasn't looking were you? Because if you are you are a dirty motha fucka you know." Nahjee continued to jest his potna,

"Anyways, well when you weren't paying a whole lot of that damn attention, there was the little hottie with the red bangles and the wavy hair up there with them, you know. Well anyways she messes around with this cat named William who works at the post office from what I gather but so what she all lovey dovey with playboy regardless, got that."

"Yeah, I got it."

"And Miss. Sexy Mama, the one from last night, the one that got you so tied up that got you scared to go to sleep and shit, and probably haven't ate shit either, well she goes through a thang with her dude, some Mexican cat that 'pose to had put a whopping on her, one of those black and blue beatings, hear me?"

"Yeah, yeah," oh Nahjee was really interested now, at first he was regular interested but shit just got real. This conversation took a turn that he was not ready for, shit, all through the night those bangles played funny games with his cool, and badgered the fuck out of his sleep so much that he was now running on fumes.

"Anyways, ole girl with the redness go and save the girl from a shelter you know, the one for battered women and nurse the girl back to health. I mean, from what Tahj say little red riding hood is some kind of smarty when it comes to that medicine shit, I mean she 'pose to become some kind of doctor…" Nahjee interrupted,

"Alright already Ra' what happened," Nahjee didn't need all the details he was already hanging on to every word. So much, that he needed Rasaan to hurry the fuck up and carve the fat so they can get him to the meat of this shit.

"That's what I'm trying to tell you if you stop interrupting me, fuck." Rasaan thought to make Nahjee wait a little while longer so he said, "Shit, ok, now where the fuck was I before you kept distracting me?"

"You said that she; the red one nursed her home girl back to health."

"Yeah, yeah so in order to do that she had to bring her to the flat that she shared with this William motha fuck and the thanks that she get, this bitch, the woman of your dreams decided that she wants to start fucking on this William nigga, not in a motel, not in the back seat, but in the same house probably in the same bed."

"Is that right? That shits crazy, so what did little red do?" This question brought Nahjee to the edge of hope.

"Well, from what I gather her name is Tamia, little reds name, the scandalous one the one that you like so much, her name is Marva, but we'll call her Ms. Marva now that she cribs at your place on the smooth, probably ain't fucking on dude no more but she probably is. The damage is already done from what I gathered, but I know you and you're gonna do whatever it is that you're doing. I just thought I'd put you one up on her, you feel me?"

"Hell yeah, but let the record reflect that I appreciate you even more so, but I'ma need you to trust me on this one."

"Alright, if you say so but now when are we gonna get together, I mean I could set everything up for this evening, any idea who would carry yet?"

"I'm thinking around three, and from what 'Cel and them saying they got the perfect carrier."

"And what if,"

"What?"

"What if they bring the sixty grand?"

"They're not, but you're right just in case huh? You got any ideas?"

"None, none at all,"

"Well, that's something to work on, would Tahj do it?"

"Hell to the Naw, Not Tahj, I can't believe you would say that shit?"

"Why, you think it's gonna be some rough stuff or something?"

"From what that nigga Chris was talking about hell yeah."

"And you think they'll go as far as offing some women?"

"I don't know, but we sure as hell ain't gonna use Tahj to practice finding out with, must have lost your mind."

"Yeah, you could say that again, well let me do this and you figure that out." Nahjee closed the phone and nodded his head in the direction for Marcel, Scope and Stomp to see the fella come from the rear door of a shop going to toss a garbage bag into the dumpster.

"You got 'em?" Asked Nahjee to the other three,

"Yeah, we got 'em, so you say he's the main one?" Marcel spoke for the other two then listened closely as Marcel tied it all together.

"Ok, the other two shops belong to dude right there." Nahjee nodded again towards the man that was now making his way back inside of the shop and through the same door to which he come, then Nahjee said,

"It's like this; this dude could fence anything, diamonds, arts or people, anything of extreme value. I'm talking about paintings that could reach seven digits no bullshit." Oh, Scope and Stomp was paying serious attention now and to prove it Scope said,

"And you say the only thing protecting all that is a safe, Dog? If that was me it'll be a squad in that bitch and everywhere that I go."

"Remember, there's the alarm so it's important that you make them deactivate that or it would trip to the police station." Nahjee looked around to make sure that he had their attention and went on, "Unless you knew what to look for then you would never know that it's there which is the reason you wouldn't need a squad, because the "secret" is the best security in the world, if nobody knew you were a baller, tell me, would anybody ask you for some money?" All three understood the science of which Nahjee was speaking from. So now they were on to the next one. In order to get a real idea on how to approach each mission, one needed to case and plan which for Marcel, Scope and Stomp this was as easy as 'A-B-C, and 1-2-3 because this was their element, this was what the fuck they do.

William was in hog heaven; his mistress to his other mistress had used her key to walk in and take care of her business and boy what a lustful business. Marva was clad in a maxi coat, heels and nothing else had took to the stairs and to the room where she found William sleeping, doing everything she could trying not to awake him until she had took him inside of her mouth. Still with her coat caressing her nude body she nibbled until William had awoke and loved his self even more for doing it, this day more than he did yesterday. He felt...Powerful...Untouchable. He held her head as he sent his powerful thrust in and out if her mouth until he found a rhythm that would bring him to the brink of total satisfaction. Then he released his grip and backed away allowing her to stand and let her jacket fall to the floor. Nothing but pure beauty he thought, not bad for a wakeup call, not bad at all. He watched as Marva crawled slowly across the bed and never exhaled until she was straddled over him, even though Marva was getting paid for her works, still she loved riding William. If he wasn't such a sucka and belonged to 'Mia and Lord knows whoever else, then he would have made the perfect toy for her. Although, she was still in love with Javier and she knew it, but variety had never hurt anybody. She rested her hands on William's chest and rode him slow sending a very, very sensual sensation through the moment adding the lust needed to something so forbidden as borrowed love. She stood in the bed, her high heels were all she wore, she switched positions, she still straddled him but in reverse, giving William the perfect view of her sexy well shaped back end and this is how she performed for him until she came, came and came again never once allowing William to come. She knew that these two had all afternoon so no rush was even necessary.

Tamia was out of the house sooner than usual. Normally she would have cooked for William before she left, this time, well he'll be alright. Normally she would have written him a note to confront him about his messiness this time she figured this would be a sit down and face to face. Not only did he come home to her in the thug hours of the morning, but he came in smelling like mint toothpaste and Angel perfume the Halo fragrance, a brand that she would never buy but she knew somebody who does. She wouldn't have cared if William decided to lie to her because now his lies were lies, when normally she would allow his lies to be truths.

"I had all that I could take." Tamia said to herself tossing away her food cartons as she left the fast food restaurant and headed off to school. Tamia thought of the progress that she had made with her life, she thought of every reason to quit and to surrender to the likes of misery. Yet her foot stayed on the gas pedal and her hands still navigated her automobile in the direction of the University of California Davis where she was gonna let her studies be the distraction that she needed. Focus on your assignment and not the troubles of the world outside of medicine, she figured. Still Tamia navigated towards her destination even though the task could be impossible when one's world had just come crashing down beside them. Still she knew that she must journey on, for she has always been pushed by the spirits before her, by that of her Mother and Nana, and by the likes of those run down tenements that she has always despised. The drug addicts and high school dropouts who hung out with no other destiny than to rob people of their nothings or barely anything had proven to be a good lesson. It was always true; misery has always loved company for misery has always needed company. Tamia was so far into thought that she barely heard her cell ringing, picking it up from the cup holder pressing talk she said,

"Hello."

Marva has never felt this rhythm before, the spell was a dizzying and yet a fulfilling one. William held her waist then he toyed with her breast bringing each nipple to its stiffness. Erected from pleasure and stabilized by the pain once he pinched, then sucked, then bit. Marva found paradise hid behind the folds of their lust, their very, very forbidden and impermissible desires were at its limits and threatening to forego even the boundaries of being rabid. So their fornication though bought has proven to be flames none more than uncontained.

Marva rode William until again she exploded sending juices flowing; it was something about being in this crazy place, this daring, yet awfully crazy place that sent her senses to haywire. Hard was to rationalize with the fact that her excitements grew when she was being her most deceitful. Oh how the world owed her so much and so does everyone in it, just like last night she made William give her oral pleasure just moments after Javier had hopped up and down inside of her, now it would be Javier's turn. She figured she would only be the liaison between the two. Oh, she was in love with Javier, but it was also her rough reality that Javier was out for his cake, he wanted his family and his nigger bitch to remain a token, yet on the sideline. Well, in case he's been overlooking some stuff, maybe she needed to remind him that she was too boss of a bitch to be sidelined from anyone or by anyone. Yes, she really loves Javier in her own little way and although she has her own little way of showing it she made herself a promise to love herself more than anything. From the outside one could see her new way of seeing life to be reckless and self-loath, but this was her thing. She ran her, not Javier and not anybody on this earth, she answered to the dough, which she was now getting plenty of. To this thought she crawled up William and straddled his head so she could feel his tongue inside of her.

Tamia had replaced her phone into the cup holder and directed her car into the turning lane where at the light she made a U-turn and headed for home, her class was cancelled for the day which she figured could come in handy. Well for starters she could use the time to prepare an even better presentation which she was scheduled to deliver on this very day until her study partner called to inform her that their class had been officially canceled. Ruby, who was as smart as a whip, was also about as shy and fainthearted as they come, had the best research method, but lead her to the podium and you would find it easier pushing a bear to the slaughter house. So the pact was made, Ruby would point the directions and, Tamia would do the explanation and, this pact was sealed and joined at the hips. Ruby had perfect attendance on hers and because of her phobia of speaking and of doing much of anything else in front of people she had made damned sure that Tamia's' attendance report was just as spotless, impeccable and a fraction just past perfect. So Tamia knew that if Ruby told her that class was cancelled then dammit class was cancelled. Tamia only had one class for that day would now have for property a very much needed day off. One that she could use to rearrange her life and send it into a more organized direction because, well as it stands her comforts had been blown to pieces, her security has now been threatened along with her beliefs in people for she had been let down over and over and long enough. She could now practice being her own best friend, even more so now that she sees Marva's' rental parked in front of her place.

"Geez, what do we have here, some old fashioned disregards for anything other than themselves and their own selfish agendas, crazy, crazy, crazy," Tamia said while exiting the car.

Marva was enjoying this little game that William was playing with her high heels; she was now on her back so William took control of her. He kissed each heel all the way down her legs and up her inner thighs sending voltages in the high millions as he kissed her rectum down to her vagina then back up her thighs and to her heels again. This game was intense, so intense that either she or William heard as Tamia entered the house. Marva's moans were so resounding and discordant that neither of the two heard as Tamia took to the stairs either. William dove in again and again; he sent the high voltages to his now tamed dominatrix. His rhythm was splendid, his tactics were incredible, high maneuvers were gallant and majestic and all of his cylinders was hitting, in fact everything was perfect, his performance was wild enough to make even Marva call him "Big Daddy." Everything was perfect, except the timing. The timing was not perfect, in fact it sucked, there's a proverb that says that there's a time and place for everything and Lord knew that this, was not the time and it sure as hell was not the place, not by a long shot. Yet, neither William or Marva knew this, for it was hard for Marva to see Tamia standing in the doorway because William's ass was hiked up making it hard to see anything past the lust and the crack of his ass and William damned sure couldn't see anything from where he was looking because he had his head so far up Marva's vagina that his eye lashes blinked near her small intestines so he didn't see Tamia, but they both heard when she walked in and opened the closet door. At first they were just a little frightened then relaxed once they saw that the only thing that Tamia withdrew were hangers with clothes draped around them before heading out of the room only to return for more of her possessions.

"Oh my God Tamia, I'm so sorry," William said through his embarrassments. At least he didn't say "It's not what it looks like," Tamia thought before saying

"Oh, no, no "Big Daddy" excuse me I'm in y'all way, I'll only be a second. Marva don't mind me at all I promise to be real quiet I only need a few more articles then I'll be out of y'all hair." Tamia said all of this without even breaking her rhythm of unhooking hangers from the closet and creating a pile in the walk way leading to the stairs. Marva needed not to dress much all she needed to do was add her maxi and she would be presentable enough to make her exit, which she done without second thought towards the predicaments that she was now escaping nor did she bother to explain anything to her friend, her sister for years. As far as she was concerned nothing would ever change the fact that it was indeed everything that it looked like and whatever happened between Tamia and William was all on them for she had enough problems all on her own. For starters she needed to find another sucker with product which way she would then still is able to keep some bait on the traps that she tried so hard to set.

CHAPTER 13

LIFE COULD BE A CRAZY thing sometimes and for Marva, events could have never unfolded in a stranger fashion. A day that begun with an extreme amount of pleasure, a pleasure that came from an intercourse unmatched by anything or anyone, shit, it was something about the way he sucked her heels that gave her a large power rush, then the twist of fate. It was the beginning of all the worst case scenarios, for starters she was just busted on her back with her legs up and wide open by someone who had no business discovering her secrets, a skeleton that she now wished a hundred times remained hidden had fallen out of the closet. Once a justifiable secret, I mean once the dough or the product made its way to her possessions there was nothing left to talk about. A secret that now bore the nakedness of its own bones. She recalled a feeling so intense, so sheer in its energy that Marva never bothered to apologize to her friend, pretty much her sister and confidante, whom she has known all of her life but she did find it necessary to stick her hand with the wavy fingers out to collect her just do before making her exit. She thought about Tamia for a split second and not much longer than that, a true friend indeed but "we are headed in different directions baby, you could have this life here in this bitch ass town I need the fireworks sweetie" then the thought was gone for the only pangs that Marva was experiencing was that of William.

Marva knew for sure that she knew exactly no one of William's ilk, his makeup was indeed different. He was the type of person that could be in the streets as long as he has and remain dumb as a son of a bitch and no matter who tried to straighten him out, he'll just remain nothing more than stupid. Marva knew that if push came to the good ole physical stuff, that she was gonna just fork over the dough for the packages but the thought alone was spooking the shit out of her because she hated the idea of doing business with the dealers in Oak Park enough to keep her second guessing all the way to Green Haven. Seems like Marva was suffering a greater loss then she had projected in the case that something this horrible was to happen. What was bothering Marva the most, as crazy and as fatuous as it all may seem was the calm to which Tamia was displaying, almost as if she had known all the time that her lover and her friend were being as they say, intimate. Thinking further that if Tamia had known then the same must be true for Mecca, Tahj and Lerin. Although this thought was supported by evidence as unstable and feeble as a wild guess. Marva felt the paranoia from her acts and started to wish that she could start her life from scratch but as it stood the reality of it all was unchangeable so what the hell. Next on the list was to invite Javier to lunch and she was sure to whip up the right dish, soggy coochie on a platter with a side order of William. A smile creased her lips before she said,

"What's good for the goose Javier has got to be good for you too," She reached for her ringing cell phone knowing that it would only be one or two people, it would either be William, in that case he may feel bad so Marva knew that she would invite him over instead of Javier. If so she knew just how to cheer him up seeing that he had already paid enough for one day or it could either be Javier who wouldn't mind making a pit stop between his bush trimmings. Reading her callers ID did she know that she was wrong on both counts for she was now looking at the name and number belonging only to Tahj. She hesitated before answering finding it best to just go on ahead and get the guilt tripping out of the way was surprised when she heard Tahj say,

"Girl, I know that you be getting your hustle on, so, if you need a hand at that my dude got a line on a few grand if you up for it." Shit, the fuck kind of question is that Marva thought for a moment before saying,

"Girl, you know how badly I need the money, I'm pretty much up for anything short of murder and that all depends on who supposed to get it."

"Ok, ok well listen, from what I gather him and his dude is having problems keeping a transaction innocent, he doesn't trust them they don't trust him, girl it's a mess. So, all parties elected to use women this way the scale balances off that way and everybody happy with each other. I mean if you're like yeah and all don't panic because you're gonna have a lot of security, I mean considering..."

"Considering what, the sensitivity of the merchandise?"

"Nuh uh, considering that Rasaan's potna we believe got a thang going on for you. I mean the rumor has it that ever since the other night at the club that the Dom bottle broke a record and a lot of hearts. You know the dude that I'm talking about right, now I got to tell you that the brother from the club, well he was against the idea the whole way. So I got to tell you the bad part too. It was Rasaan who mentioned that they should use you seeing how they was gonna have to take you on some test runs any way to check on your trust worthiness their words not mine. Uh uh, mines were that if my home girl doing anything it's gonna cost you and I mean really, we stopped negotiating at a few grand seeing that if you say yes, then you could spot your girl a few of those damned ducats." Tahj was hitting her notes, exactly how Rasaan said that she should, listened as the line gone quiet, knew that Marva hadn't disconnected, but that Marva's wheels were spinning and smiled at Rasaan whom played the conversation as the umpire, made the hook symbol with his finger and stuck it in his mouth. Tahj gave Marva a moment to digest the hook before saying,

"So, what you want me to do?" Marva barely heard this, because her wheels were indeed spinning so much that her thoughts were racing. First she had to conclude that Tamia hadn't reached out to Tahj as of yet, but was sure that was in the making, so Marva thought "I may as well get all that I could right now." Second, there was the idea of getting next to Mr. Man which indeed could be the prize winner.

"Marva.... Marva, you there,"

"Yeah, I mean I hear you, tell them that I'm game what do they want me to do though?"

"Drop off a briefcase, pick up a bag and all of this under the watchful eyes of some good dudes."

"And the briefcase, what's in it?"

"I would say that I didn't know, but I'd be lying, I mean with you being my girl and all I needed to make sure that you wouldn't be on any gung-ho shit, but from what I could see, it'll only be paperwork, some information that one group is willing to buy from the next is all I see, and nothing more."

"Ok, so, when is all this going down though?"

"In a couple of hours, I mean I just now found it all out, seems that nobody wanted to leak that part, kept everything spare of the moment so nobody could make plans ahead of time to mess the deal up you know." Tahj finished and Marva liked everything she was hearing, concluded that Rasaan and this Nahjee character must really have their thing together. Looks, smarts, dope and taste which was everything that a woman wants in a man, no matter the woman, Marva smiled at the thoughts she was having then said,

"I mean; I appreciate that you taking my safety into consideration. Regardless of anything we're girls first so whenever you need me just hit me whenever, I'm ready."

"Ok, that's what I'ma do." Tahj hung up before Marva leaving Marva to really consider now all the eccentricities that played out in a span of a day finalized that in some kind of crooked way happiness was headed in her direction. She knew that if she played her cards right that soon she'd be pushing her a BMW, a navy blue one already equipped with everything, rims, music style and the boss who bought it. So she thought, "Who needs friends when I could have power," she mumbled to herself while she reached for her phone once more, thinking that since the card game hasn't begun yet that she could play her other game so she placed a call to Javier and offered up her lunch knowing that his tongue would help her to relax. Which was everything that she needed at the time because in a few hours she would be dealt her first hand and she sure was gonna hold her cards close to her chest, "for a few thousand please,"

When Tahj hung up the phone after speaking to Marva, Rasaan picked up his phone and called Nahjee who picked up after the first ring and listened as Rasaan told him about Marva being on for the ride and that it would be her who would accompany Aretha for the swap.

"I'm scared to ask you how the hell you pulled that off," said Nahjee.

"Shit, I got awfully motivated when you said let's use Tahj, who by the way said that she would do it if nobody else stepped forward."

"How the fuck did you approach Tahj with that, you know I was only fucking with you when I said that, right."

"I didn't approach her she was getting her nosy on when I was on the phone with you, the bits and pieces that she heard helped her use her own inferences the rest of the way. Since she heard me being so adamant about us not using her for practice she automatically drew up that we were on to something too dangerous for her. Well if that was the case then it was too damned dangerous for me too you should see this shit, I'm talking about leave it up to her then I can't go anywhere."

"Ha ha, Ha ha, if so she wasn't gonna let you out the house without her."

"I don't know what you think is so damn funny, at first I was suppose call you and have you come through, you know so she could lock both of us in the house."

"What, nah, don't call me for no shit like that, not for some shit like that and especially now that we come this far?"

"I had to, she had me cornered and I panicked. Where are you?"

"Shoot, I was on my way to your place, but I think I'm on my way to the waffle house."

"Nah, come through."

"Shit naw, I smell a rat way over here."

"Naw, its goods, but there is a rat which is what I need to explain to you."

"Shit naw, I could hear you just fine from over here."

"I mean, it's just this little bitty part that I left out."

"Figures,"

"You know how I be manipulating people."

"Yeah, so,"

"So, I tell ole girl, I mean I had Tahj do the talking, but we sold her on the idea that we were gonna kick in a few grand."

"Ok, ok, that's what's up."

"That's not it."

"Somehow I didn't think so but were gonna cook the bushes pretty soon I hope." Nahjee had noticed that Rasaan was taking his time about coming forward decided that he needed to brace himself when he heard Rasaan say,

"So, she was game to go through once we leaked that you had a thang for her and really didn't want anything to happen to her and how we were gonna be extra careful on this considering such a prized possession, meaning she was at stake."

"Ahh, that's the way it is, let me guess you need me mushy for the moment? A few tears, I can't believe that were using her and how it has to be somebody else and that's how you need me?"

"Yes,"

"Maybe a few hugs and shit, you know warm the moment up a bit."

"Hell yeah," Rasaan was getting excited seeing his plan come together.

"How about I promise her a nice little dinner after the job is done, somewhere special, a dinner for two, just me and her you know." Rasaan was in rhythm now, excitement over floweth, marvelous, fantastico.

"All the time I'm popping my whip on her; I'm giving her the briefcase and sending her on a mission impossible."

"Heeee, Heeee, Heeee," Nahjee pictured Rasaan doing his Michael Jackson impersonation, labeling that his happy dance where he'd spin around a full 360 degrees, stop, grab his crouch, grab his pants and then kick his leg out and this was his happy dance. Then he pictured Rasaan flying around like a balloon once Nahjee let the air out of him by saying,

"Shit naw, hell to the uh uh," and "You got me what they call, fucked up." Rasaan stopped in mid action as if he was just stonewalled at the gates of heaven said,

"Wha-wa-what do you mean, I don't understand."

"Sure you do, no, is the easiest and the hardest thing to say, but never misunderstood... Only got one meaning but is recognizable in many languages and they say it in many different terminologies as in fuck that, uh un, nope, oh you must have lost your motha fucking mind, or even nigga please......."

"Fuck that shit." Rasaan interrupted this educational spiel.

"Fuck that shit is also on the list, see I knew that you knew where I was going with this

"Dog, you can't do this, what are you doing?"

"Gee whiz, if that wasn't some confusing shit? How you gone tell me I can't do some shit then under the same breath ask me what is it that I'm doing, now I'm gonna need you to get a hold of yourself."

"Man, you need to come through here quick."

"No sir'ree Bob, you see, even that was a slick way to say no."

"You gotta come through, what are you doing?"

"About to go and get me something to eat like I said earlier before you started acting like you forgot what the hell "no" meant."

"You gotta come through time is wasting."

"My point exactly, as far as I know Tahj right there waiting on me to come through just so she could sock it to me for some of those promises that she knows I hate to make but know that I'ma keep. Oh, and if you already forgot to remember, this is business that we gotta do, remember, and who knows, it just might not be the good business that we're used to. Which is the only reason that I'm not gonna bait this lady into taking the ride. If were gonna pay her then that's her getting down for the paper and I'll have no problem with forking it over. But never, not even for one iota of a second am I gonna con somebody into biting a bullet for me. I just don't need that shit on my conscience. Contrary to popular belief, I really do have one of those, you know, a conscience. I mean, don't mix me up with "he who do gooder" all holy and shit because I'm not and I'm hip to the reasons why this is a good idea for ole girl to go and pitch the switch. I mean with her being scandalous like she is and by the way that's something only God could judge not you and not me, so we won't. What we are gonna do is stay true to it, you feel that?" Even though Rasaan really did stop giving a fuck about Marva once he saw the connection between her and Nahjee, still he had to rationalize that Nahjee spoke a truth that was ever so far from being common place in today's teachings. Because today the anthem is "ain't no love" and many, many people in today's hustle would pledge their allegiances to such a sorry way of seeing life. Trapped now Rasaan said,

"Ok, now this puts us back at square one, hmmm. So, what are we going to do?"

"I'm going to eat, I don't know what you're going to do, I mean if you got Ms. Ma'am on for the dough then I'm not tripping as long as she knows the risk and wouldn't be going in blind and mislead then I'm good with that."

"My nigga," the two disconnected.

The time William was dressed or even presentable enough to approach Tamia, who turned into a fast walking, clothes piling, merchandise sorting speed demon. Caring oh- so less about anything that William had to say, as far as she was concerned he already said enough. So, when he reached for her arm to stop her from heading to the door saying,

"Mia, you don't have to do this,"

"Is that right, so, what do you suggest for me to do if not this, William?"

"Well, you don't have to leave like this."

"So far I'm going by car but if you know a quicker way then I'm open for suggestions."

"That's not what I meant."

"No, then I'm gonna have to ask you to please release me so I could be gone now."

"No, 'Mia, oh God I was so wrong."

"That's nice of you to figure that one out on your own. Now if you would, you know, be kind enough to excuse me? I mean you still sort of reek of some kind of shellfish."

"No, 'Mia at least listen to me for a minute."

"Let me guess, this is where you say that if I didn't work so much or if I didn't study so much and maybe if I paid more attention to your needs then I wouldn't have to find you with another woman, right. Maybe it was because I didn't behave like a slut, you know some good ole fashion role playing, let you suck my high heels until you throw up. How much do that cost, because I know that Marva wouldn't have done this for free. How would you had wanted me William, dressed up like a runaway slave, yell Massa' while I'm playing like I'm scared of you while you prepare to choke the shit out of me and rape me? What do you really think that I should listen to William? I mean for real, because I'ma need you to hurry up and blame me for everything because I have a really busy day ahead of me not to mention, so do you. I mean, don't you got some "rocks" that you're sup-posed to be somewhere poisoning people with?"

Took aback by the knowledge of his other way of living being revealed by Tamia, so stunned was he that the only thing left to do was release Tamia's arm and allow her to pass knowing that he'd have to live with the fact that she'd be hurt forever. He concluded that his stash was gonna take a major hit if he were to remain living there in the townhouse without her and the best thing for him to do was vacate the same premises as well. So, when Tamia re-entered the house she found him packing his belongings. Tamia cared less about his actions, she went along gathering her items and was long gone the time William made it to the window to pull back the curtains to look for her.

Tamia hadn't had a full proof plan to what she would do, but she had a very strong feeling that starting over was gonna be one of the hardest things that she has ever done. So the very first thing that she done was pull into a coffee shop where she booted up her laptop, the same one that she made these special plans not to pack into the trunk, leaving that on the front seat for easy access. Once her computer came to life she immediately scanned for places that she could rent that was in her budget. The one thing that the internet has always provided was a wide range, yet fast paced way of reaching out to people, places and things. So, armed with this long list, Tamia made one call after the next, she was beginning to become more and more disappointed as one prospect after the other failed to provide fruition.

Tamia remained steadfast with the true belief that if Marva could pull it off then so could anyone. Although Tamia knew that she wasn't willing to go to such drastic measures as Marva but she knew that she was gonna take the same determinations and channel that until she prevailed. The day played itself out until the night time found Tamia checking into the Motel Six on Stockton Blvd. Once she became settled in enough to call her study partner, she had done so only to hear a line go unanswered. So, she sent her a text message asking that Ruby be ever so kind to cover for her in the morning. Tamia was sensing that her new found spotless attendance streak was about to come to a screeching halt, because no way as she explained to Ruby in full detail would she be in the least little bit, prepared enough to cover for herself.

The text message struck gold because Ruby texted back saying that even though she was in a place where she couldn't talk but if she was, she said that she would be screaming her head off yelling "shit no" and "don't do me like this" then finished saying that Tamia had better find a way to make it in the morning or else. To this Tamia finally found laughter, it was the thought of Ruby hyperventilating at the podium just before the presentation. Tamia did tell her that she was in an inescapable situation so she begun to see fainting in the forecast for good ole Ruby and this is what Tamia texted back in return. Ruby fired back with a text that she made sure to include all capital letters when she wrote "NO, NO, NO, NO, NO' then 'SEE YOU TOMORROW AND DON'T BE LATE." Shaking her head as if shaking off the inconsideration that Ruby was displaying for Tamia's predicament. So, Tamia tried once more because she needed Ruby to understand that other things exist other than her fears of approaching a damned podium and speaking with diction and strong conviction to a crowd of many, and that it was settled. Tamia was gonna have to leave her classmate alone out there on her own, especially if she continued to fail to understand. Her phone buzzed again and again in rapid fire intensity "What kind of predicament first, at least tell me that lest I disclaim you as a friend forever without knowing all the details, come on Tamia don't do me like this. The thought alone is killing me, don't do me this way," so Tamia fired back in a way that even an idiot would understand she said,

"Ruby I am right now in a motel room scared to death and out of my wits. I am sure to be up all night, and I'll promise you that much. I am so close to homeless that I must check out in the morning with a one tracked mind and that is to fix my living situation lest I fail to find sleep forever." Tamia pressed send and this time the text came back even faster than before, it read.

"My god, Tamia are you ok, listen I'm at Mass and can't get away but soon I will call you back. Don't worry my folks has a few places, I know that you are strong headed but let me help you?" So, that's where she's at Tamia summarized, those darned Catholics didn't care when they get theirs in, early in the morning or in the wee hours of the night. Never one to argue the whys' or the when's that a person decided to call on God. Tamia stuck to the business at hand, said.

"Thank you, I could use all the help that I could get; only I can't afford much."

"Why the motel though?"

"William and I just broke up, it's ugly right now." Tamia fired back.

"OMG" came the response then another text followed "I'm on my way, where are you?" This was all Tamia needed was someone to help her feel sorry for herself, but did tell Ruby her location and later found out that Ruby didn't walk in feeling sorry at all, hell no. Ruby walked into the small motel room with her phone pressed to her ear and was conducting some kind of aggravated full court press about her business. Relentless in her approaches, leaving Tamia feeling some kind of way for the person that Ruby was talking to, then couldn't believe it once she discovered that Ruby was in a conference call with first her mother. Who then dialed in to her grandmother due to being under so much pressure, and a grandmother who too took a little of the heat before telling Ruby to call her uncle, who was asleep but gladly awoke to hear the grievances from his favorite niece.

Ahh, Ruby, the apple of his eyes, who pled for a place that one of her classmates could rent with just one slight problem. He would have to wait for payments seeing that her classmate attends school full time. Tamia listened to Ruby and shook her head. She couldn't understand for the life of her just how Ruby talked so well on a phone, but would clam the heck up at a podium. Tamia listened as Ruby sold her situation to her uncle, concluding that she was on her way to pick up the keys. Tamia couldn't believe her ears. Ruby told her not to thank her yet, because the place which was all she could squeeze with absolutely no money now or even for a while was located in Oak Park. Still, Tamia found reason to thank Ruby, and told her that she was more than grateful.

If love was a baseball game, then the only time William reached base was when he was getting hit by pitches. At first he wasn't tripping, shit, if Tamia wanted to leave then go. Hell, if Marva never called back, then so be it, because he had a place to go, which was way better than this wretched situation that he was walking away from.

Lose a bitch gain a bitch was the name of the game, oh he was a playa now. So once he was packed up and leaving the house he was heading to a bitch that had the freaky tendencies that he always loved in a bitch. She had her own place and wasn't asking for much just a few nights of his undivided attention and now she could have that every night. We're not going to even mention how he could get his 'stack up' game going on. "Oh yeah, I've been playing the fool for so long" he said to his self before pulling into Aretha's drive way. William knew that this was the moment that Aretha was waiting for. She was gonna be so happy with the decision that he made to call her place, his. So, when he ran up the stairs to Aretha's, he thought of ringing the door bell, but then decided against that and searched through his key ring for the key that Aretha had given him ever so long ago.

Finding it he unlocked the door and walked into the house aiming to sneak up on his baby girl. Well he found her, and when he did she was asshole naked on the sofa surrounded by naked men. He started to feel a little sick to his stomach as he watched as his baby girl performed expertly. "You punk bitch," William yelled to Aretha. Scope turned to see William, but thought "so what." Aretha heard William, but she couldn't stop now because Scope wrapped his hand around her head and pounded his dick so deep into her mouth making sure that she allowed it. "Dang trick, how about closing the mother fucking door nigga," Scope said to William without giving Aretha a break, who really didn't care if she had one or not and to prove it she revealed her deep throat game to them all. "You fucking whore," William ran to Aretha so that he could slap the shit out of her but by the time that he arrived to striking distance, Stomp had the drop on him with his pistol was drawn. This giving Scope and Marcel plenty of time to get their shit together and once they got their shit together, the three beat the holy shit out of William. They used feet, hands and pistols and anything else that they could get their hands on. Aretha just laidback and watched, she was getting turned on by this ruckus so she began to masturbate while watching William getting beat to a bloody pulp. Once they were finished and all of Williams' pockets were turned inside out with him out cold. Scope walked over to Aretha and offered up his penis and she took it. She performed orally while masturbating herself for she knew that only one nigga called the shots in her life and he kept her on her knees and back and her broke. She knew that her life belonged to him and if Scope made her stop breathing then albeit because scope is tried and true and a slow death, would be the moment that she discovered that he failed to love her anymore. And for William, a day has never ever been so screwed up.

CHAPTER 14

NAHJEE AND RASAAN HOVERED OVER the briefcase and done everything necessary to disguise the plates within the folds of the briefcase then done as Rasaan suggested by placing documents that meant exactly nothing to anyone inside. So, when Marcel, Scope, Stomp and the ever important Aretha made their showing the briefcase was revealed to the four then it was sealed and locked, and the combination was given to Aretha and her alone. Who was left behind with Nahjee and Rasaan as they awaited the arrival of Marva? This way they could head out to McClatchy Park where Aretha and Marva were to wait for the buy to come through. Nahjee and Rasaan would be located at McClatchy Park as well, only they were tucked away at the baseball diamond in perfect view of the parking lot which had been strategically selected. It was a good place for pay and leave or even a take and leave, but a horrible place for a murder and leave due to the heavy flow of foot traffic as well as police traffic which discourages this. Marva was to drive Nahjee's BMW and Aretha was to do the transactions, and this was the part that Marva found especially attractive, you know driving the Beamer and all but it was something in the warning when Nahjee said, "if something cross presents itself to be really smart and just give up the briefcase and fuck the money." Now that part wasn't attractive but she was told not to worry there was still dough in it for the two so she was back to feeling comfortable again. Aretha knew that Scope, Stomp and Marcel were on their way to get the real money just on the strength. Aretha thought it best to leave Marva in the dark thinking that if anybody wanted her to know that part then they would have said something to her instead of having her show up late when they were putting all the plans together.

Now plan B was the highlighted area on the map. Plan B is where Scope, Stomp and Marcel waited on the words of good business or fake business, though all three of them voted on the latter they all vowed to honor good business with their agreed payoff but secretly they all rooted for the skullduggery. If some fuck shit went down, then they would walk right up in those pawn shops and pay their motha fuckin selves. With all the players in position waiting for the trade to take place. Nahjee and the girls occupied their time with last minute instructions concerning their walkie talkies. Saying that to keep Nahjee and Rasaan informed just in case something or someone cross made its appearance a direct line was to depress the talk button once the pickup guys showed up, just in case time would be a luxury that either one could afford.

It was instructed that Marva worked the mechanicals and that Aretha dealt strictly with the transactions. Secretly, Marva had a thing stirring inside of her, each time Nahjee spoke she found that she held on to every word, especially his commanding tone. The fact that he stood not even fifty feet away in garbs looking like a mighty hungry and homeless gentle-man, only added fuel towards her fire. She has always liked a man of deep ingenuity, and Nahjee appeared to have this in abundance, and the fact that he played his homeless role so well told her a lot. She smiled at the way that he was staggering around with an automatic weapon, seeing this Marva was all the way turned on, so much that she was becoming para-noid. All she needed was Nahjee to reject her for her yesterdays, somehow she was gonna have to convince him to take a chance on her. "Man, this man has his shit together," she was thinking before her box came to life.

"Alright you two, heads up, to your right a bit, black Sedan see it?"

"Got it," said Marva.

"Ok, nobody stupid, nobody super heroes, do you copy?"

"Copy," Marva could have sworn that she heard a weapon being loaded.

"Remember, we want the bag first, then the case."

"Copy,"

"Alright, here they come, easy, easy roll the window down, nobody panics."

"It's four guys, see them?" Marva was told to expect two.

"Yes, yes, remember if its cross let them have it, it's all good."

Marva felt this deep, deep driving urge to say "Yes daddy we got it" but the urge was rudely interrupted when Aretha began speaking to the single gentleman, who've exited the car, she said,

"I was told to receive first, then I'll up the case, other than that I'm afraid that we'd have to try again later."

"Oh, ok no problem, I was expecting somebody else is all," said the Spanish looking man. So, Aretha looked past him to the car then said,

"So was we which is the reason that I'm gonna need the bag first, you know just like everybody drew it up or should we leave and like I said the first time, try this shit again later." Marva was extremely confident that Aretha had already done this type of work somewhere before, and she wasn't the only one who was entertaining this thought, for Nahjee felt his self, smiling at the bluntness of the woman his self.

"Oh, no, no we could get all of this out of the way now, if it's the bag that has to go first then a bag it is," the Spanish man had gone back to the car to which he made his exit from and opened the rear door and removed a small black bag. No way could sixty grand fit in such a tiny bag Rasaan thought, not even if it showed in large bills, Nahjee had to be thinking the same thing because he was up and staggering. Allowing the men to see that there were witnesses in the event that this deal had gone terribly wrong. The first man made his way back to the car and Nahjee heard through the walkie talkie as the man said,

"Now, this ma'am is the only bag that I got and in it there's a ten millimeter pistol do you know what that is?" Aretha nodded her head. "Now, I must ask you have you ever been dead before?" for this Aretha shook her head in the negative, while the car was being surrounded by men of Spanish decent. "Now, I don't want to kill you, but I really would if you decide that the bag that I have isn't enough to pay for the case that you have, do you understand what I mean?" Aretha nodded once more and instantly Nahjee began to will her to give up the case. His telepathy was awarded as he watched as the case was handed over, to a very, very professional character that was not in any hurry to leave, without first checking the contents of the brief.

"I'm gonna assume that you have the numbers to unlock this case here," The fellow raised the case in indication, for his reward Aretha gave him the folded piece of paper that Nahjee had given to her. Which was to Marva's relief who exhaled heavy enough for Nahjee to hear through the talk box? While everyone watched as the man tumbled numbers until the case was open. He searched the case until he found what he was looking for before closing the case. He stood then nodded to his partners who decided for an encore was to pull out a blade and stab the tires of the BMW before leaving. Marva, watching as the Sedan pulled out of the park, was now more confused as ever before. For not only was they just robbed, but now they were handy capped with four flat tires and all of this was done right in front of two brothers who held guns under their coats. She was thinking that it should have been at least a shootout around this motha fucka. Nahjee was the first to make it to them, he walked around the car to see and confirm what he already knew. Then he stopped at the driver side window and squatted low enough to speak to Marva, he said,

"Are you alright?"

"I'm just a little shaken is all,"

"Ok, its ok, you guys did well, I'm proud of you guys."

"Why did you let them get away so easy?" Marva just had to ask, for she was troubled by the composure that everyone held but her. Even Aretha's expression held a slight tent of a smile to it.

"Let who get away so easy?" Nahjee asked before pressing send on his cell phone and began talking while walking out of earshot distance. Marva learned quickly and one of the things that she learned was that this man, this really fine and awfully handsome man, possessed a depth that went past mystifying. For every move that a lesser man would make this man done took off three steps ahead. So, the best thing that she could do was to hush and let him do his thing. "Hmmm, whatever the hell that is" she thought before getting out of the car and joining Aretha and Rasaan, whom also awaited Nahjee to walk off his phone call. Marva saw as the three exchanged concerned looks before Nahjee broke into a smile, one that immediately relaxed Aretha. So something really slick was going on because no one, none that Marva knew had ever taken getting robbed so merrily.

"Look, I got something for you guys," Nahjee said while keeping his end of the deal, forking over the two envelopes, one for Aretha and the other for Marva whom only temporarily accepted for she glanced through the hundred dollar bills before handing the envelope back to Nahjee and shaking her head in the negative. Rasaan could have sworn that Marva found a scorpion in her envelope as fast as she gave it back to Nahjee before saying,

"How about helping me out with a cab or a lift so I could get to Stockton Blvd. considering that this car is disabled and you insisted that I should leave mine at The Waffle House. I believe that I've had enough excitement for one day." Marva watched as Nahjee tumbled his thoughts in order to mentally arrange each one, before dialing another number where he spoke rapidly into the phone before disconnecting. Five minutes later a car was brought to carry Marva where she suggested. Nahjee wasn't nowhere close to ready for the stunt that Marva just pulled off handing him back the envelope like that, in fact nobody was, not even Aretha. Rasaan didn't give a fuck still under his breath he called her a punk bitch and a few other things because now he knew that the bitch scored a point with his potna. Nahjee, who was in awe of the whole thing still found humor in watching Rasaan attempt to make some sense of it all.

"Hello" Nahjee said, then, "Are you all right playboy?"

"Yeah, yeah, I'm good."

"Well, we have to go now; do you think that we could finish what we started?"

"Yeah, so we just leave the car here?" Rasaan knew that his answer would tell if his potna was thunderstruck, had one coming once he heard,

"I mean, while you were trying to figure out every reason to hate Miss Lady for her guts, me and Aretha had already sprung a deal you know, you must have blacked out from all of that red rage," Nahjee laughed at his friend.

"What the fucks so funny?"

"I mean, here this beautiful lady is over here thinking that you are just the handsomest devil ever."

"And, that's funny nigga?"

"Nah, that's not funny, but once I told her not to worry about you because you like the 'mans' and shit and to you I said ain't that right and your ass said yeah. Now that shit was funny nigga I don't care what you say, soon as you said that she started looking at you like a muscle bound homosexual ever since." For a response Rasaan flipped them both the bird then headed off towards his car leaving Aretha and Nahjee to finish working out whatever details that were being made about the car. During Rasaan's out of body experience, he drifted like a sleep walker all the way to Marva's neck and squeezed it awfully hard and asked her over and over, to die. Nahjee fell in step with Rasaan and the two walked in silence a moment then Nahjee said,

"You know that I was only playing about that gay thing right?"

"Whatever man, so where do you think them niggas at?" Rasaan unlocked the car door remotely granting them access to the interior.

"I don't know yet, but I want to give them a minute before I hit those niggas back. Shoot, all I know is that they were some happy motha fuckas to have received the go ahead."

"I'm hoping that they clean it all out, wish they make it in everywhere and leave 'em all broke as a bitch. I'm talking about buzzard broke, next door to starving to death.

"Dang, the venom in that strike was better than a Rattler, now here I am thinking that everybody was cool and stuff." Nahjee ridiculed his potna.

"Hardy, har, har"

"Be for real, if those niggas didn't come crazy like that, would you still feel the same way?"

"Not at all, the truth is, those niggas cashed us out enough to eat like we do. I mean, I've known you forever and I haven't heard your stomach growling not once since we were little."

"But don't you get this terrorist feeling?"

"Terrorist, nigga hell naw,"

"Dig, you remember those stories that Uncle Jay used to tell us about the bombs that the terrorist would travel with, and how they carried such a pride, even knowing that one day the very bomb that they would carry, would be meant for them with this being the tradition of a suicide bomber. Even here, tell me do you see where I could see how they were only just fattening up the frog for the damned snake?"

"Now that I think about it bro, we were probably getting played the whole way for all those years." Said Rasaan,

"Could say that again, but like you say my nigga they provided food. I won't go as far as saying that they were playing us all along, no. But, I would say that it came a time in their plans for sacrifices and I'm thinking that this is where we come in at."

"Shit I almost fucked our plans the fuck up just a minute ago, liked to pulled out the 'thumper' and aired this motha fucka out as soon as I seen the bitch start with the tires, something about hearing the air seeping out that made me almost lose it."

"Well, I'm glad that you were able to control yourself, boy you would have done some shit like that I would have been forced to shoot you my-self. Ra' whatever you do never lose it upstairs because the moment that you do, is the very same moment that you had just ran out of game and never, whatever you do, never run out of game."

"Tell me you didn't want to flat line them motha fuckas?"

"I really didn't, no. Me, I want to beat them at their own shit and I wanna be justified while doing it. I wanna out 'rob' the robber and out scam the scandalous. I mean, I was sort of scared that they were gonna force my hand for a moment."

"Which was why you hobbled your fake drunk ass out there in the open like that, huh?"

"For real, but, I need you to pull up over there for a second so I could make a few of these phone calls. Shit, we would either interrupt something or it's time to mosey on to the next one" Rasaan pulled into the 'wicked wheels' motor cycle club to the suspicious stares that were coming from the bikers. Nahjee was connected immediately to Marcel who brought him up to date, seems as if they were rounding third and headed for home.

"This nigga got shit" said Marcel, then "My nigga, you ever see an M-4 before?"

"Nah, I can't say that I have."

"My nigga this motha fucka got a Grenade on the bottom of this bitch, I can't wait to find out how to let one of these thangs go." Marcel was running on high voltage.

"Then where are you going to get more ammunition once you let it go, only thing you'll be able to do is scare the mess out of some body and nothing else after that."

"Nuh uh, that's what I'm saying, this motha fucka had shit. He had a box of these motha fuckas, we found them, I'm talking about these bitches looked like a box of gremlins at first, shit we didn't know what to do."

"Whoa, my nigga be safe with that shit, it sounds scary."

"My nigga I feel like Bin Laden in this motha fucka, I mean say the word and the bitch in the trunk gets it in the kissers, the whole motha fuckin' boom."

"In the trunk! My nigga who in the trunk? You niggas got somebody in the trunk? Y'all just a riding around and shit, well is the nigga making hella racket back there. Listen to see if his ass is back there kicking and yelling and shit?"

"Nuh uhh, we got the beat turned all the way up if he is back there kicking and shit then he sounds like four fifteens to me shoot, you probably right, but now, what you want us to do with this nigga?"

"Hmmm. Hold on a minute," Nahjee looked to Rasaan and said "they want to know what you want them to do with cat daddy that they got in the trunk?" Nahjee heard when Rasaan said.

"I don't give a fuck what them niggas do, that's on them." said Rasaan. Nahjee was back on the line, he said,

"My man says it's on you how you do that part, what I'm concerned about is the drop, how you wanna do that. I mean if you like the thinga-ma-jiggas then keep that and I see you when I see you, but, if you like suit cases then that's where I come in at."

"My nigga, I have never questioned you on your get down and I damned sure ain't gonna' pick today to start; we drew up a plan so, with all due respect playa. I mean, we came this far sticking to that so I'ma suggest that we stick to that all the way out nothing changes over here daddy. Although it's killing me because these are some nice thinga-ma- jiggas, a lot of pretty stuff going on right here fella. My nigga I'm having a hard time trying to fight the temptation to put a damned grill in my mouth. I would be so blocked up I'll shit sprinkles of raw cuts for a year straight."

"But"

"But, like I say we came this far."

"Same place?"

"Yelp, same place I need a drink and Scope surely needs a drink. I don't know what happened to my nigga, he's been in shock ever since we found the rockets. I'm thinking that he was just scared to trust his self around something like that. I know because I almost passed out once I found out that they weren't gremlins too. Shit, get this nigga a bottle of Remy and we'll sit that nigga ass in the corner somewhere."

"Ahh Nah, tell him he got it that goes without saying, bottle and a corner, holla when I see you."

"Yelp," the two sounded off then Nahjee turned to Rasaan,

"So, you don't care how they finished?"

"Uhh uhh, in fact you know what I was just doing just a minute ago? I was selling my car. I mean since you always try to keep up with my style I figured that I may as well tell you. I mean you gonna find out anyhow."

"Is that right, your style, when you get some of that? Boy do Tahj know you out here talking like this, or is this one of our secrets? Talking about me riding your shit nigga you didn't even know that you could put duce's on this raggedy motha fucka. Who you gonna sell it to?"

"I don't give a fuck I'm just gonna erase every trace you know?"

"I could dig it, crazy but I fell out of love with my little thang too. I'm talking about a motha fucka could give me eight dollars for my shit, could you just imagine our reach now?"

"There is absolutely nothing wrong with my imagination thank you, futures look bright as a bitch, and speaking of a bitch if my life is still the same bitch as before then that ugly duckling done turned into a beautiful swan didn't she man?" Rasaan found it necessary to place his call to Tahj whom he knew was a total wreck by now. So, he dialed then started the car and chucked up the peace sign to the bikers and drove off heading to The Rendezvous. Tahj, who was already in the area made it to The Rendezvous before them was already, sipping on a Long Island Iced Tea when they both made their entrance and spotted her at the bar. By the smile she gave made it easy to tell that she's been worried to death ever since he left to go meet Nahjee. She just accepted tradition, the kiss upon arrival, just as there was a kiss when they departed.

"Howdy handsome," she said.

"What are you drinking?" Asked Rasaan,

"Lerin sprung for me a drink, said something about me wearing my heart in my hands. You would think that if that was the case the bitch would have sprung for a Bacardi Rum huh, the pink cap, the 151."

"Oh, that bad huh, so why didn't she?"

"Because the bitch is fast, she done already put together that I was gonna meet you here, and that if I was gonna meet you here then I must have some work to do. Which, if I had some work to do then I don't need to drink on the job, could you believe that mess?"

"Hell nah," the truth was that he really didn't, in fact while Tahj was explaining it all to him she noticed that his eye balls was swimming in his head, racing from one side of his head to the other, then wandered off in order to locate Lerin, The Great.

"I don't know how she does it either, she could be one of the best reporters this city has ever seen, I tell you."

"Ok, so where is she at now? That's what I want to know," chimed in Nahjee who have grown out of patience.

"She's gone to the back for a minute, she'll be back."

"Ok, so are you?" Asked Nahjee,

"Am I what bra- bra?"

"Are you gonna drink on the job if so, I could get you that fire water?"

"Well, that all depends on the job don't it?"

"A little bit of safe driving is all," said Rasaan.

"Are you guys tailing me or no?"

"You better know it Mah."

"Then I guess a little juice won't hurt, maybe just enough to settle the nerves a little bit."

"That-a-girl," the three left the bar and settled into the horseshoe booth and took light drinks while waiting for Marcel, Scope and Stomp to make it through the door. Tahj was always one for details minus the gory stuff begun to inquire about her assignment. Whenever Rasaan and Nahjee felt like discussing their business in her presence she was most of the time awed by the conclusion. Once Rasaan told her how Marva pulled all of this off was one thing but once he told her that she done it as a favor was a whole other thing by itself. Shaking her head unbelievingly, Tahj said.

"So, you mean to tell me that she gave the money back? Now that's the Marva that I remember, but something's telling me that now we'd need to listen for the slither. I'm nervous, don't know about you two but your friends need to hurry up so we could get to the "Goose" and bra I could tell that you're impressed. I saw that gleam in your eyes before. I would never tell you what to do and even if I did you wouldn't listen anyway because like I said, I've seen that look before. But for the record I want to be remembered for telling you to be careful," Tahj held Nahjee's eyes long enough until he nodded his understanding. Then looked to the door before saying, "is that them?" Nahjee and Rasaan both sought and agreed simultaneously.

"Good, I would love the juice now, baby." Tahj looked to Rasaan with the indication of drink and the other unspoken gesture that only someone of such close relation would have picked up and fully understood.

"No, stay, it's good for you."

"Nahjee, you comfortable with that too?" She asked,

"If he likes it I love it," was all he was able to say before the two men arose to embrace the three men who'd arrived. Tahj forever the lady and the perfect mate for a hustler remained seated and let the boys be the boys they were. Right off the bat Rasaan recognized the way Nahjee explained the reason for the Grey Goose. Scope still wore the look of a non-believer so it was Rasaan who asked; "My nigga is you alright?" Although he nodded in the affirmative nobody in the booth believed him. Stomp was to his rescue right away he said, "I've known this nigga since forever, I'll swear to God that I have never seen him like this before and in the very same breath I would swear to the same God that we ain't never seen a play like this before either so forgive us."

"Well, shit since you put it like that, but know that there is always a surprise at every turn.

"That's why he looks like that right now, he's trying to figure that shit out, that's his "we've just been woo-doffold," look. Never mind that, but now check this out," snapping his fingers and pointing at the bottle he said, "I think we all know why we're here."

"No doubt, my main man you could do the honors," Rasaan said. Stomp obliged cracking the top and pouring the rounds, satisfied that even the lady at the table accepted graciously. In unison the six threw their shots back then laughed once Scope said,

"You niggas ain't gonna believe this shit."

"Yeah, we heard," Rasaan said smiling.

"I mean, umm, it's like, ah…"

"I could dig it," this time Nahjee released his humor. "So should we, you know, get to the good part," Nahjee finished knowing that the faster they done the business the safer everyone would all be.

"What about the bottle?" Marcel reminded.

"You guys could have it," Nahjee said then located Lerin to tell her that he'd bring her back the tab. Waiting until she agreed before the men left. Tahj headed back to the bar, no one needed to know that she was transport.

CHAPTER 15

IT WAS NEARLY FOUR O'CLOCK p.m. the time Tamia and Ruby unloaded the
final box in to the tiny apartment. Both of them were beat, both of them
looked at each other in brand new lights. After conquering such a hor-
rendous night, morning and now evening the two collapsed. A full day
was already behind them. Yet, a full day still awaited them. Everything
was done in haste, by three O'clock a.m. Ruby returned to the motel room
waving keys to Tamia's new place, reminding Tamia not to blame her for
the conditions of the place in the event that Tamia just absolutely hated
the apartment. Tamia was way more impressed at the notion of Ruby riding out to Fresno to grab the damned keys in the first place. She never ever
told Ruby that she had herself grown up in Oak Park. So the condition of
the apartment would just be a condition that Tamia would be forced to
live with. Tamia felt so sorry for Ruby who appeared as if she hadn't had
a full night of sleep in ages. She decided that she would clear off the bed
in the motel room and force Ruby to power nap. Ruby, who was way too
tired to even put up a suitable argument just collapsed onto the bed and
in minutes she was asleep, her soft purr was heard under the fast pecks to
which Tamia slid over the laptops key board with.

By six o'clock a.m. the two hit the door like war horses, armed with
a sense of determination, grit and a resolution unmatched by anyone or
anything. Operating on fumes, a muffin and a cup of coffee they set out to
conquer their busy day. These two caravanned to 'Y' street in just enough
time to drop off Tamia's car which was filled to the max with merchandise

and would look to be just as out of place on a school campus as the new Catholic Priest would appear behind bars. But these two were reputed for their wit and unchallenged intellects, had known this already so they agreed to car pool to school. Which they did, and to the naked eye one would of thought that the Russian looking white lady who took off like a bat out of hell was doing such a thing because she was scared to death of being in Oak Park, where other white people either showed up with all the windows rolled up and all of the doors locked, or they'll arrive with the Sacramento's Police Department to guide them to a horrible scene. None of this was the case for Ruby who was not Russian, though her Slavic features could lead one to think so, but the truth has it that Ruby was Jewish and true Ruby was into Mass and Torahs and things of the religious nature. But, that was about as far as her fears would have it. White, yes. Scary? Nope. Hood? Oh my goodness. Tamia had to wrestle with the idea of a violent church girl who too, doubled as an avid, Wocka Flocka Flames, Plies, Tupac, Jay-Z and Birdman fan which confused the hell out of Tamia who remembered when she once said,

"Girl if you don't give me this canister right now, you're gonna kill him."

"And, that would serve him just right," she smiled to Tamia.

"What did he do to deserve you emptying the whole can of pepper spray on him?"

"He took my iPod, it's in his pocket, hold him steady while I get it back," Ruby rolled over the villain.

"Girl, how do I know that you're not robbing him?" Tamia asked.

"Don't worry, I'm not," maybe it was the fact that Ruby was smiling the whole way through which made it hard for Tamia to believe her.

"Are you sure that you're not robbing him, I mean this doesn't look right?"

"My iPod is pink, with some pink head phones. You're not scared to hold him now are you? I got another can in my purse. Maybe we should soften him up a little more." Tamia thought for a minute that this white girl had to be kidding and because of her thoughts she missed it when Ruby withdrew an additional can and began to spray the unlucky villain, who found it in everyone's best interest especially his, to just give the woman back her iPod. Satisfied with her recovery she returned to her modest and normal self. She knelt beside the villain and apologized to him, said that she was awfully lucky that he was such a fine person or she would of never saw such a prized possession again. Without offering any treatment what so ever, the white girl stood and placed one ear bud into her ear after the other. She scrolled down her play list, pressed play and walked away leaving a wounded villain plus Tamia in her rearview.

Tamia couldn't believe a minute of it, any of it, really none of it but she was already running late for her first class of the day which wouldn't be a good look at all so she couldn't stay to help because the professor in her Neurobiology/Neuromuscular class wouldn't tolerate late at all. In this class late or absent was basically the same thing. It was explained and hammered home that to save a life if but one life at a time requires the super natural, people that possess uncanny abilities to always be available, punctual and efficient. These were the base ingredients that would be compromised by no one, living or dead. So, with this for an understanding, Tamia really wanted to help the villain, wished that she really could oh how God would bless her heart for this one but it was "peace out" fella on this one. She took off in a trot to make up for the precious seconds that she lost and held her pace until she made it through the door of her classroom where she said a small thanks and took her seat. Through her peripheral Tamia's attention was caught by a very cheery white girl waving her arms while wrapping her cord around her iPod in order to put it away and ever since then Tamia and Ruby has been campus cronies. White girl, ahh, and ok yeah this is true but, scary white girl? Shit no and this was all right with Tamia because Tamia only had one genuine fear and that was of failure.

So, for three years and a few days these two has known each other and during this time Tamia has only heard stories of Ruby's family history but never and never had she ever been to Ruby's place. This was some awfully strange shit to watch as Ruby slammed the car into park and ran to the front door of a very tiny house which was not what Tamia was expecting at all by the way. Tamia knew that Ruby came from a financial family, a lot of smart money going on over there, unlimited capabilities and this she knew. Each venture nets large sums after large sums so there was no financial aid for Ruby. Then there were the other signs which gave her away. So, Tamia concluded that this must be some well off white people shit to have all the money and got the nerve to live like they check to check. Whatever, Tamia thought; this is a good person never mind her pigmentation or social backgrounds, culture or whatever. Ruby was a good person and Tamia was glad to say that this is "my girl right here." Tamia thought of Marva and of Lerin. Who would have believed that their girl Marva was capable of such treachery? Maybe Tamia was even jealous seeing that she couldn't recall a time that William performed orally with so much energy while lying with her. Tamia shook the thought away then returned to Ruby. The last person on earth that Tamia expected to come to her rescue showed up to help the emotionally battered Tamia land on her feet. Right when Tamia was thinking that she was on her own again, Ruby not only drove her back to Oak Park, but she helped Tamia empty her car into the apartment. Seeing that no way would Tamia be able to survive solely on clothing, well, there were toiletries Ruby said sarcastically bringing up a bright side.

"Nuh uh girl, you need pots and pans at least. If you don't want the couch that's one thing and I know that you don't want the bed. I mean I wouldn't want that bed either but you're gonna need more things than this, come on."

"Come on, where we going?"

"To your other house,"

"I don't want to see that house ever again Ruby, or him."

"I do, you think he's still there?"

"Why? You wanna mace him?"

"You better know it."

"I'll be all right pretty soon."

"Ok, then what did you bring to eat?"

"Nothing, perhaps we'll order out."

"That's all I ever do is eat out, plus I already found out that black people could cook hella good. So, let's just go grab something to cook before we go to the hospital, at least we could get there on a full stomach."

"I almost forgot about that."

"I don't know how, you only owe another seven hundred hours of field training, far too soon to catch amnesia no matter how selective."

"Shit."

"Hmmm,"

"I was just about to roll out on the floor and catch a few winks."

"Well I'll run and do the shopping, while you knap a bit, but you have to promise to cook."

"Oh my God Ruby, I can't let you do that."

"That's what your lips are saying but the look that you are giving me is saying oh Ruby you are such a Saint and an awfully true friend and all you would have to do is go to Broadway and take 99 North.

"Well that's what you'd have to do but how about you let me just cook for you tomorrow?"

"Pa-lease, girl this is Oak Park tomorrow don't come all the time around here."

It took William all the strength that he could muster in order to get on his feet before stumbling down again. Determined, William regained his balance and felt his way around the darkened room. He waited for his instincts to kick in before he realized that he was inside of a closet. He felt the clothing, the shoes and other miscellaneous products. William felt his way all the way until he found the door knob and relief that it was unlocked.

Pushing the door open the room still appeared to be black, and the hardest thing for him to do was raise his eye lids. "Oh shit" he said to his self "my eyes are swollen so bad that I'm blind." William had to concentrate really hard, for he knew that his life depended on it. William viewed the structure of the house in his mind's eye and his keen sense of awareness allowed him to find the front door. He un-locked it and stepped out of it half way expecting Aretha and all of her boyfriends to halt his progress. He felt the breeze and was blessed to have heard the traffic from the cars passing by.

"Ok, here come some steps, now don't fall, watch it, hold it, one at a time there you go" then he was down the steps. Now his next move was a gutsy one but he knew that it would have to be. So, with one foot in front of the other he walked towards the street. Nervous? Yes. But, he kept walking straight until he was either hit by a car or he reached the attention of some one that would help him. He took faith with him and this was the real meaning of letting the Lord be your guide. Our Lord had delivered William into the middle of San Jose Way without being struck by an automobile though he did receive a few scares from screeching tires and horns blowing loud enough to shoo him back to the curb but William knew that back to the curb was definitely a place that he just couldn't go. William stood in the middle of the street until somebody decided to help him and they did, it was a crack addict that lived down from Aretha who wanted to know if William had anything, meaning drugs for sell.

"Ain't this about a bitch" William said, then "I'll tell you what, if you call the ambulance for me I'ma give it to you for free, you know that I'm a man of my word."

"What the hell happen to you?"

"A car accident, now I need you to hurry up."

"Are you sure, because I could just go to Eighth Avenue to cop some stuff right now?"

"And leave me like this, man you're cold blooded but yeah I'm sure, soon as I hear the sirens I'ma give it to you."

"Ok, but at least get out of the street."

"No, just go and hurry lest somebody beat you to calling them, then our deals off."

"Ok," the woman said then bolted towards her place and later the sound of blaring horns and impatient motorist told William that if he didn't move that they were just gonna run him over. That right there was a chance that William was willing to take, because as dangerous as being hit by a car could be he knew that if he wandered off then his assailants could easily attack him and end his days for him. William knew by the way he was beaten that each one of those dudes had killer written all over them and if they were going to make a showing then they were just gonna have to down him in front of everybody. Then the sound of the sirens played in the sky, William was relieved and freighted with anticipation.

"Ok, I did what you said so what's up?" Said the lady, who had the feeling that she was getting burnt by William, a feeling now confirmed when William said,

"Mah, thank you, but I'm gonna have to see you when I get back." William heard footsteps then he heard voices,

"Sir we are gonna need you to lie down," said one of the EMT personnel, who took a hold of William to guide him to the ground. William felt relief, he felt that by him being in the company of these professionals that he was indeed going to live which was basically, all that really mattered. Before long William was loaded onto a waiting ambulance and was receiving treatment the moment that he was situated inside and to the hospital he was rushed.

The emergency room was crowded; here is where the ill came to roost, at the UC Davis Medical Center. This is the one place that everyone must go but hate that they had to be there. Here you could check in complaining heart burn and leave with the advanced knowledge of terminal cancer. A blood check had checked out to be some other stuff to scare the shit out of you telling you some mess about a suggested H.I.V test. Like they knew something and this being their slick way of telling you while remaining within the boundaries of the law.

The other reason the Medical Center is a hated place, is because it takes forever and a day to be seen by anybody else other than an RN and all they'll need is a decent blood pressure reading and you could be hanging on until tomorrow. For William, who was beat up an inch away from that shiny light, didn't quite qualify him for special treatment. The X-Rays confirmed the broken eye socket and cracked ribs though, so the nursing staff figured that he'd be alright. The suspected head trauma was visual though no one knew how severe with Cat-scan being next on the list.

William had been under nearly six hours and during this time the doctors performed efficiently, they came about as close as they could to re-pairing such a battered mess, leaving all sorts of bandages and stitching in their efforts to send away a happy customer, while William slept through it all. One procedure after the next still William slept. The doctors called him a weary soul, even gone as far as saying that it was the rest that would be his best medicine and the solidifier of his recovery. William slept not knowing the full extent of his surgeries, all he knew, was that they gave him some nice shit in reference to the medicine. The anesthetics were powerful, so powerful that William replayed his days through his uncon-sciousness. This is where he saw Marva, the very person who never really cared about anything, except Marva. He knew for sure that she didn't care about his future at all or what so ever.

Then there was Tamia, my God how long was she standing there watching as he broke her heart with each moment of pleasure. Bigger than that was how she appeared to be unfazed, or even hurt by his ac-tions what-so-ever. In fact, it was as if she has been waiting for a mo-ment like this to occur, maybe she wanted to move on all along. Then there was Aretha, who masturbated to the sounds of his agony, who handled three men at the same time with the expertise of a prostitute and a seasoned one at that. "Oh me, oh my, what have I done with my life" William said in such a small whisper but a whisper loud enough for Tamia to hear him.

"Now that is an awfully good question," William didn't need to open his eyes to know that Tamia was present. So, with his eyes closed he mumbled,

"What are you doing here," even though he asked the question with venom on it deep down he was glad that she came, at least until she said,

"What am I doing here, well this is a hospital ain't it and I'm always here, remember? What are "you" doing here is a better question? Looks like you really got kicked around pretty good this time. I hear talk that someone knocked the memory out of you, or was that just something that you tossed in to avoid the deputies?"

"Whatever man,"

"Ahh, snappy, snappy aren't you, if I didn't know any better I'd say that you sound like you are mad at me about something. Whoa, they did beat the memory out of you, let me go and inform them that I found a full proof way to tell that you are full of shit and that one good burp and you'd be cured."

"I don't have to talk to you,"

"Uhh uhh, noooo, in fact I just came to read your chart then I'm gone and now that I have, you have a nice day."

"Wait, Tamia."

"What is it William."

"I'm sorry you hear."

"I know."

"No, really,"

"I know it just took me a while to see that."

"Are you being sarcastic again?"

"Not at all, you are sorry and it did take me a while to see that, loves blind you know, had I saw this sooner I would have been gone."

"Like that?"

"Mm, hmm, like I say have a nice day." Tamia walked out of Williams's room and gone next door to visit another patient so it was there when she heard William vent his frustrations. Then the sound of a phone being tossed across the room was heard by the whole floor.

"Now that miss Kim, is none of my business," Tamia said to the elderly patient who hunched her shoulders in response then said.

"None of my business either,"

"Maybe I should call security, you think,"

"None of my business, but there go phone right there," Miss Kim pointed towards the phone and watched as Tamia dialed up security to handle the commotion coming from room 402 and hung up.

"Now to you miss Kim," Tamia lifted the chart so Miss Kim could see the evidence to which she spoke from. "This looks like you should be on your way home, you got somebody coming to get you girl?"

"Yeah, my boyfriend, 'him' come right away."

"Your boyfriend? Miss Kim," Tamia donned a suspicious look towards Miss Kim.

"What, it says there that I don't need boyfriend? It says so there, him no more, no good." Miss Kim slid her thumb across her neck.

"No, it doesn't say it but Jesus Miss Kim, that can't be healthy."

"Yeah, for me healthy, for me really good, no,"

"How old are you?" Tamia scanned the chart.

"Fifty-Eight, five eight is how much."

"And your boyfriend he healthy too I hope."

"Yeah, yeah, healthy too, him three five, really healthy, huh,"

"Miss Kim, oooh, you go girl, shoot don't let him hurt you too bad now."

"Ok, not too bad but I like it hurt."

"Miss Kim!"

"Oh, hush, you five eight you hump like rabbit, me too, ehh."

"Uhh uhh, I'm going now, you take care of yourself and stay out of trouble."

"Ok, ok you beautiful, you Gods girl."

"Not all the time, not as much as I should."

"Well, God bless you Tamia."

"I sure hope so Miss Kim, I sure hope so." Tamia replaced Miss Kim's chart then headed out of the room where she ran into Ruby who wasn't cool with the fact that Tamia was holding out on her.

"Ah, there you go, mmm hmmm."

"Why are you looking at me all cheesy for?"

"Is there something that you wanna tell me, that you haven't told me, afraid that I may look at you different, maybe?" Ruby used her hands to communicate that it was now time for Tamia to enter with the missing pieces.

"Ok, you win; I do not understand what you mean, which ain't hard for me to do right now considering that I ain't been to sleep since last Friday. Blend that together with the fact that I just found out that one of the oldest women I know is more sexually active then the both of us. Maybe not you, but I'm sure that she's better than me."

"Ahh, so you think I'm a freak-a-leak do you?" Again Ruby was with the cheesy smile.

"Ruby, with you there is no and I mean noooo, telling."

"Ok, enough of that, how about you take a guess who's right in that room over that a way a bit?"

"That's an easy one I just left from down there, crazy, huh."

"Yes and girl guess who've just been black listed from the entry gates?" Ruby's smile grew broader,

"Me, Nahhh," Tamia began to laugh.

"Yeah, what's so funny?"

"So, I've been kicked out of a house, a relationship and now a hospital room. How does a person do such a thing? Normally it's Doc these pills aren't working I need you to increase the dosage, or Doc please get me out of here, never is it don't come to my room ever, that has gotten to be a first."

"Well the police helped out a whole lot."

"The security, I'm the one who called the security."

"Oh yeah, them too, they asked me to locate you to inform you that you are wanted on the third floor," Ruby finished, shaking her head not believing a thing that's been going on with her friend.

"Gee whiz Ruby,"

"You could say that again, I didn't even know that you could attract so much attention, do you have a gun?"

"No, what the hell I'ma need a gun for, geez?"

"Well, shoot, he's in there singing like a bird, he said that he went to his girlfriend's house, but she was already entertaining some other guys. You never told me that you liked the guys two and three at a time. You should make a movie, Tamia that's awesome; I'll be your camera person you know."

"Girl, if you don't leave me alone, ain't you got some work to do?"

"Uhh uhh, not as exciting as this I don't. What's it like though at least tell me that?"

"I don't know."

"Don't make me have to go and try it on my own."

"Ugggh, you are so nasty, listen to you."

"You got your nerves Miss house full of men, they probably wore gun belts like on "A fist full of dollars" on some shootout at the OK Corral shit, what were you guys doing, role playing or something? I like role playing, let's pretend that I'm black and a whole lot of gang bangers ran in and belt the shit out of my cheating boyfriend and send him to the hospital, now you fill in the blanks, what else happened?"

"You're disgusting, so I'm on the third floor you say, the maternity ward, are you serious?"

"Uh huh,"

"And, what you gonna do?"

"Well, since you're not gonna tell me anything I'm going back in that room to hear some more of your dark secrets."

"Well, ok, see you later then."

"Wait, did I already ask if you were really masturbating while they were beating him like that, shit you're a sick-o."

"Girl go on," the two separated. Tamia was waiting for the elevator when the two officers came out of Williams room in full sprint, well, so much for Ruby learning more about her dark secrets Tamia thought readying herself to render the elevator to the desperate looking officers. Who suddenly felt that the need for an elevator was useless when there was a door that read 'stairs' just right across the hall, and both officers recognized this simultaneously and bolted for the stairs and all Tamia could hear after that was the "ding" coming from the elevator.

Tamia had gone about the rest of her day in an up-tempo fashion allowing nothing to steal away her joy; she enjoyed the new mothers and adorable babies on the third floor. Tired she may have been, even hungry for the muffin and pizza slice wore off hours ago, but the patients kept her going. To this she was grateful and even more so when the bell sounded and Ruby saying.

"Guess what? You and I are having a slumber party."

CHAPTER 16

RASAAN STAYED DIRECTLY BEHIND TAHJ thinking how he always liked the way Tahj handled her business. She never missed a turn signal, she never bypassed the speed limit, and she was always aware and on the lookout for dangers. Never has it crossed his mind to use anyone else to do the driving, and even though he was certain that Tahj could pull it off by herself, still he knew that he would never let her. As for the merchandise it was always valuable, whether it was in monetary value or sentimental value, never the less the values never wavered past the state of extreme. Did he trust Tahj alone with the merchandise? Of course, trusting was never the issue but Rasaan never underestimated the hunger of the streets.

He was thinking about Lerin as he drove, how in the hell did Lerin know so much, she was notorious for her street wit and if Rasaan didn't know any better he would of swore that the whole world was mic'd up just for Lerin. The good thing was that Tahj and Lerin were friends or Lerin could be awfully dangerous as an enemy. Even in his reverie Rasaan stayed directly behind Tahj and traveled just as flawless through the traffic. The music was turned down low and Nahjee was talking on the phone to Aretha which was Rasaan's most educated guess because all he kept hearing was Pirelli, Pirelli, Pirelli, maybe Aretha couldn't understand that someone would pay so much for some damned tires.

"Dog, could you believe this shit, like what the fuck did we do to be so blessed," Nahjee said while shaking his head in disbelief.

"Well, we crossed every 'I' and dotted every 'T' so far," the two found the humor in Rasaan's charismatic's.

"Nah, for real though, I'm still feeling like life is a beautiful thing. Like it's become automatically easy all of a sudden, could you feel that? We catch somebody at their shit then "Bam" life is a synch; I mean what more could you ask for bro?" Said Nahjee,

"I don't want to sound ungrateful or anything because I am but out of all this shit that's going on, as easy as it all may seem. You know the beauty of it and the part that you like so much, well, all of that scares the shit out of me. We're brothers; I'm saying that you're that more than anything, don't get me wrong. Even with the closeness I know that it's impossible for me to know everything about you and it's the same way the other way. So, let me share the little bit that I've been keeping from you; you know the part that makes me my own unique individual, this is gonna just crack you up. Listen when my Universe is lined up like this you know what I do, I panic and get nervous and shit, you think I'm scared of wealth?" Rasaan's smile gave him away.

"You lying, I know you, I could tell when you're playing, ain't you?" Asked Nahjee,

"Hell yeah,"

"I knew it,"

"Shit, you were acting like life being easier was a bad thing so I just thought I toss something up. Shoot, life ain't 'pose to be hard it's 'pose to be explorative."

"I like exploring but I think I like being alive to do all of this journeyman shit, it's something about the air I breathe that I love the most, you dig?"

"Ahh, living is good. Don't worry you'd live forever."

Oh my God, this is wrong hot dammit this is wrong. Fuck, fuck, fuck, what the fuck. Scope couldn't believe it, police on the left, police were on

the right and right in front of them and they were behind them. Oh yeah, Scope knew how to drive but this was some new shit. His car thieving, cop chasing training days didn't show him how to handle a situation like this at all so he questioned his luck.

"Dog, tell me this shit isn't happening," he said.

"Oh yeah, mm hmm, this is happening all right, now I done seen you pull off some nice shit, but I swear to God you pull this off my nigga, I'ma kiss you in the mouth," Marcel said still sizing up the situation.

"Me too," Stomp rose up from the back seat to say but couldn't keep his eyes from the rear window.

"I mean, I really don't see us giving up right here like this but tell me bro, you know me if you say it's so, then it's so. So 'Cel, do you think those niggas set us up though, because if they did I hate to say what I'ma do when I see those niggas."

"Scope, there are a lot of things to worry about, but not those niggas, that shit we gave them niggas Scope was crumbs and a favor to us and nothing else and, I need you to believe that." Marcel finished holding Scope's eyes with his own until an understanding was formed.

"How about we figure this shit out once we get the fuck out of here, because our chances are getting smaller and smaller." Stomp had some other concerns but none bigger than the moment he was in now. Surrounded by cops with a body in the trunk and a smoking weapon trumps the who's, and the why's of the moment.

"I mean, I wanna press the gas but I think that I'm gonna need a little help. Don't stop thinking, because I haven't worked it all out yet except crashing through that fucka up there. So, if anybody sees something else now is like the perfect time to say something."

"Dog, do what the fuck you do and get us the fuck out of here because, I'm starting to get scared all of a sudden." Said Marcel and Stomp agreed fully but said,

"My nigga if this is it, then it's it and fuck them niggas, but the longer we sit here the worst off it's getting and nothing else so push us up a little closer and 'Cel I got everything left, you do your rocket thang over there and Scope the first light you see my nigga take it and if God want to see us about something tell me, what could we do to stop it? As I walk through the valley of the shadows of death" were Stomps last words before he stuck his rifle out of the window and sprayed shots in three round bursts, one repetition after the next, swinging his weapon from right to left, and then left to right until the drum was empty. The sound of Marcel working his weapon was all that remained. Until Stomp was back in business using Scopes.40 Caliber to send well placed shots at the officers. When Marcel finally figured out the rocket the explosion was felt on the concrete. Scope saw an opening, not a very big one, nor even a good one, but never the less it was one and a very dangerous one. In fact, it was the only one the Sacramento Police Department used as a trap, in the event that this stop and arrest wasn't as routine as it was drawn up to be.

Once Scope headed through the opening with Marcel and Stomp licking shots along the way did the police come to life with deadly vengeance? Hundreds of rounds fired at the car, Marcel was hit first, his head was tossed back violently and blood gushed from his forehead and rolled down his cheek. Even though, he was dead immediately, his body was still receiving rounds fired by the police. Still, Scope made it through the hole that offered him a bit of light. Only there were two lights, one that offered them freedom and the other was offering him release of his ghost because even his body was riddled with bullets. A crash of thunder sent the Chevy Malibu through to the other side.

"Stomp, you cool my nigga," Scope yelled to the back but no answer was to be given because Stomp was felled, slumped in the corner of the car. A phone was ringing on the floor board, it was Marcel's, and When Scope swung a tight left the phone slid under his foot so he picked it up.

"Hello," he yelled into the phone.

"Playboy, this Nahjee…What the fuck going on over there?"

"Dog, 'Cel is dead, Stomp is dead, hold on," Nahjee heard tires screeching then Scope was back on the phone, he said "and I'm dying my nigga, I could feel it."

"What the fuck, where are you right now?"

"I'm on 12th Avenue by Oak Park Market."

"Alright then, cool, head towards Martin Luther King, hold on." Scope heard Nahjee barking orders then he was back on the line, he said really slow for Scope to pay attention really good when he said,

"Right before you get to Martin Luther King you're going to see us. We're in a black Benz that would be on your left coming from the freeway, right by the Snake Hills. Do you know where the Snake Hills at?"

"Yeah I do, I'm on my way right now."

"Listen, you got to make the left on snake hill and there's a Benz jeep, a maroon one, it's waiting on you. We're going to run interference for you, for just a short minute, that's how long you got to get out of the car into the jeep. The lady is going to drive you out of there, do you hear me?"

"Hell yeah, is that you with the lights flashing?"

"Yeah, is that you with a gazillion police behind you?"

"You got jokes."

"I know, remember, one short minute is all you got my nigga."

"And that's all I need too."

Rasaan timed Scope just right before he filled the lane so no one else could pass before killing the motor. The time the many cops showed up they were stalled long enough for Nahjee to hop out of the car with Rasaan and push the car out of the way manually, as if the car had stalled on its own. The flashing lights gave the moment credibility and a nice enough of an alibi for the two to avoid questioning, still they waited for the last cop car to clear out before Rasaan started the car and took off immediately placing a call to Tahj.

"Hello," she answered right away,

"Ma, talk to me?"

"Uhh uh, go to my place I got Tamia on the phone, baby hurry ok he looks like he's fading fast." She was off the line.

"See that's what the fuck I mean, shit dog it look like we going to lose Scope too."

"Shit!" Was all that Nahjee could say.

"You should call that girl and have her meet us at Tahj's."

"Who, Aretha,"

"Yeah, Tahj say that he doesn't look good, that he looks pretty bad actually."

"Shit!"

"Could say that again," Nahjee placed the call to Aretha who too answered her line right away.

"Mah listen, something has come up, and I need you to get a ride or just jump in my car and get on the freeway and do a million to the south area."

"Why, what happen"

"Listen, I can't talk about it right now, but take the Sheldon exit and call me as soon as you do that, hear?"

"The only way is to drive your car."

"Than do that and hurry and I need you to trust me on this one."

"Take Sheldon you say, I'm on my way, is Sean all right?"

"No."

"Oh my God,"

"Yeah, hurry," Nahjee was off the line watching as Rasaan was switching lanes as if he was trying to locate Tahj on the freeway, moments later he spotted her doing everything that an ML350 could do as far as speed was concerned. So much for such a safe driver she was. Nahjee was holding on and never said a word of complaint, not that it would have mattered much anyways. Because Nahjee knew what Rasaan was doing, he was clearing the way for Tahj using his horn and his powerful motor to aid him, all the way until they were off the exit and headed in the direction of Tahj's place.

Tahj had the garage door raised in seconds and in seconds Rasaan was through the door first to grab Scope, who was smiling and conscious but awfully bloody. With Nahjee there to help, the two carried Scope into the house by way of the kitchen where Tahj cleared away the table of its decorations, giving Scope a clean place to lay. Tahj ran around the house with the phone pressed to her ear taking mental notes of everything that Tamia had to say for she knew that it had to be something that she could do to stop this man from dying on her table or in her house, so, she tuned in closely.

"Oh my God no, no, no, no, this can't be happening," Tamia yelled into her phone scaring the shit out of Ruby and to Ruby she said, "Girl, I'm sorry, but our slumber party has just been canceled,"

"Oh, why, what happened?" Ruby asked and Tamia thought for a minute then said.

"Can I trust you?"

"With anything, my God what is it?" Tamia remained silent for she was still skeptical a moment then said.

"I need to go and help someone who's just been shot a bunch of times." Ruby looked to Tamia for signs of a joke. Not finding any, she said,

"Wait a minute, I'm going with you." She ran into the nurses' station and cleared it out of bandages and tools that they were sure to use for removing bullets and all of the antibiotics. So much for the "on call" nurses because now these two were the "house call" nurses and neither one of them possessed a license to do what they had both set their minds to do and like rams they hit the door.

"Tamia, are you all right?" Ruby asked.

"Sure, why you ask?"

"I just wanted to be sure."

"I'm cool,"

"Is that why you're driving like there's nobody waiting on you, I mean shit. I'm glad that it's not me over there, gosh, you getting your grandmother on right now girl."

"I got my girl on the phone helping me with the prep work."

"Oh, well that explains everything. I was beginning to think that you were sort of hoping that whoever it is over there died before we got there, this way you won't have to show what a horrible doctor you'd be?"

"Oh, is that right,"

"No, the truth is you are a good Doctor or soon to be anyways I just wish that you were as good a driver because as much as I don't know what's going on I really do want to help this person."

"Which reminds me, you know that we're not supposed to be doing this right?"

"Yeah, I knew already, but why do I feel like we are though."

"Because you're so black market like that,"

"The medical cape crusaders,"

"No, but for real, not a word of this to anyone,"

"What if he dies?"

"Don't say that, but not our problem do you got that."

"Yeah, you're right. I am really excited; we could do this I know we can."

"This is what we signed up for, I know that much."

"Ha, wow this is crazy," Ruby had to laugh at herself.

"What's so funny, the hell got into you?"

"My mother would shit purple Twinkies if she ever hears of this."

"Mmm, then you better not let her find out, look we're here just follow my lead, then we're directly to work, you got that?"

"Yes, and may God be with us?"

"My words exactly," Nahjee was the first to greet them which was at the door. He appeared to be unstable as well as confused to what he should do now that the two arrived, he said.

"Tamia, hopefully and ma'am,"

"Yes, where's Tahj?" Tamia asked.

"In the kitchen, oh my God would you please save him?" Nahjee cracked and his worry became evident enough for Tamia and Ruby to blow past him removing their jackets and running to the sink to wash up. Seeing Scope on the table with most of his clothing cut off of him already, Tamia noticed that Tahj had followed her instructions to the letter.

The bandages were applied nice and snug in order to slow the bleeding, Immediately Ruby and Tamia went to work under the scrutiny of such a small audience of Tahj, Rasaan and Nahjee. Ruby checked Scope's pulse then shook her head. Nahjee didn't know what that meant, but knew that it didn't look good though. Tamia stopped what she was doing and nodded to Nahjee to follow her where she led him to the entertainment center and pointed to the radio and said.

"The oldie station please," then the radio came to life "Nuh uhh you have to turn it down some, that's fine, thank you," then she was back in the kitchen pointing at tools until Tahj was in possession of the right one before handing it over. As Rasaan and Nahjee looked on, one bullet after the next was removed, and everyone heard as they rattled in a cup. Ruby and Tamia made cuts from educated guesses. Anti- biotic was administered with hopes of a remedy, pain pills of the high narcotic variety were taken by almost everyone in the house and then Scope was offered a few. Rasaan was happy for the fact that Scope was alive; each breath his friend took reminded him of Gods works. He knew that Scope wasn't out of the woods yet. Still, Rasaan needed to believe that life wasn't supposed to end this way.

Nahjee on a lot of occasions found himself getting blitzed by his telephone so he never quite saw the magic form completely, didn't get the chance to see Tamia manipulate one of the rounds with a tea spoon, but he heard the cheers and this gave him hope. That damned telephone and all of its well-wishers. Thank you, but good lord how could he had missed such a skill set as Ruby dove in with her scissors and syringes until the repair of an artery proved to be the turning point to everyone's expectations. Nahjee heard the cheers and knew for sure that he had just put his final call in the bag while standing in the middle of Tahj's drive way, therefore he never saw as Scope begin to get his color back either. Still in the drive way he prayed, which was nearly a more difficult task then even calming Aretha who proved to be more of a distraction then supportive. Even she heard the cheers in between being panic stricken and heard when the radio was cranked up towards house party capabilities too and this sent them both a running. It seems as if everyone had all prayed the same prayer, a prayer titled "Lord Please Send Us a Miracle."

"Wait right her ma' and hold that thought," Nahjee froze Aretha at the doorway. "Let me go see what all that's about first."

"Uh uh, I wanna go and see for myself," she contested quickly.

"Like I say, wait here and I'll be back in a minute," Nahjee ran through the door in time to find that everyone held a glass in preparations for a celebration. He sought Scope and found him breathing, if the little oxygen can that was strapped over his face meant anything, then it looked like a good fight with Scope the winner and gaining momentum, in- fucking- credible. Tahj was looking over Nahjee while sipping from her glass smiling as if to say "you missed it" catching that, Nahjee waved her over.

"What's up," her brows came together in concern.

"His ole lady is outside and would love to see him."

"His momma outside," her confusion apparent,

"No, lady friend,"

"Do I know her, I mean I don't want to stop nobody from, you know, because lord knows if that was Ra' in there, Nahjee I don't know two people that would have kept me outside this long, but a lot went down here today and a lot goes down here Nahjee did you consider that?"

"I don't know if you know her, some chick name Aretha and yes I'm hipped which is the reason her ass is still outside."

"Aretha, hmm, can't say that I … wait a minute, same girl from the club the other night when you and Ra' got back?"

"Yeah, I believe so…"

"Oh my God I can't believe this shit, what the fuck kind of day am I having?" Tahj asked the heavens. Rasaan seeing Tahj for her agitations came over and said.

"What's going on over here?" Tahj pointed to Nahjee who didn't know what the hell was going on either shrugged his shoulders.

"Tahj," Rasaan said,

"Rasaan, Aretha's outside," and Tahj took the hunch that her man hadn't the slightest idea to what she was talking about and was sure of it once she saw him as he too shrugged his shoulders and attempted to toss back his beverage before Tahj said.

"Boy, Aretha the one from the club, Aretha and William silly, Tamia's man." Oh now he remembered and the drink that was once going down the hatch was now being sprayed over Nahjee.

"What the fuck..." immediately Rasaan began to explain the situation. Tamia and Ruby sensed that there was a pink elephant in the room with Ruby saying that she could tell that something weird was on the horizon though her exact words being "now this can't be good" each time Nahjee looked over to them then Rasaan would give them a gander.

"Looks like they want to eat us up now, huh?" Said Ruby,

"Yes!"

"Is that normal, you know, regular?"

"Nope,"

"Ok, now I'm nervous."

"Me too, hold up a minute," Tamia walked over to the huddle with Ruby in tow, the two stopped and Tamia said.

"Is everything ok," and for this one question Tamia received three different answers. She heard the customary 'yes' then there was the ever so truthful "no" then there was a definite "shit" which called for a little humor on Tamia's part.

"Ok, which one is really the one?" Tamia said scanning the faces of her friends and anything that she may have missed Ruby was sure to catch. So far the two Ruby and Tamia knew that this joke was somehow on them. Tahj told her that a very abnormal situation was upon them, Tahj also explained to Tamia that the best thing to do was to remain professional before filling her in on the situation. Tahj started with the fact that there was an ailing person in her kitchen awaiting proper transportation to the hospital. And that normally she wouldn't entertain the thought of inviting the very person that helped ruin her friend's life into her home. Yet this situation was not a normal one to now she was at a cross road. Now that Tamia understood the dilemma and so did Ruby, who wouldn't stop smiling until she heard Tamia say.

"Oh, by all means, Tahj let her in."

"Yeah," said Ruby "let her in, wait, first let me get my purse." Nobody was ready for Ruby at all; she bounced around until she was back rambling through her tote. "Ok, now I'm ready."

"For what?" Said Tahj, her confusion was evident "Tamia, what is this girl ready for?"

"Long story," Tamia said shaking her head.

"Girl, what you got in that bag? A gun or something," Rasaan asked.

"Nah, she ain't got a gun," Tamia interjected then said "Shall I go get the girl; lord knows that she probably out there worried to death."

"No, I'll go and get her," Nahjee headed for the door still not believing any of his day and returned leading Aretha through the house and to the kitchen where she collapsed upon seeing Scope, never saw much of anything else but the many wounds, before she headed straight into vertigo.

"Listen I'm gonna need you to get a hold of yourself Aretha. There is a lot and I mean a lot going on here, do you understand that?" He let her nod her response before saying "Good, I have some people that I need you to meet" Nahjee finished then led her out of the kitchen.

"Is Sean...I mean... is he dead?"

"No."

"Well, I need to help him Nahjee!"

"Exactly," Nahjee was happy to see that the two was on the same page. This was operation "get this nigga the fuck from out the kitchen."

"Ok, ok, so, what do I need to do," she asked.

"Well, that's what we're all trying to figure out now, come on." Nahjee led Aretha through to the living room where everyone sat quietly nursing their drinks with the music turned down low enough to hear them enter.

"Everybody this is Aretha. Now umm, Aretha it is about to get really uncomfortable in here but we're gonna deal with it right now though, all right?" She gave a hint of a nod which Nahjee took to be her way of saying yes so he went on "Ok, see that lady over there, her name is Tahj, this is her place and she's also Rasaan's girl of many years and you already know Rasaan. Now the white lady, ahh, I still don't know her name, but you owe her a great big thank you and so do we." Nahjee turned to Ruby and said "Mah, I believe I speak for everybody in here when I say thank you." Then back to Aretha he said "Now the lady sitting next to her may ring a bell, her name is Tamia." Nahjee noticed that either Aretha was a class act with the lying or even stone faces or the lady really hadn't the clue to Tamia.

"I can't say that I know her, but thanks for everything," Aretha was very cordial. "Never mind that bullshit," Ruby was thinking while rocking back and forth doing all she learned about professionalism to control herself. She held her bag really tight and this brought on an immediate concern especially once she blurted out.

"How about William, ahh, do that trigger anything bitch!" Ruby stood with her hand in her bag daring two things to happen. One that Aretha started to lie to Tamia face to face and the second she was daring anyone to put their hands on her before she finished saying what she had to say. Which nobody gave her any indication of interfering, but was relieved truly, once they saw as Aretha collapsed to the floor and Ruby re-take her seat.

"Oh my God, William, no, no, no, this can't be happening..." Ruby was on a roll now so she interrupted her by saying.

"Uh uh, hell no bitch, it is happening. What were you thinking was going to happen? Look I ain't even the smartest person in here but let me help your whore ass out. So, William must have walked in on you while you were entertaining all your men friends in the craziest fashion that I've ever heard of... Then these guy's beat William to a pulp, just a square inch from his life and my best guess is that the same guy in that room was one of the guys who is responsible for a lot of events that happened today. Personally I don't give a fuck, but medically, he needs a hospital or he's going to die.

Now, I know that my delivery may suck but so what; it's the way it is. Does that man deserve to die? I don't know him nor would I ever judge him if I did. Now judging from the likes to which he staked his life for," Ruby paused to look Aretha up and down as if to hammer home her point then said "I would say that Lucifer bought him at a generic bargain, but then I don't know you all the way either. Still in all with just a little bit of brains you would be able to heed what I say when I say that he can't be moved a whole lot. You need to make a splint big enough to fit under him to act as a brace for him to carry. I would recommend a hospital a few counties over or they will link him at the hospital to all that's transpired in this city today trust me, with that you are now on your own." Tamia stood along with Ruby and the two embraced Tahj then shook hands with Rasaan, Nahjee and to everyone's surprise Aretha before the two headed through the door.

"Gee, Tamia is your life like this all the time?" Ruby asked once outside.

"Yes it is, girl I'm telling you, never hang out with black folks, you hear, never!"

"I mean there's never a dull moment. I'm seriously beat. Well, now that it's midnight what are we gonna do?"

"Hold up," Tamia retracted her steps and ran into the house and returned with a bundle of quilts and pillows and tossed them in the car.

"No food though," Ruby reminded her.

"Hold up," again Tamia ran into the house only to return empty handed.

"No luck huh,"

"They ran me out of there, she said give you this," a big wad of cash landed on Ruby's lap, who looked at it like it was a baby dragon.

"Who said give me this?"

"Tahj, I think she likes you."

CHAPTER 17

NAHJEE, FOREVER COOL IN PUBLIC was catching plenty of hell in private. Once again he tossed through the night, even with the fact that he took to the mattress fatigued from worry, stress and from lack of sleep, still rest evaded him. His night was long and gruesome, eventful and it was crazy as hell. The horrors of his recent past still replayed in his mind and overrode everything.

Nahjee couldn't help but wonder how Scope was fairing, was he in the hospital, was he handcuffed to the same bed that he was dying on? Nahjee looked to the suitcase and hated even the shadow that it casted against the wall in his dark room, still haven't looked inside to view the contents to which many had died over. Though he knew that he would, just not yet. His body was tired, his mind the same, his spirit was weary and so were his ideas, sleep was an item that he needed badly but would never come. It was the way that her fingers operated so effortlessly across Scope's body, the confidence that she projected on each and every turn. The way she had gone from tense to calm in the matter of seconds. She was made to take care of life and no matter the life. She left embracing her friends and shaking hands with her enemies both death and Aretha and this was by far one of the most impressive things that Nahjee had seen in a while.

"Mah, I don't know who you are but would you please leave me the fuck alone," Nahjee yelled towards the ceiling before getting up to go and work out and once he found sleep he knew that he would sleep in no matter the business, it was gonna have to wait is what he was thinking right before his phone buzzed. Nahjee wanted to send it to voice mail, everything in his body screamed voice mail, but his mind told him that they have just finished losing.

"Hello,"

"Bro, you are not gonna believe this shit," it was Rasaan.

"You don't even have to tell me my nigga, I think I already know."

"This bitch, I'm talking about fuck! Dog, never ever fuck with a stupid bitch, this bitch tried to run that nigga to Oakland, the nigga in Highland Hospital right now DOA"

"Nah,"

"Now, didn't we draw up Stockton? Something about San Joaquin Hospital, now who said that? We all said that right? Didn't we all agree to Stockton though?"

"That's how I remember it too, where's she at now," really Nahjee didn't care if the girl was in Sacramento, Los Angeles, the Bay Area or floating in a river some damned where, all he knew was that he was too far out there to even care for much of anything.

"Tahj said that she called from the hospital, something about a lot of police asking a lot of questions and 'pose to call back soon as they were finished"

"What, I bet you cleaning up shit right now"

"Like the house on fire, I done already promised Tahj a new jeep"

"Know that's right,"

"I'm talking about, Tahj got bleach flying everywhere, she already looking for another place, shit. I'm proud of my baby though, you seen her acting all doctor's assistant and shit, you see that shit my nigga? Let them had asked me to do some shit like that and we would have lost that nigga a long ass time ago."

"I'm hipped, yeah; tell her that I'm proud of her too."

"Yelp,"

"So, when you think you guys gonna be finished over there?"

"We already bleached everything even the garage"

"My nigga, don't miss shit, make sure you get it all because them forensic bitches is hella good."

"Shit, they ain't better than Tahj, we got niggas calling from two blocks over talking about the neighborhood watch want a call for evacuation due to Clorox bleeding through the vents saying some shit about Osama still alive."

"You see the news?"

"Not yet, but it's all they talking about on the radio though."

"Is that right, it is what it is with me, did you hear anything on your other potnas?"

"Ooh, one was in the trunk and two bodies inside of a car of question they're saying on the radio, all DOA but the one in the trunk they believe was alive and a possible kidnap victim until the gunfight, lot of speculations there,"

"I could dig it, I mean you see that car, like it was running on bullets, it's a wonder how he kept it pushing"

"For real, three hundred and something rounds they say,"

"What!"

"Mm hmm, that's how many shell casings were reported so far that and a rocket, shoot those niggas wasn't playing huh, and they were calling for the Nationals the last that I heard."

"Guards, whoa, the big guns,"

"Yelp, same thing I said and guess what? I'm going out just like those niggas let them bitches come knocking at this door, for real."

"Man, let me hit the showers and I'll holla in a few."

Marva couldn't believe it, she was numb, and she didn't know what to think or what to do. The news unfolded before her eyes. The car was bullet riddled and surrounded by cameras and law officials. Dead bodies were being carted off while a spokesperson begged the public for help. Seeing it, and still she couldn't believe it. No matter how many times they ran the story, still she couldn't believe a minute of it. Four people dead three are suspect until further notice, ok, which three were dead is what she was dying to know. Marva thought to call Tahj then thought against it, as far as she was concerned all of her ole school friends were through. She climbed off of the sofa, awaking Javier as she done so.

"Marva, what's going on, you all right?" He asked,

"Yes, I'm just going to the store, you want anything?"

"You already know what I want, come here,"

"I'm just going to run to the store ok, I'll be back before you know it,"

"Well, ok hurry back I'm so horny for you it ain't funny"

"Oooh, you're so nasty," Marva snaked around him and headed to the door and out to her rental, the same one that needed a payment soon. "Hell, even I need some things," Marva verbalized her thoughts because of all things that she needed, what topped the list was Javier out of her house, somehow his company was more exciting as long as she played the middle between he and William, but straight up was bore city. Drats, she was gonna have to pack him up and quick too or for excitement she would practice killing herself for crying out loud.

When Marva arrived at the store, one of the first items on her list was the Sacramento Bee, the newspaper has often been a trusted source for information which was exactly what Marva was in desperate search of, you know, some information hot dammit. She was in hot pursuit for answers. "Who" were the dead ones is what the newspaper needed to let her know. She leafed through the pages hurriedly until there the riddled car, and there was also three other pages of pictures and gruesome reports but nothing said anything about "who" and her phone ringing was getting on her damned nerves. Fearing that Javier was calling, Marva screened her callers ID.

"Hello," she said into her phone while holding her breath.

"Dang miss lady, you are a hard person to catch up with," well it wasn't Javier. Marva began to smile once she recognized the voice

"Oh, is that so, how hard am I to reach?"

"Very, I mean I've been calling everybody that could help me run you down. I just said forget it and called the cops, shoot they know everything, good thing you got caught shoplifting as a juvenile or I would have never found you, do me a favor and don't do me like that again. First you deny my gifts then you make yourself awfully unavailable"

"Sorry," Marva gave her best innocent school girl impersonation. Her pulse had its own rhythm though her heart had its own melody, it sung a whole "nother other song," one that was spirit lifting and soul massaging.

"Ok, I forgive you, this time, and only this time you hear that, and that's only if..." Nahjee left the rest out there for Marva to eat and she did,

"If, if what,"

"If you spend the day with me,"

"Ooh, what are you up to handsome man, I don't know that I could trust myself around you uhh uhh, no thank you."

"I think that you said that wrong..."

"No, I said it right trust me."

"You'll be fine, trust me, my intentions are innocent I promise, though I do have a confession to make, I mean the moments of my life haven't been so kind lately as you may know by now that I lost a few friends, still even in that I am innocent. Although I don't know why, but I've been desperately seeking the comforts of a woman. I fear because for me not any woman would do, I mean she too must be handsome, not to mention through and through. Her eyes would reveal the truth of her real beauty each time she smiles at me. This world right here would be reminded of a divine intervention because her medicine is pure and heaven sent. I mean pay me no mind, when I say that deep in my mind, I'm nothing more than a dreamer, but in my dreams I chase the best of everything, the best home, the best car, eat the best food, travel on the best flights, wear only the finer fabrics and not one flaw on any of my jewelry pieces, but now this is my dream you know. So, before you poke holes in my balloon and fly me all around 'til I'm out of air let me finish.

You see those were only the dreams that I've run down already, converted into my realities, you hear that. If so tell me, why is it that I was happier when I was barely able to buy a burger, you ever been to Red Lobster alone, ain't it funny but everyone that walks through the door are couples together and for just one fleeting moment they are happy. I'm alone because it wasn't until recently did I see the very eyes to which I love so much, in them I could see the birth of my sons and my daughters and even my future. Mah, since the day that I met you though telepathic it may have been, I knew that I would go a long way to see you smile at me again. My soul has found warmth, but it is my spirit that I want to talk about, it is that same smile which encourages me, it gives me confidence and belief that I could conquer everything when at first it was some of the things, and like you I too find it hard for me to trust myself around you as well."

"Whoa, you don't give a girl room to operate do you, what are you reading from?"

"Ahh, it's because I speak with eloquence, hmm, do that bother you? I mean I'ma go ahead and be for real because that's how I'ma be and note that I don't know anything else, but a man of my cloth if you've been listening adores only the finer things in life mommy. Santa clause gotta bare it all everything from silk draws to cover all's, my house like a castle, my woman once I get one like a queen, everything from the air I breathe to the foods that I eat speaks elegance not because I was born this way, but because I was raised this way, and, to answer your question I am reading from something..."

"I knew it, what is it? It's cute, it's..."

"Not what you think though, so let me explain just this little piece, what you think it's a greeting card or a missive from Michael Angelo is only my heart, you see, when I was a tiny tot to a micro dot. I was taught how to follow my heart and in my heart is a map of my life, my personal GPS you know, and it is my belief that if you were in touch with everything about "you" then you would be able to read the tablet of your own heart too, let me ask you, have you ever followed your heart before?"

"My heart is stubborn, I'm scared of it, and it hurts like hell most of the time." She confessed,

"And if your heart had eyes it would cry, right?"

"Exactly,"

"Then this means yes, you have followed your heart before, it just led you to a dark place is what you feel like but that's ever so not the case, the actual fact is that your heart has been manipulated by your mind, your mind says go even in times when your heart says no. It's the biggest evil in the world, your mind could be wicked, yet your heart would always be a loving instrument, you know. When your mind fails you it's your heart that breaks, it pays the consequences for both lanes; mistakes, no matter who made the mistakes it will be the heart that pays, could you hear that so far?"

"Yes, I really can, and you say that you don't have a woman and that you are single, right. Well, if that's the case then I think I know why."

"Oh, is that so, why?"

"Because there isn't a woman in this life good enough for you, in heaven maybe and perhaps she's an angel or something probably."

"Thank you and maybe you're right, and maybe it was me that has made the mistake this time, if so, please pardon me."

"Oh, and the mistake that you made was what again?'"

"For explaining to you my desires for a queen, when it's an angel that I should be looking for. As I said before, mommy I'm a man of the finer things and to undercut myself would indeed be hypocritical. So you have a wonderful day and I'm sorry to have inconvenienced you."

"Wait, no, don't hang up. I didn't mean it that way, Nahjee I wanna be better and enough, I wanna be held by a person such as the person you explained yourself to be; I wasn't trying to belittle you at all. But in my defense picture men that approach often, and always in their most shallowness, anything low budget just name it. So much that it's hard for a girl to see the difference in selections then in ten minutes you shatter every belief that I ever had in men, because your delivery is so authentic that you are more amazing then believable."

"So?"

"What, what are you asking me?"

"Just to spend the day with me,"

"And the night and the rest of my life to all of those I would say hell yeah, but would that be my heart being manipulated by my wicked mind as you say?"

"The only way that you would ever know the answer to that……"

"I'm listening…"

"Well, you'd have to listen to your heart."

"Oh my God, you're driving me crazy."

"Perhaps,"

"No, literally,"

"Well."

"Well, if it's my heart that I should follow then I may as well be as real as possible by telling you that I have this one flaw that I can't seem to shake."

"Is that right, and you need me to know this so that we don't go in blindly."

"Exactly,"

"Ok, I could dig that, so tell me."

"I am independent to a fault." She blurted quickly,

"I learned that the other day, so what."

"I don't have a job so I hustle hard."

"Ahh is that right, ok, again I'm going to have to say, so what."

"You think I'ma whore hun?"

"At first I didn't but now that you brought it up."

"No, I'm not a whore I don't sell my body."

"Oh, ok, so…"

"Does this bother you?"

"Not at all, anything that I could help you with," Marva couldn't believe her ears, she was playing every card that she had in the fashion of a genius, and she has never shot this hot ever, not that she could remember. "Well, just wait until I wrap my legs around you Mr. BMW, once I juice then I got 'em right where I want him" she was thinking then said,

"I don't know many street people if you know any, then that could help me out a whole lot, if not then don't worry I'm sure that I would manage."

"Oh, ok, whatever's alright with you, like I say if you need my help just say the word, I know how independent women like doing things on their own and all."

"Do I keep sticking my foot in my mouth?"

"Yes…"

"Well, I say the word then, if you could would you please help me out of this one situation."

"Yeah, I could do that, just tell me all about it face to face though, you got that, so my situation is I got a van that I need to take back but I'm having trouble driving my car and the van at the same time."

"You want me to help you with that poppy?"

"Would you please, plus there's a lot of shopping that I want to do, do you smoke tree?"

"Sometimes why,"

"I was thinking we blow the tree and sip the grapes all day until the moon comes, then talk all night until the sun come."

"Oooh, just like me in High School,"

"I got an hour for you if you're not ready yet."

"An hour is fine, let me get myself together is casual all right with you?"

"I'm jeans, white Nikes and a T-shirt."

"I got you; I'll call you when I'm ready."

"Bet it up," when Marva got off the phone she couldn't remember a time when she was this gassed up, so rejuvenated and ready to go more than she was now. Man, was the stars shining down on her in such a pretty way, the only thing now was to go and get Javier out of her house which was exactly how she walked in.

"Javier, I'm horny for you too darling but trust me on this one, something has come the fuck up so, I need you to get the fuck out" and all of this Marva said on the move from one room to the next doing what she called "getting her shit together" and never had Javier ever been dismissed so cheaply.

"Well, in that case I need some money, I mean ain't no sense of me going home empty handed, bitch got me fucked up talking 'bout the light bill and I need to do something about that seeing that I'm 'pose to be on a job and all."

"If you don't let me get out of here either one of us is gonna have any money or any lights."

"Well, I'm not going then,"

"Listen, all I got is two hundred bucks and I swear that I'll give you more later on, I promise."

"You promise"

"I promise"

"Ok, I'll make it work, love you."

"I love you too poppy, here kiss me." The two kissed and Javier dressed quickly and left, Marva thought, the best way to keep him out of the way was to toss him a few crumbs, and seeing that Marva was indeed on her way up and on the fast track too, she better save her a jar of crumbs, enough to keep him gone.

"Get ready Mr. Eloquence, here it comes," Marva soliloquized while looking in the mirror. She added the finishing touches to her appearances, loving the fact that she was killing her "tom boy" look, black sweats, Raiders jersey and black and silver Nike airs, black hat with her pony tail bouncing behind all of that, I mean after all, this could be a White Remy and Purple Haze kind of outing far as she knew and she was surly comfortable and casually built for a real nigga. And what 'Mr. Follow Your Heart' didn't know was that Marva liked the finer things in life too "Well, let our king meet his queen" she said while placing the ever important phone call.

"Hello,"

"Ok, I'm about as ready as I'm gonna ever get,"

"Great, where are you?"

"On my way out to the car, why what's up,"

"I mean, that don't tell me a whole lot, West Sac., East Sac. You suspicious about something I should know about?"

"No, not like that, I'm in Green Haven, you know where that is?" She asked,

"Nah, I can't say that I do," he lied

"Ok, if it makes it easier how about you telling me where you're at."

"I'm on K. Street right now."

"You're on the mall; oh you're already shopping then?"

"Nope, had to pick up the van here on K. Street," now this was true

"So, you're waiting on me then," Marva felt immediately important to Nahjee.

"Yes, unless I need to pay somebody to follow me out of here."

"Where is your car?" She asked,

"Right here with me,"

"Oh, ok, I got a car, and you got a car and a van, do you see anything wrong with that?"

"Ahh, yeah I do, so who car do you have,"

"It's a rental,"

"Perfect,"

"Oh, why is that?"

"Not only do they come with full coverage insurance but they love when you bring them back."

"I'm not gonna take it back, then what am I supposed to do?"

"Well, that all depends on what you say right now."

"To what,"

"Rather or not you think that we could get along well enough to have a future together."

"That's moving kind of fast don't you think."

"Yeah, I do, still the question remains."

"Truthfully, those are my intentions exactly, to succeed at being queen enough for you." Marva smiled at her own wit,

"Great, then take the car back,"

"If you say so poppy,"

"Now where are you?"

"On my way to K. Street like you said."

"Ok, I'm where the Hard Rock Café used to be."

"Yes, do me a small favor?" She asked,

"Anything, what's up?"

"I love those Jamba Juices; would you cop the Mango with extra boost for me."

"Yeah, something's telling me that you're gonna need the entire boost, all that you could get." Nahjee chuckled into the phone,

"Promises, promises," she retorted

"Trust me on this one, how long do you estimate?"

"Another ten minutes or so,"

"Ok I'm in an all-white cargo van surrounded by motor cycles,"

"Ok, see you when I get there, poppy." The two disconnected,

CHAPTER 18

"WAIT A MINUTE, WAIT JUST a minute, I can't understand two words you guys are saying," Mecca said looking from Tahj to Lerin then back to Tahj again, and couldn't figure if the problems she was having keeping up with the conversation was due to Jetlag or the fact that each time she asked them to hold up the two would only pause and then restart the procession of hurried words simultaneously. The jetlagged teamed with over excited psychobabblers just didn't make good for listening.

"Now Tahj you were saying?" Mecca said then again the two took off. Mecca raised her hands and said,

"Ok, the problem that I'm having is that I can't understand what both of you are saying at the same time. One of you are saying Nahjee, the other is that girl and Marva did what to whom, I'm thinking maybe I just need a small nap so I could get past the fact that none of you guys even asked me how was the Islands. Oh my God I could have stayed there forever. I been drinking Rum out of a coconut ever since I got there, man I love that place." Lerin gave way for Tahj to speak and was glad as hell that she covered the part about Marva first which sent Mecca into a hot rage. She couldn't believe for a minute that Marva would stoop so low as to fuck William, who she knew was Tamia's heart. Tamia had never loved any man before him and had never loved any man as much as him since. And right when it appeared that Mecca was beginning to simmer down, Tahj told her about Aretha which sent her right back to record level temperatures, more like torrid or sweltering. Neither Tahj nor Lerin was able to recognize her after a while. Never have they seen her in this light before and to prove it the two decided at the same time that the best thing to do was to shut the fuck up, and they did.

"Dang; all of that happened since I been gone," the two nodded their responses.

"So, does the girl know that I need to see her about something?" This time the two shook their heads in the negative. "So again I'm back at square one, gee thanks."

"I wouldn't all the way say that." Tahj's bravery restored.

"Oh, so there's a chance for me to talk to her then?" Mecca asked and for a response Tahj replayed the last two nights after swearing Mecca and Lerin to secrecy, saying that a promise was necessary due to the fact that she didn't want to get caught betraying Rasaan's trust in her, ever. She emptied her mind of mental pictures, only after the two had promised, she told them about the shoot out and the kidnapping. Told then about how Marva and Aretha was robbed by some white folks at gun point, and how she had to rescue Aretha's man from a high speed chase, and how Tamia had to come and patched him up although he managed to die later on anyways. She told them that it was not Tamia's fault, and that the fault lies strictly on Aretha and her alone. Lerin listened on like "how in the hell did I miss all of this shit" when any other time she'd gotten the news way before even Barbara Walters. Mecca listened on like she could barely believe all of this shit happened in one week, just said,

"Now, wait a minute ok, you mean to tell me that you had this bitch in your house, you even rescued her man even though she's been fucking our girls man how could you do this shit Tahj, if that ain't the most hypocritical shit that I've ever heard,"

"Mecca, I ain't even gone ask you to take that back," said Tahj, then, "Because as you say you need a nap right now so this must be the reason for your selective hearing, but if that's how you really feel, you know, me being a hypocrite and all, then I recommend that this is where we part, because the last thing that I need is a friend who sees life so selfishly as to think that nothing in this life matters more than her and what she's going through. You see, "my man" and I repeat "my man" the very same one who sticks his neck out for me every time, not half of the times or some of the times sweetie, but every time, told me to go and pick up a man that would surely die if I didn't and it was "my man" the same one that I was explaining to you earlier who invited that girl to my place so she could come and carry "her man" to the hospital. So, now that there's a whole bunch of man shit going on I would expect that to go over your head, considering that you don't have a man. And, before you cross your wires all the way up and figure to further disrespect me or "my man" know that I would fly your ass around this club right away if you do."

"I'm sorry for...." Tahj interrupted Mecca by saying.

"Wait a minute, let me finish, before you look at me in any way as hypocritical first put yourself in my shoes, I live like I do and know that I'm speaking of the happiness, baby, is because of the way that "my man" who goes ever so far out of his way to be a real nigga. What he says, he does. What I had hoped he was, he is. Not one time in all the years Mecca, not one time had I ever caught him in a lie or caught him cheating. If he looks at me and say go and rob a bank, well guess what, all I need is a mask and somebody to drive, because I'll be just-a robbing do you got that? Well you should, because if you need to get your hands on this lady so bad guess what you need to do, you would have to go through my man." Without giving Mecca a moment to breathe Tahj just picked up her purse and headed for the exit. Lerin, who heard every word, though she held her head low looked to Mecca and said.

"Oooh, you were wrong, wrong, dead wrong, you sure have a way of pushing people away from you, don't you"?

"Didn't mean for it to come out that way," said Mecca.

"Yes you did, it even had the perfect form when you said it."

"Really, I didn't.'

"Noooo, really you did. I saw your expressions forming before you said what you said. I didn't come close to thinking that Tahj was gonna let you get away with that one, how could you ever doubt her? Tahj! Really Mecca, Tahj?" Lerin finished shaking her head.

"Shit, I just ruin everything don't I?"

"Sometimes your ass sits on your shoulders but so what that's the reason why we all love you, the main reason we're all scared to leave you alone too, fearing that you may get yourself killed but for the most part it's the reason why we love you though."

"And you say that I was dead wrong?"

"Christ, did you just hear the story that she just told us? I mean for real, one of the worst things that ever happened to Sacramento she was a part of. While you were on the Island she was in a world all on her own and ever so dreadful. Do you remember hearing yourself say 'Oh my God Tahj are you ok' or 'what could we do to help you?' Because I don't remember hearing you say that shit either, for you it was 'help me' 'represent me' 'didn't you guys even care about me', while I was gone getting all jiggy with it on the islands, globetrotting, complaining about jetlag and shit.

Before you left I felt like killing you myself over this same person, because you felt like I should have informed you sooner overlooking everything that I said only to satisfy your own blood lust."

"I gotta get him out of there really I do, I'm his last hope, I'm really his only hope and the only chance that he got."

"I know that, he knows that, Tahj knows that, Tamia knows that, Marva knows that…"

"Girl fuck Marva," Mecca interrupted.

"Oh my goodness, you're hopeless, you make me wanna pull my hair out and run away from you."

"I was just saying though."

"Me too, I mean help me out, how is it that you work in a place where game gets passed out and you don't get any of it. How is it that you come from Oak Park where we have no choice but to keep our heads up and the first thing you do is drop yours. And the part that keeps driving me nuts is how is it that you don't have no game but you constantly push away your girls who have plenty of it."

"Bitch, I got game don't even say I don't."

"But I can say that it doesn't seem like it."

"Why you, what made you say that Lerin?"

"Ok, just for the sake of record keeping. Let's pretend that I'm the bitch that got you acting all weird and shit, what do you need from me now that you got your hands on me?"

"I need you to go and talk to my brothers Lawyer and help him win his appeal or get him the new trial that he wishes so hard for."

"And, why should I do that?"

"Because, you know that you lied so much to get him there."

"So, what,"

"What do you mean so what?"

"Yeah, you see how that gives me even more of a reason to stay the hell away from those white people, what is it that you got for motivation?"

"Oh, I'll pay her; Desmond's been saving up for this moment."

"Some money, ok that's a start but how much money?"

"Oh, I don't know a few thousand, five or six."

"Hmmm, now that'll make me think but what happens if after I thought about it and still I don't want to do it? I mean I wanna do it but I'm scared to do it, hell they might hang my ass up over there fuckin' with those white folks."

"Then I'ma beat the living shit out of her for locking my brother up in the first place. Decorate her up real nice and stuff you hear me." Mecca didn't know what to read in Lerin's blank stare, as if she could see past her and through her. It was as if what Mecca had said had somehow pressed a stop button on the whole conversation. Slowly Lerin shook her head and said,

"I told you that you don't have any game."

"Well, that's the only plan that I got."

"Well. I don't see that plan working at all."

"No?"

"Hell no, even if you beat the mess out of her did you really accomplish your goal?"

"Hell, one of them."

"Ha, so you mean that one of your goals are to beat the shit out of this girl?"

"One of them, one of them, bitch that was my first one, as soon as I got my hands on her I was gone ring her fuckin' neck, so much that when I let her ass go she would look like she just left the spin cycle the time her neck corrected its self." Mecca finished,

"But, would that have accomplished the ultimate goal, the one that you are so badly after?"

"No, no, I have to say no, gosh Lerin I don't know what to do I'm so serious I may only have one shot not to miss. I was really counting on the fact that since she's a hoe that she would just take the money."

"Or, she would take the money and run,"

"Then I'ma kill her ass,"

"Then who's gonna help Desmond?"

"You're getting on my damned nerves"

"I know, I'm just playing devil's advocate and the reason you don't like it is because the devils winning."

"So, what would you do if you were me?"

"Oooh, girl I thought you would never ask, first I would pick up my phone and call Tahj back here, and that would be the first thing. Then I would put everything in order starting with my positives, one being that I know I'ma see her again, and then I know that I'm going to need the skinny on this lady, you know why? Because money or the threat of violence never made it all the time, but you know what do? Pressure, see pressure always makes people get right. You know who taught me that?"

"Yup, Nahjee told you that the night you kept loading him up with free drinks. I thought you was trying to get him drunk so you could take advantage of him remember."

"Bitch, those drinks weren't free, I paid for every one of them and would have continued to pay if he would have asked for more all the way until my whole check was gone."

"You're crazy as hell," Mecca laughed at her friend.

"No, bitch you're crazy as hell, wasn't you paying attention to the shit that he was talking about? Shoot I used some of his strategies and came up on some nice stuff. I could listen to him all day and all night but like I was saying before I was so rudely interrupted that I would line my shit up, I would work with the money last, way after I put a squeeze on her. The time I finish with her she'd take thirty dollars and a train ticket."

"I know that's right. The only thing wrong with that is that I'm so slow on the skinny."

"I'm not."

"I know that you're not, by the way I saw how you was looking at Tahj when she was explaining her past week, you couldn't believe that shit huh?"

"I needed me some popcorn for that one."

"I was saying, the look that you wore said something else."

"Is that right, like what?"

"Like where the fuck was I when all of this was going on."

"For real though, I couldn't even believe that shit, but anyways let's say that there's no skinny on the girl."

"Then we're fucked right?"

"Or you could call Tahj and have Tahj have Rasaan call in a favor or something; I'm saying that you never know maybe a little honey is enough sugar after all."

"I could hear that, I mean let's hope so, now I really feel like an asshole for pissing Tahj off like I did."

"Well, welcome home, and glad to have the real you back."

"Ok, now if you could hold this sheet up towards the light you would barely see the ghost figure because it's so transparent but still you could see it. What's important here is the numbers, could you see any?" Rasaan held the sheets into the light switching from one sheet to the next, barely seeing what he was looking for, but seeing though never the less, said.

"You're right, I could barely see them," Rasaan passed the plates to Nahjee, this way he'd be able to keep up. Watching while Nahjee held the plates into the light then said.

"I see them, barely, but I could see that these ones are flawed,"

"Exactly," Rasaan heard Christopher say before picking up a plate to give it the twice over, still not getting it he said.

"I tap out, help me,"

"Nahjee you want to do the honors?" Said Christopher and for an answer Nahjee pulled out his wallet and removed a one-hundred-dollar bill and handed it to Rasaan then said.

"Now, how do you know that this is a real hundred-dollar bill?" Rasaan stuck the bill in the light then said.

"Because I could see the ghost"

"Which also shows up on the plates," said Christopher

"And I see USA100 on the line streaking down the bill."

"Which you don't see when you look at the plates," said Nahjee as he and Christopher waited for Rasaan to scan the plates once more and just as Nahjee said, the line was not present.

"You get it now?" Asked Christopher,

"Yeah, yeah I'm up now, this shit crazy."

"Good, now pull out your plates." Christopher pointed to Nahjee who brought the briefcase to the table and opened it and remove the plates, instantaneously holding them up towards the light and became gratified immediately once he saw the ghost, the numbers and the ever so important, lines across the plates.

"Now, these aren't flawed, uh uh, buddy this looks like money." All Nahjee had to do if he wanted to pass Rasaan the fuck out was stall another thirty seconds before reporting his findings and that would have done it because Rasaan was holding his breath so long that when he finally exhaled it was heard throughout the room.

"Gee whiz son what was you thinking, that he was gone say that I gave you guys the flawed ones too?" Christopher said shaking his head in disbelief.

"Nah, I don't know what I was thinking, my bad."

"What I'm trying to say is, these plates that are flawed are what you gave to your friends back home. They are no good, anybody in the money business would figure this out right away, and who shall ever pass them has a cell in the Unites States Prison for them waiting. What we are gonna do, you know us three, we gonna approach this situation here the correct way. So, we know the difference between the plates, now look at the numbers on the real plates." The two stuck a plate into the air, Nahjee was the first to speak saying,

"Ok, the numbers."

"Now picture every fifty-dollar bill that we print to have that same serial number, could you see the problem with that?" Christopher asked the two hoping that he had them in rhythm which he did, once he heard Rasaan say,

"Every bill has a different serial number and if all of ours have the same number, then anybody in the money business would figure that out too, huh."

"Exactly, so what does this mean?" Christopher asked Rasaan.

"Oh, this means that we gotta bend it over, we're fucked, and oh we have to get the KY Jelly on this one."

"No it doesn't, no it doesn't, and I need you to see the magic in this whole thing. Now, those numbers represent where that bill was made at, what we are gonna do is play around with those numbers, you know, knock them out of sequence and chronological orders."

"Uh, sounds slick but how we gone do all that?" Nahjee asked.

"It's what I do, I'ma printer by trade. My brother, well he worked at the mints up and down the United States of America which is the reason why those plates look like the real deal, because they are the real deal. Now what I'm gonna do is scan these plates and send them to my computer like I was taught how to do. Then I'm gonna play around with the numbers like I said that I'ma do until I could print over a million sheets of each set, now this is where the balls come in at. By now you should be getting your arithmetic together, we're gonna need ten thousand sheets of good paper and guess how were gonna do that?" Although Christopher asked the question loud enough for the two to hear he only drawn blank expressions for a response, remembering that these two were virgin to the white collar stuff, he decided to fill them in.

"Well," he continued "I made a bleaching solution and what we are gonna do is make a small investment let's say thirty-three and a third percent of the ten grand that we need, thirty-three hundred dollars each. I do the work you spread the hustle, deal?"

"First, we need to know what you mean by spread the hustle," Rasaan was quick on his feet, never has he ever made a deal a hand shake or a back alley deal without knowing the whole deal in its entirety.

"Stay with me, a million sets of prints, a bleaching solution, we need paper, guess how we gonna get it?"

"Well, I'm hoping that you're not saying that we need to bust into the mint or something. Because other than that I don't care how we get it, if we got to have it then tell us where it's at," Nahjee said in an effort to get their friend to realize the severity.

"The bank…"

"Oh, hell nah!" Nahjee backed out right away "Dog, I'm not running in nobody's bank, thank you, but no thank you."

"You guys are hopeless; I'm not talking about knocking off the place. I'm saying that we could buy a few bricks of single dollar bills, bleach those, presto there's the paper. In respect to the Presidents and all the other influential people, who were fine enough to grace the cover of one of those fine bills, we are gonna run thousands of each note starting with a five. Two thousand fives, two thousand tens, two thousand twenties, two thousand fifties, two thousand in hundreds, allow them to dry…," Christopher left the rest to their imagination.

"And our goal on this is what exactly?" Rasaan was still confused.

"Nahjee, get him before I stab him with the first thing I get my hands on. Silly our goals are unlimited, whatever we wanna do we're gonna do it; Gulf Streams, yacht boats, your own Island if that's what you wanna do it won't matter, it's all on America and if that makes you feel bad need I remind both of you guys, that you guys are actually a long way away from home yourselves. You know Africa is hell of a ways from here and I was hoping I wouldn't have to explain the rest to you guys." Christopher's words, each one hit the two the correct way like he knew it would, Rasaan recovered first then said,

"Ok, let's say we walked in with fifty thousand singles then what?" Rasaan asked.

"Whoa, could we raise those kinds of ducats?" Christopher asked.

"Let's just say that we could, then what?" Rasaan asked again.

"Then we'll need a place to work, preferably a warehouse with a lot of space. Then we could purchase the industrial printers, which would give us the maximum yields. So if we got those kinds of numbers than those are the plans that we need to be making." Christopher said through an intense expression as if he had other concerns as well.

"Ok, we have those kinds of numbers and we have that kind of space and you have an idea to the equipment right?" Nahjee spoke up.

"Yeah, yeah I do."

"But, you have other concerns?" This time Rasaan addressed Christopher.

"Hell yeah, um that's a whole lot of Money you know that right?"

"Ok, so what?"

"Well, normally the more money the greed becomes untamed. I'm saying, I could work, work, work for days on in, a few shots of dope then I could work for a week without decreased production, but how do I know that, you know, that my hard work would pay me too?"

"Well, let's get it all right, right now, easy it is to just be friends and we could all eat, all three of us. Right now we have an opportunity to reach really high up enough for twelve of us more than plenty for just the three of us. You look for security, you have it, but we also ask for the same security. We need to believe that our days are safe from harm of any kind. There's a gag order that I'll strongly suggest, I have real estate everywhere, I have friends everywhere as well. Rasaan just so happen to be the only one that I trust, I've known him forever but for five years I was doing business under his nose without him knowing because I too needed security. Now for you Chris, maybe I won't trust you so much but I would surely need to believe in you, do you understand what I'm saying to you?"

"I do, so are we business partners or what?" He asked.

"Which is my proposition, security is job one this way you could work without worry just grant us the very same luxuries. Leave here and order your equipment, all that you're sure you are gonna need and I'll call you with an address that you could work from, perhaps you would find it suitable. I mean you could give it a gander and if it works then you could have everything shipped there. Rasaan has a line on a few bankers and so do I, we'll get a few bills right away and we'll bounce them around the country and even out of the country for a test run, if it all pass like I believe that it will then we will come back here and work, work, work like you say. Your job is to make the money, our job is to channel it through our creative ways, so now what do you say?"

"I say hell yeah, and the fifty?"

"All singles right?"

"That's what I said." Christopher couldn't believe it.

"Well, you know that turning that kind of money into all singles would take some time."

"I'm not in a hurry up kind of hurry, but I know that it would be hard for me to sleep knowing that there's so much work to do. With these kinds of perks involved it's hard to understand how anyone would be able to sleep."

"For real, for real," Rasaan said. "Give me the money right now, I'll go and melt it all down to singles and have it done by tomorrow I swear to God."

"Yeah, you sound excited son, but not like me I been waiting for this moment ever since I left that ole grass over yonder where I left my brother at. It was sure a mess out there where you two are from, wowzers, the way the news report stuff from over that a way, I'm almost scared to come down even to work, that ole guy in the trunk shot so many times. What in the hell was he doing in that ole trunk is what I'm trying figure out myself, but this morning there was a picture of him in the paper surrounded by two African American gentlemen which is why I should be saying thank you two on behalf of my brother and my family and his. But that would only mean that you two have a knowledge of this and I wouldn't dare think such a thang as that, never the less without me thinking anything I'm gonna say thank you and to stipulate our deal in case I over look something with security being job one no one speaks the safer we'll all be, right?" The two nodded.

"And exactly how much do we each bring to the table because it seems as if my first deal gotten shot out of the water."

"Christopher, the deal is this, we bring the dough, you mix your solution, go just a thousand sheets at first and we all split evenly, your work, our dough, even split and no words to anyone, not your wife or no body, no matter how bad or happy you feel. This secret gets out we're gonna crumble which is a bad thing you got that?" Nahjee looked to them as they both agreed.

CHAPTER 19

OVER THE PAST THREE WEEKS Marva lived a life that she had only read about in books or saw depicted in the magazines and every day on TV. She had known God before but not like this. Shining all bright and stuff in her life but uh uh, not like this. A lot of people despised the way that she lived her life, but by the way it looked she must have been forgiven, to now she has become the envy on all walks. She couldn't understand most of the hate that she was getting, but had a feeling that it was Nahjee related it's the way that God has made it so, to hell with each and all of them was how she concluded her summations of her past and near past experiences.

Ever since Nahjee entered her life it's been good bye to the rentals, it's been 745li everywhere she went, imagine the heads that turned with that change of events. A fox she was, by some freak of nature she received the perfect mix at birth which gave her a life on easy street and some wished that she died because of this, then, there was Nahjee. Connected everywhere, the packages that she was humping to get, with one phone call she was in touch with a guy who gave it to her on the house, saying something about a player's contribution. Easy street was by far a world class understatement, flights across the country, this State, that State, this club, that club, one jewelry store after the next. 'Oh' her ear rings and bangles and 'wow' was her necklace collection of diamonds, pearls and emeralds. Last week marked the very first time that she'd ever been to a furrier, yesterday marked the second. The first time she left with knowledge of a Black Sable Coat that was the finest one on display anywhere was how the sales person sold them. The second furrier offered up a Mink Coat of golden brown and sported the softest texture that Marva had ever felt 'oh my' she thought of how she would look in that damned Mink, if only Nahjee hadn't gotten his sizes screwed up she knew that she would rock that thang out everywhere she took the beamer, but as it stands she has to suffer the re-order. Both coats bought and paid for, on delay due to sizes and then there was the labeling issue that seemed to be ever so important to Nahjee, in fact everything that they have shopped for bore the exact same labeling that he told her was meant only as a reminder to whoever wears that coat to shoot for his heart as the label read "aim at my love" why so ever was this so important to him was beyond her knowing, but she knew that it was exactly what she was gonna do, every day of the week, and that was aim at his love.

The one thing that she would have to hold close to her chest was the fact that she already had a love; it was her very first one. In her heart she knew that she should let it go, only her heart kept getting in the way. She hustled hard just to be able to afford to help him without jeopardizing her thing with Nahjee, who just two days ago walked her into The Diamond Exchange and ordered one thousand milligrams worth of pink diamonds that wrapped around a band for her and this made her nervous, under the impression that Nahjee was going to propose soon. The jeweler told him that he'd have his order filled in a week, for Nahjee told him specifically to engrave the piece just in case it was lost or stolen.

The time that the two made it back to Sacramento, she opened up the rumor mill that said that she and Nahjee were on the calendar to wed soon, not knowing what she would say if Nahjee was to confront her with it, just as long as he knew what she was shooting for was all that mattered here. It was too much in Nahjee that she liked and was comfortable with to ever give him up and she knew it, her sexual prowess's were useless to a guy like him, for many of nights had he spent the night only to suit up in his silk pajama bottoms and with his bare chest revealing his muscle tone which drove Marva crazy on a regular would roll over and seek sleep. His strut of confidence along with the way that he held her ever so protectively counted for everything, it made her want him even more. The way he talked, he sexed her mind. The way that he caressed her sent tantalizing waves of pleasures throughout her body. Only he always disapproved of any sexual advances nor did he provide any indication that he was along merely for the sex. Now she knew that there truly was a difference between him and every other man that she's ever met. Never mind the coats and the jewelry, cash, cars or the prospects of having much, much more to come, Marva was going nuts and she found herself slipping away into a bliss of love overload. All of which comes with fears that she was gonna lose herself as well as Javier in the process which meant in large that Marva the great has gotten herself "in too deep and way too far out there for her comforts."

"If I'm gonna go way out there I may as well sock it to the trap for all that I could," just in case, she thought, and, by the looks of it she would have to strike with a heavy blow too because there seems to be so much in there, oh, the rewards were plenty. Especially once you add that she now had a steady line on the packages. No, these were her wishes from life; her prayer has been granted for her.

Marva smiled at the thought of catching his eyes roving over her body, all the way from her painted toes to the tip of her head. It was always hard for him to do business with her less lone hold eye contact with her so she never knew all the time what he was thinking, but she knew that if and have he was the type to leave and take everything with him, she was sure to be a million miles and a bunch of dough in front of him, she knew that much. Although the thought of this ever happening was a crazy scary one, and one that had her driving on instinct on her way to meet in a place that she had gone over a dozen times in the past week, over to her old house.

For Tamia, life was just a little bit different; when she awoke her mornings always took a while to do it for the kinks were often hard to work out after sleeping on such a hard floor. Even though she had promised herself that she would put her place together soon, she had never come around to do it, figured that she would rather save her monies just in case another emergency presented itself unexpectedly.

Often were the times that Tamia would find herself drifting through the nights, entertaining the many thoughts of the way her life has taken shape and couldn't help but wonder what was it that our father expected from her before she goes. The life that she had thought of was ever so far away, financially. Tamia knew that all she would have to do was stay focused and patient then the hard work would pay off sooner or later. Spiritually, she couldn't believe the cosmic ways of this world, here she was, the closest thing that anyone could come to Christ like, the old fashioned way 'God' first and his works next and then there was her life.

Tamia thought about Marva and couldn't help but wonder if and have she herself was on the right shit with this Christ like business, it's the scandalous and the deceivers that are the ones that are winning here, the eviler, the more rewards and wealth and all of this went against the ways of her Nana's teachings. Still it was a challenge to hold her religion. It was the thought of Marva getting married, Tamia couldn't believe it, and what was that poor man thinking, she thought 'what could he possibly see that the rest of the world didn't to make him want to marry her. Oh my God all anyone ever talks about now a day is her flying this way or flying that way in Nahjee's car, running her errands, and each place in luxury. Then there were the sightings of the two of them out together going from one mall to the next, one jewelry shop after the next 'perhaps ring shopping' they all say. Then there were the bracelets and ear rings that everybody speaks so highly about. So, whatever was going on over there it must be pretty serious.

Tamia attempted to rationalize with the whole idea and nearly cracked up into a million pieces. 'God, how could the same person that has ruined my life be so happy in life, what did I ever do to warrant such a punishment, tell me, this way I know to never do those deeds again. Tamia sought a sleep that she knew would never come. She thought 'maybe if I do next week's assignment then I'll burn the stresses of her right now's', even that was to no avail. It has been a long time since she donned on her sneakers to run, running was her past time in high school and through her freshman and junior years at UC Davis, but became too busy to entertain such a past time, still she suited up in her sweats and sneakers and ran around Oak Park, this was the perfect night for a run.

The moon was full, the breeze was soft and the stress level of her mind was high. When all of these elements were combined into one moment, a good run seems to remedy all. She wore her Nike air shocks for the red reflector trimmings that allowed automobiles to spot her once the lights hit and just in case someone was driving impaired, she wore her white shorts. In her mind's eye she recalled the news how the events unfolded on Bigler Street where hundreds of gunshot casings were found. So she ran down Bigler until she got to 38th Street, she gone up 38th headed towards Fourteenth where the roads swerved, creating a snake like image which was why the neighborhood called it 'Snake Hill'. She visualized Tahj waiting there to pick up the man who was as tough as nails to have been shot so many times and had survived even if for just a little while.

Tamia hated the mere mention of him later dying. 'Why had Aretha picked Oakland' Tamia's guess was as good as anyone's, whether or not it was the best pick for her, the facts were the brother was dead and gone. Tamia ran as if she was tireless, Ruby said that William spoke really heavy about Aretha living on San Jose way which was where William spent a lot of his nights. Tamia ran until she found San Jose way and Eleventh and then she ran down San Jose way.

Nothing was on San Jose way but dope addict's and drug dealers standing on the corner, still she ran fearlessly and tirelessly and in rhythm. Tamia used track for therapy and her trots still proved to be therapeutic. Tamia thought about William moonlighting on this very street of tenements, both the buildings were cheap and so were the people who sold themselves cheap. 'Why would William cash in all of his marbles on the count of what this street had to offer? By the time Tamia made it to Broadway and San Jose way, she had saw prostitutes getting in and out of cars, drug deals being made in the open, drugs being used in the open with no regards for neighbors no matter how nosey. Tamia jogged across Broadway and through Fourth Avenue Park avoiding the sprinklers until she made it to Fourth Avenue, she ran down Fourth Avenue until she reached Thirty Seventh then ran up Thirty Seventh where she made it to Y Street and eventually to her apartment. Mentally she calculated her distance speculating it to be nearly eight miles if not more. Whatever the distance she needed a shower.

It's been three weeks of rapid running and melting down the merchandise that Marcel, Scope and Stomp had left behind. Tahj, Rasaan and Nahjee spent all day running down their list until most of the merchandise was either traded or fenced, every favor and every stop was called in by them. Nahjee and Rasaan worked "over time" at the warehouse on Florin Perkins with Christopher, watching as he performed one form of magic after the other. Tahj had an idea that something was going on, but didn't know quite what, but once Nahjee gave her one of the most beautiful rings that she had ever seen she found all kinds of reasons to occupy herself by doing something else other than worry about what they were doing. Tahj had spoken to Rasaan about Mecca and her situation and the only thing that she heard about that was that Mecca had to wait until he finished doing what he was doing.

"But tell Mecca that I got her and not to worry" he said so Tahj thought 'whatever him and Nahjee was doing was bigger than Mecca's situation by far. Then there was the big concern that Rasaan had for Nahjee, the streets were killing Rasaan by the way the streets were talking, he wanted to confront Nahjee so bad that it used to keep him up at night. Tahj held the same concern which is why the two would talk on the phone until the wee hours of the night when they weren't both together.

They both thought of ways to knock off the wedding, they both thought maybe they would just get Marva knocked off then the wedding would die all by itself. Both Rasaan and Tahj gave the statute of limitations time to run out on this night, where a better understanding must surface. Not the one that the streets had spoken but the way Nahjee had spoken it. It's the way that it always should be and it would be. Which was the main reason why Tahj refused to sleep until Nahjee and Rasaan had walked through that door which didn't occur until four nearly five o'clock in the morning, but so what Tahj paced back and forth across her living room in front of the television which was on, just the volume was cut all the way down as one commercial after the next played on, each one attempting to sell Tahj or whomever else was stressed out enough to be awake in the small hours of the morning, some goods that may be used once or twice before it began to collect dust. Still Tahj paced energetically.

Scared to even sit down for she may even drift off and miss an opportunity that was too ripe to pass up. As she paced she was preparing herself, the words that she would say, and the careful way that she would say them just in case she was jumping the gun a little bit. She really didn't want to ruffle Nahjee's feathers because of the deep, deep respect that she has for him, the love that she has for him as a brother and one of her truest friends. Somehow had flew out the window all but quick once she heard the keys fit into the door knob, her pacing had halted she heard two voices coming through the kitchen, she felt herself coil.

Once Nahjee and Rasaan was in her visual she pounced, with a flurry of blows one after the other, both men were un-expecting. So much that Nahjee never saw it coming, neither did Rasaan who was took by surprise but managed to wrap up Tahj and swing her out of harm's way, but not until she had scored real big with dead on accuracy. Never once did she hit Nahjee anywhere else but his nose, with every shot.

"Dammit, Tahj what the fuck you do that for?" He shouted through his now blood soaked palms. "Could you at least get me a towel?" No one moved, Rasaan didn't know what to do he was in shock. Tahj knew what to do, but she was damned if she was gonna do it.

"Nigga fuck you, you could bleed until you pass out and I hope you do so I could kick the shit out you!" She yelled at him from across the room. Rasaan snapped out of his shocked filled trance to say,

"Go get him a towel, right now what the fuck wrong with you?" Then to Nahjee he said, "Are you alright my nigga?" Nahjee who was just complaining about being tired was fully awake now, looked to Rasaan and said, "Ra' what's going on over here?"

"I do not know." He said waiting on Tahj to bring a towel which she did. She tossed it to Nahjee's feet while looking him up and down in disgust and said,

"You make me sick."

"What the hell did I do?" Clearly Nahjee was confused.

"Tahj you said that you wanted to talk to him." Rasaan reminded her.

"Well, I guess I said all that I had to say didn't I?" Tahj was still in combat position.

"So, you just bust my nose like this without even telling me why?"

"I did tell you why, I said that you make me sick."

"What the fuck is going on, why you do me like this though?"

"Nahjee I swear to God Tahj said that it was high time that we all need to sit down and Talk, this part was brand new, Tahj you better apologize to him right now, and I mean it because that was not talking that was something else."

"Well, shit I panicked, I'm sorry bra but you get on my nerves so bad that I could choke the shit out of you. Oooh you make me so damned mad I could kick you in the balls."

"And what the fuck is that gonna do?" Nahjee said through the big towel.

"I don't know yet, but I'm sure that it will make me feel better," Nahjee looked to Tahj, the pain crept into his eyes as he released the towel from his nose, he gave the towel to Rasaan and prepared to leave, which he would have if he didn't have to wait on Rasaan considering that Rasaan was how he got around ever since he gave up his car to Marva. Although Rasaan was sure that Nahjee was hurt enough to take off walking, said.

"Hold up, Nahjee truthfully I don't know what has gotten into Tahj, but I know her this isn't how she wants to see you, hurt you know, and neither do I all the way until right now Tahj made me promise to bring you over so that we could 'talk.' I would have never brought you over here for this shit, but since we're all here, I have some concerns, and Tahj has some concerns, but it appears that her concerns are bigger than mines. I'm upset, but I'm your motha fucka, your nigga, nothing less than brothers. Yet somehow you've found a comfort into letting the streets beat you home, so to say. My respect for you limits my ways of questioning what you do with your personal life; I just don't think Tahj shares in this belief. Tell me could you forgive Tahj for her behavior, before we leave?" Nahjee looked to Tahj and said,

"Sis' I've always valued your opinions, even beyond rational ways of seeing things, and even though I'm arguing with myself rather to grab you by both of your ankles and swing you around this fucka like Barry damned Bonds. I just can't see you behaving this way without reason, even though I feel as if 'my personal life' shouldn't be reason enough for such a reaction due to the root words in all of this being 'my' personal life. And this should exclude any and all things, reducing your intrusions to be nothing more than opinions. But, as I say, I value your opinions so, if there is anything about 'my' personal life that you don't understand why don't you guys just say something. Ra' was right; this physical stuff was indeed a bit much." Nahjee finished holding Tahj's eyes with his own and he waited until her expression softened before he let it go.

"Oooh, you make me so mad shit, Nahjee, I'm sorry I really am, I didn't mean to hit you like that."

"Well, could have fooled me."

"I mean at first I didn't, but like I say I panicked. I've been pacing here all night looking for the right words to say to you, it was like the more that I paced the angrier I was getting. I can't believe that you are being so stupid as to get down with Marva like this. She is only playing you and I don't like it in fact when I see her I'ma bust her motha fucking head is what I'm gonna do. Anything that she wants, you buy it then she come down rubbing it in our face like she's Queen of the Nile and we ain't shit. The car, the jewels and the clothes are one thing, but running off to marry the girl Nahjee, hell to the hell no. This is why I'm so mad because you are so stupid. I wanted to kick you in the balls for being so stupid; at least I would have done the world a favor and stopped a bunch of dumb, heartless, evil little fuckers from taking over. Like I say I am sorry because I know how stubborn you could be when it comes to your personal life as if that shit don't affect other people namely me. Try me, I'll go over there and stab that bitch so many time when I get out they'll give me a job at Raley's Super Market working in the butcher shop, and what the fuck is you smiling for, call me on that shit? Like I don't know that every time you "peck" her with some change, that she ain't sliding that shit to Pedro or whatever the fuck his name is. Like I don't know that while you're walking out the front door that she ain't sneaking him through the back door and I hate that you're cool with the shit, and what the fuck is you smiling for Nahjee this shit ain't funny." Nahjee followed Tahj far enough but knew that this gig was up for she had painted him into a corner. The one thing for sure if Tahj became physical with him then poor little Marva wouldn't stand a snow ball's chance in hell, not to mention that his play was gonna eventually call for his friends to forgive him sooner or later. So he knew of no other time to confess then right now.

"Ok, ok you got me, Ra' I know what you're thinking, but it's not like this. How about we'll just all sit down and I'm thinking that we're gonna all need a drink for this one. Tahj you got something nice and strong in here?" Tahj looked at Nahjee's' cheesy expression then said,

"I think that I'm gonna have to say no. I mean if I need a drink to hear it, then, I think I'd rather hear it sober." Rasaan, who has never and he meant never, seen Nahjee this way knew that a bomb was on its way, looked at Tahj with a questionable expression then back to Nahjee, still unable to read anything which was even more frightening because, normally he would be able to. Tahj saw Rasaan's concerns then said,

"Well, alright but this better be good because you already know how I like my Crown Royal." Tahj left the room leaving Rasaan to finish trying to figure what could Nahjee be up to, which didn't happen. Rasaan took himself straight to the worst case scenario. He thought to himself 'this nigga done already married this bitch', but he kept his thoughts to himself figuring it's best that he just hears it from the horse's mouth. When Tahj returned with the bottle and the three glasses Rasaan took the bottle from her, unscrewed the cap and took a long swig before releasing the bottle, then said,

"You already married that bitch huh Dog?" Tahj didn't like the sound of that at all, she didn't need a drink, but she did need the bottle so that she could bust a niggas head wide the fuck open. She looked to Nahjee and with a deadly whisper said,

"Well. Nahjee did you?"

"I should say yeah just to croak you two, but I'ma have to say, no."

"So, you didn't marry her yet?" Rasaan needed to know right now.

"Ra', how dumb do you really think I am?"

"I'm listening," said Rasaan.

"Me too, and I wish you'd hurry up about it." Tahj reached over and took Rasaan's glass and poured liquor in it, and the same for Nahjee then herself. She looked at Nahjee and said,

"Well...."

"Ok, shit um, ok I need some promises right here..."

"We promise now go ahead...." Tahj interrupted.

"You don't even know what I need you to promise."

"Bra, tell us the shit, damn!" Rasaan grew tired of waiting.

"First I need you to promise that no matter what I confess to you that you wouldn't see me no less and that we'd still be brothers." Tahj was knocked off guard.

"Confess, oh my God Nahjee what did you do?"

"Now, that was not a promise." Said Nahjee, Rasaan sized up the situation before saying,

"Did you do something that's gonna hurt us, you, me, Tahj?"

"I'll never do that Ra' not even drunk and you know that bra."

"Well, hell we promise then," This was simple because it was always fuck the world outside of these three, everything was forgivable this way.

"Ok, umm, Ra' I always knew that you thought that I had a thing for Marva. The other day when you asked me what I thought of Marva, I said that she was incredible and bionic and you almost wrecked us into the fire hydrant remember that." Rasaan nodded and Nahjee continued on, "Well in a few words I was telling you that she was unreal, meaning fake. Yeah I knew all the time that she was doing her extras but I'll be for real with you like I always am. That girl doesn't know if I'm a man or a woman. I mean she has never felt me naked or seen me naked not even in my sleep. I told this girl that I knew everybody in just about everywhere did that stop her from her treachery? Did that stop her from plotting, hell no! The only thing that she heard was when I said that I was on my way to the jewelry store, the mall or the galleria. Now, I need you to ask yourself, both of you guys, why was I doing all of this to begin with? We needed to melt shit and you know it?" Rasaan knew and so did Tahj. "Now, let's be for real, the other day when her and that girl got robbed in the park only told me that she was a down ass bitch. She was a scandalous one, but she was a down ass one and I couldn't think of anyone better to carry the goods on this one, and Ra' you already know why I was flying her back and forth across the country. So let's don't act brand new to that all the work that we doing. Ok, now hold on to all of that for a minute. Now let's start with the place. Tahj that was you that said give the girl the place, remember?"

"Yeah, but that was then and she was my girl then."

"Well, even now she doesn't need to know that I'm her landlord. Now the car Ra' you wanted to kill them motha fuckas when they flatten the tires, what makes you think that I wanted that car after it's been violated like that? Yeah it's a nice car for anyone to have. Ra' you said that you were selling your car, what did I say?"

"That you were gonna sale yours too."

"Right, I said that I didn't give a fuck about that car and that a nigga could give me eight dollars for that car, well, that's because I felt like killing those niggas too for violating my shit." Rasaan nodded and Nahjee went on. "When you told me to be careful and that the girl was a snake, you remember that right it was the day she was took for the drop and refused the paper? I told you that I needed you to trust me huh?" Rasaan seen it all coming together and began faulting himself for doubting Nahjee. He shook his head as if trying to erase the thought of it all. Tahj knew a buildup when she heard one; she took sips from her glass pleased at the direction in which the conversation was now headed.

"So, by the looks of things now I could see that you didn't trust me, but that's cool though. What I need you to know is that even though I heard all of this cross shit about Marva, I gave her plenty of chances to be like 'I've done this and I've done that, but all of that because of this', but the only confession that she ever made to me was that she's independent and that she's a hustler. Not that she was remorseful about the people that she hurt or the lives that she ruined no. Her confession was that she was a hustler. Now had she come clean; I swear I would have spared her. So by saying that, I gotta tell you that I've done something a few days ago that is so unlike me and everything that I say after this is gonna be so unlike me. Ok, so there's this girl, a woman really, I mean every day I think of her. I could never go to sleep without wishing for her to see me like I see her. Since the very first time that I saw her she's been killing me soft, the way she wears her hair, the shape of her fingers. She wore a perfume scent a month ago and I could still smell the scent of her as if she's in the kitchen right now."

"Oh my Gosh," Tahj stood up, "its Tamia ain't it?"

"How did you know?" Nahjee confessed.

"What the fuck! How the hell! Hell naw." Rasaan didn't know what to say, but Tahj did.

"I knew it!" she said jumping up and down in her happy dance "I knew it, I knew it, and I knew it."

"Yeah, it's Tamia, the other day when she was here working on Scope I felt suffocated in her presence, I never felt so nervous in my whole life. Each time she comes around it normally takes me days to rid myself of anxiety enough to go to sleep. I saw how her life has been wrecked by Marva and William so much that it hurt me inside as well and I really took it personally a little bit."

"Uh oh." Was all Rasaan could think to say, but not Tahj though.

"Bra, what did you do? Where is Marva?"

"Tahj, contrary to popular belief I have never killed anyone. Sure I took it personal because even though I don't know Tamia so much, somehow her enemies became mine, her friends became my friends. Somehow I wish her dreams and aspirations were also mine."

"Ok, I still have the same question, where the hell is Marva?" Asked Tahj,

"Where is Marva, as far as I know she's at home?"

"Um kay, and?" Tahj needed more clarification.

"And you wanna know the trap that I set for her don't you?"

"Yeah, that's what I wanna know," said Tahj.

"Hell, me too," Rasaan always liked how Nahjee formulated his paybacks.

"Ok. A few days ago I got a call from Mecca and Lerin, both of them were in the market to talk to Aretha so tough that they were beating down aisle five saying something about Aretha being the reason that Mecca's brother is doing three dimes and an eight piece in the pokey. Lerin was looking for the skinny on Aretha and I didn't see any way to help only calling a favor was all that I could think at the time. So, Lerin reminded me of a conversation that we shared about pressure. I had told her that it was pressure that could push water up a hill a long ass time ago and she called me on that shit."

"Rasaan remember when I told you that Mecca needed to speak with you, well this is what it was about." Tahj reminded him and he nodded his affirmations.

"Anyways," Nahjee went on "something kept bugging me about the way Scope died because if Tamia and her friend felt that it was something that Aretha needed to be careful with doing then they would have hipped her to it. I'm sure they would have told her how to manage and what to look for, something about the intelligence in those two, just seemed unwavering. So I had my lawyer call down to Oakland to find what he could, and he scored on the autopsy and guess what the autopsy came back with?" The two suspected the worst, but said nothing. "It seems Scope died of

Suffocation and I sort of believe that Aretha killed him and if so, I wonder why. I didn't know then nor do I know now far as I know he asked her to do it, but that's how he died. So I get back on the phone with Mecca and told her to go visit her brother and tell him not to worry much longer, that I drew up something that may bust him out of there. I told Mecca that it would definitely have to go favor for favor. She has a problem with Aretha and I have a problem with Marva, if she could help me with Marva then I'll press Aretha, do you follow me so far?"

"Uh uh, what does all of this have to do with where's Marva?" Tahj needed to know.

"Tahj, far as I know Marva's at home bagging up her hustle so she could take to the prison, you know how she do."

"So, now you got Mecca's brother hustling for you. Is that it?" Tahj took on a despicable look as if accusing Nahjee of stooping so low.

"I don't got Mecca's brother doing shit, but Marva has been taking him packages for a while now. I just asked Mecca to find a way to interrupt that is all and just yesterday she said that she worked it all out, something about one of the officers had a crush on her up there and would be there to wait on Marva to show with the goods. Her brother is set to refuse the order and walk away from Marva, see the trap in that? Mecca said that her brother saved a few pennies, that he was saving to make sure his lawyer stayed paid up for his appeal, some oriental dude that was good a long time ago, but so bummed out now that it's a wonder that he's on his shit like they think he is. So now that you hear that, you mad at me still?"

"Hell naw that's what that bitch get, now here I was thinking you was kissing her ass but here you were killing her ass. See that's why you're my bra bra. I love you so much I just knew that you lost your motha fucking mind getting ready to marry that bitch, man I was spooked. Don't do me like that no more," rattled Tahj.

"Tahj, I don't even know where the marriage shit came from; I'm just scared to death that Tamia probably heard that shit."

"Oh, she has. She was pissed more than me." Tahj said.

"So, you've been holding on to all this shit and you didn't even include me on none of this shit, how long you been carrying on like this?" Rasaan wasn't as forgiving as Tahj.

"Ra' you never asked don't blame me. When I'm curious about something I always ask. If I felt like I was gone be pissed off I'm still gon' ask, it ain't my fault bro. I'm the one that told you to trust me."

"Anyways, so at the club it was Tamia that gave you that struck by lightning look and not Marva then?"

"Those red bangles were driving me nuts; you think I'm a sucker now huh?"

"Nah, so why send Marva the Dom, especially the Rose' then?" Nahjee wasn't all the way off the hook, Rasaan needed more before deciding.

"What, play boy I sent that out to Tahj and lady red bangles."

"Forget all of that, what are you gonna do about Tamia," asked Tahj.

"Well, if she already got her hands on the bullshit, then I don't see me doing no smoothing over any time soon. Especially if she's more pissed off then you Tahj, we see how that worked out. I may as well just hang it up if that's the case. I just couldn't pass up the moment to let Marva know what it felt like to love something so much or to cherish something so badly, only to have someone else come and take that away from you out of spite and without reason. Ra' you should have seen the energy that I put into that girl, you would have really gone Ape shit, I mean I got her nose wide enough to park a fleet of school buses. She's been putting the moves on me dreaming of sexing me and I ain't ever budged. She said that I confuse her, I'm different, unlike anybody that she's ever met. She said that I give her chills when I'm not around, what you think of that? She often reminds me of a married life, ooh, I'll die first, but somehow the rumor hit once we made it back from the Diamond Exchange, where I was getting Tamia a ring made."

"What the fuck, ring, my goodness, you do got it bad." Tahj knew the symptoms.

"Girl, you heard me. Shoot, you think that's something it's Minks and Sables and a whole bunch of more shit coming, I'm talking about I bought something every time that I thought about it, but now that was all part of the buildup."

"A ring bra- bra" Tahj was excited.

"Yep, five caret Pink Diamond, Princess cut."

"Hmm. Better than the one that you gave to me, better not be bastard."

"The one that I gave you was flawed, now, this all pink thang, flawless."

"Oooh, you shit, I'm not even mad at you though, I'm mad at Rasaan, he better get it right pretty soon. What I want to know is not only how but when you're gonna approach Tamia?"

"I ain't got the slightest idea, I mean if she's pissed and all..."

"Uh uh, leave that up to me, I'll handle it from here."

"Tahj," Rasaan interjected.

"No, actually it's a good idea, if you could; bring her over to my place after Marva leaves to go do her sneaky poo poo, could you do that? If so, then I'll forgive you for busting my nose."

CHAPTER 20

THE TIME RASAAN DROPPED NAHJEE off in front of his BMW it was nearing Seven o'clock in the morning; once again sleep has avoided him. Marva saw as Rasaan pulled up, release Nahjee from the car, and then pulled away. This was one of the things that Marva liked in Nahjee, he respected her space. He was the type that would call before he'd come by, each time without fail. What Nahjee didn't know was that Marva spent most of the night thinking about him, she concluded that Javier would never rid himself completely of his baby's mother; she even felt it necessary to knock off her hustling, it was something about all the sneaking that she was beginning to feel uncomfortable with.

Marva made herself a promise that she was gonna be a better person and a suitable enough mate for Nahjee. It was the slow songs that played through the night that helped her realize that she really found something strong enough to hold on to forever. When Nahjee rang the doorbell Marva found that she was quick to get it open, she wanted to tell him that she was on her way to a prison, which was really how she got rid of her packages. She knew that Nahjee never cared how she got her dough as long as she wasn't whoring around; she was, but so what. What he didn't know shouldn't hurt was how she saw life before, but not now, Marva wanted to brief Nahjee on it all and she was, but, once she got back.

"Look at you, looking all tired and stuff, did you over work yourself again?" she asked and for a response he nodded.

"Do you want me to cook you something to eat before I go?"

"No, where you going?"

"I need to run a few errands before it gets too late in the afternoon; by the looks of it you need a power nap anyways. Don't worry; I'll be back before you wake ok honey?"

"Mm hmm, do you have to go though?"

"Yes, I have an important meeting that I need to get to and I have some very important stuff that I need to talk to you about when I get back, it's pretty serious and I'm scared a little."

"And, we can't talk about that right now?" Nahjee tried to give her one last try, in fact his body screamed 'lady now is the time and no other' found himself shaking his head once he heard Marva say,

"Nah, it could keep until I get back, but barely. You go ahead and rest, sweetie you look beat, I'll see you when I get back, ok?"

"Of course, ok then, I guess I'll see you later then." Nahjee headed for the room where he collapsed on to his old bed that's been passed down to Marva and lord knows who she passed it down to. Never the less he lay in the bed with his eyes wide open. He waited until he heard the car start up and drive away with the music blaring before rolling over. Nahjee thought of the last conversation that he shared with Marva the other night; he told her that he was the type of person that would never let the primitives push him off his square, ever. He told her that he knew people everywhere. People that do everything, he shared stories with her that spoke of Cancun Mexico, and of Rome, of Paris and of England, but he also saw when his words flew through her head without stopping.

The point that he was trying to make was that it took game to get to those places, which should have told her that he had a whole lot of game, but it didn't. Because she only heard and paid attention to the down payment that he said that he was gonna put on that new Bentley thang. He told her that he had so many connections due to the fact that he eat these streets, breathe these streets and drink these streets. Did she take for knowledge that Nahjee had sent a guy through to grant her a free ride no matter where with the packages, no. She was selling herself short on all turns and overlooking the big prize, because her eyes where always on the little bitty small rewards and this made her very ugly.

The way Tahj was bamming on Tamia's door so early in the morning, Tamia's whole apartments should have become rudely awakened. It took a minute for Tamia to get to the door, but once she did, she wore two looks that Tahj was aware of. One was a look that Tahj knew ever so well, that Tamia had cried herself to sleep, and the other look was of strict confusion.

"Girl I need you to get dressed right away." Tahj said hurriedly overlooking her revelations.

"Tahj, what the hell are you doing here, what time is it?"

"I don't have a lot of time to explain, but I need you to come on, you could get dressed in the car." Tamia looked past Tahj into the black car that she came in and said,

"Girl ain't that Rasaan in the car?"

"Alright scratch getting dressed in the car, but I need you to toss something together and please hurry up and come on."

"Tahj you are scaring me." Tamia backed away.

"Tamia, I'll cut you deep if I have to ask you to come on one more time."

"Well, gee, in that case let me put on my shoes, but do tell me am I being kid napped or can I at least know where I'm going."

"You, my sister, is on your way to Paradise."

"Yay, I mean I've never been to Paradise before what should I wear?"

"Would you come on? Mecca and Lerin is already gone and we sort of need to beat them there."

"And where is there?"

"Green haven, we need to get to Green Haven in a hurry, so um, Tamia, would you please just get your shoes and come on with me."

"I thought you said that I was going to Paradise." Tahj fished through her purse and Tamia couldn't help but to laugh at the Thought of Tahj searching for her knife said, "Hold on, here I come."

Rasaan drove through the traffic with expertise, all the way to Green Haven, while Tamia sat in the back seat and wondered just where in the hell was they really going, but as long as Tahj and Rasaan was with her, she knew that it couldn't be anywhere harmful, then recalled her words immediately once Rasaan pulled into the condominiums that she knew Marva lived in.

"Tahj, what you guys doing?"

"Just come on, I need you to trust me ok," the three got out of the car and ran up the steps together and waited as Rasaan rang the doorbell, moments later Nahjee opened the door to see Tamia standing next to Tahj, the two locked stares.

"You guys come inside, Tamia I got to say thank you for coming, I know that this is all a surprise to you."

"It is, what's going on here?" For an answer Nahjee swung the door open and stepped into the interior of the house to allow the three to gain entry. Tamia's gestures of rebellion were questioned by Nahjee who said,

"I could tell that you don't want to be here." Tamia held his eyes then said,

"I know that Marva lives here, and I wish to go."

"Wait a minute Nahjee" said Tahj, then to Tamia she said "Tamia, you can't think of the first time that I ever bullshitted you and I promised that I would never. Girl, but now is the time for you to listen ok. Um, you see, this isn't Marva's house, this house and the other three around it are his, he let Marva rent as a favor to me. Tamia, Nahjee as you know is like a brother to me and I've known something has been going on with him for a while now and I just learned earlier today that his illnesses comes from the fact that I think that he's in love with you, not Marva girl. What he's done here I'm so embarrassed to say, but this idiot decided to put some stuff on Marva due to the fact that she found it so easy to sock it to you. It was all crazy when I heard it and I trust that you would call him an idiot too, but anyways he done built a whole world around that girl only to snatch it away from her sort of like what she did to all of us. However, I'm sure that he's worth the listen if you decide to."

"Tamia, from the first time I saw you, I knew that I was made to love you. When you come around, I can't breathe freely, eat with satisfaction or sleep. I made wishes that you didn't hurt so much and that your focus would never stray due to your pains. The way that you look at me, there I could see the truth when I look in your eyes, I feel so vibrant and alive and, like I got my own heaven, you know? I reflect on the day that I heard your name for the first time, it's been like a love song that plays over and over in my head ever since. Ma' I could go anywhere and do anything, but in my heart I know that I wouldn't be happy or complete in the process if you weren't there with me. I've sought far and wide for eyes like yours, the very eyes that hold my future. Never mind my immaturity when it comes to Marva, I just needed her to know that rewards come from doing good, and she is bad. If you could forgive me, I'll promise that such the immaturity would fail to resurface."

"Ahh, if that wasn't some holy pimping, some designed macaroni Tony around this motha fucka," Rasaan has never had the chance to see Nahjee express his self in this fashion.

"What are you, some kind of ladies' man or something?" Tamia asked.

"You mean like a womanizer?" Tamia nodded her head.

"Uh uh, girl, I vouch for this one." Tahj followed the conversation like the line judge at the French open. Tamia turned to Nahjee and said,

"How come you never said anything then?"

"Hell, if I had known what to say I probably would have said something, I just found out today that my time ran out, and had to do something, anything and really fast too. I mean, now that it's the end of the game the timing proves to be perfect."

"What you mean by that," said Tamia, then the door bell sounded off.

"Hold on for a second," Nahjee ran to the door and opened it to the loud voices of Lerin and Mecca who jumped into Nahjee's arms before going to greet the others. Mecca stepped away from Tahj and turned to Tamia and said,

"Bitch, I know that you ain't in here playing hard to get is you, because I know your ass."

"Nuh uh, bitch I ain't playing nothing." Tamia said to Mecca, then to Nahjee she said, "What did you mean by the end of the game?" Again the door bell and again Nahjee ran to the door only to return holding a box, he sat it down then said,

"What I was trying to say..." Again the sound of someone at the door, "Shit, hold on a sec," and again Nahjee ran to the door and again he returned with a box. Mecca was the first to address the pink elephant in the room by saying,

"What is in the boxes?" She came to stand in front of the boxes, curiosity told her to open one and she did and pulled out the loveliest coat that anyone had ever seen.

"What the fuck," was all Mecca could say, not Tahj though who said to Tamia, "Girl you better get your coat." Tamia's eyes lit up and she walked into the coat, Nahjee saw that he was just an inch or two off with his measurements. Tamia's breath was taken away from her as she turned around for all to see, while everyone applauded her. She took the jacket off and, Nahjee said.

"Please, try this one. I'm curious to know how far off I am, I missed a little on that one?" And they all watched as Tamia tore open the other box and pulled out the Sable coat, this time she let Nahjee put the coat on her while tears filled the wells of her eyes. She mumbled the words thank you to him; the two was ready to kiss, when the doorbell rang again. Nahjee who grew tired of that bullshit, just turned to Tamia and said "I think that's for you too," they watched as Tamia walked to the door and this time she returned with two boxes, she held one in each hand. Everyone in the room wanted to know what the hell was in the boxes, but didn't care as much once Nahjee came back into the room with Marva's jewelry box and opened it. Tamia knew that she would never wear anything of Marva's, until Nahjee pulled off the coat and showed her the labels.

"Aim at My Love," Tamia didn't get it so Nahjee told her to follow the banner from right to left and she did, then it all made sense. The twisting banner like label made it simple to read, the banner was made to go right to left on top and left to right on the bottom "Tamia My Love," it read then Nahjee opened up the jewelry box, everyone grabbed pieces and read the clips for stamps and each one of Marva's prized possessions bore the same exact stamp, that when read correctly said, "Tamia My Love." Lerin looked around the room until she settled in on Nahjee and said,

"Now how long has this been going on?" then "Ain't this about a bitch?"

"Well, it took a couple of weeks for the coats, a few weeks for the necklaces and a few weeks for the ring and the ear rings." Everyone's attention had gone into the jewelry box, not seeing any rings or ear rings just necklaces. Nahjee pointed to Tamia, who was swimming by now, just handed the boxes to Nahjee who opened the smallest box, which bore the ear rings, four hundred milligrams of pink diamonds that he placed merrily into her ears. Again the room became elated, Nahjee then opened up the other box before showing it to her he said,

"I am mindful to the pains that you've endured, it is said that the hotter the heat, the harder the steel, the more pressure to coals, the finer the diamonds, I have in my hand Mah, a promise, that I would never intentionally hurt you. I will never desert of give you any less than my all, and I say these words in front of Rasaan who is like a brother to me, in front of Tahj, who is like a sister to us both, and in front of your friends, though one hurt you, allow us to restore you, and in my hands is more than a promise, but a wish that you would be my wife forever and ever. Until death has separated us and until death I will be everything I say I am. You could deny and I'd feel no different than I do right now for if God wanted me to be happy he would deliver you. Before I show you I need to ask you, would you marry me?" The room fell silent and the only thing that Tamia could do was cry, then the room began to chant. "Go, go, go, and go." Through her tear filled eyes Tamia said,

"Yes!" and the room erupted, so Nahjee opened the box and removed the ring, Tamia offered him her finger, then marveled at the sight of the pink diamonds that had wrapped themselves around the band. Her fingers were thin and the ring fit loosely but inside was a card which invited her to go and have her ring fitted to her size, the same went for the coats. Lerin walked up to Tamia and said, "You are a lucky bitch, what did I tell you, tell me that I don't know my shit."

"Nah, girl you know your shit, I ain't never doubted that for a minute."

"So, are we gonna kick it tonight at Club Rendezvous or what?" Mecca yelled over the commotion. Nahjee and Rasaan didn't know what to say, because as far as they knew they had work to do.

"Ra'," said Nahjee.

"I'm thinking we should treat Chris to a good time," said Rasaan.

"Hell yeah, let's do it, I'ma only get married one time huh?"

"May God be with you bro."

"Right now I'm sure that he is, I'm sure of it." The room grew loud, then awfully quiet once the phone began to ring. All of those present looked at the phone like it was the boogey man calling. Nahjee slid next to Tamia and said,

"Mommy you know that's for you right, however you behave yourself is all right with me."

"Who is it? You think it's Marva?"

"Member the end of the game that I was telling you about, well there it goes." The phone stopped ringing, then moments later the ringing resumed and the whole room waited as Tamia gone to the phone and picked it up and said,

"Hello." She listened as the operator gave her instructions to follow in order to process the call. "Hello" she said again then "Marva where are you? In jail, what the hell are you doing in jail, wait a minute you have to stop screaming or I'm not gonna be able to hear you. Who's all here, well it's me, Tahj, Lerin, Mecca, Rasaan and Nahjee. What you mean what are we doing? Well, first we were celebrating the fact that me and Nahjee are getting married, wow these coats, you should see them, but never mind me, this is bad. What are they gonna do with you? Huh, get out of your house? Oh my, Marva I just found out that this house really belongs to Nahjee or did you know that? Girl me either, now if that wasn't some slick stuff, you already know how good Tahj is at keeping a secret, I would have never known. So now that I got the coats, the jewelry, the man and the house, I'ma take a wild guess and say that you left all of your money hid somewhere in here, huh?" Tamia moved the phone from her ear as Marva screams was heard clearly through the room, "I'ma take it that is a yes, I'll tell you what, if you tell me where it's at, I'll give you some of it back. If I have to find it myself, then I'ma blow it all on shoes, me, Tahj, Mecca and Lerin. You better hurry up and tell me because they all done took off on their scavenger hunts. I'm sure that they'll find it. Fuck me? Well alright then take care of yourself ok... Oh. Well." Tamia said, "I think she hung up on me."

"Got it," came the sound from the room and Lerin came in with a shoe box saying, "I wish people stop working these damned shoe boxes." Lerin emptied the box of its contents. "Girl is you sure we're going shoe shopping?"

"You guys go ahead, it's all on Marva I told you that she had our backs."

"Tamia, make sure that she got our backs, but way back there?" Mecca said, then "this is enough to pay my brothers lawyer." The room grew quiet again, sensing that their shopping spree has just been canned.

"Well, we may as well." Said Lerin,

"Hold up a minute," Nahjee left and came back with a number scrawled on a piece of paper and said, "Like I said, favor for a favor. Have your brother get in contact right away? Aretha would play her part don't worry about that." He finished.

"Well, I want to know the squeeze that you put on her, I mean I just have to know," said Lerin with more excitement than she intended.

"Mah, I want to, but I can't tell you. I already gave my word, but she really got us though, you trust me?"

"You know what, I love real niggas, but sometimes they get on my mother fucking nerves." Lerin said and stomped off. Mecca couldn't believe it so she said,

"Nahjee, is this guy any good though?"

"Mah, he's one of the best in the country, the crack lawyer that you have, no offense but we'll get you a refund, just get ready to have your brother back, trust me alright?"

"Are you serious, I mean please don't play with me like that, please don't. I can't take it Nahjee for real." And for real Nahjee, stared at Mecca. Tamia watched, Tahj just shook her head then Nahjee said.

"Mah, I know that you don't know this about me, so I'ma hip you to me, never do I ever make a promise that I can't or won't be able to keep and never and I mean never do I ask someone to trust me if I couldn't be trusted, as I said, you need to get yourself ready to have your brother back and again I'm gonna ask you to trust me." Mecca saw Nahjee for what he was, a grown man and a believable one. She cracked, Tamia just hugged her friend.

"Y'all I don't mean any offense, but I haven't slept in a few days and this crying shit ain't for me, plus from what I gather, tonight is a really big night right. So y'all need to get out of my house." Although Nahjee laughed, the house began to empty. Rasaan and Tahj were the last to leave, and Tamia didn't know what to do, until Rasaan looked her up and down and said,

"No, no sweetie I've been with him the last few days, I need some sleep too I ain't going anywhere but home. If you don't like it here, then you have to call a cab." And that's how they left Tamia standing in the middle of the floor.

"I was thinking about selling this place?" Nahjee told her. "A lot of bad memories you know."

"You want to tell me about it?"

"Can I?"

"Nahjee, you could tell me anything."

"Ok, but tell me, is it a penalty if I didn't?"

"Would you do it to save me and my feelings?"

"No, I sometimes feel as if it's not about what is said but what is done, if I said I loved you and shown you that I didn't. Which one would you believe?"

"I understand, but tell me, did you mean everything that you said to-day though, I mean really, really mean it?"

"With all of my life, you're my passion; I could do you all day every day, several times a day."

"I have a passion you know what that is?"

"Yes, God gave you a set of hands to save and repair lives with."

"How do you know that? That is my passion though?"

"Because, I'm the one who turned the radio on for you remember?"

"What does that have to do with anything?"

"The music was only the sound track, so that meant nothing, but the way your fingers danced around Scope, the way you relaxed yourself after only seconds of anxiety, the way you shook hands with your adversary, meaning the loss of life, and all of this gave you a homely feeling as if you were right at home while doing it all."

"You noticed all of that?"

"I'm pretty observant."

"So, you wanted to sell this place?"

"Yes, this place is bad, nothing is good here."

"Can I ask you a question; I mean I said what I said already. I honor my words like you do, but…"

"No!"

"No, I can't ask you a question?"

"No, that means me and Marva had never."

"Well, that was sure my question."

"And that was sure my answer."

"I believe you even though you are unbelievable."

"I think I'm confused by that, now the car that I overheard you saying that you wish for its return. I really hate that car."

"Oh, that's a nice car."

"Well, too many bad memories."

"So, you wanna sell that too?"

"Yes."

"Ok, so are you telling me all of this because we're partners?"

"Yes and the other thing."

"What's that?"

"Our living arrangements."

"And you propose?"

"The place in Galt, make this place look like a Cracker Jack box, I'm really thinking Galt."

"I just moved into a place…"

"I know in Oak Park."

"Well, I'll eventually need an office."

"The house in Galt has two of them. I have gym equipment in one of them, but I could arrange you a good place to study."

"What should I do with my car?"

"Is it sentimental to you?"

"It's a lemon."

"Hey, I have the very first car that I ever bought."

"What kind of car is it?"

"It's an old pacer."

"Ha, is that right, where's that at?"

"In Galt, California."

"Are you serious?"

"Yes, so do you keep your car or no?"

"Do I have to?"

"Up to you."

"If I say no?"

"Then I'll say that you're thinking up grade."

"Yes, I really will pay you back."

"I believe you would, but upgrade to what?"

"The Lexus GS300,"

"Ok do that tomorrow, alright."

"Are you serious?"

'Are you?"

"Yes."

"Then so am I."

"Then there's the other thing."

"What is that?"

"I really haven't been to sleep."

"Are you tired?"

"Very."

"Ok so what do you expect from me now?"

"Help me? I don't understand what you mean?"

"Are you expecting me to put out, so to say?" Nahjee took on a worried look then said,

"In exchange for what?"

"Nahjee my fruits are for you as a gift, I don't do the in exchange for anything. You ask me to marry you and I said yes that is my word. I married you twelve times before you asked me."

"Your fruits, I like that, but trust me if and when you decide to share…. Your fruits as you say sweetie is entirely up to you."

"No pressure?"

"None at all mommy."

"I like that. "Mommy" that's cute."

"So are you."

"Well, a nap is what you want and a shower is what I need may I please, I ran all night yet before either one of us go our separate ways you to sleep, me to a shower, I wanted to tell you that I would never intentionally hurt you either."

"I know," and for that the first time they kissed.

NAHJEE AWOKE TO THE SOUND of the phone ringing, which was disturbing him so much. He could only think that the caller would be Marva, wanting to know how could he do this to her. This to him would have been a simple answer. He despised scandalous people, the grave yard he would say is full of good people, because the scandalous had sent them there, feeling as if Marva was the culprit for intruding on such a needy item as was his sleep, made him decide not to answer right away.

"Do you want me to get that?" Nahjee turned to Tamia and smiled at her.

"You don't have to if you don't want to, you could unplug that thang if you want."

"Why are you smiling so much for?"

"Somehow, I thought this was all a dream, what about you why are you smiling so much for?"

"For the same reason this is unbelievable, you make me happy."

"That's good to know, we have a big night the only thing is we don't have a way to get there should I order a car?"

"You mean like a limousine?"

"Mommy, I never do the limousine ever, and I sort of like to keep it that way, but I do have a few connections you know how to drive a stick?" He asked her, and then smiled at the double meaning.

"My car is a stick; I mean if that's what you meant."

"It was; so do you wish to cop or should I cop?"

"If you cop what would it be?"

"They have a SLK that I could have sent over right away."

"Is it the two-seater?"

"The one and only,"

"Then I'm with you."

"Just out of curiosity, if you were to order, what would it have been?"

"My budget would have brought us a PT Cruiser, but we would have to go get it." Nahjee tried to envision the two arriving at Club Rendezvous in a PT Cruiser.

"What, you ain't down with the PT Cruiser?" Tamia asked.

"I mean, if that's what you want to do." The phone began to ring again.

"Should I get that?"

"There's a voice mail on that thang."

"You know a lot of times people complain about their spouses and their need for a phone."

"Yeah I know, don't worry, my phone is very seldom on. I'm the voice mail kind of guy."

"What is on the agenda for today?" Tamia asked.

"Well, right now were stranded, we'll need to do something about that, then you'll need to transfer your things to Galt, I mean if that's what you really want to do."

"It is."

"Are you sure?"

"Yes."

"Well, could you drive a truck?"

"Yes, I've drove one before."

"Then, we'll order a PT Cruiser and a truck." He laughed at himself.

"I was in love with the Mercedes idea."

"Ok, red with the butter scotch, good for you?"

"You could order a car just like that, the color and all the stuff?"

"Just like that," Nahjee snapped his fingers to emphasize the swiftness. Tamia stared at him then shook her head at him and said,

"Listen, Nahjee I try really hard not to judge people, but I need to know, how is it that you make such an enormous living? A lot of this stuff people talk about while describing their dreams. I said a Lexus then you say cool go get it tomorrow, at first I was playing around with you, I mean, how could I pay you back I'm only a student and could barely afford life, it'll take years to pay you back. I believe that if I'm gonna be your wife then I shall reserve the space to ask this."

"I could dig it, no problem at all. But do understand that it'll be oh so hard for me to explain every dollar, but I could ease your worries by telling you that I'm an entrepreneur. You know a business man."

"That deals in what business, that's what I'm asking?"

"Cocaine, heroin, guns, kid naps, ransom notes and murder," Tamia began to turn blue in the face and the more she listened to Nahjee the darker blue she became but managed to say,

"Are you serious?"

"Not at all, are you alright I mean gee I was only playing." She socked him playfully on the chest and said,

"Well, don't play with me like that."

"For real though, listen to me, I'm an honorable man never have I ever sold drugs and never have I ever killed anyone trust me."

"Well, what about the kid napping and ransom notes?"

"Mondays and Fridays you're safe the rest of the way."

"You're playing around again. Do I have to worry when you leave the house is what I wanna know?"

"I haven't the slightest idea what tomorrow brings I just do 'em one at a time, I wanna say no but who am I?"

"Ok, so your money doesn't come crooked then?" she asked.

"Tamia I'm gonna have to ask you to define crooked because there is a lot of definitions to the word crooked. Someone who works minimum wage, for crumbs would work so hard to make his employers millions, tell me, do you see anything crooked in that? You get millions I get hundreds? Really though mommy here's the thing, you could ask me anything you like and we could dance around what's wrong and what's right all week, and the answers to who's wrong and who's right will always be in the eyes of the beholder. Do you wanna know how much dough we have; I mean I could better answer that for you than how I get it?"

"You said we?"

"I know what I said. Are you used to the mine, mine, mine and I, I, I kind of guys?"

"Yes."

"Well?"

"Should I know?"

"It's up to you."

"Would you be upset with me if I wanted to know?"

"Nope, but if I tell you, would you promise not to crack my head open about the how's and the where's that the cash comes from?"

"That's a deal, so how much is there?"

"I don't even know." He smiled.

"What you mean by you don't know, how silly is that?"

"I mean that I never count it, I just make it and throw it in there."

"In where?"

"In the bank, some in the safes or wherever else it lands, really."

"So, you got that much money that you don't know how much is in the pot?"

"I mean if that's the way you wanna put it, but you're spooking me, ok so our day consist of, that's what we were talking about."

"Ok, I'm going to Galt and then what?"

"Are you upset?" He asked with a smile of confusion on his face.

"A little bit." She said.

"So, are you upset because I don't know how much money I have? I don't know about you, but sweetie where I'm from that's a good thing."

"That's a horrible thing Nahjee."

"I never saw the need to balance my books, in a way I still don't, but if you are the type that likes order then I could show you where everything's at and you could line it all up if you want to."

"Where it's all at? Nahjee what are you saying?"

"That you would have to sort out a few places, I mean there are the Caymans, there's Switzerland, there's a few bucks in Tel Aviv, a lot of numbered accounts up and down the country mainly on the East Coast."

"Are you serious?"

"Very, now like I said any time that you want to arrange all of this then feel free."

"You're making me dizzy."

"I know, I could tell."

"How do you manage to live so devil may care?"

"I didn't know that I was living devil may care, mommy I only concentrate on living, as you shall, if there was something that I want or need, it would always be a phone call away. You know why? Because my word is good, the dough is cool, but a lot of times you would see us go places and we'll be compensated everything. Very seldom do I reach for my wallet, you know why? Because of the people that I know, Jewelers, real Estate Moguls and brokers from all walks, I could go anywhere, to Germany, Asia, Paris, France, Rome and England and I'll manage no different than I do now."

"I'm awe struck."

"Because you judged a book by its cover, huh,"

"I believe I did; by the way you speak I feel as if God delivered you almost as if you are way too good to be true. Aren't you scared a little bit that marriage would ruin you?"

"That would always depend on my selection right? Marva or her type is always a bad selection for me."

"How do you know that I'm a good selection?"

"I follow my heart and even if I fail, I will still continue to follow my heart."

"I like that. So, if I'm going to Galt, this means that you won't be there to help me then?"

'Not at all, I have Aretha, and then I got a friend down here from out of town…"

"Chris right?"

"Yeah, how you know that?"

"Because I'm pretty observant as well."

"Ok, well yeah I need to hang out with him and Rasaan for a bit, and then I'm off to Galt."

"So, should I wait for you out there?"

"I would think that to be best, I wish not to come back here ever again, so take whatever it is that you need in here, and what you don't, call Goodwill and donate it to them. Listen, just do me the one favor, and try as hard as you could to not make Galt look like this place. The pictures on the walls, the couches, the plants anything that gives this place character, give it away."

"I understand."

"You'll see when you get there. There's a lot of work for you to do as far as decorations. I have a few places in mind that you could use to bring your visions to life."

"It's that bad, is it?"

"You'll see, but now I need to shower, try your hand at calling these numbers tell them that you are Mrs. Nahjee Markel, then place your orders, start with the car and truck, and then when you get to Galt you could order whatever would make you comfortable."

"You do know that it's almost five o'clock right?"

"Ok, um, what that mean?"

"A lot of places are closing soon."

"Ahh, nah sweetie, a lot of these places are closing to the public."

"Are we not the public?"

"Not at all, do you think that you could get use to that?"

"I'ma try, but I know that it must be nice."

"To be fortunate or Mrs. Markel?"

"To be both."

"Well, see if you could get a handle on it, they may think that you are a crank caller at first, don't be offended by that because never has a woman called on my behalf before. The code to my phone is an "N" shape which will unlock it, then scroll through the contacts. When the car come just take my phone and if you need me hit Rasaan's phone and you would find his number under Bra-bra."

"And, you wouldn't have all kinds of women calling this phone while I'm doing the business though?"

"Did we cover the womanizer part yet?" Nahjee asked sarcastically, knowing full well that they had.

"Ok, just double checking that's all."

"For the last time I hope."

"For the last time, baby is you for real, or has some one cloned you from the early sixties?"

"I'm gonna take that as a compliment, I think."

"It is."

"Well, let me get in this shower."

"Can I get in the shower with you?"

"Of course, but who's gonna order the cars?"

"Like you said, those places are closing to the public."

"I'm so much in love with you." She reached for his waist and planted a kiss on him and said, "I know," which she did and to the shower they've gone and could have stayed forever.

The shower water was hot, the jets were powerful, and so was Nahjee and Tamia. With her being such a small frame compared to Nahjee, he lifted her into the air and there she wrapped her legs around his waist and accepted him. Their lips stayed on each other. She bit his neck and his chest in fine nibbles, which sent his excitements to soar so much that his thrust became ever so aggressive. She screamed out his name and told him over and over that she will be there. She told him that she loved him the moment that she saw him and the two came together in one grand explosion. The two shivered and convulsed violently, "I love you too mommy," was all that he could say.

Aretha has been waiting on the call from Nahjee for a few days now; he said that it was important enough to change her life completely. Her financial situation was going to improve drastically. This she had an idea of already, because she already knew that Scope had left her something. She just didn't know what it was. The impressive part was Nahjee being willing to give it up to her, for a while she was thinking that he was gonna play her out of her part, but was happy as hell when the call finally came.

Although it wasn't Nahjee that called the message was just as good, tonight she was invited to celebrate at the Club Rendezvous. The celebration was called for all friends and all family of Nahjee and Tamia. Whatever the hell that meant all she gave a fuck about was the payoff that she was going to collect and then she was going to blow the scene and leave Sacramento so fast. She thought, maybe head back to Nevada. "Yeah, that's what I'ma do," she said to herself. "I'ma blow this town and start all over again."

Tamia, hadn't recalled being so busy in all of her life, she was a mover, a secretary and a party planner. She was in mitigations, a liaison and a truck driver and she was all of these things at the same damn time. Nahjee's phone buzzed and buzzed the minute that she turned it on. "I don't know how you do this thing here Mr. Man," she said to herself but this shit is driving me crazy already. Mecca called with Desmond on the line, who couldn't believe a thang that Mecca told him, not even when Tamia told him, but the two knew that he was happy which made Mecca happy which in turn made Tamia happy who said,

"Mecca, before you hang up I need both of you guys to listen to me really good. Everything is going down tonight, Des' the lawyer is coming down and Mecca, Aretha is coming to. I tell you guys this because Mecca I know how you feel about the girl and we're afraid that you would let the way you feel get in the way. We need you to stay away from her and I need you to promise me that."

"Sis," it was Desmond "sis we need this right."

"Yeah, we do Desmond, I really want to choke this ho the fuck out. I really do."

"But, sis from what I could hear that is no good though."

'I know, shit, I know, what if she doesn't listen, then what?"

"Mecca," Tamia interjected "Are you gonna trust Nahjee or not because if you're not, then for Des' sake, we'll need to make other plans."

"Mecca" Desmond said "Sis' all we're asking you to do is behave, if there's a lawyer coming in let him do what he do, if Nahjee or whatever his name is has planned all of this, why not trust him? Because you know just like I know that he could have sat down like everyone else. Why is he doing all of this to begin with? I really don't know, but I'm not dumb enough to look a gift horse in the mouth. All we need you to do is behave, could you do it because if you don't think so, then say that shit and let them make the other plans, all right?"

"Ooh, I'll behave." Mecca snapped.

"Uh uh, promise right now, me and your brother."

"Alright, I promise."

"Good, now listen Nahjee got a cold skinny on the girl and he's gonna squeeze the shit out of her tonight. I promised that I wouldn't relay the method, so don't ask. What I know, he had to tell me because I'm part of the play, Desmond it's gonna work trust in that, it's a lot of pressure in this play. So much that the idea is for your lawyer, who is now one of the best in the country to haul the girl to his office, where there are court reporters on hand and an old retired judge, who is there to make an affidavit. Whatever the hell that is so if the girl takes off running she'll be in way more trouble than if she confessed to lying. There's been a lot of work put into this whole thing already; everyone is in position waiting on tonight. So, Mecca I need to ask you again, are you sure that you could behave?"

"And the squeeze goes down tonight?" Mecca said now excited.

"Yeah, and its brilliant too girl, I'll tell you what I wouldn't want to be on this man's bad side, it wouldn't surprise me if Des' be back in Sacramento tomorrow. I know that this lawyer dude was spitting mad once I told him everything, he said something about tearing the girl a new asshole. He can't wait to get his hands on her, I told him to meet us there at eleven, but he's probably up there right now."

"Sis, we got this right?" Said Des' who've become now concentrated.

"Yeah, we got this," said Mecca.

"Well, let's go get 'em," said Tamia then the three exchanged their farewells, and Tamia called Rasaan. Already she was missing Nahjee. Once Nahjee was on the line she said,

"Hey baby, how you doing?"

"I'm high as hell." He responded.

"Wait a minute what y'all doing over there?" Tamia's concern was evident.

"Nah, I'm high as hell off you."

"Is that right? That's always good to hear, let me know when you start to come down, so I could send you back up there, ok."

"Will do, what's going on though?"

"First I started to miss you, then I wanted to touch you, then you tell me this stuff and I got all horny for you, but I know that you doing you. So I withdraw all of that to tell you that the lawyer said that he will see you tonight, Aretha said that she would too. The lawyer said that he'll call the judge and have everything lined up for midnight. He didn't understand why so late, but when I told him that Aretha was a flight risk he put the rest together himself."

"And Mecca?" He asked.

"Her and her brother called, my guess to say thank you, but all in all I iced her."

"For real, because we don't need emotional business do we?"

"No, daddy, business is business."

"Daddy, ooh would you listen to you."

"I've been waiting all night to say that."

"What about that one girl, the white one?"

"Ruby, what about her?"

"Did you invite her?"

"No, do you think I should?"

"Is she a friend of yours?"

"That's my girl."

"Then, yes I think you should, how is you making out though, are you alright?"

"Yes, this phone is killing me; I don't see how you do it."

"I told you how I do it; I always turn that fucker off and play the voicemail."

"I see why you do that, but now my concerns are, how do I reach you when I need to hear or see you, how do I reach you? Or do I have to leave a message too?"

"Not at all, tell me, how is it that you got me on line right now then?"

"Because you told me to call Rasaan if I needed you."

"Like I would tell you every time we part, don't worry you got VIP all day, every day."

"So do you baby, are you still high or should I come through and break you off a little something, something."

"You wanna get it in the truck? Ooh kinky,"

"On top of the hood of the truck,"

"Oooh, kinky, kinky, kinky, but nah sweetie run your routes and I'll be wrapping things up here pretty soon and I'll be out there shortly."

"Ok sweetie," she disconnected and though she wondered where he could have been, even wondered who he was really with, she knew that she was gonna eventually have to trust him, regardless to the pieces that William had stolen from her. She knew that she wouldn't give him that kind of power over her, where as she would cheat Nahjee out of his just due and with that she held her head and followed the GPS all the way to Galt.

CHAPTER 22

THE RENDEZVOUS WAS FILLED TO capacity for the news spread awfully quick that one of the most eligible bachelors in the whole town was getting picked off of an awfully short list of available bachelors. Once the city heard that the lucky guy was Nahjee, the town had gone bonkers. "Oh hell no," was all the ladies were caught saying. The fellas needed to see who this gypsy woman was that hypnotized their fellow brethren, because she would have to be stopped, she must be brought down on all stops. The buzz was heard all over town, so much that Mecca and Lerin often entertained the thought of going outside to scalp tickets. It was a crazy mob out front who needed to get in but couldn't because there was so many people invited that were gonna get the priority passes already. This kicked the idea of hustling right on out the door for these chicks even though the two knew that they could make a killing at the door alone. Loving the fact that they'd get the rest of night off, once they've worked the doors until the doors have been closed, due to the "private party" light that kept blinking on and off over the entrance. All of which made this mob even more dangerous. Ten o'clock showed and Mecca began to grow nervous, and everyone knew that the time was drawing near. When Ten Thirty p.m. showed up, Mecca's phone began to ring.

"Is that you girl?" Lerin barked.

"What?"

"Is that your phone ringing?" Mecca had barely heard Lerin, never mind her phone ringing, but once she retrieved her phone she not only noticed that her phone was ringing but she already had three missed calls.

"Hello," she yelled into her phone trying to fend off the loud music.

"My name is Geoffrey Larva; I'm looking for Mecca ahh…." Mecca helped him out by saying,

"This is she."

"Well, I'm having a very hard time getting in the club."

"Where are you?"

"I'm out front in my car, I came to the door they said that it was a private party and was sure that I wasn't invited."

"Ok, come back to the door; stay on the phone though so I could recognize you when I see you."

"Uh uh you have to come get me, no offense, but I barely made it back to my car. My poor chauffeur didn't know if he should run over as many people as he could to get us out of here or to call the National Guards."

"Well, I'm glad you called me first."

"This is why I make the big bucks you know, I got the brains."

"I hope so, use your flashers and I'll be there in a sec." To Lerin she said, "Guess who's outside?"

"Ahh is it the lawyer dude."

"How you know?"

"You've been rubber necking everyone that came through the door looking for two people especially. One of them I was hoping to God didn't have your number."

"Well cover for me, I'm going out to get him because somebody gave him a hard time at the door."

"Probably Ricky,"

"My guess too, I'll be back." Mecca went outside looking for flashers then she found some on an all-white, stretched Lincoln town car. She walked over and waved the lawyer over. She saw as the interior lights switched on and the rear door was opened by the chauffeur and a very powerful, smartly dressed individual stepped out of the car. Right away Mecca recognized "important person" as it seeped from the pores of the lawyer. Immediately Mecca knew that freedom fighter better fits this guy and not that other guy that she was doing business with. He took powerful strides to cover the distance between them then he stretched out his powerful paw and formally introduced himself. Mecca took his hand and shook it, then said,

"Follow me," and he did, he marveled at the way Mecca handled the crowd of people who not only wanted in, but wanted in right now. Though he didn't feel all the way safe until they were in the confines of the club said,

"Is it always like this?"

"Not all the times, but a lot though."

"You handle yourself pretty good. What's the occasion why is everybody so desperate to get inside; they are offering money and everything? It must be something very big going on"

"Who was offering money? You mean I just missed some money?" Mecca said jokingly "Nah, I'm only kidding, that line is normally long, but this is the worst. The clubs already filled to maximum capacity"

"They are celebrating what again?"

"Nahjee, they are mainly celebrating him."

"Ahh, yes, I see how they could do that. Special kid I tell you, I just about owe him everything, my life included, all of it now that I think about it."

"Looks like he pays you pretty good, you look real high class." Mecca sized up the lawyer,

"Oh, no, no, no sweetheart, I'm not for hire like that, he pays me nothing ever, but to anyone else yes, my prices are out there quite a bit. Granted that if you heard anything that I said Mecca, then you'd know that if Nahjee calls, I come running. One o'clock, two o'clock, or three o'clock in the morning I won't care I'll be there. You must have never heard the story about the drunk lawyer with the gun in his mouth have you?"

"No, I can't say that I have, but don't tell me that you're the drunk lawyer are you."

"The very one but not the only, law is a hazardous profession, so, your brother is Desmond, yeah?"

"Yes, but let me clue you in on what's going on…"

"Something new has come up I need to know about?"

"No, it's just that everyone is scared that I'm going to screw this thing up. I'm not supposed to be seen talking to you or anybody else for that matter."

"But, we are going to have to talk eventually right. I'm sure everyone agrees on that, no." Said Geoffrey

"Not until after you did your stuff we ain't. I got my girl at the door willing to give me the heads up for right now, but trust me there are a lot of nervous people hoping like hell that I get away from you. So, what are you drinking and I'll bring it over?"

"Well, how about a Cranberry Juice?"

"Everyone is gonna think you're the FBI or the Fire Marshal, how about a Scotch on the rocks?"

"Whatever, but you should trust me, I make a horrible drunk, then there's the drunk lawyer thingy that we should consider, you follow me on this?"

"Yes, Cranberry over rocks it is."

"My dear, that was a very wise decision indeed."

"Don't worry I'll keep them coming."

"Thank you," the crowd came to life in a very loud exhibit and the excitement had told Mecca all she needed to know. That Nahjee and Tamia had arrived.

"Ok, I have to go now, try to remember, you never saw me, got that?" She hurried away from the law man as fast and as far away as she could get.

The DJ made announcements that followed one banging track after the next one. The club vibrated, screams and woops were heard blocks away. The place to be was "right there" and the time to be there was "right now." Mecca knew that Aretha had made her showing because; Lerin used her blinkers to weave through the heavy traffic in order to reach Mecca.

"She's here huh?" Mecca didn't need to be a rocket scientist to figure this one.

"Yeah bitch, I'm telling you right now, the bitch is here. Don't come with the bullshit later on, because you know how you get. But anyways, Tamia made me promise that I would babysit you. No matter where you go, I go or she made me promise to cut you. Now Mecca, I don't want to do it but I will do it."

"You don't need to babysit me, girl go ahead and enjoy yourself."

"Nah, I'm cool, whenever you need to pee let me know, I'll flush it for you."

"That serious, huh,"

"Hell yeah, when the white man leave your bail is set and you could do whatever you wanna do. Until then, we're gonna sit here and drink and I'm gonna teach you how to read lips all right."

"What are we drinking?"

"That-a-girl, I knew I could count on you. Hennessey straight, I got them on repeat, so, take a seat and pull out your pen and write really soft on that napkin. It's time for us to crack us a case do you hear me? You know I'm the one to show you how to do it, girl this is our house god damned me. Wait to they sit down and we're gonna...what the fuck are they doing, is they leaving...fuck." Lerin has never been so disappointed in all her life. She watched as Nahjee, Tamia and the powerful built attorney lead Aretha out of the club meaning that Lerin's case was now closed.

Aretha didn't know what to think; all she knew was that whatever was going down, whatever the payment it all had to go down in the back of a limousine. "Shit" she thought "this is gonna take some getting used to." Once the four were comfortably situated inside of the car the briefcase became opened for all that was present to see, then Nahjee said.

"Aretha, this is a good friend of mine, he's a lawyer to oversee that you've received your payment. It's like a Will all right, this way you can't continue to ride us for dough once we part, could you dig it?"

"Yes," was her response so Nahjee gave her the document to sign and she did so without reading it then the lawyer signed on as the witness. The next maneuver was a little puzzling, but when the lawyer opened a small black box and placed his thumb into the ink then placed his print next to his signature and advised Aretha to do the same he said "this is quite a bit of money." So with a smile on her face Aretha performed in the very same way and left her print.

"Ok, now that piece of business is behind us, let's go to the next piece. Aretha you remember this lady right here, right? She was the one that saved Scope and put him back together." Aretha nodded then accepted the piece of paper that Nahjee said that she really needed to pay attention to. As Aretha read the autopsy she began to tremble, and as she read on the tears rolled down her cheeks, so Nahjee said.

"I'm gonna recommend that you don't say anything right now. Why you did it is between you and Scope, that you did it is between you and God. But, we need you to know that we know that you did it. Now, this dough is enough for you to run with, twenty thousand bucks ain't bad it was Scope's cut. I'm sure he would have wanted you to have it. But, this next piece of business may make you wanna run just know that in front of a court officer you gave him a full confession, signature and print, which is the reason that I suggested that you read the autopsy carefully. Seeing that you were willing to sign so freely, I suggest that you pay a lot of attention from here on out. Tamia as you know is the doctor who would swear under oath that she repaired Scope then released him to you for you to care for him, which means that you were the last one to see him alive." Although her tears flowed heavily still she managed to say.

"But, you don't know..."

"Again I'm gonna suggest that you don't say anything lest you mess yourself up really big," Aretha hushed quickly for she now knew that the best that she could do for herself was to remain silent.

"Ok, now there's another piece of business," immediately Aretha began to hate when Nahjee said those words "Now this piece of business could either free you or it could mess you up more than anything."

"Ok, I'm listening," I know your ass is thought Tamia but refused to interrupt Nahjee while he was leading her to the point of free or fall, Aretha chose free.

"Good," Nahjee said, then "A while ago you testified that a friend of mine raped you, but we know that you testified because he refused to pay you. You were working out of Reno then, right." She nodded, now knowing the reason for her discomforts and decomposing mind state. Just how was it that she had gone from euphoric to awfully miserable in the matter of seconds was the mystery that was way bigger than her, and she knew it. Here she now stood, in the court room of "hood justice" to answer for an offense that happened ever so long ago. Somehow, in the back of her mind she has always feared this day to come, her worse fears were now confirmed, it was now official.

"I'm so sorry," was all that she could say.

"Yeah, me too," said Nahjee "Listen, Aretha a lot of lives have already been screwed up, what has happened, has happened already. There's nothing that we could do about that, but try to salvage as much as we could. Me, myself I'd rather that you take the money way before I wanna see you take a deal for murder or go to trial and lose for even a lesser charge. Like I say what you've done is between you and God, what do you say, would you help us out?"

"What would I have to do? I don't know what to do."

"Just go with my lawyer, we need you to answer a lot of questions, you do it right I'll tear this up, no bullshit, and the money goes with you. If I was you I would put it up so that you would have something to land on when all of this is over. Or like I say Mah, you could run but twenty grand isn't a lot of money to be on the run for murder, believe me."

"Am I going to jail Nahjee, you don't have to lie to me?"

"If you do it won't be for murder unless you leave us out there. But, if you do go to jail don't worry about that, like I say, keep quiet and he'll come and bail you out and you'd be able to fight that from the streets which is a big difference by the way. I would also say that if you had some game about yourself you'd put all of this on Marcel, Scope and Stomp. I'm ever so sure that they wouldn't object to your freeing yourself at their expense; tell them it was the victim's award money that made you do it once your dude threatened your life if you walked away from the dough. Offer to pay the dough back and go on about your business, easy."

"Ok, I'll do it; can I call you when this is over?"

"Nah, don't worry about me, though I'm flattered, but you go far away from here and start again. What's wrong with that, huh?"

"Ok, you are truly a beautiful person."

"Thank you," Nahjee collected all of the papers, he shook hands with Geoffrey then nodded to Tamia who took the cue and lead them out of the car and the two walked side by side towards the entrance of the club moving aside only to let the big white powerful car pass. The two saw as the car made its way out of the lot.

"I think that went over pretty good," Tamia smiled to him.

"Me too, look," Nahjee gestured towards the door. Tamia looked to see Ruby having trouble at the door. The two walked over to the bouncers and Tamia spoke first.

"Is there a problem here?"

"Tamia, oh my God would you look at you… look at this coat it's fabulous." Nahjee nodded to the bouncer and watched as he moved aside to give the three, Nahjee, Tamia and Ruby entrance into the club.

"I've been calling you all day," said Ruby

"Girl, I have never been this busy, guess what?"

"Nuh uh, tell me,"

"I'm getting married," Tamia showed Ruby her ring as if the coat wasn't enough. The two yelled their over whelming excitements over the music.

"I'm not gonna even ask you who was dumb enough to do that for you girl, I need me a drink and it sounds like it's going down in here."

"It is, you remember Nahjee right, from the other night?"

"Yes, he was the nervous one, right?"

"Yes, honey, this is Ruby, a friend of mine."

"Honey, so you're the stupid one, please to meet you."

"I guess that I am, but now you girls go and do your thang. Ruby I sure hope that you could step, I mean this place is unforgiving when it comes to two left feet." Nahjee decided not to send her in blind so he tipped her ahead of time.

"Oh, I get it, I get it, it's a joke right? You think that because I'm white that I can't get it in, huh?"

"I don't know about all of that, but I said what I said. You guys be good, mommy I need to find Ra' and Chris ok."

"Have fun baby."

"I will," Nahjee stepped away from the two women and found Christopher first, and to him he said "Where's Rasaan?" Christopher pointed towards the dance floor and said.

"Him and the ole lady, you know."

"Thanks for coming, enjoy yourself,"

"I am and guess what, I done already passed six fifties. I gave tips away so much and so many that I think the girl over yonder has a crush on me, get a load of that."

"Well, be careful."

"Nah, don't worry about me, as long as they got Johnny Walker in here I'll have company."

"Well, don't get too drunk this place is notorious for its sharks."

"That's who I'm waiting on, maybe I should drink some more and make it look a little obvious, what you think?"

"Whatever man, keep your head up though." The song ended and Nahjee excused himself and gone to Rasaan "Bro," Rasaan looked Nahjee up and down then said

"What's up ain't you supposed to be somewhere celebrating?"

"I am, listen, we need to get Chris laid tonight he looks lonely, could you pull that off?"

"How come you don't pull it off?"

"Tamia, remember her don't you?"

"Hmm, yeah, ok I got him. Did you know that we've been passing dough?"

"Yeah, he told me,"

"Dig, they pulled the pen out on his ass right in front of me, and right when I was just getting ready to grab him and take off, the bartender gave him change back, so, guess what I started doing"

"Hell nah,"

"Got me fucked up, been done bought the Dom Rose', fool we're on our third one, you want some?"

"Whoa."

"Could say that again, and its six boxes of it dry already too. Nigga move!"

"I'm hipped, hah, ok now I'm scared to death for Chris though."

"Why is that?"

"That's a lot of dope money ain't it?"

"Way too much, he's on his way to rehab; we've already talked about this on the way over here."

"My nigga, man I like how we're thinking," said Nahjee.

"I see that the white girl made it in, look at her, oh, oh she go look at her."

"She's holding her own that's for sure." Nahjee was impressed,

"So, you're getting married, wow, I can't believe it."

"Yeah, it's about time though."

"She'll make you happy I'm sure of it."

"She's doing pretty good so far."

"I don't see Aretha."

"We pulled her over already."

"Ok?"

"She took the money."

"Good girl, I was sure hoping that she would, you know for Mecca and all," Rasaan shook his head then said "You know that she's gonna be able to pass it right, the money I mean."

"That'll be good for her."

"I mean we gave her some money that was good as money, you know this right?"

"Like I said, that will be good for her, we are all doing ok, I have no complaints."

"Me either, I've been thinking about marrying Tahj, what you think?"

"Oh, shit, are you serious?"

"Yeah, I'm not getting any younger she ain't either."

"Plus you guys go good together."

"Yeah, toss that in there and I could smell cake right now."

"And rice."

"And a new suit, a Tuxedo with cake on it."

"Don't forget the rice in the pocket."

"And the rice in the pocket,"

"Don't mean to sound like a pooper, but I had enough for one night."

"Yelp, don't worry about Chris' I got him, he's a good dude."

"Yeah, I fucks with him. Let me get the ole girl, if she ain't ready than you got your hands full, hear." Rasaan nodded though he couldn't see why she would want to be here without her man. Nahjee found Tamia, and said.

"Mah, I believe I had enough, you ready to go?"

"I thought that you was never gonna ask. Man I'm tired, my feet are killing me, I'm horny as hell and I'm sharing you with too many people right now."

"What about Ruby?"

"She knows her way home."

"Has she been drinking a lot?"

"Just enough to get her shoulders and feet into it, I been watching."

"Ok, I'm sold, do your farewells and I'll be waiting for you in the car."

"Yes, I'll be there shortly." Nahjee left the club and headed to the lot. Tamia went to thank everyone for coming out than bade her farewells. Nahjee was going over paper work when Tamia opened the door and got inside of the car.

"You ready?" Nahjee asked,

"More now than ever before," The two left the club and headed straight for the freeway, the same one that would carry them home. As Nahjee flowed in and out of traffic he thought about his life and the changes that have entered his life both with and without his permission. He knew that he was prepared for a life of this magnitude "the sky's the limit" was how the game came. He looked to Tamia then he knew that prayers really made it to heaven.

"What are you thinking about?" Tamia asked.

"Yesterday"

"Me, too,"

CHAPTER 23

THIS TIME WHEN NAHJEE AWOKE he done so in a panic, he thought he was being robbed. His gun was in the drawer on the other side of the room and out of immediate reach. He knew that he had to concentrate and zero in on the banging noise. "Hmm" he mellowed a bit because whoever was breaking in was doing it in rhythms. How did he forget that Tamia had come home with him? Oh, it was the alcohol that's what happened. His memory slowly came into focus, a half of a fifth of Remy and a lot of late night talk had taken its toll. The contents of such a conversation warranted the alcohol, and he knew that it would. Tamia was a good listener and Nahjee was a horrible drinker. The rhythm continued pat, pat, pat, pat, so he rolled out of bed to find Tamia in the weight room.

"Hey sleepy head, ahh, did I wake you?" Her pace never slowed, her sweat made her sexy, giving her the athletic look.

"At first I thought that someone was breaking in. I almost ran in here and drew down on your butt."

"Well, I'm glad that you came to your senses in time, how did you sleep?"

"It was amazing, much needed and deserved. How long you been up?"

"Since eight, that's what I call sleeping in for the weekend. I have a lot of work to do, seeing that the only thing in here is weights and work out equipment, a few electronics, and a bed. No food, no television, no couches or love seats, how you live like this is beyond me..."

"Listen lady, I'm not gonna stand by and listen to you complain about my ain't gots I worked hard for all of this and for your information I do have food."

"Oh, you do, do ya, where is it then, huh?"

"In the ice box, where else," playfully Nahjee rolled his eyes at Tamia.

"What, a half a pack of sausage, a quarter dozen of eggs and a tub of "I can't believe it's not butter" and two of those little mustard packets?"

"Well, that's food ain't it?"

"But, anyways, I've been thinking."

"Oh, you have, huh."

"Yes, silly, I've been thinking," Tamia shut the tread mill down and begun to power walk, she said.

"I love this room right here."

"Me too, I love to work out, you know, keep my sexy up."

"Me too, so I was thinking that maybe you wouldn't object to us, you know sharing an office, and the one upstairs look plenty of big enough."

"That's because you haven't moved your things in there yet. I know you doctor types; you'd have stuff everywhere. You'll need another room, one medicine referring to another and all; I could see it now, uh uh, shit no."

"Well, sweetie, something awfully wonderful and need I say convenient has come around since those days' sugar, it's called an internet. Don't worry, you'd like it, you'll have your corner and I'll have mine. Then, when our works become frustrating, we could come down here and work it off. You know, keep our sexy up like you say."

"So, you say there's an internet that could fix all of this?"

"Yes, silly I would have thought you were seriously out of the loop, but all I kept hearing all morning was "you've got mail." Speaking of which, you missed your appointment yesterday. Doctor Summers called, well the doctors secretary anyhow. I started to curse that bitch out for calling here all misty voiced, I think we got an understanding now though. Then she had the nerve to try and change up, ugh."

"Well, I'm glad you didn't curse her out, like I say never has a woman done anything on my behalf before. Don't worry it'll die off pretty soon."

"That's what I was thinking, so do tell me?" Nahjee's eyebrows lifted, not quite getting what Tamia was talking about and Tamia found it evident when Nahjee said,

"Um, what?"

"This Dr. Summers, what's that all about?"

"Dr. Summers is a good friend of mine…"

"Ok." Tamia interrupted.

"She's a very, very smart and beautiful person, incredible I used to say. She has a way with words…" Nahjee saw Tamia's eyebrows knit themselves together then she said,

"And you see her because?"

"I don't think I should answer that, in fact I'm not gonna answer that I'm exercising my Fifth Amendment right to remain silent."

"And if you do I'ma exercise my right to bear arms."

"And which amendment is that?"

"The one that says that you have one more try before I run in the kitchen and come back in here and cut you for playing with me." Smiling Nahjee said,

"And how in the hell you gone do that, huh, it ain't no silverware in there remember, just a fork, a spoon and a butter knife. Come here you could spoon me any time you'd like."

"Oooh, why do you need to see this Mrs. Summers?"

"No, Ms. Summers, she's not married."

"You better stop playing with me."

"Why ever would I do that when I'm having so much fun with you?"

"Ok, you know what; I just want to give you something to think about. I know every vein in your body, every one of them. I know what their uses are, and what happens if they're interrupted or ruptured. In fact, I could give you a shot that would paralyze every muscle in your body and you would have to answer me with your eyelids. I'd tell you to blink once for yes and twice for no. I'd torture your ass so much I'd have you in here blinking like a big dog which would mean hell no. So, if you wish to keep playing with me you go right ahead."

"Dang, you're playing hard ball ain't you, all of this because I don't have any silverware?"

"So, who is Dr. Summers and why is she calling you, and what kind of appointment did you miss, and that's my last time asking you or I'm going to get my bag."

"Dang all of this…"

"Who is she?" Tamia snapped.

"Whoa tiger, easy there booga, now, now, now, ain't you the one who answered the phone? What did the secretary say? How come you ain't over there shooting her misty ass up with the eyelid syrup? No, you're looking for a reason to fuck over me." Smiling Nahjee said, "You're sexy as hell when you're pissed, are you hungry some?" Tamia looked him in the eyes and said,

"You didn't answer my question."

"I know, neither did you? I'm starved plus I have an appointment that I missed and it just so happens that I never miss my appointments."

"In that case, yeah, I'm famished."

"You're not hungry you're just nosey that's all."

"Sort of, soon as I heard misty I've been on guard ever since, what the hell you keep smiling for?"

"Because you're so cute, look at you, all aggressive and stuff, but there's something I need to share with you real fast and I need you to hear me good ok? I have absolutely no control over who finds me attractive enough to sound or look misty. I have absolutely no control over the way anyone behaves themselves, but what I could control baby, is me. The way that I behave, I mean if I have to remind you over and over that I love you and want only you, then Tamia you need to know how time consuming that'll be. Plus, it'll be like me defending a relationship instead of just being in love with one. I believe that what you are doing is letting your downfalls and disappointments enter us already. I'm afraid that I won't be able to contend with that."

"Oh, Nahjee I'm sorry, I said that I wouldn't let that happen. I'm so sorry, I mean it."

"I think that we should get dressed and go get us a bite to eat."

"Then we're coming back here?"

"Nuh uhn, why?"

"I ordered a bunch of stuff; it should be coming any minute now.

"Well, we can catch what we can, if not leave a note on the door that way they could get the key and unload it and we could put it all together once we get back.

Tamia drove the Red Mercedes carefully, refusing to be responsible for any accidents of any kind. Nahjee appeared to be unfazed by the slow driving of Tamia's as long as he pressed the buttons on his phone. They've gone to the steak house, him and his buttons, when they went to the PO Box, him and his buttons. In fact, the only time that he looked away from his phone was to punch buttons on the GPS for Tamia to follow which she was doing with extreme caution. Arriving at their destination on Alhambra Blvd, in Midtown Sacramento, Nahjee said,

"Mah, go around the back, you'd be able to pull in and park anywhere." Seeing an empty lot save for a car and a cargo van, Tamia said.

"You think anyone's here?"

"Sunday, that's why it looks like this, believe me, there's always someone here." The two made their exits from the car and Nahjee waited for Tamia to fall in step with him before the two were admitted into the clinic by an elderly woman who Tamia took to be Doctor Summers. Upon introduction did she then discover her speculations to be true? Doctor Summers took Tamia by the hand then said,

"You may not think so, but I am pleased to finally get the chance to meet you."

"Oh, well here I am," Tamia wore a look of consternation.

"Thank you for coming as well as making sure that he received the message, please follow me." The elderly woman turned on her heels and led them down the long hallway. Tamia could tell that Doctor Summers was a powerful woman. She could even tell that growing up she was a very beautiful woman. Tamia sized up the good doctor, listened as her heels echoed down the hallway. The perfume that would linger long after she had gone, Tamia knew the expensive toilette waters and this lady sure rocked the good stuff. Doctor Summers turned to Tamia,

"I have heard a lot about you; so, please feel free to discuss you with me all right?"

"If you don't mind me asking, what kind of Doctor are you? I didn't see the name anywhere."

"That's because you guys came through the back, but to answer your question I'ma Psychiatrist."

"Oh," Tamia was taken aback.

"You look surprised, so I'm going to take it that this boy didn't tell you that."

"No, I can't remember a time that he did."

"Well, now you know the man that I know. It's my understanding that you too are in the practice of medicines." Tamia nodded her answer; the doctor sized her up, and then said,

"Good, the world could use more of us. Ok, now that we are here, since this boy didn't tell you that you were coming with him to see the crazy doctor, hence the look on your face. Let me lay the ground rules. One, everything inside is always recorded but never released. I don't care who ask, never. Two, inside there are no such words as I don't know, I can't or please stop. Now three, since I learned that you were coming, there is a station set up for you as well. This is what we call group therapy. The rule is this, for number three, when I ask you questions, he would hush and can't answer for you, and, the same goes for you while I'm speaking to him. I must warn you that either one of you may hear answers that may make you uncomfortable; you won't like what you're hearing. I need you to know and understand that it is only life and this is where we'll deal with it, are you ready." Tamia nodded "Cookies" Tamia began to answer with a no thank you until she heard Nahjee say,

"Yes ma'am," although he took to an embarrassed demeanor still he stood with his head poised in confidence.

"Good, come on in," Doctor Summers opened the doors to a very plush office. She led them inside then turned to them and said,

Tamia, shoes off you'll take this one, head here, and feet here." The Doctor pointed out the positions most effective. "Boy, you take this one, your head next to hers, feet out." The two removed their shoes and took to their couches respectively. Tamia's and Nahjee's head were merely inches apart. Tamia couldn't believe that she was even going along with this foolishness. This was just outright ludicrous, preposterous even and silly. What in the hell, as soon as this was over she knew for sure, that she would thank the good doctor and run like hell. Still she managed to relax on the couch and while staring at the paintings on the walls of the good doctor did she notice that her interest was piqued a bit once the doctor began to speak.

"Ok, the recorder is now going on and I'll open first by saying that this is the meeting between Nahjee Markel and the visiting Ms. Tamia and I am Doctor Summers here at the Alhambra Psychiatric after care and follow up. So, now that we've erased the preliminaries I will now explain the reason why we're here. I have been the primary doctor for Mr. Markel ever since his twelfth birthday. He was recommended to me by the county of Sacramento Juvenile Center, due to the mental and emotional trauma to which he's experienced over the loss of his parents, in this case it was a murder suicide. With this in the open, I'll start with Nahjee first." The doctor asked one question after the next one, and for long periods of time. She would switch tapes then begin again. Tamia listened on and the only thing that kept coming to mind was just how professional this doctor was "man, she's good" she caught herself thinking. Now she knew how Nahjee was always so professional with his actions and so eloquent in his vocalizations. Seems as if he was practically raised by a very intelligent woman, and one who reminded Tamia so much of her Nana, that it was killing her. Tamia heard as Nahjee spoke so freely of his past month, the people that had come in and out of his life. He spoke about Marva, of Stomp, Scope and Marcel. He spoke of Tahj and Rasaan, he spoke of Aretha, most of all he spoke ever so deeply about his feelings, those for his self as well as Tamia. By the time the tape stopped Tamia was blown away.

"Boy, that was good, I'm comfortable knowing that you shared so much, still I must ask, is there anything else?" He shook his head and opened his eyes, which by now Doctor Summers knew all too well to be the punctuation mark which signaled the conclusion.

"Ok," she said, then "Tamia."

"Yes, ma'am."

"You saw and heard the procedure am I correct?"

"Yes ma'am,"

"Ok, please close your eyes and we'll have, well a conversation." Tamia acted as instructed and Doctor Summers powered the recorder once more and begun her "conversation" with Tamia. After a moment Nahjee knew that Tamia was crying, but he couldn't help her. He knew that the doctor was tapping on some raw territory which made it hard for Tamia to answer even then he knew that it was nothing that he could do about it. Nahjee knew that Dr. Summers was gonna heal her, as she has healed him. Therefore, even if there was something that he could do, he wouldn't bother to intervene with someone as professional as the great Doctor Summers. For he knew that there was nothing in the world as dangerous as a woman scorned and by listening to the two women communicate he now knew that Tamia indeed had been scorned by so many avenues in life, that her being scorned was indeed an understatement. Nahjee listened as Tamia cried and she sobbed until one tape was replaced by the next tape. Then even that tape was replaced. The only thing that Nahjee could think of at the moment was how much he was gone love her even that much more. Now, he couldn't believe that she's been carrying so much weight on her shoulders. He now knew that she was so much stronger than he gave her credit for. Good thing Dr. Summers warned him ahead of time about some of the answers he wasn't gonna like because he sure didn't he was relieved to hear the tape stop and Dr. Summers say,

"I believe this is enough for right now, boy this is the time for you to ask or tell this girl whatever it is that you want," for an answer a tear rolled down his cheek.

"Well, that's what I thought you'd say when you got home, but I guess it'll work here." Said Dr. Summers then, "Child what about you anything you want him to know?" For a response Tamia reached over to Nahjee's face and with her thumb she wiped away his tear.

"Oh my goodness, you two were made for each other. I wish you guys quit it or I'm gonna cry. Look at you two just as cute as some pretty buttons. Ok, now that the tapes are done and before I give you the summations, boy tell me is there anything that's got you now scared of her or scared for her?" He shook his head in the negative. "Child what about you are there some things about him that got you scared of him or scared for him?" Tamia waved her head yes.

"Oh, well it ain't a better time than right now," said Doctor Summers.

"Truthfully, right now I'm living a dream, just to be in his company is rewarding enough, but he has showered me with so much already and I mean I been raised by my nana like I told you and…"

"So you wonder if its bad money that he's spending on you is that it. Your nana raised you well I can tell."

"Exactly, I don't know how he gets his money and so much of it that I fear that I would marry a man that'll only make me a widow faster than he would make me a mother."

"Now, you are even more of a beautiful person than I gave you full credit for, but maybe I could help you with this a bit. You're scared because you don't know where his monies come from, don't be because I do. You see those paintings right there both of them I got from him. The one on the left the painter painted that somewhere between 1498 and 1500 A.D his name was Leonardo Da Vinci that was one of the last paintings to have made it out of Italy from him. The one on the right is a classic as well just not as old, but just about as prestigious, that one was painted in 1880 by a French painter by the name of "Monet." I tell you this, because I too am old fashioned and would never take dirty money, nor gifts. No matter how precious, but you see that boy over there? I raised him; his mother and I were thick as thieves. There wasn't much that I could have done in the way of being a foster parent for him with me being a student still and awfully broke, but I did manage to give him wisdom which surmounted his twelve years. I taught him how to speak, how to dream and how to invest his valuables, time and monies. He's nearly thirty now yet you are the very first woman that he's brought for me to meet which means to me that he holds you in high esteem.

"This boy, I call him "Cookies" because you know why?" Tamia shook her head no. "I call him "Cookies" because every time he finished a project I baked him cookies, then I found that he kept me wearing an apron. I mean his learning was in the greedy section; his education was far past anyone in middle school. His IQ for business would satisfy Harvard, Yale, or Brigham Young all of which is Ivy League. The type of person that he is, I mean his spirit is accepted in all walks of life. Has he ever told you the story about the drunken lawyer with the gun in his mouth?" Again Tamia shook her head in the negative. "What about the jeweler that was robbed by his own brother, have you heard that one?" Again Tamia shook her head. "Well there are about thirty other stories maybe he'll entertain you with that one day. The facts are even that this place here was built with the money that this boy has earned in favors alone. So much that even those paintings were a gift to him which is the reason and the only reason that I haven't sold those thangs yet. So, to you my dear child I'm gonna tell you not to be scared of him, but be blessed with him. He's no saint by far, and perhaps he is involved in things I am not aware of, but I doubt it, and if I would have ever caught him selling drugs I would have killed him myself."

"Yes ma'am." The two women locked their eyes on each other. In this they formed a womanly bond. Far as Doctor Summers knew she was trusting Tamia with a hot ticket item and she needed to be sure. Tamia looked to her as if reassuring her that she could be trusted.

"Ok, now let's get to the fruits. By listening to the two of you; I could see that there is a bridge that connects the both of you. Both share juvenile loses pretty much the same way, both has been introduced to pains inflicted on to you by others who were once friends or even associates. From listening to the both of you guys I could honestly say that I heard it not only before, but I hear it all the time it's like a broken record. I myself call it "THE GETO LOVE SONG." It's a record that plays loud with no meaning and it plays loud all the time. In this song, there are different stories yet somehow they all remain the same. Nahjee who is Scope, who is Marcel and who is Stomp and who is Aretha? I tell you, they were all artists and all except the woman is dead, but have you stopped to think of how some people are alive only once they are dead? All three of those men aren't dead they used their lives to make a legend, a street legend but a legend never the less."

"Billy the kid has been dead since the 1800's. Yet kids today know who he was which, was the thought process of these three gentlemen. They were in love with the streets and nothing else, and the lady Aretha well from what I could see she didn't kill Scope as you call him, because she hated him. No the contrary speaks out here. She loved him, so much that she performed with whoever and however if that's what he so desired. No, she couldn't see him reduced so bad as being vulnerable she needed to love him like he was. Young lady to you," she turned to look at Tamia then said, "There's nothing in the world like a broken heart, especially when the ones who love you are the ones to do it. So I need to ask, no, I need to beg you not to break his, lest you undo what took years to heal." Doctor Summers pointed to Nahjee then continued. "Especially when it's the people who loves you are the ones to break it, William it is right? Well his greed over shadowed his love for you in his life. He needed more and more and more sexual gratifications and his stimulations have come from a variety of partners.

Some men pride themselves on being honorable. Some pride themselves on the notches that they are able to put on their bed post. Even if it took money to do it because through orgasm is how they'll find happiness, not pride solely, but sexual conquest period. Now, there's Marva right, really I should go over and hit this boy in his face because he knows better."

She stared at Nahjee then continued, "If God wanted that girl to suffer from her inequities then God would have done it. I'm not all the way mad at him because I know him. He has always fought fire with fire so to say. As he said today, he was hurt by the ways people hurt you, and that's the only reason why I haven't knocked him down yet. What I want to tell you, is you could go through life hating the people who've hurt you, but guess what? All through life, that one pain had and would if you let it, control you many years after it has occurred to you. My suggestions are to forgive yourself first, then forgive those who've hurt you. Then release their spells and go on about living your lives, such beautiful lives they are too. Remember there is a "GETO LOVE SONG." Every time, it'll play loud, yet it'll have absolutely no meaning. Marva was a fool, William was a fool, Scope, Stomp, Marcel and Aretha were all fools. Marva loved money more than life, now she's broke, foolish. William loved sex more than life, now he's lost everything, foolish. Those three boys chased a name and street fame in a few years very few people will remember their names, foolish. Billy the kid had Hollywood or he would have died foolishly. Only love for God and love for yourselves and for one another is the only way to be genuinely alive on this earth, now that I said what I could see, you two could get out of my office and Cookies miss another appointment you hear?"

"Sorry Aunty Karen."

"Doctor Summers."

"Doctor Aunty Karen Summers."

"And you, child you come back to see me, don't have me hop in my car and come find you, do you hear?"

"Yes ma'am, thank you so much, I didn't even realize how bad I needed that."

"I knew that, we all do baby, it's called life."

"Ok."

"Cookies, you know the way out."

"Ma'am," the two kissed their farewells then Nahjee and Tamia headed towards the exits. Once outside Tamia noticed that it was late in the evening, for the sunlight began to grow a tint on the day.

"Wow, that was uplifting," Tamia said then stopped short of their rental. "You didn't, Nahjee you didn't," Tamia was now jumping up and down in excitement around her new car, an all-white with gold leafing sprinkled around her Lexus GS 300. The red bow on it meant that it was gift wrapped, just for her.

"Yes, I did, you were killing me with your grandma driving, man. I couldn't take another minute of it."

"I love you so much baby, I really do."

"Just don't let it play loud."

"I won't, with no meaning right?"

"Right, The Geto Love Song."

"Race you home, Cookies."

"Ha ha, very funny, ok I'll give you a ninety-minute head start."

"If that's the case what do you want to eat, that's plenty of time for me to cook."

"There ain't no food, remember?"

"But, do you remember what I said about the internet?"

"In that case I'll see you when you get there I'm starved."

Tamia woke up the next morning in the arms of her happy. She had learned so much about Nahjee. "My God" she thought "I really love this man, God thank you, thank you, thank you," but to Nahjee she said,

"Baby, baby…. Nahjee?"

"What's up?"

"You up?"

"At first I wasn't then I had a dream that you were waking me up because you caught the house on fire."

"I've been thinking."

"Oh, oh" for this he sat up in the bed. "So, the house ain't on fire then, ok I'm ready."

"You make me happy, baby I thank God for you. I do, really I do."

"Oh, oh."

"What is wrong with you?"

"Look, I'm just gonna need you to just go straight there baby whatever's on your mind let it off."

"I don't want you to sell the place in Green Haven, there I said it."

"Well, um, I don't know what to do with it Tamia, trust me. I really don't know what to do with it because I really and truly hate that place."

"It's like a museum over there."

"Ok, then give it to the county for a museum then."

"You know what I think is incredible, you, you are unbelievable. It's how you could give away what so many people will kill for."

"That's because you're looking at it the wrong way, if that place was like a yoke around your neck and it felt like a threat to kill you, would you "A" continue to wear the yoke or "B" give it away or sell it?"

"There's four units over there, can I give away one of them?" Nahjee looked into her eyes, then turned away from her and said,

"Tamia, I don't care if you gave away all four of them ain't you listening." Then he was up and headed to the restroom. The time that Nahjee returned Tamia was getting dressed. She said "Baby listen, I've been doing a lot of thinking ever since we left Aunty Karen or Doctor Summers. She's been heavy on my mind. There is something that I need to do." Nahjee nodded his understandings. Tamia was dressed and headed out to her car.

Tamia made it down to Solano County Jail in time to beat the traffic for the afternoon. She was registered to visit Marva by one thirty. Tamia saw as Marva walked through the doors of the visiting room clad in the orange two-piece jail attire that already made her look convicted as she made her way to the visit booth. Her head was held low, still she showed. She took her seat and picked up the phone.

"Hello," she said then she cracked, tears refused to stop flowing Tamia just let her cry, just as Nahjee and Doctor Summers had to let her cry. "Oh Tamia I'm so sorry." Then again the tears flowed down her face.

"I saw that you still had both of your visits. So no one has even bothered to come and see about you? That's cool though, you'll be alright.

"I'm sorry Tamia."

"Like I say, don't worry about it. Right now Marva your bail is only twenty thousand dollars. Ten percent of that is two grand I brought five grand, every penny that I ever saved. I just put it on your books. I don't know how our wires got crossed like they did, but they did. The place that you left in Green Haven is yours, you don't owe anybody anything, and it's all yours. You've been my sister as long as I've known life, but you killed us. In a way, I've always been responsible for you, but know that this is the last time that I'm gonna reach out to you. I need you to go your own way. I need you to stay the hell away from me and may God be with you. I would leave the key in the mail box. Every bail bonds man said that they could take the money off your books to post you. Take care of yourself Marva." Tamia stood and even though Marva banged on the window, Tamia ignored her and walked out of the visiting room and got on the elevator, to herself she said "Girl I released you so that I could live."

Tamia made it back to Sacramento before three o'clock. Something told her to drive up San Jose way. So she did, something told her that William just might be standing around, and he was. Seeing him, she could tell that he was reduced to a shell of the man that she once knew and even admired. She pulled up alongside him and called his name. Seeing her William walked over to her, and he had a strut as if he knew Tamia would come back for him.

"How are you 'Mia? Ooh look at this car, it's a nice one, it makes you look even more beautiful. I hear you moved back to Oak Park, Y Street yeah?" Must be a rental car he thought.

"Yeah, I did, but that's not why I'm here. William I came to tell you that I forgive you. I need you to take better care of yourself and so do you and may God be with you, ok."

"Wait a minute that's all you have to say to me?"

"I believe that this is all I will ever say to you."

"Ahh, you punk bitch, you come through in this bullshit car like I need your bitch ass."

"Good bye William." Tamia drove up San Jose way, until she found her way heading to the freeway and on her way home. The time that she arrived in Galt she saw Rasaan's car and another white Jeep parked in the front of her house. Once she made it inside of the house her once heavy heart was now up lifted as she saw Tahj, who was happy to see her.

"Nuh uh, girl look?" Tahj modeled her ring finger.

"Oooh, uh uh, Rasaan she's lying?"

"Nah, we were just going over the plans right now." He said.

"Baby, what are they saying?" Tamia asked Nahjee.

"That it's starting to smell like cake and tuxedos in here."

"And rice," finished Rasaan.

"Nah," Tamia couldn't believe it.

"Yeah, so far we got you and Nahjee leading off. Then we'll switch, you know. First I'm the best man, then he's the best man and so far we have the church on 42nd and Broadway. Oh and we got the longest limo ever. The cake is taller than all of us. The dresses, now this is where we left off, mainly because you weren't here and I hope you could see that me and bra have no idea what to look for in a dress. We were leaving that up to you and Tahj." Rasaan updated Tamia.

"Oh, my God Tahj this is serious."

"I know did you see my new jeep out there?"

"Yeah, I just parked my new Lexus next to it."

"Uh, uh, you are lying."

"Uh uh." The two women ran out the door.

"So, how is Chris holding up?" Nahjee asked now that the girls were gone.

"Shit, he's been laying under Cali since the other night."

"Is that right?"

"He's in love all over again," said Rasaan.

"What about his program, what is he saying about that?"

"They're coming to pick him up in the morning, so he's trying to do as much fucking and partying as he can."

"Ok, it was nice meeting that dude, I fucks with him."

"He's funny as hell, got a lot of jokes and shit, you know. He should have been a comedian." The girls came back inside equal amount of loud and the same amount of happy.

One of the biggest wedding ceremonies in history took place in the county of Sacramento. Newlyweds of a certain kind defined the true meaning of love while in the pursuit of happily ever after. United Airlines would take them to South Beach where they would spend weeks drinking Margaritas and assorted Cocktails was there plans, at first. At first they were going to tour every club in South Beach just the four of them. They were going to spread the word across the country that what each club was getting was the benefits of celebrating two newly married couples that were there to spread happiness and glee to even total strangers. Now, these were the plans that were made with impeccable energy, plans that had each member of this happy society who couldn't keep their hands off of one another, at first. Tahj held Rasaan like she was never going to ever let him go and Rasaan held Tahj like he got so much paper that he didn't have to go anywhere but on vacation whenever his heart desired. Tamia held Nahjee like he was indeed her final destination and Nahjee held Tamia at a distance because he couldn't believe what the fuck just happened.

"What! Oh hell naw, well do they know that we are on our honeymoon, I'm talking about we just got here the day before yesterday. I mean whatever happened to… ah hell naw uh uh, postpone that shit… what you mean you tried...fuck. Hold on a minute," Nahjee turned to his fellow globetrotters as if what he was about to say was going to kill at least two of them and said. "Guess what, y'all ain't going to believe this shit..."

"Hell naw, uh uh, hell naw," Rasaan who followed the conversation long enough to already know the symptoms of a letdown waiting to happen. Gave every indication that whatever or whoever was on the other end was going to get a hard sell out of him.

"Honey," was all Tamia could offer.

"You ain't going to believe this shit, Desmond has a court date, but guess when? In the morning, next month has just been bumped up to tomorrow and Mecca wish us to be there and Geoffrey says that it's a good idea, if not but to make sure that Aretha could see us in the audience just in case."

"So, what are you saying, that we have to go back to Sacramento." Rasaan needed more clarification

"Exactly"

Nahjee and Tamia walked through the doors of court room 19 just in time to take a seat next to Tahj who was doing a horrible job at trying to convince Rasaan that to support their friends was indeed a good thing but it is something about a court room to a thug though. Nahjee watched as Aretha sat in the witness chair and cried her eyes out. Some real killers made her behave this way she cried, while Geoffrey Larva took her in and out of scenarios. The District Attorney didn't like one bit of it, he accused Aretha of everything except being a child of God, which Aretha didn't care much just as long as she wasn't being accused of being a murderer. The new jurors heard the stories of how Marcel and Stomp died and was sure that if Aretha was forced to be a prostitute then guess what, they all believed her. It took exactly six months for Mecca to be rewarded her brother back after a long and steady fight. What Nahjee,

Tamia, Tahj, Rasaan and Lerin were able to see was the love that Mecca has for her brother, so much that she would have risked her very life if that was to restore her family. Oh what a crazy, crazy love and a loyalty almost unheard of, and this in turn has to be at least the chorus to the very song that Nahjee has learned so much about, "THE GETO LOVE SONG."

Authors Notes: PM Don is the Author of other fictional works including the prolific titles, The Capital of California, 1.6 Million, A Hint of Jasmine and Paper Boi which is due to arrive soon.

PM Don is a native of Sacramento California, where he studies Theater Arts and Cinematography. His histories consist of long extensive years in both creative writings and song writing. His library of other Authors that motivates him and his writing ability listed are Dan Brown, James Patterson, Donald Goines and Alex Haley. When asked what motivates him the most? Simply to show a generation that there are other methods to be successful than to fall victim to the poisons injected into our inner cities and our youths.

PM Don resides in Sacramento where he is currently at work writing new novels.

www.ingramcontent.com/pod-product-compliance
Lightning Source LLC
Chambersburg PA
CBHW071259170626
46809CB00001B/289